Take Me Back to the Start

Also by Jeannie Choe

Best I Never Had Series

Best I Never Had

No Place Like You

Take Me Back to the Start

A ROMANCE NOVEL

JEANNIE CHOE

Take Me Back to the Start
Paperback Edition
Copyright © 2025 by Jeannie Choe

Love N. Books Press
An Imprint of Wolfpack Publishing
1707 E. Diana Street
Tampa, FL 33610

www.lovenbookspress.com

Character illustrations by Martin Barnes
Internal graphics design by Rachel Chaya Design
Edited by My Brother's Editor

Paperback ISBN 979-8-89567-966-1
Ebook ISBN 979-8-89567-965-4
LCCN 2025935746

For all the women out there
supporting and uplifting other women.
This is a sisterhood I never want to live without.

Note to the Reader

Hello Reader!

Thank you deeply for being here and for taking a chance on Teeny and Everett's story and myself. I like to start my books with a little icebreaker, if you will. If this were a first date, I believe this is the part where we exchange details about our immediate family and favorite colors. Mine's pink by the way. All jokes aside, I want you to know why I wrote this story and what you need to know before diving in.

You'll meet Teeny at a crossroads in her life. She's saying a mournful goodbye to her current one and a very hesitant hello to an old one resurfaced. I wrote her character so that those who feel that rock bottom is a place where redemption is impossible can see how incredibly untrue that is. Also to know that we are all flawed. And despite being flawed and a little broken, we deserve to be loved in the way that we expect to be.

There are elements to this story that may be a bit controversial, and it may stir some beliefs and viewpoints you may not agree with. And that is completely okay! We are all allowed to have our own opinions, and this is a safe place for all. With that being said, we can now move on to triggers. I generally prefer to share them via links to maintain a level of mystery, but I feel there are some elements to this book where I would feel more comfortable being up front with them.

So here are the triggers as listed:

- Cheating (not between main characters)
- Manipulative ex-partner
- Abortion (off page)
- Panic attacks
- Divorce (not between main characters)
- Brief mention of postpartum depression

I hope you enjoy! And always have a safe reading journey, no matter what fictional (or nonfictional) world you dive into.

Love always,
Jeannie

Take Me Back to the Start

CHAPTER ONE
Teeny
NOW

WHEN MY BEST FRIEND, Grace, got married, I told her I'd wear whatever maid of honor dress she wanted me to wear. Strapless, floor length, even tulle. Whatever the bride-to-be wanted, I was prepared to give it to her. But, deep down, I secretly hoped she wouldn't pick pastel. Baby pink, lavender, sky blue, canary yellow. All of it made my pale skin look even paler. And with my jet-black hair, round face that made me look about ten years younger than I actually am, and the strong Wolverine-esque anti-aging genetics my mom passed down to me, I knew I would look like a practical child attending church on Easter Sunday instead of a thirty-year-old maid of honor.

Luckily, she picked a deep ruby red A-line floor-length gown. It was flowy with a strap across one shoulder. My husband, Leo, thought it was beautiful. We were child-free for the night in a fancy hotel room with room service and thick walls. We were in love.

That was six years ago. A lifetime, it seems.

"That green one looks amazing on you, Teeny."

I turn to look at Mina from the reflection in the large mirror of the changing room. "Well, it's your wedding," I tell her while she dangles a skinny champagne flute in her fingers. The giant three-carat diamond ring my brother proposed to her with glints off the lights around us.

"I still want you to wear something you like."

I smile at her. "I'm really not picky." *As long as it doesn't make me look like the Easter Bunny's going to be walking me down the aisle.*

"What do the other bridesmaids want?" I ask, running my hands over the deep emerald tones of the dress. It really does look nice. The chiffon material feels light and airy while looking luxurious. Too bad I won't have a husband to tell me I look nice in it this time around.

"They liked the darker shade of green rather than a lighter color. Said it would make my eyes pop in the pictures."

I nod, agreeing. "Okay."

I try on another two, one in mint and another in a rusty sage color, before we decide the darker tone is the best way to go. We set up appointments for the other bridesmaids and leave the bridal store.

"So, what other wedding errands are we running before dinner?"

Mina hooks her arm through mine and looks at her watch. "We have time for one more stop," she says. "Maybe a quick Sephora run? I could use your help deciding on a lipstick shade. I need something pink and neutral. Something that says blushing bride."

"Sure," I say, smiling at her. "Dinner's at seven?"

"Seven thirty," she answers. "Is Leo coming?"

I shake my head. "It's mainly wedding party, so I told him he's on his own tonight," I tell her, averting my eyes to my purse where I pretend to search for something. ChapStick, hand sanitizer, the ruins of my marriage. Maybe if I keep my head ducked low for another minute or two, she won't be able to tell I'm lying.

"You really don't mind going with me to Sephora?" Mina asks. "I mean, you'll tell me if I'm being total bridezilla and demanding things like your time, right?"

I laugh, finally looking up at her from my deep tote dive. "Of course, I don't mind."

"Okay," she answers, pausing a moment before adding, "Because I have another favor to ask."

"What is it?"

"I have a cake tasting to go to in a few weeks," she explains. "But I can't go. I have to go out of town for work, and it took ages to set up this appointment with the bakery. Can you go with your brother? I just know he's going to pick some weird childish flavor like confetti unless an actual adult intervenes."

That sounds pretty on brand with Josh Cohen and his taste buds. "Yeah, that's fine," I tell her with a breezy laugh.

"You sure?"

I nod. "Of course," I assure her. "I don't have much going on, work-wise, and I have some free time in the coming weeks. Just let me know when exactly and I can move things around if I need to."

This is good. Wedding errands, work, distractions. Busy is good.

We finish shopping, Mina opting for the shade "Honeylove" at the register at Sephora, giving her the perfect bridal look against her skin tone and iridescent turquoise eyes. We make our way to the restaurant where we're meeting the rest of the bridal party.

The room reserved for the dinner is small and intimate, making it difficult to avoid small talk. As soon as we walk in, Josh spots us right away. "There she is!" Mina blushes, bringing her shoulder to her cheek, as her husband-to-be rushes to her side. "Did my punk kid sister take care of you?"

"Whatever, Josh," I argue, rolling my eyes in his direction. "I'll let you do the bridesmaids' dress shopping next time. See if tulle looks good on you."

Mina laughs, looping her arm around his neck. "Did you miss me?" she whispers against his ear.

He whispers something back, something I can't hear over the low rumble of chatter, and I walk away, leaving the betrothed couple to be.

"Hey."

I turn to see my other brothers, James and Andrew, fingers firmly gripping fresh drinks and sly grins of amusement on their faces.

"Getting the party started?" I ask, gesturing between their occupied hands.

"Josh is picking up the tab," James, my oldest brother, comments, raising his glass.

"And you know we can't say no to free alcohol," Andrew, the baby of our family, adds.

"Well, if that's the case, order me a chardonnay," I request coolly. I take a step closer to the row of empty chairs and sink into the soft cushioned seat. Andrew walks away toward the bar, and James takes the seat next to mine.

"Where's Leo?"

I shrug, peering at James with a look of boredom. "Enjoying the single life?"

James's brow furrows. "Where's he staying?"

"At his brother's, I think."

"I take it you haven't told Josh?"

"Nope." My wedding band suddenly feels like a hot brand, the small diamonds shimmering as I fidget with it around my ring finger.

"You know you can't keep it from everyone forever," James comments. "You're going to have to tell them. Especially Mom and Dad."

I respond with silence.

"What are they going to say when Leo doesn't show up to the wedding in a few months?"

I sigh deeply and a little dramatically. "I guess I'll tell them he got caught up." *Yeah, with his dick inside another woman.*

James only knows about Leo's infidelity, or momentary lapse of judgment as Leo calls it, because my husband also happens to be one of my big brother's oldest friends. While I decided to kick Leo out at the first whisper of his admittance to his affair, James has tried to keep a neutral ground. He hasn't badgered me into letting Leo back

4

into the house, but he also hasn't cut all ties with my soon-to-be ex-husband. And I'd be lying if I said it doesn't bother me even the tiniest bit, but it seems James's friendship with Leo is the least of my worries in the thick of our separation.

"Where's your other half?" I ask, changing the subject and even taking a small jab at the fact that I'm not the only one who showed up tonight solo.

"Sophia was running a fever," he explains. "We think she might be teething."

My face softens at the mention of my niece, eight months old with chubby cheeks the shape of shiny bao buns and fat Michelin man arms. "How's Kendall?"

He bobs his head. "Hanging in there."

He and his wife, Kendall, welcomed Sophia into their lives last year. And while the joys of parenthood have been a wafting presence in their home, postpartum depression has been its loyal companion. It seems all of our homes have been replaced with glass ones. Fragile and vulnerable, cracking with every shaky shift or rumble, disrupting our already frail lives.

"You know, Sadie can come by and babysit any time," I offer. "She'll take any excuse to play with Sophia."

"Yeah," he answers with a soft, appreciative smile. "I'll let Kendall know." After a pause, he looks around the room and adds, "Is she...?"

"At her friend's house?" I finish his sentence with a knowing eye roll. "She practically lives there now that she's on summer break. But she's going to summer camp in a few weeks so maybe I'll get her back once she's back home."

"You did good with her, Teeny," he says, the low tone of his voice showing how much I've grown. How much we've both grown. "You and Leo both did good with her."

"At least we got something right."

Our conversation is cut short as people start to take their seats. Josh and Mina settle in somewhere in the center, where they can spread their attention throughout the table, along with the other bridesmaids. Andrew returns with my chardonnay and sits in the empty seat next to James, leaving the seat to my right empty.

Dinner starts, introductions are made. The one other bridesmaid is Mina's cousin, who seems pretty friendly and normal. The maid of honor, Mina's best friend from college, is the only one missing. She's set to arrive a few days before the wedding from New York City.

It isn't rare or uncustomary for my siblings and I to come together for dinner like this. And it isn't even always for things like wedding celebrations or birthdays or anniversaries. It can even be for something as menial as an impromptu weekend barbeque or beach day with the kids. But the one glaring sore thumb we can't seem to ignore is the fact that my husband isn't here. There's no excuse of a sickly baby at home to take care of. The continuous mentions of work and long hours at the office are wearing thin. I could almost feel it on the tips of everyone's tongues. Where's Leo?

My entire body feels worn, too tired from making up excuses.

"He's working late."

"He had a meeting with some clients that's taking longer than he thought."

"This case he's working on is taking up a lot of his time."

After all these years, filled with lies and months and months of multiple "momentary lapses of judgment," all I want to do now is throw in the towel.

"Hey, is Leo coming?" Andrew asks, nodding his head to the empty seat, as if he's reading my damn mind. "He still owes me a hundred bucks from our last round of golf. Or did he not tell you how badly I kicked his ass last month?"

I catch James glancing at me, a solemn look of concern and discretion keeping him from saying anything. "No, he's...at home," I finally answer, my words spoken in a whisper through my lie.

"How about you stop placing bets every time we hit the golf course," James cuts in, flicking Andrew's fork so it loudly clinks against his small bread plate.

TAKE ME BACK TO THE START

The sounds of James and Andrew bickering fade into muffled words of, "You're just jealous of my stroke count." I drown out the noise with the light drum of my fingers against the clothed table. My hands start to feel clammy, and the room starts to feel like it's closing in on me. I stand from my seat, turning to James and pointing my finger toward the much more crowded dining area. He nods, accepting my signal to excuse myself to the little girls' room, and I walk the narrow walkway.

My phone buzzes in my hand, and when I look at the screen, I see an alert for a new text message from Leo.

LEO

I came home to get a few things and you weren't here. I was hoping to talk to you.

My entire body sags and I feel like what little energy I had left dissolves into defeat. What does he expect? That he could cheat on me, ruin our marriage after fifteen years, and simply hope I'd move on from it? Forgive him? How are we supposed to move on from this?

I toss my phone into my bag, hoping it'll get lost in there where I won't be disturbed by it for the rest of the night, and continue my way toward the ladies' room. I didn't need to pee or do anything bathroom related but I needed some air or...something to take my mind off Leo's barrage of messages.

I need to talk to you.

I'm sorry.

Please let me come back home.

"Oof!"

A large body, one clad in a dark navy suit and brown oxfords, crashes into me. I stumble a step back, slapping my hand against the nearest wall for support.

"Ohmigod," I say with a gasp. "I'm so sor—" I pause, looking at the dark eyes of the stranger peering down at me with a sharp

7

jawline and a slightly crooked nose. Only, it's no stranger. Far from it.

Everett.

"Teeny."

"Wh-what." I feel disoriented. My knees buckle and the bottom pit of my stomach feels like it weighs two tons. Everything around me feels like it's spinning. Twisting and turning on a tilted axis like a spinning globe.

I turn away from the direction of the bathroom I had no real business going to in the first place. From the rest of the wedding party, from my past in the form of the biggest heartbreak of my life. A gust of fresh air hits me in my face when I exit the restaurant and I rush to my car, not bothering to tell my brothers I'm leaving when I feel a warm hand grip my elbow.

"Teeny, wait."

Everett was always able to catch up to me. With his long legs and agility on and off the basketball court, there wasn't a place I could go to outrun him. And twenty years ago, I never wanted to. I always wanted him to come find me. To make things right, to fix whatever wrong had happened between us. Until I waited and he never came.

I tug my arm from his grip, ignoring his protest, as my heels continue to click against the sidewalk.

"Teeny!" He rounds me and blocks my way, stopping me from getting to my car.

"*What*, Everett? What?" A tremor starts to slither up my fingers, traveling all the way to the dip between my shoulder blades. I feel like I'm having an out-of-body experience. He's really here. I'm not imagining this.

He takes a deep inhale. "Hi."

I scoff, crossing my arms and turning away from him. "What are you doing here?"

"Having dinner? I'm here to meet—"

"No, I mean *why* are you here? Why did the universe have to bring you here right *now* when *I'm* here? As if—"

8

"Josh invited me."

My mouth clamps shut. *Josh invited him?* "Tonight?"

He nods. "Look, I'm already late," he says, running a hand through his perfectly wavy hair. "But...can we talk? Maybe after dinner?"

"Wait a minute," I say, ignoring his question. A scowl twists my features, and I glare at him. "You're here to see Josh?"

He nods again. "Did he not tell you?"

"Everett!" We both turn toward the entrance of the restaurant to see Josh greet Everett. "I just got your message." He holds up his phone, waggling it in his fingers in Everett's direction. "I thought maybe you got lost."

"Uh, no." Everett glances at me before facing Josh. "I just ran into Teeny."

"Man, it's good to see you!" Josh exclaims, pulling Everett for a hefty embrace. "Let's go inside. James and Andrew are here too."

Everett takes one last look at me, so much implied yet unsure in his slightly agape mouth and dark, pensive eyes.

"Teeny, come on," Josh calls. He doesn't ask what I was doing outside, why I look distraught, as if I've just witnessed a crime. Instead, he guides Everett past the hostess booth, and I reluctantly follow behind. By the time we've made it to our table, I've had about ten different discussions in my mind. Ones that feel confusing and angry and outright frustrating.

I should've just left, driven off in the safety of my car. Why did I foolishly come back inside like everything would be fine and dandy and I'd be able to sit through a whole meal with Everett in the same room? And what the hell is Josh thinking, inviting Everett here? Is he the third groomsman I never bothered to question my brother about? And why wouldn't he tell me this? And let's say Josh just randomly decided to ask Everett to be a part of his wedding. Why did he agree to it? After all these years? He had to have known I'd be here too.

"Teeny?" I hadn't realized I was just standing there, my hands

9

loosely braced on the back of my chair. As soon as I hear Josh's voice call my name, a confused and concerned tone laced into his voice, I realize I'm practically glaring at Everett. "Is everything okay?"

Everett's eyes follow Josh's gaze, taking in the way I'm frozen. A gentle smile softens his entire face, and it makes my breath hitch, remembering all the times he looked at me like that. When I'd catch him watching me paint or doing my homework. It was always that smile that opened my heart up just for him. And it's been closed since the last time I saw him.

"Yeah," I say meekly. I take my seat and Everett hovers over the empty one next to mine.

"Mina," Josh calls from across the table, his hand gripped over Everett's shoulder. "This is Everett."

"Ohmigod!" Mina exclaims. She shuffles out of her seat and rounds the table to meet Everett. "Josh has told me so much about you. Thank you so much for coming."

Everett smiles warmly. "Couldn't miss one of my best friend's wedding."

I catch Everett's eyes when I look up at the three of them exchanging introductions, and I regret it instantly. I didn't know I could feel angry and sad at the same time. Those two emotions start this violent back-and-forth quarrel trying to overpower the other, but neither one is winning. The second I feel like the anger's going to bubble over, this deep ache stabs at my heart. It's resurfacing from years of searching for some level of closure while scared to face the reasons behind it.

Everett settles into the seat next to mine, the only empty one. I catch James shifting uncomfortably to my left, nudging me carefully with his elbow.

"You good?" James whispers. He glances at Everett quickly, acknowledging him in a way that only I notice before his concern refocuses on me.

Unable to speak, I nod. Even though all I want is to tell him no. To beg him to get me out of here. Somewhere safe where I can shove away this entire encounter like it never happened. Where the existence of Everett can be completely ignored instead of sitting inches from me, where I can study the shiny buttons on his jacket sleeve and get an intense whiff of his cologne.

"Yeah," I finally say, my voice barely above a whisper. "I'm fine."

There's a small stain on the tablecloth. Something that was once red, like marinara or ketchup. It looks like the fabric has been washed and bleached, but this stubborn stain somehow sustained all those efforts. I focus on it, hoping that maybe it'll help me. Take me away somewhere on a mythical journey to teach me the ways of being so relentless it could withstand the harshest of products. But then I feel a warm hand perch on my shoulder. A consoling squeeze comes from James's touch, and I realize I don't know how to be that stubborn. I don't know how to banish someone I loved to the point that I thought my heart was going to explode. I only know how to feel broken.

CHAPTER TWO
Everett

THEN

I REMEMBER GETTING car sick when I was six. It was a long drive, a thoroughly planned out road trip from Monterey all the way to Vancouver where my parents made overnight pit stops to national parks like Mount Rainier and Olympic. I threw up a few times, surviving off Gatorade and saltine crackers until my body somewhat adjusted.

Now, at seventeen years old, it seems I've outgrown those stages of motion sickness that come with long car rides. Instead, I'm able to ride out the boredom through the drone of my parents' playful bickering in the front seat and the rubbery hollow thump of my palms against the basketball cradled between my thighs.

But this time, my view isn't rows and rows of colorful foliage and mountains that hide the outside world with columns of thick forestry. Instead, I'm surrounded by the coastal breeze and the oceanic blue horizon as we leave Orange County.

"You're going to fit in just fine, Everett," my mom calls from the front seat, her fifth attempt to reassure me since we'd left Sacramento with a small U-Haul hitched to the back of the car eight and a half hours ago.

"And if those kids give you a hard time, you tell them to shove their shiny BMWs up their asses," my dad chimes in. "Right along with their rich people money and fancy houses." He swivels his head, throwing a quick glance in my direction as he changes lanes on I-5 heading into Carlsbad.

"Yeah, Dad," I say, running my nail along the dark silicone lining on my basketball. "I'll make sure to put them in their place."

He ignores my sardonic tone, keeping his eyes on the road ahead of him. My mom asks him something about the washer and dryer back home in Sacramento, something for him to take care of when he flies back up next week while she and I get settled down here in Del Mar Heights.

Senior year certainly isn't turning out how I thought it would. I thought I'd be starting my last year of high school up north, finally breaking the "new guy" curse. I think this'll be three schools in four years? Or was it four? I lost count after sophomore year and first period English when Mr. Moon had me stand at the front of the class to tell everyone "two truths and one lie" about myself, which resulted in the most embarrassing guessing game that centered around the big question: Was I really abducted by aliens? (Was it not obvious?) Maybe it's the difficulty of forming any sort of status in a school full of teenagers eager to stake their place and ready to rip you to shreds based on judgment and popularity. Or it could simply be the fact that any sort of label or standing in a social setting sets off warning bells in my head like a fire alarm. One full of smoke signals and a fiery heat ushering me away from group gatherings.

"You are still trying out for the team, right?" I catch my dad's gaze through the rearview mirror, meeting my eyes again, but now with a more concerned edge.

"Yeah, Dad," I say through a deep exhale. "Of course."

"Maybe I should put in a call to the coach. If they know who I am—"

"No, please don't do that. I don't need people knowing who you are."

"Come on, Everett," he argues. "What's the point of this contract and name-dropping rights if not to get my son on the varsity team?"

I respond with an eye roll.

"I can even throw in a meet and greet with Peja Stojaković," he offers, his voice sing-songy.

"Wow, using your players for personal gain. Is that how you're going to start off the season as the Sacramento Kings' new head coach?"

"I dare them to question their boss."

"Thanks, Dad, but I think I'll avoid the use of nepotism to 'fit in,'" I say. "Wouldn't make me any better than those spoiled kids with their BMWs."

"Just give it your all. And make sure that Coach lets you try out," he adds. "I know they always say their rosters are full, but they can always fit—"

"Eddie," my mom interjects. "Let him figure it out." She runs her hand along his arm, gently putting a stop to this conversation.

"I just want to make sure he gets in. Those coaches at UC Davis are tough. Much tougher than high school coaches."

"Dad, I'm not even sure I'll get in," I protest. "And I already said I'm not going to play in college."

"I know." He presses the heels of his hands to the steering wheel, holding his palms and fingers up in surrender. "But if you do change your mind, you need to have all the resources at your disposal. You can't join a college team if you didn't even play your senior year."

"Yeah, well, if I stayed in Sacramento, I wouldn't have this problem."

"Everett," my dad protests. "We already talked about this."

"I know, I know."

"Everett," my mom adds, throwing in her two cents. "If your dad wasn't so busy up there with this new coaching job, I'd love for you to stay, but—"

"But you need to move here. I know, Mom."

My mom awkwardly twists her arm to reach me in the seat

behind her. Her fingers lightly tap my knee, a little pat of gratitude for my fluctuating sympathy.

The guilt of my frustration causes me to lay my hand on top of hers, a silent apology for my outburst. The truth is, I do feel bad. It's not like she decided to move down to sunny Southern California for a year of sunshine and the easy life. And if it weren't for my grandfather passing away two months ago, we wouldn't even be in this predicament.

"How close is it to the beach?" I ask as my mom pulls away.

"About six miles. No more than a five-minute drive."

"You're going to love it," my dad says. "And whoever decides to buy it is going to love it too." He exits the freeway, finally feeling like we're seeing the finish line after our last restroom break in Irvine.

"Eddie, we'll wait to see what the realtor says," my mom warns. "You said give it a year, and I am going to fully enjoy the house for a year before we have to sell it."

My dad reaches for my mom's hand, giving it a firm squeeze. They've been doing that a lot lately, exchanging secret glances and polite smiles, both reassuring themselves that this year-long separation is a good thing. While it isn't ideal, it's the best option considering the current circumstances.

When my mom was handed the deed to my grandparents' house, she didn't want to sell it right away. In fact, she wanted to move back home, finally plant roots back where she grew up. But with my dad's work and the unpredictability of it, it wasn't possible. So they compromised. He'd stay up in Sacramento while he completed his first year as the head coach for the Sacramento Kings, and me and my mom would move down to San Diego to finish out my senior year before I head off to college. If I looked up the word "compromise" in the dictionary, I'd probably find an image of my parents amicably shaking hands with firm, agreeable smiles.

The car slows as we turn the corner into a short cul-de-sac. My mom leans forward, peering through the windshield while watching the rows of houses pass by. "Ah," she exclaims softly. "Here we are."

My dad slows to stop in front of a two-story house that looks so much bigger than the memory of my four-year-old self. The driveway alone can probably fit four cars, five if the person driving knows how to parallel park. The tan paint looks freshly coated and the dark brown shutters siding each window make the house look homey and rich at the same time. My dad parks the car in the driveway, and we exit.

"Why does it look so much bigger than I remember?" I ask when the three of us meet at the hood of the car. We're peering up at the house, our necks strained to the sky as we take it all in.

"Probably because the last time you were here, you were still using a little training potty," my mom comments, gently patting my back.

"Come on, Everett," my dad calls. "Let's get the luggage down."

My mom continues her way into the house while my dad and I walk to the back of the U-Haul. Just as we're wheeling the first of our luggage up the driveway, we're interrupted by a high-pitched squeal followed by the urgent pitter-patter of feet.

"James!" I hear a loud shrill screech call from the house next to ours. My dad and I both look toward the sound of the noise at the same time.

A girl, who looks to be about my age, runs out of the two-story home that's a lot smaller than my grandparents—or, ours now, I guess. There's a basketball hoop in the driveway, mounted high above the garage, and a few loose basketballs sitting in the grass off to the side. A Pathfinder sits in the driveway with a glossy CD dangling from the rearview mirror right next to a pearly white SUV.

"James!" the girl calls again over her shoulder. "Don't hog all the Sour Patch Kids!"

More footsteps follow. "I want some too!" calls another voice, this one more playful and innocent coming from a boy about seven or eight. They race each other to the SUV, two more guys following behind them, and I suddenly feel out of place in my loose basketball shorts and plain gray T-shirt as I watch them walk out of the house in buttoned-up shirts and ironed khakis.

"Shotgun!" the girl announces with a smug grin. Her hair picks up with the breeze, and I see the glint of her smile shine against the late afternoon sun. The dress she's wearing follows, the hem fluttering around her knees. Jesus, she's pretty. Even from the distance across a driveway and a patch of grass separating our two homes, I notice the freckles lining her cheeks and nose and the way her dark eyes peer innocently at who she's silently taunting with her hand on her hip and a cheeky grin.

One of the guys, already at the door to the front passenger seat, groans. "Oh, come on!" he complains.

"You can get shotgun in mom's car." She flicks a hand in his direction like she's shooing away a bug, her wrist thickly adorned with bracelets and her nails painted a dark sparkly shade. A quick glance in my direction and we meet eyes, her smile disappearing behind the curve of bare skin where a single strap cuts across her shoulder.

"Hello!" a man calls, just as he approaches the SUV and joins his brood, noticing me and my dad awkwardly standing in our driveway. "You must be the new neighbors. I'm Jasper."

"Eddie," my dad answers as the two meet at the property line dividing the two homes. "Nice to meet you."

"Welcome to the neighborhood." Jasper turns to face the car where all the doors are open and the chitter chatter fills the air with chaos. "Those are my kids. James, Josh, Christine, and Andrew."

My dad chuckles. "You got your hands full."

Jasper smiles warmly in response. "You have no idea." There's a small pause and it's interrupted by one of the kids approaching his side.

"Dad," he calls. "Mom just called James. She asked us to pick up the cake before we head to the restaurant." He has a full bag of Sour Patch Kids held loosely in his hand, the top ripped open and a dust of sugar smeared over his thumb and index finger.

"Uh, Josh," he says, facing him. "This is Eddie and..."

"Everett," my dad answers. "This is my son, Everett."

Josh shakes my hand. His hands feel equally confident and shy through the small pause of hesitance and the lack of eye contact. He's about as tall as me, hovering at around six feet, with the light, almost reddish-blonde hair his dad has. They have the same eyes too, blue with hints of copper, the complete opposite to his sister sitting in the front seat of their SUV.

"Are you new to the area? Or moving from around here?"

"We're moving down from Sacramento," my dad answers. "Though my wife is from here."

"Sacramento! Where about?"

"Right around Land Park and Richmond Grove."

Jasper exhales a long, drawn out whistle. "That's some fancy roots you have there."

My dad lets out a nervous laugh. "We just moved there about two years ago from Monterey," he tells him. "Work has me going all over."

"Wait a minute," Jasper says with a slight rise of surprise in his voice. He has a loose hand pointed in my dad's direction, and it's the face that we've seen one too many times back home. I just didn't think it would happen so quickly here. "You're the Kings' new head coach."

My dad huffs an awkward laugh. "Sure am," he answers with a polite smile.

"I thought you looked familiar." He turns to Josh. "Josh, we got a celebrity next door."

"Oh, no. No, no. I'm no celebrity. Just doing my job."

"I'm a huge fan," Jasper adds. "Though my kids have been trying to convert me into a Lakers fan for years."

"Are you from up north?"

He nods. "Grew up in Santa Cruz. I moved down here after me and my wife got married."

My dad's face lights up. Though we've been all over Northern

California, it's the vast area that spans from Monterey to Sacramento that's home. So while we have no small tight knit community, it's the familiarity of the area that we feel attached to. "Hey! Nice to meet someone from back home," he says, adding a friendly handshake and hefty pat to Jasper's shoulder.

"So are you taking up a different job? You didn't back out of your contract? Or is that confidential information?" Jasper asks, poking fun at the level of discretion my dad has to keep in relation to his job.

"Oh, no. Nothing like that," my dad assures. "This is my in-laws'. Was," he corrects. "Ours now, I guess. Anyway, my wife's going to take the year to clear it out, enjoy it one last time before we sell it and this guy goes off to college." He hooks a hand over my shoulder, grinning proudly at me.

"I'm sorry," Jasper offers with a stern face of condolence. "Mr. Allen was a nice man. Always let the kids back there when one of their toys flew over into his yard." He juts his chin toward our house.

"Daddy! What's taking so long?"

We all peer at the car with the doors still open, a blast of radio music streaming out from the speakers. I see the girl, Christine, look in our direction with a set of curious eyes. Her lips are pressed together and twisted to one side while she sits impatiently.

"I'll catch you later," Jasper tells my dad. "We got a birthday thing to head out to, and now we've got to pick up the cake." He chuckles warmly, extending his hand to my dad again. "It was nice meeting you both."

"Nice meeting you too," my dad answers. We turn back to our waiting bags as Jasper hops into the driver's seat with everyone buckled and waiting. I glance back at the front passenger seat as Jasper pulls out of the driveway, only to see Christine peering at me through the window. I see her lips lift in a small smile, the sentiment reaching her eyes as they soften, and I smile back.

CHAPTER THREE

Teeny

NOW

WHEN LEO and I were house hunting eight years ago, we weren't picky home buyers. We just wanted something modest where we could watch our daughter, Sadie, grow up. Somewhere safe with a decent school district and enough room for us to eventually bring home a yellow lab like I've always wanted. We finally found one not too far from my parents' house, the place I'd grown up and where my brothers hadn't strayed too far from as well. We could still stop by on the weekends and drop off Sadie for an overnight stay at Grandma and Grandpa's house. James and his family could come over for Sunday Night Football or a random weekend barbeque. While it needed some work, it was perfect for our growing family.

Now, walking into the vacant house that suddenly feels too big, it feels empty. There's no yellow lab to meet me with a wildly wagging tail and the pitter-patter of happy paw steps. There's no husband to ask how my day was or what I want to do for dinner. I'd spent almost half my life building this life and this home, putting up the walls and filling the space with memories, only for it to feel like it's no longer mine.

I set my purse down on the floor somewhere on the way to the kitchen, tossing my keys on the counter as I flick on the overhead lighting. My coffee mug from this morning sits half empty next to the sink. Sadie's headphones and ChapStick are left on the stool tucked under the kitchen island, forgotten and probably being searched for at this very moment. Piles of mail are scattered in a disorderly heap, and my laptop sits left open with a blank screen and invoices resting atop the keyboard.

With Leo's partnership that came shortly after we bought this house, we experienced a level of financial freedom most couples our age didn't get to. Leo's ambition gave us this home and a life that allowed me to pursue my work at a pace I was comfortable with. I studied architecture in college and shifted my career goals toward interior design and decorating once I started working and found more opportunities. I worked freelance and took on clients without the pressure of constantly having to work. Looking back now, it seems it all came with a price. Late nights of Leo courting clients and opportunities to expand his reach. "Networking," as he called it. Maybe I was too trusting. Maybe I thought our marriage, while it wasn't perfect, didn't have enough ups and downs for Leo to consider a greener pasture. But maybe we needed those ups and downs. Because living life in a straight line was boring. It was uneventful and listless. Something so quick to get tired of.

My phone rings just then, vibrating violently inside my purse. When I look at the screen, I see Sadie's name flash on the screen.

"Mom," Sadie calls as soon as I answer. "I don't need you to pick me up. Lauren's dad's going to drop me off."

I glance at the time glowing off the microwave. "It's almost nine," I comment. "Are you sure?"

"Yeah," she answers. "We're putting on *Mean Girls*."

"*Mean Girls*?"

"Lauren's mom is showing us some old-school movies. We just finished watching *The Notebook*."

"And those movies are considered 'old school?'" I ask rhetorically, unable to hide the criticism in my voice.

"Mom! I gotta go!"

21

"All right. Text me when you're on your way home."

"Okay. Bye!"

I smirk, hanging up and staring at my phone screen. Moments like this are where I'd tell Leo our fourteen-year-old daughter thinks the movies I watched as a teen are now considered "old school." Or that Sadie's out late with her friends and we have the house to ourselves for a few more hours. And suddenly, I can't remember the last time I had a conversation like that with Leo.

We hadn't been Leo and Christine in so long. And I don't have the heart to mourn us. Not when there are so many things to be angry about. How Leo and I both used work as a buffer to fill the cold, empty space between us. How our attention veered more toward Sadie even though she'd long outgrown the stage of her life where we needed to baby her to death. How I'd even ignored the way he'd spend more time on his phone or on drawn out "work calls," most likely scheming a quickie with his mistress.

How did I end up here?

Instead of contemplating and reexamining my marriage, I trudge into my en suite to shower. Maybe running my body under scalding hot water might melt some of the tension off me. And quite possibly even the nagging questions making me wonder what I could've done differently with my past.

I tossed and turned all night. Every time I closed my eyes, I kept seeing Everett.

Everett sitting in the driver's seat of his BMW with the windows rolled down and the breeze blowing through his hair.

Everett running across the hard cement of our driveway as he and Josh did practice runs on weekends.

Everett chasing me across the sandy beach in nothing but his board shorts and sun kissed skin, laughing at me whenever I splashed water in his face.

He's back. I tried to erase all thoughts of him from my mind last night but as soon as my head hit my pillow, I failed miserably. And now, it feels as if the last twenty years was this long stretched out chunk of time that didn't even really happen. Sadie, my marriage, everything feels like it happened in some hazy alternative universe and suddenly, I'm sixteen again. I'm waiting for the boy next door to come over and flirt with me under the guise of hanging out with my older brother.

I'm thinking all of this, all the moments that could have been if Everett stayed, when I pull into my parents' neighborhood with a box of fresh donuts nestled into the cushioned seat behind me and Sadie sitting next to me in the passenger seat.

"Mom," Sadie calls for my attention with her head bowed down to her phone. "Lauren's asking what time we're going to pick her up?"

"We should be done by one, so about one thirty?"

She silently nods, and I peer at the back seat where my canvas tote bag filled with my bathing suit, a beach towel, and the latest edition of *Better Homes and Gardens* pokes out the top.

"Are you girls still okay with Mission Bay? Or did you want to go to a different beach?"

She shakes her head. "It's fine." She swipes her finger along the touchpad on my dash to change the music before adding, "Lauren said her mom can pick her up around six."

"Okay."

"Would it be okay if I spent the night at her house?"

"You're going over again?"

She nods, looking up to face me. "We're watching *Clueless* and *She's All That* tonight."

I smirk. "You know, when I try to get you to watch those movies with me, you always say no."

23

She pouts and her already round eyes turn into giant saucers. "I promise I'll watch one with you before I leave for camp."

There's nothing like a true set of puppy eyes, mastered through years and years of practice, to get a pushover mom like me to say yes. "Fine," I say, rolling my eyes.

"Dad's still dropping me off at camp next week, right?" she asks. "He's been really busy. Is he even going to have time?"

"He's a little busy, but I'll make sure he'll be there to pick you up on Thursday."

"How long is he going to stay at Uncle Javi's? I didn't know home renovations needed this much attention."

We—or, Leo—used the lie that his brother, Javier, had home renovations to take care of in his new house up in San Clemente and required the desperate help of Leo. While it wasn't necessarily a lie since Javi's fixer-upper required a lot of fixing and Leo has some experience handling most of the revamping to our home, it's enough to fend off Sadie's curiosity. That plus the added advantage that teenage girls have the tendency to make the world revolve around themselves and Leo's already glaring work-related absences that she and I've grown accustomed to over the years, it's made the beginning stages of this separation less stressful on my end.

"I think maybe another month or so," I answer after a long pause of silence. One that I try to hide by peering at road signs and streets I've driven through a hundred times.

I finally pull into my parents' driveway. Their cars are parked inside the garage, but I notice a fancy BMW parked in the empty spot next to me. I peer inside, hoping to find any clues to who the car belongs to as I walk up the walkway to their house. I ring the doorbell with Sadie trailing behind me, and I'm honestly impressed with the level of dexterity she has balancing the tray of coffee she'd been holding on her lap the whole time while tapping out a very rapid text message. I'm holding the pink box of donuts in my hand and when the door opens, the last person I expect to see is standing on the other side.

"Hi, Teeny."

There's a long pause where I'm just standing there, speechless and gawking. I blink multiple times, hoping if I do it enough times, what I'm seeing right in front of my eyes will just disappear like some illusory magic trick. Over and over again, while I try to understand why Everett is answering my parents' door.

Sadie peers up between Everett and me, a confused furrow forming between her brows.

"Sadie. This is Uncle Josh's friend, Everett," I finally say after we've stood there in this long embarrassingly unpleasant pause of silence.

The corners of Sadie's mouth turn up in a forced smile, and she swipes her phone occupied palm in the air, giving him an awkward wave. "Nice to meet you."

"You too." He answers her calmly, a tone of authority plaited into those two simple words. I don't understand how he looks so cool and collected while I look like a frazzled mess with bags under my eyes and my tattered jeans I purposely wore to spend a day elbow deep in dirt and my knees rooted in grass stains and soil.

Sadie tucks her head down and angles her body sideways to fit through the door with Everett taking up more than half of the doorway. When she's out of earshot, most likely beelining for the kitchen where my mom always keeps cold stashes of Yakult in her fridge, I falter under Everett's observant gaze. "Is that your daughter?"

I nod. I shift the donuts in my hand, and Everett's eyes focus on my left hand, right where my wedding ring glints even under the shaded awning above my parents' entryway.

"She has your eyes."

I don't nod this time. Instead, my eyes narrow, unsure how to interpret his observation. Is he just trying to make conversation? Or is there some weird underlying meaning behind his comment that my daughter inherited some of my looks?

"You're a mom now," he adds. There's a tenderness to his voice, and it makes something warm leak into the rigid anger spreading through my body, making it malleable and soft. He pauses before adding, "Motherhood looks good on you." Another pause. "But, you know, everything has always looked good on you."

A blazing fury starts to kindle inside my chest, and I feel like my fingers are tingling. Whatever crack in my anger that made my heart give in to his words is immediately filled with the remains of my resentment.

"Even heartbreak?" It wasn't the first set of words I wanted to say to him, but it spewed out of me. What the *fuck* does he mean?

He sighs, and a line between his brow fissures, something that wasn't there before. Something new yet old and weathered, showing how twenty years isn't a short amount of time. "Teeny," he protests.

"Excuse me." I briskly pass him, walking to the kitchen. Sure enough, Sadie is standing at the far end of the island, the side closest to the refrigerator, with a small empty Yakult bottle sitting in front of her and a fresh one in her hand. I slide the box of donuts toward her, to which she silently opens and takes the twisted glaze sitting on top.

"Mom! We're here!" I call, setting my purse down on the kitchen counter along with my keys and the remains of my reason as I try to grapple with the fact that my ex-boyfriend is in my parents' house.

"Good morning," my mom sings just as she enters the kitchen. She glides toward Sadie with open arms and pulls her into her bosom, nuzzling her cheek into the top of my daughter's head. Sadie responds with a firm embrace of her own.

"Hi, Grandma."

"Hi, my baby." She pulls away and squishes Sadie's cheeks between her hands. "Thank you for coming today."

"Of course," Sadie answers. While at fourteen years old, Sadie's main concerns are getting a second lobe piercing, an all-expense paid shopping trip at Sephora, and apparently diving into a 2000s nostalgic time capsule, my mom is one of the only people who can pull her out of her own world. Those two are peas in a very tight pod.

"Can we have some *mandu* for lunch?" Sadie pleads, her eyes shimmering with a pout.

"Yes!" my mom shrieks. "I just went to the Korean store and got some the other day."

Sadie beams, and I swear I've completely disappeared from her periphery. "Is Dad here?" I ask, smiling at the two of them.

My mom turns to me, finally acknowledging the person who brought Sadie into the world. "He's coming right down." Her eyes flash to the coffee on the counter. "You brought coffee," she says, reaching for it. "Just what I needed."

"And donuts." I poke a finger toward the pink box sitting in front of Sadie.

Everett stalks into the kitchen and eyes me. I'd almost forgotten he was here. Almost.

"The Amazon guy just dropped this off," he announces, placing a small package envelope in front of my mom.

"Oh, thank you," my mom says sweetly. "Have some donuts while you wait for Josh to get here. Everett can have a coffee, right?" she asks, turning to face me.

"Actually, one was for Dad."

"He doesn't need it." She slides the coffee toward Everett and scoots a few packages of sugar and cream in his direction as well.

"Thank you," he says to me in a low voice.

"I didn't get it for you, so—"

"Teeny," my mom chastises. "Don't be rude." I roll my eyes as my mom asks Everett, "Have you gone to your old house next door?"

"No I haven't," he says, cupping his hand to the back of his neck. Something somber and nostalgic flashes through his eyes. "I didn't want to bother some strangers just to check out the place."

"Nonsense," my mom responds, waving a hand in his direction. "Mr. Tran is really nice. He'd let you check it out. I'm sure your mom would love to hear about how different it all looks now. I'll walk over with you and introduce you."

Everett smiles politely and nods. "Thanks, Mrs. Cohen."

"How are your parents?" My mom reaches into the fridge for another Yakult as Sadie finishes her second one. I throw a wary look in her direction, warning her that that's enough sugar. Of course, my mom ignores it.

"She's doing well," he answers, his eyes watching me. "She remarried five years ago and moved to Seattle. My dad's still up in Sacramento."

My mom smiles a genuine smile. "Oh, that's nice." She takes a quick sip of her coffee before adding, "Tell them we said hi."

"I will."

There's a short moment of silence, bits and pieces of my past left unsaid while my mom presents herself with politeness for an old friend she's lost touch with. She fills the awkwardness by busying herself with the package in her hand, ripping it open and peering inside. "That's what this is." She looks up at me. "Your dad's been waiting on these cable ties. I'll be right back."

My mom leaves, disappearing up the stairs with Sadie close at her heels, ripping open the foil seal on her drink.

"I want to say hi to Grandpa!" Sadie exclaims, the third person in that little pod she and my mom share.

And it's only Everett and me in the kitchen.

"Teeny—"

"Look," I say sharply, interrupting him. "I get that you're here for my brother's wedding. I can't change that but please, can we get through this without doing this?"

"Doing what?"

"Acting like we can be civil with each other."

"We can't?"

I scoff. "Everett, we can. With a *lot* of effort, we can. But I really don't want to. And I think if we just avoid each other, it'll make things easier. I really—"

"Then don't."

I scowl at him. "Don't what?"

28

"Don't be civil with me."

My scowl deepens, and I almost want to take him up on his offer. Maybe swing the big frying pan sitting on the stove into the side of his head. Or grab the hot coffee from his hand and splash it all over his perfectly pressed polo shirt and chinos.

Our silent staring contest filled with animosity on my end and sincerity on his is interrupted by the sound of the front door opening and closing. It's followed by the annoying jangling of keys and Josh's bright voice.

"Everett, you're already here." I throw a quick glare at him. *Traitor.*

Everett turns to face him with a carefree smile. "Yeah, I thought I'd come by a little early and say hi to your parents."

"You got your clubs in the car?"

He shakes his head. "I didn't bring them down, so I'll probably rent some at the country club," he says, his eyes back on me.

Josh nods at the same time the front door opens again. It's starting to feel crowded in my mom's relatively small kitchen. Like the barely comfortable distance between me and Everett is becoming smaller and smaller with the growing scrutiny that may or may not be there.

Mina rounds the corner, an adorable set of overalls swallowing her small frame along with a large straw hat and thick-rimmed sunglasses. "Hey!" she exclaims when she sees me. "I didn't know you were going to be here today too."

I nod. "Looks like Mom's recruited quite the workforce." I peer outside at the beaming sun, showing the increasing temperatures in the mid-nineties by late morning. "Probably too late to enforce labor laws."

"Aw, Mom's first little labor unit," Josh comments with a teasing smirk.

Everett coughs a laugh mid-sip, and my deadpanned look transitions into a death stare with narrowed eyes and a clenched jaw.

"Dad!" Josh calls in the direction of the stairway. "We gotta go!"

A muffled "I'll be right down" echoes down from the second floor and the room falls silent.

"So, how's the hotel? You get checked in okay?"

Everett tears his gaze away from me, and I feel like I can finally breathe. I start to fiddle with the tiny coffee stirrer in my cup and busy myself with tucking away the donuts in a corner next to the sink.

"Yeah. It's not too far from here so that's pretty convenient."

"You really didn't have to come down here this far ahead of the wedding," Josh adds.

"I had some things I wanted to take care of anyway," Everett answers. He glances again in my direction, and I almost want to jerk my head in his direction with my hands extended out in front of me like I'm challenging him to a rumble. Why does he keep *looking* at me?

Luckily, I don't have a chance to throw a silent non-verbal threat at him because my dad bounces into the kitchen. He's wearing his plaid golfing pants and a soft yellow polo shirt with a beaming smile on his face. Golf days are Dad's favorite. Nothing gets him excited like a day at the driving range with only the lush grass and eighteen holes in front of him.

"I'm ready," he announces, reaching past me for a donut. "Good morning, Teeny Weenie."

"Hi, Daddy."

"You brought the donuts?" he asks, already stuffing half a maple bar into his mouth.

I nod. "I brought you coffee too, but Mom gave it away."

He frowns in mock disapproval. "How dare she."

"I tried to warn her."

"She's just showing Sadie some smocks to wear while you girls work out in the garden today." My dad finishes the last bit of his donut like he hasn't eaten in weeks and turns to my brother. "You kids ready to go?"

"Yep," Josh answers. "James and Andrew are meeting us there."

My dad reaches for yet another donut and winks at me. "Don't tell your mom."

I smile at him as he walks away. Josh stoops down to kiss Mina, and Everett glances in my direction.

"See ya, Teeny," he throws over his shoulder as the two follow my dad.

I don't answer or even look in his direction. Instead, I take a long soothing sip of my coffee while keeping my gaze on the flimsy plastic lid. My phone just buzzes in my purse. When I set my coffee down and reach for it, I'm greeted with the one name that could lighten my mood after a morning of it being soured by my past literally opening a door I didn't want to be opened.

"Hi, Grace," I breathe into the phone, letting a whoosh of air expel out of me like a sigh of relief. I saunter toward the living room for some privacy and catch Everett settling himself into the driver's seat of the BMW I now know is his, and something in my heart squeezes, causing it to twinge and ache.

"Hey, Teeny. What are you up to today?"

"I promised my mom I would help her plant some begonias in the backyard so I will be up to my tits in dirt and back pain until about one. What about you?" I peer in the direction of the hallway to check if my mom or Sadie have made their way downstairs, wary of my verbiage in the same living room I used to open Christmas presents in.

"A little bored, and I think Buster wants to get out of the house. He keeps eyeing his leash and giving me those puppy eyes." I hear a low whimper from the other end of the line.

"Well, I'm taking Sadie and her friend to the beach after this, wanna join us?"

A loud bark interrupts our conversation. "Oops, you said the magic word."

"Beach?"

31

"Sadie." Another loud bark.

A calming grin has fully replaced the irate scowl on my face, and I realize this is the perfect remedy for that continuous spasm making my chest feel somehow hollow and heavy at the same time. "I'll call you when I leave here."

CHAPTER FOUR
Everett
THEN

"YOU WANT SOME OATMEAL?" My mom lifts a small pot by the long handle, showcasing lumpy slop inside with the faint rise of steam above it.

I shake my head. "I'm good with cereal." I've always hated oatmeal. The texture and bland taste make me feel like I'm eating mashed up animal feed. I'd much rather stick with my sugar-filled breakfast cereal.

My dad walks in, clicking his thumb against the pad of his flip phone. He reaches my mom's side, swooping down to give her a quick peck at the corner of her mouth before snapping his phone shut and reaching for a freshly brewed cup of coffee. "Some oatmeal can't hurt, Ev."

I ignore him, helping myself to another heaping spoonful of Frosted Flakes.

"You about ready?" my dad asks before taking a loud slurp of his coffee.

I nod. "Are you dropping me off?"

My dad peers at my mom and the two share some secretive glance before looking back at me. "We thought maybe you could drive yourself."

"Oh, am I taking mom's car then?"

He reaches into his pocket before tossing me a set of keys. I catch it against my chest and peer at the key fob. I run my thumb over the plastic buttons and look at my dad, throwing him a puzzled look. "What are these?"

"The keys to your new car."

My brows shoot up. "A BMW?" I lift the keys, pointing the round blue and white logo in his direction.

"I thought you should fit in with those spoiled rich kids."

"Dad!" I bolt for the door and run outside. Sure enough, sitting in the driveway is a brand-new black BMW. The shiny paint glistens in the sun, and I can see the tan leather interior through the faintly tinted windows. I jerk the door open to the driver's side and sink into the seat, inhaling that new car smell. I hear the footsteps of my parents follow as I'm running my hands over the soft leather lining the steering wheel.

"It's a manual transmission," my dad explains, leaning his arm against the door frame. "Which I'm sure you'll manage just fine. Power windows and locks. Stereo's the best kind. All the bells and whistles."

I look up at him, my hand still gripped on the steering wheel. "Are you sure, Dad?"

My dad laughs. "Of course."

"I mean, it's a really expensive car."

"So drive it carefully."

My mom tucks herself under my dad's arm and they both watch me take in my new car. "Thanks, Dad."

"Happy senior year, Ev."

I step out of the car, testing out the key fob with the locks and car alarm, and follow my parents back inside. I grab my backpack off the counter, say goodbye, and rush back to my car, throwing another "thank you" over my shoulder.

I tinker with the stereo system a little, figuring out how to program radio stations and stuffing my CDs in the glove compartment. It was one of the few items I actually unpacked. That along with some of my practice gear and DVDs I tend to watch on repeat. While the boxes sit unopened in my room, it feels inefficient to unpack when I'll be moving at the end of the school year. And from past experiences, the less I unpack, the less I'll have to repack when I leave.

As soon as I turn the ignition, the engine starting with a low purr, I notice Josh from next door leaving his house. He's trailed by his sister, both wearing early morning scowls. It suddenly occurs to me they probably go to Torrey Pines too.

Josh sees me watching them, and he waves a hand before getting into the driver's seat of his maroon-colored Pathfinder. His sister's eyes follow the direction of Josh's greeting, only to see me watching them. Her scowl softens, and she offers a tight-lipped smile.

I back out of the driveway ahead of them, following the detailed instructions my dad gave before I left the house. Right on the second street after the stop sign, a left on Durango Dr. until I turn onto the main road. The directions are pretty simple, and after I spent the last two weeks making short drives to the grocery store or getting takeout while we were still waiting for our stove to be replaced, I've familiarized myself enough to know which streets to look for. Just as I'm driving past intersection after intersection, I notice the same red car Josh is driving in the rearview mirror with him and Christine in the reflection. She's laughing at something at the same time Josh sneers at her. She pinches his cheek, and he lifts his elbow to get out of her reach. I smirk, watching them tease each other, just as the red light I was stalled at turns green.

When I pull into the large parking lot of Torrey Pines High, I see Josh still trailing behind me, pulling into a parking spot not too far from mine. We move in synchrony, getting out of our cars and our doors closing with a thud at the same time.

"Hey," Josh calls, quickly eyeing my car. We walk down the dark pavement to the large building of the school, our steps slowing as we meet at the sidewalk.

"Hey." I tilt my chin toward him at the same time I loop my backpack over my shoulders.

"Teeny, this is Everett. He lives next door," he says, tapping the back of his hand against his sister's shoulder.

"Hi," she says softly, waving a shy hand in my direction.

"Teeny," I repeat. Her lips pull into a straight line as if she's holding back a smile, while her name flutters around my head. Like thousands of brightly colored confetti. I thought her name was Christine this whole time. Ever since I met her dad and he'd slipped in that minor detail about her. And I've been whispering it to myself in my head, wondering what it would sound like out loud. While I called it to get her attention or while she learned my own name, enunciating the T at the end or dip after the first syllable.

Teeny.

Her teeth poke out from behind her upper lip, the front two bigger than the rest, and I don't know if this little detail about her is a flaw or if it's a likeness specific to her that only she can wear effortlessly. If without the small glimpse of her wide teeth peeking like they're curious, would her smile appear less fascinating?

The three of us walk away from the parking lot, Josh leading the way, with me trailing behind, and Teeny trudging next to me. She's stuffing some things into her backpack, letting the straps hang from one shoulder while she maneuvers her arm into the deep pockets of her navy colored Jansport. A calculator drops from her bag, and it lands on the hard ground with a harsh clack.

She doesn't so much as huff or let out a frustrated growl like I expected. Instead, she flinches at the sound of hard plastic hitting concrete while I bend down to reach it for her.

With my knee bent and back slouched forward, she peers down at me. The slight breeze flicks her hair across her face. She smiles at me, and I notice she smiles with her eyes. Normally round when she's quietly thinking to herself or observing her surroundings, they curve and sparkle when she smiles. They match the small wrinkles that line the bridge of her nose and the amusement bouncing in her eyebrows.

"Thanks," she says, gently taking her calculator from me. When I stand upright, she looks up at me, her round eyes turning curious. Her smile doesn't change, and something about the way she smiles softly, with the corners of her lips lifting just enough to let me know repulsion or disapproval is the furthest emotion she's feeling as our hands sit between us with the calculator acting as a buffer of space.

For some reason, I feel like I can tell her anything. My deepest, darkest secrets, like I'm not a huge fan of chocolate ice cream. Or that when I told my mom I lost my lunch bag when I was nine, I actually chucked it off a bridge on a dare.

"You're welcome," I say awkwardly. "Is it Teeny? Not Christine?"

She looks at me with a confused tilt of her head and an amused smile. "No one calls me Christine."

"Oh." I rub a hand at the back of my neck. "Your dad told me your name's Christine the last time I saw you guys." I feel a flush creep up my neck, and my heart turns fuzzy as I realize what a fool I'm making of myself. Why couldn't I just play it cool? Call her Teeny and call it a day? Instead, all she knows now is that I remember her name like it was lasered into my brain the second I laid eyes on her playfully pouting at her brothers on her driveway.

"Teeny's fine," she corrects me, her words pushed through a suppressed laugh.

"Teeny it is." A smile twitches the corners of my mouth, and that embarrassment dissolves.

Teeny.

I have my class schedule burning a hole in my back pocket, itching to be looked at for the twentieth time. Walking into this entirely new territory feels a little like I'm walking around in my underwear, and not knowing where I'm supposed to go is really adding to the unwanted attention I may have looking like a lost puppy in the school hallways.

We continue walking into the school, finding a lot of the students are pulling up in shiny new cars that match mine. The kids look cooler here, more confident, more breezy. Maybe it's the ocean air that's glided in from the coast all the way to the campus. Or the simple fact that most of these kids likely live in a home similar to the one I just moved into, too big and wide for my parents to know what to do with it. My skin starts to feel exposed, making me insecure as I saunter carefully into the main building.

"So, uh, do you play?" Josh asks, looking at me with a sideways tilt of his head. "I just thought, since your dad's a coach and all..."

"Basketball?"

He nods.

"Yeah, I do." My answer sounds just as unsure as I feel, and I'm sure it confuses Josh.

"Are you planning on trying out for the team?" He asks this question with hesitance, probably catching onto my lack of enthusiasm.

I nod. "Yeah, that's the plan. Hopefully the varsity squad isn't full."

"We are," Josh answers. "All the spots were filled during tryouts over the summer, but I'll put in a good word. If Coach Martinez likes you, he might move some of the guys over."

"You play too?"

He smiles proudly. "Team captain."

My brow shoots up. To think, we moved in right next door to the team captain. My dad's going to love this.

"Where's your first class?"

I pull out my class schedule from my pocket, smoothing out the wrinkles to hide the evidence of how badly I've been studying it. "Uh, room thirty-six."

"Mrs. Fix? French?" Teeny cuts in, overhearing our back and forth.

I look back at the crumpled paper. "Yeah."

"Oh, we're in the same class," she says.

"Great! Then Teeny can show you where it is," Josh says excitedly. "I'll see you later."

Josh walks off, joining a crowd of students in the main quad, leaving me and Teeny alone.

"It's um, it's this way," she says, lifting a hand in the direction of a wide hallway to the left. I nod and follow, dodging a few people hurrying through the thickening crowd now that it's getting close to 7:40.

"Are you a senior? Or..." I ask, trying to make small talk.

"Junior," she answers. "Josh is older by, like, eleven months, but he'll treat me like I'm eight for the rest of my life."

I chuckle.

"Do you have any siblings?"

I shake my head. "Only child."

"Lucky."

I chuckle again. "Don't you guys have another brother? He doesn't go here?"

"He's at UC Irvine," she answers. "He was just visiting for the weekend."

"Oh." My chest untightens as we both smile and continue to stroll our way to first period.

"You know, that old couple that used to live in your house, Mr. and Mrs. Allen, they were really nice. They used to bring us donuts on the weekends and pump my brothers' basketball when it needed air."

"Yeah," I respond, a little taken aback by the sudden mention of my grandparents. "They're—were—my grandparents."

"Oh," she says softly. "I'm sorry."

"Thanks," I say quietly.

"My parents visited often after Mrs. Allen passed away last year. They helped him take out the trash bin and stuff when he couldn't really do it on his own."

We arrive at the classroom marked "36" and round the corner in the room that's already almost full. It doesn't look like there's any sort of seating arrangement or silent agreement that certain seats are saved for some considering it's the first day of school, so I follow Teeny to a seat at the far end near the windows.

"Thanks for walking me to class," I say in a low voice, leaning in her direction.

She smiles with her teeth exposed, and the two front teeth stand proudly in the middle of her smile. "No problem."

CHAPTER FIVE

Teeny

NOW

"THIS IS SO MUCH BETTER than playing in dirt," I comment, leaning back in my beach chair with a deep sigh. "I think I'm going to be digging soil out of my nails for a week."

Grace reaches for her plastic tumbler filled with ice and something of the wine variety. "You're such a good daughter," she says. "I would've hired someone to do all of that."

"And waste money on something us adult children could do? Have you *met* my mom? I would never hear the end of it."

Mina, whose ears perked up the second Sadie said "beach" back at my parent's house, laughs from my other side. "I think she'd disown you."

Sadie and her best friend, Lauren, frolic at the water's edge, a mere fifty feet ahead of us. She's tossing a tennis ball for Grace's border collie as he barks and jumps to catch the ball midair. A bubble of laughter and amusement slips through my lips when Buster tackles Sadie to the ground and slathers her face with kisses.

I shift positions, stretching my back from the achiness of being slouched over weeds and tulip bulbs. And I'm pretty sure I experienced some level of a heat stroke after spending four hours in my mom's backyard with gardening gloves on and a hand trowel

41

gripped in my fingers. After an appreciative pat on my back and Sadie's promise to be back next week to make good use of my parents' pool, we left to spend the latter half of our day at the beach.

Mina stands from the spot on her large blanket and joins Sadie out in the water, Buster greeting her with giddy recognition for another friend joining the party.

"So, this ex-boyfriend of yours," Grace throws nonchalantly after a moment of silence now that Mina's out of ear shot. "What did he want to talk to you about?"

"I don't know, and I honestly don't care." I gave her the Cliff Notes version of my encounter with Everett and his pleas to hear him out as soon as she arrived at the beach while we unloaded and Mina and the girls lathered themselves up with sunblock.

Grace's small knowing smirk turns into a disapproving frown at my flippant remark. "But he's going to be here for the wedding?"

"Looks like it."

"Leo's going to have a field day when he finds out."

I shrug.

"You know, I think this is where I pass onto you some of my divorced woman wisdom," she comments, throwing a cheeky smile in my direction. "Entertain it."

"Entertain what?"

She flings a hand in my direction, clarifying nothing and making her words sound off handish. "The ex-boyfriend. See where it goes, and if it turns into a little summer fling...voilà!"

"What?" My head rears back at the absurdity of her suggestion.

"It could be fun."

"And dangerous," I tell her. "You don't want me to get meddled up in that mess again." She chuckles, laughing off the residual hurt from her own divorce last year after five years of marriage. "Is that what you did? Rekindle an old love?"

"Rekindle is a bit of a strong word," she answers. "More like... recharge and release."

I can't help a small giggle, and it feels good. It feels freeing to be able to laugh a little at myself, at the heap of muck that is my love life, and the collision of my present and my past.

Grace looks at me over the curve of her sunglasses. "How messy was it?"

"An absolute massacre."

Mina's phone trills from her blanket, and when I peer down at it, I see Josh's name flash on the screen.

"This is Teeny," I announce into the phone as soon as I answer it. "Don't say anything disgusting."

"Where's Mina?" he asks, dismissing my request.

"She's with Sadie in the water."

"I just got back home," he says. "I thought she'd still be at Mom's."

I shake my head, though he can't see me. "She came with me to the beach after we were done. You want to join us? I could use some chips."

"And bean dip!" Grace adds.

"Yeah," Josh answers. "Just send me a pin."

"Snacks are on the way," I tell Grace, tossing Mina's phone back in its place as soon as I send him our location. Grace and I move in unison, perching our sunglasses on our noses and tilting our breezy smiles toward the sun. Flashes of light veiled in pink fill my vision through closed eyes, and I can feel the warmth coat my skin, my arms and legs getting the brunt of the hot UV rays.

A rhythmic wave of cool ocean breeze brushes past us, soothing our pink-tinged skin. The sounds of Sadie's laughter and Buster's elated yelps assure both me and Grace that our kids are within earshot and safe.

It isn't until a shadow casts over me that I realize I'd been gradually dozing off into a lazy slumber, tired from the long day.

"Enjoying yourself?"

The warm tone, both teasing and harmless, stirs something familiar in me. Something that heightens my normally dormant fight-or-flight response.

"Everett!" I jolt from my lax state, hopping away from broad shoulders and the drifting scent of spice and outdoors.

"Hi, Teeny." Everett's eyes roam over my bikini-clad body. He takes his time, as if he's committing everything to memory. Everything from my messy ponytail, all the way down to my polished toenails.

"Everett! What are you doing here?"

I fumble with my cover-up and haphazardly throw it on, suddenly feeling completely underdressed, even with the amount of exposed skin scattered throughout the beach by other patrons, Everett included. He's wearing a pair of swim trunks I've seen on Josh multiple times, exposing all the way up past his knees to enough thigh exposure to have me looking away.

"He came with me." Josh drops two large grocery bags on the soft sand, various packages of chips and what looks like a bottle of alcohol poking out the top. I cast a glare in his direction, though he can't see through my shaded eyes.

From the distance, Sadie, Mina, Lauren, and Grace leisurely stroll toward us, Buster running circles around them. I hadn't even noticed when Grace joined them, but it looks like they're ready to take a break from their shivering bodies and enervated gait.

"That water is freezing!" Mina exclaims, reaching for a towel and wrapping it over her shoulders. She greets Josh, to which he wraps his arms around her to create some warmth and friction.

Grace approaches my side but her steps halt as soon as she takes in the scene in front of her. My tense shoulders with fists at my side and my voice caught in my throat. And this stranger of a man hovering over me with his height and authoritative aura.

"Uh, hi," she says nervously. She turns to face Everett, her back angled in my direction as if to create a shield. Maybe it's the instinctive female intuition of protecting any and all women from unwanted male attention. Or the fact that, among the growing group of familiar faces, Everett stands out like a very attractive sore thumb.

"I'm Everett." He offers a hand in Grace's direction at the same time Grace's brow shoots up.

"Everett?" There are so many hidden meanings behind her voice and a perplexed guise of confusion twists his features. "Like, *Everett Everett?*"

He doesn't answer but looks at me instead. The corner of his mouth tilts upward, but that quickly disappears when Grace takes his offered hand and aggressively shakes it. "I've heard a lot about you."

"All lies, I assure," he responds coolly, and he's rewarded with a delighted laugh from my best friend.

I walk away from the conversation, not caring about pleasantries or playing hostess to this awkward interaction, and stalk over to Josh. "Why did you bring Everett?" I hiss.

He turns away from Mina who'd been feeding him a chip.

"He was at my house, and I asked if he wanted to come when you asked me to bring over some food." He adds a little shrug, and that increases the frustration coursing through me. I hold back a groan and run my hand through my hair instead. "What's the big deal?" he asks, popping a chip into his mouth.

"It's not," I lie. "I just would like to know if you're bringing someone."

His palms face me. "Okay, jeez. I didn't think it would matter."

I return to my chair where Sadie and Lauren are ripping open a bag of Barbecue Lays and guzzling cans of Sprite.

"So, that's the ex-boyfriend?" Grace whispers, leaning toward me.

I nod.

"He's cute."

While I can't disagree with her, the look of disgust is hard to hide on my face.

"What?" she asks. "He is."

"That's beside the point, Grace."

"Obviously. He still broke your heart, but that is one fine ass man."

My eyes widen, and I smack the back of my hand to her forearm. She smirks a laugh and takes a long, drawn-out sip out of her cup.

My eye catches the long glass bottle Mina pulled out of one of the grocery bags Josh brought, the metallic red glinting off the sun with the words Smirnoff winking in my direction. I reach for it, adding a healthy guzzle to my own plastic tumbler filled with ice and soda. I might as well be drunk if I'm going to have to deal with Everett's constant gaze pointed in my direction.

"Mom." Sadie's voice perks up from the huddled whispers she and Lauren were speaking in. "Lauren's mom's here."

I tilt back the rest of my drink—vodka mixed with a splash of Squirt—before I face her. "You need me to walk you guys to the parking lot?"

Lauren shakes her head. "My mom's right there." She points to where the sand meets the parking lot to find her mom waving in our direction. I wave a hand back, acknowledging the exchange of our teenage girls, as Lauren and Sadie collect their things.

"You got everything?" I ask Sadie.

"Yup." She slings her tote bag over her shoulder.

"Make sure you wash your hair," I say firmly. "That ocean water is dirty."

"Yeah," she answers.

"And brush your teeth," I add.

"I know!" Sadie and Lauren turn to leave just as a buzz of alcohol starts to warm my blood.

With Sadie now in the hands of another responsible adult and out of my care for the night, it feels like the perfect time for a refill. I reach for the vodka, only a splash left, and add the remains of it to my cup.

"You want to take it easy there?"

"I'll be fine," I tell Grace. "This'll be my last drink, and I'll have plenty of time to sober up before I go home."

She tips a doubtful look in my direction, but I ignore it, shifting my attention to my fresh drink instead.

"Hey, was Leo busy today?" Josh asks, taking in my morose state and the way I'm drowning it in something easier to stomach.

"I don't know," I tell him. "What did James say?"

"I guess he was tied up with something."

"Then I guess he was tied up." The alcohol's starting to course through me, making me bold and my attitude thicken. I don't care about pleasantries right now, and I'd rather not talk about my soon-to-be ex-husband.

The silence lingers while Mina and Josh canoodle on the blanket that's way too small for the two of them to fit comfortably, causing Mina to take the seat on Josh's lap. Grace tears open a fresh bag of Cheetos, and I suddenly have the urge to pee.

"I'll be back," I tell Grace. "Gotta use the little girls' room."

She nods, her mouth full and her fingertips fuzzy with Cheeto dust. "Want me to come with?" she says in a muffled voice.

I shake my head. "I'll be fine."

When I stand everything seems to spin a little. The ground underneath me feels like it's swaying on a pendulum, so I grip my hand to the back of my chair. Grace hasn't noticed and neither has Josh or Mina. But I catch Everett's gaze watching my footing and how it's uneven and teetering.

I ignore him, rounding the beach blankets to the parking lot where there's a public bathroom. Of all public bathrooms in existence—shopping malls, restaurants, grocery stores—my second least favorite ones are the bathrooms at the beach. First would obviously be porta-potties. I brace myself for the acrid odor of urine that lingers in the wet cement of every beach bathroom and make my way to relieve myself. When I hit the sidewalk, a man—or a woman, I don't know—whizzes by at full speed on their bike. They nearly miss me by an inch, and it causes me to tumble backward. I expect to fall into the cool sand, but I'm caught by warm hands and a strong grip on my shoulders. When I look up at whoever it is that came to my rescue, I see Everett.

"Are you okay?"

I jerk my shoulder away from him. "I'm fine," I hiss in his direction.

I stomp to one of the individual stalls, reaching for the door, and let it swing open with excessive force. Once inside, I close it. I catch a glimpse of Everett standing where I'd left him with his hands shoved into his pockets.

Once I'm finished, I adjust my bottoms and swing open the door. It must have been the too fast sitting to standing motion or the over-powering smell in the small stall. Or even—most likely—the alcohol churning in my stomach, but as soon as I open the door, I feel every-thing rising up my throat. I turn around, heaving everything into the toilet I'd just used, not even having the time or thought to close the door behind me. So, whoever is outside of the stall can see my ass peeking out of my cover-up and the retching in real time.

Everything starts to burn. My throat, my nose, my eyes. I start coughing up what feels like my entire insides as a shiver runs up my spine. All of it, the cold, the chills, the sensation that my stomach is going to flip inside out, is all soothed by a hand pressed to my back. Specifically Everett's. I can tell it's him by the comforting strokes and the even pressure he applies when he massages his fingers between my shoulder blades. A touch I'd never forget.

"Mhh!" I exclaim, pushing my hand at Everett. "I-I'm. I'm...okay," I sputter.

He ignores my protest and reaches for my hair, brushing it out of my face and into a loose ponytail at my nape. "It's okay, Teeny. I got you," Everett's warm voice coos.

I don't have the energy to fight him. Everett can hold up my hair and pat my back. He can stand by my side until I start vomiting the inside of my stomach. I don't care at this point. I continue to heave and heave until I feel like there's nothing left to empty out of me. I reach for a small square of toilet paper to wipe my face—the vomit, the snot, the tears—before I turn around to face Everett.

I stumble off the step and Everett catches me once again to avoid a face plant onto cement. Everything starts to grow blurry. Even Everett's face. It looks a little distorted and wonky in the fading daylight lining the sidewalks.

"Come on," I hear him groan.

Next thing I know, I'm being transported through air, large arms lifting me like I'm on a big fluffy cloud. I don't know which direction I'm going. I could be headed for the moon, and I wouldn't be able to tell the difference.

My body continues to float, and my head feels heavy, causing it to fall against hard muscle. All I want to do is just sleep, to drift off into a dreamland where my life isn't in shambles.

Everything comes to a stop when I hear the sound of a car door open. I'm placed atop leather so gently I feel like I'm a coronation egg on a silk pillow. When the door shuts again and every sound is muted, I feel myself drift off into a thoughtless, worriless sleep.

"Teeny?"

"Hmm..."

"Teeny. We're home."

The drive from my parents' house was quick, only twenty minutes to get back home. I'd fallen asleep in the passenger seat with Sadie buckled into her car seat behind me. She was just as sleepy as I was, popping her thumb into her mouth and dozing off as soon as Leo buckled her in. I thought about waking her so she didn't fall asleep until we got home, but I was sleepy too. And when Leo backed out of my parents' driveway, waving a hand at my parents standing in front of their doorstep, my lids were already growing heavy off the three glasses of wine I had during dinner. And now, as he gently woke me from that alcohol induced sleep, I wanted to just stay in the car.

"Teeny?"

My eyes finally pop open. This isn't Leo's Volvo. Sadie isn't buckled in the back seat. There isn't even a car seat there. And when I look over to the driver's seat, it isn't Leo sitting there. It's Everett.

"Where am I?"

"I drove you home."

"What?"

"I told everyone you weren't feeling too well, and your friend gave me the keys to your car."

"She what?!" *Holy shit!* I can't believe I let myself get this drunk. And Grace. A wave of frustration starts to surge inside me as I map out a **"What the fuck!"** text intended for my best friend. Maybe even middle-naming her to stamp how deeply embarrassed I am right now.

"Is anyone home?" he asks cautiously.

Instead of answering him, I reach for the door handle, rushing out of the car. When my feet hit the pavement of my driveway, my entire body starts to sway.

"Whoa," Everett says quietly, rushing to my side. He has my bag gripped in one large hand while the other reaches for my waist. I start to claw at him but realize it's no use. With the entire world spinning and my house looking like it's stuck in a distorted funhouse mirror, I wouldn't be able to fight off a ladybug.

Everett wraps his arm around me and guides me to my door. Once there, I feel him fumble with his other hand before I hear a set of jangly keys and the front door open. Everett finds the light switch quickly and helps me to my couch before crouching in front of me.

"You feel like you might throw up again?"

I shake my head. My eyes are closed in an attempt to make everything stop spinning, but I feel Everett stand. He returns a few seconds later—it could've been minutes—and he places his hand on my knee.

"Take this," he instructs.

I pry my stubborn eyes open and see a blurry sight of Everett's large hands with two blueish pills in his palm.

"There's no red pill? What if I want to know all about the Matrix?" I mumble through the discomfort.

"It's Advil," he explains through a laugh. "These gel ones were all you had."

I sloppily take them from him and chug the water he hands me. Once I drink almost half of it, I feel a little less disoriented and my nausea dulls. My eyes clear through my drunken stupor, and I take in the whole image in front of me. Everett's sitting on my couch, the same cream-colored one Leo and I picked at Croft House six years ago, with his long legs tucked underneath my coffee table—that one from Crate and Barrel—with a box of Premium saltine crackers sitting on top.

"I found these in your pantry," he explains, reaching for the box and angling it in my direction. "You should get some food in your stomach."

I look at him, the look on my face somewhere between a scowl and surrender. The long pause between us is drawn out, and he doesn't back down from his offer. "I'm not going to think you hate me any less because you take the crackers."

That draws an eye roll and a peaked shake of my head. I rip open a bag and shove an entire square cracker in my mouth, and like magic, I instantly feel less nauseous. "Thank you," I whisper reluctantly.

"You're welcome."

I eat in silence, taking the occasional sip of water, and Everett waits patiently. Whatever swell of embarrassment mixed with my smothered animosity toward Everett gets tucked away. Somewhere I can ignore it and focus on the fact that he's here sitting next to me.

51

Everett's here, in my home. And the sudden realization makes a wave of melancholy sweep through me.

"This is why I don't drink," I say, cutting into the silence. "Apparently, I can't hold my liquor."

"You couldn't in high school. I doubt much has changed in that department."

I roll my eyes again, this time with less irritation and a pinch of nostalgia instead. "Remember I'd get drunk off two Smirnoff Ices?"

He chuckles.

"I was so lame."

Everett looks around the house, peering into the empty hallway. "So, where's your husband?"

I stiffen at the mention of Leo. A knot forms in my throat, and I push it down while my fingers toy with the ragged edges of a chipped cracker. "He's...he's busy."

I look over at him, hoping my omission is believable. I see his jaw tic and his brow furrow. "He's been busy all day," he comments. "He can't be here at night when his wife gets home so she's not alone in this big empty house?"

"I'm fine."

"Don't tell me he leaves you at home by yourself all the time, Teeny."

I shoot him a disappointed scowl. "I don't see how that's any of your business."

He keeps his eyes on me, and we hold this silent staring contest. One he doesn't budge from. As if he's telling me he'll decide what's his business or not. The tiredness from earlier when I stumbled out of the bathroom returns, and I realize how little fight I have left in me.

"Things are...complicated," I finally say.

"How?"

"I don't know...it just is." My lips twist to the side as soon as I feel my chin quiver, and I look away, hoping the ground will do me a favor and swallow me whole. Anything to get Everett to stop looking

TAKE ME BACK TO THE START

at me like he's looking at me right now. "Don't look at me like that," I finally say when I can still feel his gaze on me.

"I'm not looking at you in any way."

"Yes, you are."

"Like how?"

I let my gaze drift up to him, not caring that my eyes have misted over, and I can no longer hide the ache that makes my chest feel like it's going to cave in on itself. "Like you feel sorry for me."

"Teeny," he says, his voice cracking. "I'm looking at you because I shouldn't be the one walking you to your couch. I shouldn't be inside another man's home making sure his wife is safe and fed after a night out with her friends. Your husband should be doing that. He should've met us at the door and felt threatened by me bringing you home."

A tear trickles down my cheek. "This isn't his home anymore," I say through the enormous knot still stuck in my throat. "At least, it officially won't be. Just as soon as I find a good lawyer."

"You're getting divorced?"

I nod. "He cheated on me." Another tear trickles down my cheek and drops off the edge of my chin, hitting my bare thigh with a quiet splat. "I found out about three weeks ago. Though, if I had cared enough to do some digging, I'm sure I would've found out last year when it started."

"Does Josh know?"

"No," I answer. "James does. And my—Grace. But that's it. I haven't really told anyone yet."

The inner corners of his eyebrows turn up, and those wrinkles between his brows and forehead deepen, showing how not only I, but he too, has aged. "You told me."

I smirk. "Call it repayment for bringing me home. A little secret intel on my personal life."

I expect a sad smile or something of the less desolate nature but instead, he ducks his head low. "I'm sorry," he says, turning to face me with a look of pure regret.

53

My brow pinches together. "About what?"

"Your...marriage. Just, everything."

"Why? You didn't cheat on me."

A flash of a grimace passes through his face. "I can't imagine..." he says. He whispers it so softly that I don't even know if I heard him right.

"What?"

"How could he cheat on you?"

The tightness in my throat returns, and my eyes start to mist over again. I look away, peering at my toes painted cotton candy pink to avoid his gaze. "I don't know, Everett," I say sardonically, like I'm humoring his rhetorical question with an actual answer. "Men just do shitty things sometimes." I look back at him through the constant wave of tears.

So many unsaid things float in the air around us. Our past, our lives for the last twenty years that happened without either one witnessing it. And suddenly, I want to know all of it. What he's been doing since he left. If he's been in love, if he loves what he does for a living, whatever it may be. If he missed me. If he missed *us*.

I sink into the deep couch cushions, remembering why Leo picked this exact couch. It was because when we leaned our backs against it, it felt like we found a big squishy marshmallow to doze off in instead of just a simple piece of furniture we could lounge on.

"What about you?" I ask lazily, shifting the mood to something lighter. I turn with my shoulder wedged into the cushions and face him. He mirrors my movement, sliding off his shoes before resting his feet on the couch.

"What about me?"

"Are you married? Single? Swore off all women because relationships suck and being single is better than getting your heart broken again and again and ag—"

"I'm not," he interrupts.

My brow shoots up, impatiently urging him to clarify.

"Married. Or dating. Or anything, really."

I nod.

"You remember when you came over to my house and we fell asleep on the couch?" he asks, his voice turning sweet and nostalgic.

"And my dad almost ripped your throat out when you walked me back to the house after curfew?"

We share a small laugh, and Everett eases into the cushions closer to me, letting the side of his head rest against the soft curves so our eyes are level. "To be fair, he wanted to rip my throat out every time I looked at you."

"Yeah, but he got over that pretty quickly."

He smirks, and we sit there, those moments from our past drifting in front of us. I can't decide if it feels like someone's dangling those memories to taunt us or if they're sitting there, letting us sift through them, because we both need to.

For a second, I don't see the Everett that's in front of me right now. His skin a little weathered and the lines running out the corners of his eyes. Or the jawline that's grown sharper over the years with the loss of his baby fat and youth. I see that seventeen-year-old boy I loved with my entire heart. Not parts of it where some corners were reserved for other important people in my life, but all of it. My entire heart belonged to that boy at some point in my life, and I don't know what happened to that girl who loved with her entire being.

I reach up and smooth away a piece of his hair without even realizing it, only thinking about the hundreds of times I'd done it as that girl who was hopelessly in love.

"I loved you," I say sadly. "So much."

"I know," he answers. "I did too."

Not as much as I did.

CHAPTER SIX

Everett

THEN

BY THE SECOND week of school, I'd familiarized myself with my class schedule, memorizing the rooms and learning that Josh and the rest of the basketball team sit pretty much dead center in the cafeteria where they garner the most attention. Josh welcomed me into the throng of fellow varsity team members until I'd finally snagged myself a meeting with the coach. Most of it was in part due to Josh's persistence, though a push of encouragement from the rest of the team helped. With Josh's charisma, popularity, and his ball throwing skills I've witnessed once or twice outside on his driveway since the first day of school, it makes sense he's the team captain.

The guys mainly talked basketball, like how far they'd get this season with the new roster, and there were bits and pieces of upcoming parties and car talk. I chimed in here and there, answering questions like where I'm from and how I was managing the stick shift on my new car. It felt easy without the need for an icebreaker or a formal initiation.

I'm finally meeting Coach Martinez today after school during a pre-season practice meet with the rest of the team. Josh and I are heading to the gym after he sent Teeny home, tossing her his keys and making her promise not to eat in the car. She simply rolled her eyes at him, wishing me luck with an encouraging smile.

She's grown more comfortable around me, even helping me with last week's verb conjugation assignment and leaving behind small smiley faces in my notebook when I looked away. I keep finding ways to make her laugh, enjoying too much the way her entire face lights up and the small touches when she gently places her hand on my arm or playfully shoves at my shoulder. Even under the watchful eye of our French teacher, I manage to risk it all for a sliver of her attention.

"We're doing a really simple, unofficial scrimmage today," Josh explains to me as Teeny walks to the parking lot. Josh and I head in the opposite direction to the gym. "The season doesn't start for another month and a half, but Coach likes to see how we've been doing over the summer."

I nod.

"One of the seniors a few years back had a pretty serious injury, and when they couldn't find anyone as good to fill his spot, Coach kind of panicked." We approach the large double doors to the gymnasium, and Josh pulls at the clunky metal handle with a loud clank. "I think it would put him at ease if he had an extra player on the sidelines who knows what they're doing."

We trudge across the shiny, glossy hard flooring. There's a handful of other guys there, a lot of the same faces I've been sitting with at the cafeteria for the past week. Everyone appears pretty laid back, no formalities, which adds to Josh's statement that this'll be just an hour of practice drills. We all greet each other with lazy nods and even lazier high fives and handshakes, a sign of the after-school fatigue settled in our bones.

"Okay, team!" I hear a voice boom across the large gymnasium, the sternness attached to a man wearing a navy-blue polo shirt and a silver whistle around his neck. Everyone's faces perk up, that lethargy being swiped away with a wave of attention and focus. "Pair off into your teams. You guys know the drill. Four minutes, fifteen seconds on the shot clock."

Coach's eyes land on me, the newcomer that sticks out like a sore thumb and stalks toward us.

"Coach, this is Everett," Josh says, rushing to my side. "The guy I was talking about."

Coach squints his eyes. "You up for a scrimmage today?"

"Yes, sir."

A flash of approval flits across his face. "All right, go change, and Josh'll tell you where to go."

I reach into my bag for my basketball shorts and jog to the locker room.

An hour and a half later, I have a thin sheen of sweat glistening off my neck. Coach blows his whistle and gestures for everyone to gather toward the bleachers near the locker room entrance.

"All right," he announces, scanning his eyes over the symphony of haggard breaths. "You guys did good. Some more than others, but we have practice to catch up. Remember, official practice starts in a month. In the meantime, practice at home or here. I can extend my office hours if you need to use the gym."

Everyone starts to walk off to the lockers when Coach calls for me. "Hayes." I turn to him, and he meets me halfway with a fist jabbed into his hip and his other arm hanging loosely by his side. "So, I hear your dad is Edward Hayes."

I inwardly flinch at the sound of my dad's name. I have no idea how he knows, and my stomach twists with the thought that my dad ignored my plea to not involve himself when it came to my spot on the team.

"Yeah," I answer, sounding unsure and insecure. "But I want to earn my spot here fair and square."

He nods sternly. "Good," he says, the lift in his voice not matching his face. "'Cause we don't do handouts around here."

"Of course, sir."

"And I expect you to show up to every practice," he adds. "You got a lot of catching up to do with these guys, and I expect you to do that before the season starts."

"So, I'm on the team?"

He nods again, but this time with a small smile forming at the corners of his mouth. "But you aren't starting."

I beam. "That's fine," I say excitedly. "Whatever spot you got, I'll take it, Coach."

He ducks his head. "I'll see you at practice."

"I'm so jacked you're on the team," Josh says, slamming the passenger door to my car. "We can practice here whenever you have time. Or the courts at the park are good too. They're usually empty after school."

I'd driven us back home, and Josh had talked nonstop the whole way. About the upcoming season and what it means for us seniors. About the team and standings, stats, and college recruitment. His excitement was growing infectious on the drive over, making me less anxious about playing on a new team and more excited about the season to come.

"You want to come in?" Josh asks just as he heads toward his house. "My dad got this smoker last weekend, and we've been having every kind of smoked meat known to mankind."

I peer up at my house, considering my alternatives. My mom drove up to Malibu for the day to meet up with some of her friends from her USC days, something she'd been looking forward to now that my dad was back up north. I'd be home all alone anyway.

"Yeah, sure," I answer Josh.

When we walk into his house, we're welcomed by noise. I can't pinpoint what it is, mainly because it's a mixture of different noises meshed together, but also because I've never been greeted by sounds like this when I walk into a home. Yelling, music, the rhythmic clack of something being chopped on a cutting board, and even the shrill noise of a muffled chainsaw.

"Sorry it's a little crazy in here," Josh says over his shoulder.

I shake my head as we round the corner to the kitchen where I see Josh's parents at the kitchen counter. I find that the chainsaw noise, now a little more high-pitched and shrill, is a small electric carver Josh's dad is wielding. I find Teeny next to a woman, their mom I assume, as she chops vegetables on a chopping board and pushes them to the side using the blade of her knife.

"Hiya," Josh's dad calls, pulling away his focus from the large slab of meat on the counter. He's actually hovering over it, the countertop too low for his excess height, probably where Josh gets his height from. His hair, bright and wavy, hangs off his forehead and when he peers up at me, blue eyes look back at me.

"Mom, Dad. Is it okay if Everett stays for dinner?"

Both their mom and Teeny lift their heads and smile warmly at me. "Hi Everett," Teeny's mom says. Her hands don't leave the space in front of her, her grip firm on the knife and vegetables, but even with the entire length of the kitchen island between us, she's friendly and welcoming. Her round eyes, fanned at the edges with fine wrinkles, smile back at me with the same wide front teeth Teeny has.

"Did your parents want to join us for dinner?" Teeny's dad asks. "We're celebrating Andrew's birthday."

"Oh, yeah," Josh says from my side. "Sorry, dude. I forgot to mention. It's my baby brother's birthday."

I nod. "My dad's actually back up north, and my mom's visiting some friends in Malibu," I say to Josh's mom to answer her question.

"Well, that works out then. We'll make sure you're fed tonight." She pauses to move over some things into a steaming pot. Her dark hair, identical to Teeny's, is held back with a large clip, strands of white and gray making the tones of her hair silvery.

"Thank you," I answer her.

I see how much Teeny takes after her mom, with her deep brown eyes and apple-like round cheeks. Even the way she affectionately pats Teeny's shoulder as Teeny helps her with dinner seems to be a direct parallel to how warm and sympathetic Teeny is.

Soon enough, we're sitting at the formal dining room table surrounded by heaps of platters, all full of food like it's Thanksgiving dinner.

"We don't normally eat like this," Josh whispers from the seat next to mine. "It's usually just regular stuff."

Just then, pitter-pattering footsteps sound from the hallway and come to a halt at the entrance to the dining room. A kid, who I assume is the birthday boy, stands there with a Lego Millenium Falcon in his hands and his breaths coming out in sharp intake and exhales.

"Joshy! I finished it!"

"Hey! Great job, kiddo!" He stands from his seat, walking over to his little brother, and takes the Lego set from him with caution. "It looks good!"

The boy smiles proudly with a gap in his front teeth and crooked bangs lining his forehead. He looks at the table and gasps. "Where's my cake?"

"Mom's got it in the fridge," Josh explains, looking over the table to find it sans cake. "We gotta eat first." Josh sets down the Lego set on a nearby table, making sure that it sits sturdily before walking his brother to the table. "Andrew, this is my friend Everett."

I wave a hand, and Andrew gives another wide grin before taking the seat next to mine.

"Okay," I hear Josh's mom call as she appears with a large silver pot held by potholders. "Sorry for the wait. I was just finishing up the *miyeok guk*."

Teeny follows, carrying a stack of bowls. She's laughing at something her dad said, looking at him with her hands full and for some reason, it makes me smile too. When she smiles, everything about her lights up. Her twinkling eyes, her glowing skin, her rosy cheeks. Even her golden-yellow dress, covered in teeny tiny flowers hanging off her shoulder with capped sleeves and a hem that reaches just above her knee, instantly brightens up the room as she enters. Her hair is half up, two braided pigtails trailing the side of her crown, and she tosses it back at the same time her smile transitions into a full laugh, making a warm, fuzzy feeling spread through my chest.

Teeny sets the bowls next to the pot her mom brought out and settles into a seat right across from me. She gives me a smile, flashing me those endearingly charming teeth, and waves her hand in my direction.

I'm about to wave back when our silent exchange is interrupted. "Everett, have you ever had Korean food?"

I look at Teeny's mom, a long ladle scooping some kind of dark, slimy stew from a pot to a bowl.

"No I haven't," I answer. "But I'm not picky."

"Good." She extends the bowl she just served to Andrew and moves onto another empty bowl like an assembly line. "We don't eat Korean food every day, but *miyeok guk* is reserved for birthdays. It's seaweed soup, and it's a common Korean tradition to eat on birthdays. And Andrew's favorite," she adds. "It was all he ate as a baby."

I catch Teeny eyeing me curiously, observing me in a studious way as I take it all in. The genuine laughter and prattle that fills the table while the food is being passed around is infectious, just like Teeny's smile, and I find myself mirroring the teasing uptilt of her lips every time I look at her.

"Josh, did you send in your application to UCI yet?" Josh's dad asks, his voice cutting across the table.

"Yes," he answers politely. "I sent in all my applications last month."

"Good," his dad responds. "As soon as you hear from UCI, you let us know."

"You applied to San Diego State too, right?" his mom chimes in, and Josh nods. "It would be nice if you don't have to go to school too far from home."

Another respectful nod has Josh's head bobbing up and down, not giving any dispute about his future, much unlike me and my dad.

"But make sure you keep UCI in your top three options." Josh's dad pauses before gesturing a fork in my direction and asking, "What about you, Everett? Do you have plans for college after graduation?"

I feel my ears grow warm with the attention suddenly on me. "My dad wants me to go to UC Davis. It's fairly close to our home in Sacramento, and he's hoping I'll play in college."

"You play?"

I nod at the same time Josh jumps in. "He just made the team," he tells his parents excitedly.

"Congratulations!" Josh's mom says enthusiastically.

"Thank you."

"Mommy! Can I have a Death Star piñata on Saturday?" Andrew exclaims with barbeque sauce on the side of his mouth, interrupting our conversation.

Josh's dad shakes his head. "I don't know where we're going to find a Death Star piñata in three days." Andrew sulks and he adds, "But you have the very nice Luke Skywalker costume Mommy got you."

"Everett," Josh's mom says, calling my attention. "If you and your mom are free this weekend, we're having Andrew's birthday party. Nothing fancy. Just some hotdogs and hamburgers. And a jump house if either one of you is into that."

I smile. "I'll let her know. Thank you."

After an inharmoniously sung rendition of the happy birthday song with Andrew's eyes shining brightly against his candles and cutting the chocolate cake, I'm hovering over the kitchen sink with Teeny standing at my side. I'm helping her load the dishwasher as she hands me plates from the sink after she was assigned the task, and I volunteered to help. Josh's parents are putting things away in the fridge and making multiple trips from the dining room to the kitchen to store everything, and Josh has been assigned with trash duty.

"Congratulations." Teeny's gaze is on the sink where she's meticulously scraping at a dried piece of food on a fry pan. Our hips brush, magnifying how closely we're standing next to each other. "On making the team."

"Oh, yeah. Thanks." With her focus on her suds-covered hands, I watch her. I watch the way her lips twitch as she congratulates me. The silky locks of hair neatly tucked behind her ear, exposing the small diamond stud standing out like sparkles of starlight. The slope of her jaw and how it trails down a narrow hollow before connecting to the column of her neck. Even the delicate chain dangling a gold butterfly that rests on her collarbone. My hands, wet and soapy from the task at hand, starts to itch with the need to readjust her necklace so the clasp rests at her nape.

Her arm brushes against mine, and she looks up at me. Water sloshes between us when she reaches for a new plate and her temple nearly brushes against my chin. "Hopefully you can play basketball better than you can pronounce 'monsieur.'"

My brow shoots up. "I can pronounce *'mon-sur'* just fine."

She giggles. "It's *'me-syer.'* The 'n' is silent."

"That's what I said."

She rolls her eyes and nudges me with her elbow.

CHAPTER SEVEN

Teeny

NOW

MY MOUTH FEELS like the Sahara. It's dry and cracked and sandy. Ugh, and disgusting. And my neck. It feels like someone glued my ear to my shoulder, causing a serious—and a little worrying—knot to form right where my neck and shoulder connects. I don't remember the last time I'd slept this uncomfortably. It was probably during a weekend getaway to Grace's grandparents' cabin in Big Bear back in college when I was left sleeping in a recliner while Grace dozed off on an inflatable bed. My head feels like it's been squeezed and wrung out with sunlight and dehydration.

This is exactly why I don't drink hard liquor.

"Ughh…"

"Good morning."

I bolt from my prone position, pushing my hand into the cushion to sit upright. When I look over my shoulder to the kitchen where the deep, velvety voice came from, I see Everett.

"What are you doing here?"

He lifts a mug that says "World's Best Dad" in dark bold print to his lips, taking a loud, obnoxious slurp. "Having some coffee," he answers casually. "You want some?"

I stumble off the couch, smoothing out my shirt that's ridden up my torso, and stomp toward him. "I mean, why are you still here? Why didn't you go home last night?" I hiss.

He casually shrugs. "I drove your car."

"And you couldn't just Uber back to your hotel?"

"Actually, my car's at Josh's," he explains, looking too relaxed for my liking. "So, I was wondering if you could drop me off." He takes another long sip and the rattling of the coffee slurping through his lips drives me near insanity.

"Absolutely not," I answer. "You need to call Josh to come pick you up or order an Uber or something."

"Is this how you treat your guests?"

"Everett," I argue, taking the cup from him and gently placing it on the counter. "Now. You need to leave now." I round to his back and start shoving him toward the door.

"I can't even finish my coffee?"

"No!"

"Teeny!" His voice comes out all high-pitched and whiny, and I'd probably find it a little amusing if it weren't for the situation at hand.

"Seriously, Everett. You need to go. Sadie's going to be home soon from her friend's house, and you *cannot* be here when she gets home."

He swipes my phone off the counter as he walks by it and shows me the screen. "She texted ten minutes ago. She mentioned something about a movie? Said she's going to be home in the afternoon."

I take my phone from him. "Are you going through my phone?"

"The message just popped up when I was making coffee."

I glare at him before I unlock my phone and look at Sadie's message. Sure enough, she texted me exactly twelve minutes ago to tell me she and Lauren are watching the newest Timothée Chalamet movie with a couple of other kids from school. I tap out a quick response letting her know I got her message and set my phone down.

"You still need to leave, Everett." My voice has lost the urgency and panic it had a second ago, but I don't sound any less vexed.

"Come on, Teen," he urges in his most calm voice. It's the exact same voice he used when he wanted me to stay an extra hour at his house, pushing the boundaries of my rarely bendable curfew, or when he gave me the sweetest set of puppy eyes asking me to forgo the last round of reviews for our French final. "You want to grab some breakfast?"

"What." It's a question, like saying "excuse me" or "pardon me," but it comes out so flat it doesn't sound like a question at all.

"Breakfast," he repeats. "We can go to the little diner with the hazelnut waffles."

"Why?" That one sounded more like a question. Because *why?* Why does he want to have breakfast with me? What could he possibly want that requires food and an hour forced into a booth with nowhere to go besides another public bathroom that smells like bleach and the overpowering stench of toilet water?

He shrugs. "Call it repayment for watching you throw up your insides."

"You didn't see that."

"I saw enough," he answers. "But then again, I've seen you do that plenty of times." He smirks this time. The jerk smirks like he's remembering all the times he had to support the weight of my alcohol infused body while we left another party, and he let me sleep it off in the passenger seat of his BMW. And for some reason, it makes my scowl falter, leaving behind a somber pang in my chest I can't seem to ignore.

"So?" he asks again. "You can drop me off at Josh's after."

"Fine."

An hour later, after I've showered and dressed in something clean and wasn't a reminder of the night I had, we're sitting in the small booth at Marie's. It's a small mom-and-pop diner in Del Mar Heights with a wide view of Pacific Coast Highway that's been around for forty years. I used to come here as a kid, and after I brought Everett here for late night hazelnut waffles and Coke floats, it became our regular spot. We spent many nights pouring over homework and hours of comfortable silence or stories that ran on unorganized tangents and laughter.

"We'll have the hazelnut waffles and two Coke floats," Everett tells the waitress with two closed menus sitting between us.

"Can you actually make one of those a coffee please?" I add.

The waitress nods, not even bothering to jot our order down on a small notepad.

"Too cool for Coke floats?"

I shake my head. "I just..." I pause, looking at the table to avoid his eyes. "I'm in the mood for coffee." I chance a glance in his direction, and I immediately regret it, worried he can see through my lie. Like the reason I stay away from Coke floats is because it reminds me too much of Everett. Because the last time I had one is a memory I hate to revisit. And recalling all the subsequent Coke floats I had before that last memory would make me want to throw every caution sign to the wind just so we can rehash our past right here, right now.

"You always got them, Teeny," he states matter-of-factly, the raspiness of his voice making him sound vulnerable. It's there, plaited between those five words, whispered through a gravelly thickness with a realization that hits him in the face.

"I'm not the same girl you knew twenty years ago, Everett." For a moment, the anger that had balled up inside my chest dissolves. I'm so tired. I'm tired of being angry at Leo, at Everett. I'm tired of being angry at love when all I wanted to do was cherish it. I wanted to love someone and be happy. But now, I'm realizing that the only time I did cherish love was when I didn't know any better. When I thought Everett loved me as much as I loved him.

Everett looks at me, and I look at him. And we stay quiet. As if we're giving our teenage love a moment of silence so we can grieve its loss. We never had that. At least, I never did. I spent the last twenty years being so resentful, I never gave myself this moment to let go of something that gave me life. But I'm here, waiting for the moment for me to say goodbye to my past. To let it drift off into the calm waters while I watch it peacefully sink into an abyss. And I'm still not ready to let it go.

"Everett, why are you here?" I ask abruptly.

His brow scrunches into a confused scowl. "I told you. Josh—"

"No, I get that. But why?"

"What do you mean 'why?'"

"You and Josh haven't seen each other in twenty years," I elaborate. "And out of the blue, he decides he wants you to be in his wedding?"

He shrugs. "I don't know why he asked."

"And why did you say yes?"

That confused scowl returns with silence.

"You could've told Josh you couldn't. You could've made up any old excuse, and Josh wouldn't have questioned it. So why did you come here?"

"I guess..." He peers at the silverware sitting next to his right hand. The pads of his fingertips start to run over the metal handles of the fork and knife like he's stalling. "I wanted to come back home. I miss being here. I miss Josh and your family."

But not me. I nod. My throat starts to feel tight and painful. "Well, you know, those sandy beaches are hard to forget."

"Teeny—"

"Ohmigod, Christine!"

I look up at the excitedly squealed sound of my name to find one of the last people I expect to see here: Erica Davis.

"Erica!" I awkwardly call in the direction of my husband's colleague's wife. "Hi."

I stand from my seat at the same time Erica reaches my side. We hold each other in the quickest of embraces before we part, and her eyes immediately fall on Everett.

"How are you?" she asks, running a hand down my arm. "I feel like we haven't seen you in ages."

"I'm good. Just getting ready to send Sadie out to summer camp this week."

"Right, she signed up for that music camp out in LA," she says. Her eyes shift to Everett again while I do everything I can to avoid introductions. "You're going to have a lot of time on your hands."

I laugh awkwardly. "I'm taking on more clients," I tell her, though it's really none of her business what I do with all of this supposed "free time." "I think I'll have my hands full for the summer."

Erica laughs too, though her over-exaggerated chortle sounds arrogantly forced. "You working moms," she comments as if us "working moms" were some exotic breed. "I don't get how you do it. I couldn't stand to be away from my babies."

"Heh," I huff, laughing to fill the uncomfortable silence with politeness instead of with something cheeky and just as backhanded as her comment.

"Well," she adds, breathing a sigh with subtle undertones of annoyance. "I've got to run. I'll tell Marcus we'll set something up soon. I'm sure Nikki and Sadie would love to have a little girls' day at the pool." She throws another look at Everett before pulling me into a goodbye hug, one that feels more like a cold shoulder with the phony sideways peck against my cheek.

"Bye, Erica."

"Too-da-loo!"

I slink back into the booth seat and look at Everett. "What in the real housewives of San Diego was that?"

I hold back the laugh at his sarcasm with an irked shake of my head. "She's the wife of Leo's colleague."

"So does that make you one of those Stepford wives?"

I tsk. "With my cooking skills? Never."

That draws a loose chuckle out of him.

"I just have to...play the part. Be the happy wife with the beautiful family and home."

"Are you—I mean, were you happy? Before you found out..."

"You mean before I found out my husband had a side piece a speed dial away?"

Everett grimaces, but he quickly tucks wherever that expression came from and looks at me with those sad puppy dog eyes I can't stand.

"I was," I finally answer, looking away. "When we got married, and when we had Sadie, I was. But we haven't been happy for a long time."

We're interrupted by the arrival of our order. The waitress slides the steamy cup of coffee in front of me, and by the time the plate of waffles sits between us, I realize what I've just told Everett.

We don't touch anything. We don't lift a single silverware or napkin. Instead, we just sit in silence.

"I'm sorry, Teeny."

"So you've said."

"I only ever wanted for you to be happy, Teen. I didn't think—"

"You know, we should eat before the waffles get cold," I interrupt him. I can't do this. I can't rehash our past like I need another reminder of how many things were left unsaid between us. I don't need to remember how heartbroken I was twenty years ago or how the fall of my marriage was a result of so many things I couldn't let go from my past. Because I couldn't open up to Leo like I did with Everett, and my own husband never got to have the part of me I wanted to give him because I'd guarded my heart too tightly.

I start stabbing into the waffle at the same time Everett warily picks up his fork. I poke at the food, moving it around silently, while Everett stops the waitress for a glass of water, leaving his Coke float untouched. He pushes it to the side, under the glaring heat of the sunlight streaming in from the window beside us, where it falls into a messy, irreparable heap of ice cream and our past. And I can't help but think how irreparable our hearts have become in the last twenty years. We'd merely placed crappy pieces of Scotch tape over the cracks of our hearts, enough so we could ignore the ache seeping through those breaks and fissures. Maybe we can just swirl everything together, wipe around the frosty glass, and make it look presentable. Enough so that we can look at it and think about how much we loved each other. So we can finally say goodbye to those kids who unexpectedly fell in love.

The drive to Josh's is quiet. The buzz of lazy weekend traffic drifting around us, mingling with the strong ocean breeze and late morning sun, masks the words Everett and I are holding down.

The thing with heartbreak is that you believe time will heal. The days, weeks, months, and years pass, and the pain starts to lessen. They become dull and numb and something much more manageable. But what about the pivotal moments that lead to heartbreak? The ones that change you. Right down to the neurons firing inside your brain, lighting up every time something crosses your path, reminding you how you'll never be that person again. I started to measure moments in my life before and after Everett. When I got my driver's license? That was B.E. Before Everett. When I had Sadie. That was After. When I withstood thirty-six hours of labor and a C-section, and I couldn't tell him about it. I didn't have the choice to call him and tell him about the happiest day of my life, and how holding Sadie while I nursed her and shushed her to sleep only drudged up the memory of him.

"Thanks for dropping me off."

I turn to face Everett, nervously eyeing Josh's front door, when he reaches for my hand resting on the armrest between us. I should pull away, draw back from his touch, if only to remind myself that I'm still angry at this man. That I'm still hurt and sad and resentful of the past twenty years. But am I? Was I really ever mad at him? Maybe I was just hurt. And the pain seeped into a territory I didn't know how to navigate. So being angry at him felt easier. Something I was able to sit and live with.

"Sure," I answer. I finally pull away from him, feeling like the space in the car is growing smaller and smaller. And it has nothing to do with Everett's large six-foot-two-inch frame filling the seat next to me. "Look, Everett—"

We're interrupted by the front door opening and Josh's sudden looming presence. He stands there, one hand on his hip and another shielding his eyes from the sun.

"Take care," I finish. "I'll see you at the wedding."

Under the scrutiny of my older brother a few feet away, Everett doesn't push his luck. Instead, he opens my car door and steps out, leaving this emptiness in my chest I haven't felt in twenty years.

CHAPTER EIGHT

Everett

THEN

"EIGHT-YEAR-OLDS LIKE BATMAN, RIGHT?"

I look up to see my mom walk into the kitchen with a Batman figurine and a bright blue gift bag. She waves the toy in my direction, beckoning an answer.

"Uh, yeah," I answer, dipping my spoon into my cereal.

She sets everything down on the kitchen counter, taking out the tissue wrap and stuffing it into the gift bag. A blank, apathetic stare takes over the focus in her eyes. Like she's checking out, doing what she can to forget the changes surrounding us. The emptiness in her home signifying the absence of her parents. The lack of my dad's voice constantly on the phone or busy running through the house, always late to a meeting or practice or press-related things, exposing our new living arrangement, making it harder for her to ignore.

The bell chimes, announcing a guest at our door, and my mom offers a placating smile before walking away to answer it.

"Everett!" my mom calls. I walk to the front door to find Josh there with a basketball tucked under his arm. When my mom sees me, she opens the door wider. "I'll see you kids at the party in a few hours," my mom says, walking away.

"Hey."

"Hey," Josh answers, jerking his chin in my direction. "Wanna play until the party?" He tosses the ball in my direction, and I catch it against my chest.

"Yeah," I answer, throwing the ball back at him. "Let me just go change."

An hour later, I'm in Josh's driveway in my swim trunks, ready for Andrew's pool party, with Josh already sweating bullets down his bare chest. I join him, pulling off my own shirt, already soaked through, and tossing it to the side.

Josh rests his hands on his knees and smacks away the ball bouncing in his direction. "Shit, I'm more out of shape than I thought."

I laugh. "Summer will do that to you."

"Coach is going to be pissed if he sees me like this."

"You still have some time before pre-season starts up," I say breathlessly. I'm just as out of shape as him, and the unexpected workout has me winded.

"Josh! Help set up the tables!" We turn to look at the front door where Josh's mom has poked her head and is waving a hand in our direction. "Hi Everett!" she adds before hurrying back into the house.

"You want to set up some tables?" Josh asks, rolling the loose basketball toward the grass where it won't roll into the street.

"Sure."

We both walk with heavy sluggish steps into the house, still a little bushed from the last hour spent outside. Josh walks ahead of me, and I trail behind, wiping at my face using the shirt I have in my hand.

"*Oof!*" A sharp gasp and a body colliding into mine makes me curl inward and grunt.

I rounded the corner from the stairs without looking, and Teeny crashed into me as soon as she stepped off the last step, rushing down the stairs with the pitter-patter of urgent feet. Her palms press into my stomach and my hands instinctively grab her arms to stop her from falling back.

"Eww!" Teeny grimaces, pushing herself off me. "You're all sweaty."

I laugh, shaking the sweat hanging off my hair to land on her cheeks and nose. Her face scrunches, her lips pulling into a cute pout as she fakes disgust. She ducks her head to avoid my perspiration sprinkle while the bubbly sound of her laughter turns infectious.

"Ugh, you're so gross." She's pushing me away even more, shoving my shoulder, but she's all smiles and giggles. I notice then what she's wearing. A black bikini top and jean shorts. Her bare stomach is exposed, showing the evenly tanned skin on her midsection, and I can see faint tan lines run across her chest and shoulders. Like she has various bathing suits with different straps and ties, making marks based on what she chooses to wear. "You should jump in the pool. Get all of that gross sweat off your stinky body."

I smirk. "Only if you join me."

Instead of humoring me, she tilts her head to the side. "I have snack duty," she says, walking away, but I don't miss the pink flush blotting her neck and shoulders.

I follow her to the kitchen where she has a bunch of different snacks laid out. Cupcakes, brownies, cookies, candies. She disappears into the pantry and returns with a box of Pop-Tarts before removing one from a sleeve and warming it in the toaster.

I mosey over to her side and pick up the box, reading the label. "Frosted Wildlicious Wild Berry."

"You can say that without twisting your tongue, but you can't say 'excusez-moi.'"

"It's English," I argue.

The toaster jerks, spitting out the Pop-Tarts with a jolt. "Want one?" she offers.

"Aren't these breakfast foods?" I tease.

"I like them," she answers with an innocent shrug. She reaches for the freshly toasted Pop-Tart resting in the toaster and picks it up with the tips of her fingers to avoid the heat, but it doesn't seem to help in the way she expected because she plays a short game of hot potato before quickly placing it back in the toaster slot. "Ah!" she exclaims softly.

"Is it hot?"

She nods, flicking her wrist to ease the burn. I take her hand, spreading her fingers apart and blowing at them with my lips inches away from her fingertips.

Her breathing kicks up as I notice her chest rise and fall at a more rapid pace than before, her lips parting to softly exhale a breathy sigh. My thumb brushes over her wrist, and I feel the faint beat of her pulse. It's fast and thready. A flush crawls up her neck, and I almost debate letting go of her to ease her flustered state. Almost.

"Better?"

She nods, and a little bit of those nerves dissolve as her hand falls slack in mine. "Thank you."

Her fingers curl over my palm, and our linked hands sit there, hovering in the space between us. She looks at me over the curve of our fingers, and she smiles. It's soft and gentle and playful. I smile back, the upward slope of my lips mirroring hers. I want to tug her closer to me. I want to press my lips to the small spot on her skin that got burned. Maybe even throw a scolding glare and a light smack to the toaster. Payback for her injury.

Mr. Cohen walks into the kitchen, and I let go of Teeny's hand. He eyes us, the only two in the kitchen with Teeny's pink-tinged cheeks and my shirtless torso, and tells Teeny, "Can you help Andrew get dressed? He can't find his lightsaber for his costume."

She looks over at me with a knowing smile, and I see Mr. Cohen watching her. "Sure, Dad."

Teeny leaves, and I'm caught with the kitchen island sitting between myself and Mr. Cohen's stern stare.

"Hey," Josh calls, walking in behind his dad. "There you are. The tables are in the garage."

I clear my throat. "Yeah," I say, aware of Mr. Cohen's watchful gaze. "Let's go."

The smell of barbeque and sweet desserts fill the air outside in Josh's backyard. We're surrounded by the sound of screaming kids, adults laughing and talking, and the occasional giggles from Josh's cousins. All girls, who look to be about fourteen or fifteen, huddled over two folding chairs. They keep looking over at where Josh and I are, standing next to the grill his older brother, James, is manning as he pokes at it with an excessively large set of tongs, repetitively turning a spread of hamburger patties and hot dog weenies. Teeny walks over with an empty plate, and I instinctively stand up taller.

"Can I get a burger, please?" she asks James.

Her hair's wet, and she's ditched her shorts. In their place is a damp towel wrapped around her waist, and a smattering of goose bumps trail her arms. James places a perfectly prepared burger on her plate, and she slides a step closer to me and stoops next to the cooler at my feet to remove a can of Sprite.

"Looks like you have a little fan club over there," she says in a low voice as she dangles the cold soda can dripping with condensation by her fingertips.

We both peer back at the group of teenage girls, now about six of them, still stealing glances in our direction.

I smirk, too awkward for this type of attention.

She hums thoughtfully. "Are you shy?" she teases, an amused smile lifting the corners of her mouth.

"No," I answer in a low whisper, looking away and busying myself with my food.

She fakes a shocked gasp. "You are!"

I narrow my eyes in her direction. "No, I'm not."

"You totally are," she taunts with her voice at a near whisper, poking her finger in my direction. "Oh, Everett. That's no good. We can't have the hot new guy be a closeted recluse."

One corner of my lip turns up. "You think I'm hot?" I ask, the whisper in my voice matching hers.

We're interrupted by a loud splash. Josh grabbed one of his cousins, one of the giggling girls on the other side of the pool, and threw her in. Along with Andrew, who willingly jumped in with one of the other girls, they're all creating chaos in a big water fight.

"I'll jump in if you will," I dare Teeny.

"I just got my food." She holds up the plate in front of me.

I take the plate and the unopened soda can from her, and she lets me, watching me as I place it on top of the cooler.

"It's going to get cold."

I ignore her, stooping down to grab her by the waist. Her towel falls to the ground, and I rush into the pool with my arms still wrapped around her and her screaming into my ear. I see Teeny's arms flail under the water while we're both submerged and when we break the surface, she gasps in shock in my direction.

"Everett!" She laughs, splashing water at me, and I do the same. We're joined with a slew of happy screams and squeals, all drowned by the violent sloshing and splattering of water.

I feel hands on my shoulders followed by the pressure of weight pushing me down. It's not heavy so I'm able to fight it off, and when I turn around, I find Teeny attempting to climb me. I duck into the water and lift her from her hips and flip her over my shoulder. We're creating a show, and people start laughing at us before Teeny's mom announces that it's time for cake.

The pool starts to empty, but I wait for Teeny. She finds me and splashes a testy wave of water in my direction. "That was so not fair," she sulks, though a smile peeks through her anger.

"How so?"

"You're like twice my size," she states. "I'm at a huge disadvantage." She flicks more water at me, and I dodge it with my shoulder. We're the only ones in the water now, and we move around each other, wading in the deep end in circles.

"Yeah, but you speak French better than I do."

She laughs. "How does that help in this situation?"

"You could've always outsmarted me."

She rolls her eyes and starts toward the edge of the pool to join the rest of the party. "I'll get you back," she says over her shoulder. "You better sleep with one eye open, Hayes."

"You're last naming me now?" I ask, following her out.

"Only when you're in trouble. And that"—she waggles a finger in the direction of the calmer water—"was definitely last name worthy."

She hands me a towel from a stack that was set aside, and we both dry ourselves. Everyone else has gathered around a large folding banquet table near the lawn area, and we slowly make our way.

"Teeny! Mommy got me a Death Star piñata!" Andrew shrieks, running to tug Teeny toward the cake. It's a large sheet cake decorated with various Star Wars characters and figurines on top with a large number eight candle.

"Wow! That's so cool!" Teeny responds, following along with the large towel wrapped over her shoulders.

I join the crowd, all huddled around the birthday boy, standing next to my mom who has a clear plastic cup of wine in her hand. "Having fun?" she asks, taking in my drenched state.

"Sure," I answer with a smile.

"It's good to see you've made some friends," she adds, nodding a head toward Teeny and Josh who are now standing next to their parents, James, and Andrew.

"Uh, yeah," I say, my voice low and hesitant. "We go to the same school, so..."

"Well, they're nice kids. And their parents are really nice."

I nod, looking over at Mr. Cohen hovering over Andrew. "Yeah, they are."

The happy birthday song is cheerfully sung, and the cake is cut haphazardly into small squares before it's passed around. People start to scatter around the backyard holding small paper plates of chocolate cake and plastic forks.

Josh sits next to me in one of the lounge chairs outside, empty now that the giggling teens were ushered inside to watch *A Walk to Remember*. I can hear them cry and squeal while I see flashes of Mandy Moore's face on the big screen.

Teeny steps out of the house just then. She looks freshly showered and has replaced her bikini with a baby-blue sundress and sandals. She combs her fingers through her wet hair and strolls up to Josh. She has the cordless phone pressed to her ear, and she whispers a quick, "Hold on. Let me ask him," before stopping at his feet. "Did you hear about Jake's party?" she asks.

"Yeah, he just texted me about it."

"Can I get a ride with you if you're going?"

"Mom said you can go?"

Teeny nods. "As long as we help clean up before we go." She walks away back into the house, and I watch her, her mouth moving a mile a minute with the back of her dress damp from her hair.

Josh peers at me over the curve of his shoulder. "You wanna go?"

"What is it? Just a party?"

He nods. "Yeah, Jake's parents own this huge house off the beach. It's sick. Like a five-car garage and a movie screening room."

"Sure," I say, shrugging my shoulders. "I just gotta let my mom know."

We spend the next hour cleaning up and stuffing trash bags with paper plates and soda cans. Once that's all squared away, I go home to change, and we're on our way to this Jake's house with Teeny in the back seat.

I catch glimpses of her behind me in the passenger seat through the side-view mirror. She's peering out the window, mouthing along to some song playing on the radio, when Josh calls for her attention through the rearview mirror.

"Teeny."

"What?" she answers, her gaze still fixed on the view outside.

81

"Don't drink tonight," he instructs in a big brotherly voice.

"Yeah."

"I mean it, Teen," he says more sternly. "Mom's going to kick my ass if you come home drunk."

"I'm not, Josh!" She rolls her eyes.

The drive there isn't long, and when we pull to a stop at the curb, we all exit at the same time. We're greeted by a long street filled with cars and people herding toward a large house at the end of a fully packed driveway.

When we walk inside, Teeny disappears almost instantly, and I follow Josh as he's greeted by other members of the senior class. Most of them I know already, some I've met but haven't said anything beyond a simple introduction from Josh.

"Josh! You came!" It's Jake. He's a senior like me and Josh and someone that's pretty well known on campus. He drives around in a shiny black Mercedes, probably brand spanking new considering his parents are loaded. I don't know him well, but I do know he's a little loud and brash. Probably all the money that's gotten to his head.

"Jake," Josh calls, greeting him with a smile. "This is Everett."

"Everett," Jake says, nodding his head in my direction with a cocky smile. "The new guy. I heard you made varsity," he adds, folding his arms across his chest.

Josh pats Jake's shoulder. "Word travels fast."

"Come on," Jake urges, turning toward the thick of the crowd. "Let's get you guys a drink."

We walk into the kitchen where it's crazy crowded. There's knocked over Solo cups, chip crumbs, and used shot glasses all over the kitchen counter. People don't seem to bother attempting to clean up, their attention more focused on the loud music and the game of beer pong off to the side in the dining room.

Jake reaches into a cooler and pulls out two cans of Heineken before handing them to us. "There's a keg out by the pool, but you guys can warm up with these."

Josh waves his hand in his direction. "I'm driving."

"I'll drive," I offer.

"You sure?"

"Yeah." I extend my hand, silently requesting Josh's keys as he takes them out of his pocket.

"Well, since he's designated driver, you can have both." Jake shoves both beers into Josh's chest and walks away, hooting into the crowd that welcomes him with cheers and open arms.

The entire house starts to get even more crowded. Josh starts adding to the two beers he finished, harder stuff like Jameson and Jäger. People file toward the pool outside when it gets cramped inside, and I lose track of Josh. I wander around, finding myself near the pool where most everyone is occupied in drinking games or circles of rowdiness and even more drinking. There are a few chairs scattered throughout the concrete area by the pool, and I sit in one, leaning forward with my elbows resting on my knees.

"Hey."

I turn to see Teeny sitting in an empty chair next to me with a red cup in her hand.

"Breaking the rules?" I ask, nodding at her cup.

"It's strawberry Fanta." She extends it in my direction, waving it under my nose. "Happy, officer?"

I smirk. "Want to jump in?" I jerk my head toward the pool where a group of people are playing a game of chicken fight while onlookers cheer them on.

"No, thank you," Teeny responds flatly. "So, not having a good time?"

I shrug. "I'm okay. You?"

"My friends found an interesting game of truth or dare, and I lost interest after one of them got dared to use the kitty litter in Jake's laundry room."

That draws a chuckle out of me. Teeny stares into her cup, and a soft draft blows between us, pulling her hair back and exposing the darkening freckles lining her cheekbones and nose. She's wearing a little bit of makeup tonight, a swipe of lip gloss and a light layer of blush and eyeshadow. She looks less like Josh's baby sister and more like Teeny. The Teeny I sit next to in French class and share glances with when I run into her while taking out the trash or pulling into the driveway. In fact, I've unknowingly been looking for excuses to be outside my house during the day. Get something out of my car, help my mom with the groceries, check the mail. Whenever I hurriedly slip on my flip-flops and step off my front step, I glance toward Teeny and Josh's house without realizing it, hoping to see her.

"Come on, new guy," she instigates, nudging me with her elbow. "Let's ditch this party."

"I'm designated driver," I tell her. I whip out the keys in my pocket and dangle them between us.

"We'll come back," she says pointedly. "Josh won't even know we left."

I look around like we might get caught doing something we aren't supposed to and look back at Teeny. She's got these big round puppy eyes peering up at me, and I shake my head.

"All right," I surrender. We both stand, slinking off to the side door leading out to the front of the house, making our way to Josh's car. We quietly get in, almost like we'd burgled the place and we're trying to make a quick getaway, and buckle up. "So, where to?"

"Just head out to the main road, the same way we came in, and I'll tell you where to go."

Jake's house isn't far from ours, so the roads aren't too foreign, but I still need Teeny's guidance to know where I'm going. After a few left and right turns followed by a big curve into a residential area, we're face-to-face with the beach. I parallel park in an empty spot along the curb and we both exit the car.

It's about ten degrees cooler out here, most likely from the stronger coastal breeze this close to the water, and Teeny wraps her arms around herself. I peek into the back seat of the car where I saw a blanket hiding and get it for her, wrapping it over her shoulders as we reach the sand.

"It smells like stinky boy."

I laugh. "What does a stinky boy smell like?"

"I've lived with three my whole life," she states. "I know a stinky boy when I smell one."

"Am I a stinky boy?"

She takes a faux, and dramatic, whiff in my direction. "Not right now."

She doesn't take the blanket off though. Instead, she wraps it tighter around her and saunters off toward the water. I follow, clumsily trudging through the sand. When we reach the area next to a lifeguard tower, before the sand turns wet from the ocean waves, Teeny stops and plops herself to the ground. I sit down next to her, leaving inches of space between us.

"You know I haven't been to the beach since I moved out here."

"What? Why?"

I shrug. "Haven't really thought to. I'm not really missing out, am I?"

"You tell me," she teases. She bumps her shoulder into mine and waves her hand in front of her, gesturing toward the open ocean.

"It is pretty nice," I say, unable to argue the fact that I had indeed been missing out.

"You should see the sunset," she adds. "It's pretty breathtaking."

"I take it you come here often?"

She nods. "It's a little chaotic in my house. The only nuisance out here are the pooping seagulls."

"You'd take pooping seagulls over your brothers?"

"Not all the time," she answers, smiling at me. "Just..."

"I get it," I tell her, ducking my head down to the sand. "There are times when I feel like I need to get away too."

"From what? Your empty house and your mom who looks like she wouldn't hurt a fly?"

"She usually does her own thing," I tell her glumly. Her smile drops and her brow furrows into a disapproving frown. "It gets a little lonely sometimes. Just me and my thoughts."

85

"Oh." I feel her warmth lean closer into me. Possibly a gesture of sympathy or simply a reminder that I'm not alone. Especially here with nothing but Teeny and the ocean waves to remind me I'm more significant than a tiny speck on this big scary world.

"Yeah, but you know, it's nice hanging out with Josh. And I like hanging out at your house."

"Well, we got that big dining table and an empty spot without James at home so..."

I nod with a small, grateful smile.

She stands then, slipping off her sandals and dropping the blanket onto the cold sand before walking to the water. I watch her for a moment as she gently treads along the low tide until she looks back at me, waving her hand for me to join her. I stand and remove my own shoes, and when I reach her, she splashes a mischievous gust of water at me.

"Hey!"

"Payback for earlier."

"Oh, is that what we're doing?"

She laughs, running away from me, and lets out a loud squeal when I splash her back. It doesn't take me long to reach her, considering one of my steps equals about two and a half of hers, and when I do, I lift her by her waist.

"Everett!"

I ignore her plea and walk to the thick of the water.

"Everett! No!"

"I think you earned it," I tease, speaking into her hair that smells like coconut and vanilla.

"*NO!* I'm going to freeze to death!" She struggles against my grip, her legs flailing and her hands clawing against my arm. I set her down, her feet now submerged under the water, and she shoves her hand into my stomach. "Bully!"

"You started it!"

She takes a step backward, her hands up in front of her like a shield. "Yeah, because you deserve it!"

She reaches down so quickly I don't even see the splash of water until it hits my face. She darts away, and I go after her. She runs to the lifeguard tower, using it to create a shield between us, but I get to her too quickly. I catch her, just as our feet tangle and we land on soft sand riddled with shards of seashells and small branches. We tumble to the ground, my body covering hers with my thigh nudged between her knees. Her hands brace my waist, and we start to pant from the running, from the laughing, and she looks up at me with her hair fanning her face in the sand.

She looks absolutely stunning. Those dark freckles blend in with her skin behind the shadows of her face, and her eyes glisten in the moonlight, making them glow. My eyes finally zone in on her lips after I'd tried everything to avoid looking at them. Dividing two hundred and ninety-one by three, reciting the alphabet backward, trying to remember my locker combination from the eighth grade. But once I couldn't remember if my locker combo started with eighteen or eighty-one, I said fuck it. Her lips look like they'd taste sweet and soft. Like they could help me drift off to a soundless sleep while fueling an entire ten-mile run.

"Why are you looking at me like that?" she asks, her voice breathless.

"Like what?"

"Like you want to kiss me."

My own breath catches against her, finding that when my chest expands, my body pushes harder against her. "Maybe because I want to?"

"Then do it," she coaxes, her eyes so serious and intense.

"Yeah?"

She nods, and that's all it takes. I crash my lips to hers, and she reaches her arms around my neck, pulling herself closer to me. Her lips feel like silk, all soft and pillowy. And I don't know how, but she tastes like peaches. Sweet and warm and fucking delicious. I feel her knee hook over my hip at the same time she whimpers into my mouth. I respond by kissing her deeper, like I'm taking her kisses from her instead of waiting for her to offer them to me. I dip my tongue into her mouth, and she lets me, tangling her own tongue with mine.

"Everett," she whispers, pulling away from me. Our breaths start to come out in heaves. When her hands rake into my hair from my neck, I just want to keep kissing her. Over and over and over again.

"Yeah?"

"I-I don't know," she stutters. "I don't know why I stopped."

"Probably because we should."

She shakes her head. "Should we?"

"I don't know. Maybe?"

Her lips are swollen now, and a flush has crept up her neck and cheeks. "I don't know either."

My elbows dig into the rough grains of sand. It starts to buff and grind into my skin, but all I can focus on is Teeny's face. I want to trace all the little freckles on her face, connect them together if only as an excuse to touch her. I want to memorize them, note all the differences between each one. Like how the one under the inner corner of her left eye is the darkest of them all. Or how the three that trail off the side of her nose looks like Orion's belt. I feel her fingers trail my forearm, and it's a zephyr-like jolt of electricity. It zaps through me. Like a lightning bolt that bursts through my chest, sparking something vibrant and stirring.

"We should probably head back," she whispers. "Josh might wonder where we are."

I hear a tremble in her voice. It matches the reticence in her eyes.

Should I not have kissed her? Maybe I gave in too easily. I should've been the more responsible one. Waited a beat before letting my body act on impulse. Unease starts to wind its way down to my stomach, churning this fear inside me that I might have ruined whatever is budding between me and Teeny.

When she doesn't say anything else, I reluctantly agree, standing with my hand extended toward her. She tugs at it, and we start to brush the sand off from our clothes and the bare skin of our arms and legs. I see specks of sand on the back of her head and reach for her hair, dusting it off. She turns around and faces me with a sheepish smile.

"Thanks."

"No problem."

We quietly walk back to the car, the air a vast difference from when we arrived. While we drive back, it's still quiet. The only sound between us is the low hum of the music playing off the radio, turned down as if to amplify the silence between us. When we reach the party again, we sit in the car for a minute before getting out.

"Teeny," I say, my voice suddenly so loud in the stretched silence. "I'm sorry." I'm not even sure what I'm apologizing for. It sure as hell isn't that kiss. I wouldn't take it back for anything. But I need to make things right with Teeny. I care about her too much to walk away without making sure our friendship remains intact after tonight. Especially if that's all she'll give me.

"For what?"

"For what happened back there. Maybe that wasn't the right thing to do."

"You mean the kiss?"

I nod.

"Are you taking it back?"

I look at her, the regret in my words causing my voice to sound urgent. "No, no Teeny. Not at all."

"Then why are you saying sorry?"

"Because I don't want you to think I took advantage of you," I tell her.

"I'm not a child, Everett," she says coolly, followed by a bitter scoff. She opens the car door and stalks out, slamming it shut behind her. She starts stomping off without a second glance, leaving behind a residual hurt from the resentment in her voice.

"Teeny!" I jog after her, glad that I can always seem to reach her faster than she can get away from me. "Teeny, wait."

"What, Everett?"

"Look, that came out wrong. I—I just felt that maybe..."

"Everett," she says, looking over her shoulder when we hear a few people leave the party. She shoves me toward a long row of bushes where we're hidden behind its tall shadows. "I'm not some kid you lured away from this party. I asked you to leave. I told you to go to the beach. If anyone's taking advantage of anyone, it's me of you."

I huff a laugh and scratch the back of my head.

"What's so funny?"

I laugh again. "Nothing."

"You're laughing."

I take a step closer to her, my gaze set on her eyes. The only light veiling over her is coming from the sparse streetlights. The dancing silhouettes that fill her face along with the anger making her pout makes me want to kiss her again. But this time with no post-make-out apology. "I'm not," I assure her.

Her head jerks back like I've insulted her. "I don't know if you know the definition of laughter, but I think you need to get yourself a diction—"

I grab her face in my hands and kiss her again, cutting off her words. She doesn't fight me. Instead, her hands reach for my waist, wrapping her arms around the small of my back. My hands curl into her neck, and Jesus, I could get lost in her lips. Like they were made specifically for me to kiss, the grooves carved and buffed so they fit perfectly against mine.

"You are not taking advantage of me," I whisper against her skin. "Not by a mile."

She grins, followed by a reluctant frown on her lips. "You totally did laugh," she pouts, shoving her hands into me.

I stumble a step back. "I wasn't laughing *at* you. I was just laughing—" I'm interrupted by the sound of my phone ringing in my pocket. I take it out and see Josh's name flash on the screen.

"Hello?"

"Hey! Where'd you go?!"

"I, uh—I'm just outside. You ready to go?"

"I need to find Teeny first," he says, yelling over the noise in the background. "She needs to get home soon, or my parents are going to kill me."

"I actually just saw her," I say, looking at Teeny. She has her arms crossed over her stomach and her eyes round.

What? she mouths with a soft whisper.

Josh, I mouth back at her.

"I'll get her and come find you."

"Yeah, I'm in the kitchen."

I hang up and look at Teeny. "Josh is ready to go home."

"Yeah, let's go find him." She turns to walk away but then I tug at her arm, pulling to flush against me. I peck her lips, resisting the temptation to fall into another kiss.

"Can we talk? Later?"

She nods. "Yeah, of course."

I grudgingly pull away from her and follow her lead back into the house. We find Josh quickly, right in the middle of the crowded kitchen surrounded by a round of freshly poured shot glasses.

"Eyyy! It's Everett!" he calls in a slow, slurred voice. He tosses back the shot and slams the glass onto the kitchen counter.

"You sure he's ready to go home?" Teeny asks, leaning into me with a hand cupped to her mouth.

"That's what he told me."

I look at her and laugh with a questioning shrug.

"Okay, okay," Josh says, reaching us with a tomato red face and glazed eyes. "That was the last one. I'm ready to go."

"You sure?" Teeny asks.

He lazily loops his arm over Teeny's shoulders and pulls her into a loose chokehold, rubbing his knuckles into the top of her head.

"Josh!" Teeny shrieks. He laughs gleefully and lets go of her.

"Come on, Joshy. Let's go home."

I duck my head to let Josh's arm drape over my shoulders and guide him outside to his car. I safely get him in, tucking him into the back seat where he flops across the seat instead of sitting upright. I take the blanket I'd thrown into the back seat and dust off the sand before covering him with it.

I get into the driver's seat, and Teeny looks at me from the passenger seat and giggles.

"Shh! You're going to wake the baby."

She covers her mouth with her hand, and when she lets out a muffled laugh, Josh stirs in the back. "How am I going to sneak him back home?"

"Would your parents be mad if he stayed at my house?"

"I don't know. Probably not," she says, peeking over her shoulder where Josh rumbles a loud snore.

"Just let them know he came over to my house to watch movies. They can call my mom if they want."

"You're going to handle that?" She points her thumb behind her.

"I'll be fine."

"Okay."

I drive home in silence. When we hit a red light, I glance over my shoulder to see Josh still sleeping soundly, his face squished into the cushions of the seat underneath him. I reach across the center console and reach for Teeny's hand, linking our fingers together. I look at her, and she smiles at me when I bring her hand to my lips and kiss her knuckles.

CHAPTER NINE

Teeny

NOW

I NEVER THOUGHT Sadie would outgrow the fairies and princesses stage. I thought she would prance around in her frilly dresses decked out in glitter and tulle until she grew out of them and asked for new ones to replace them. I didn't expect there to be an expiration date for when she would stop wearing those cheap tiaras and plastic shoes that clacked on the wood floor.

But, alas, the day came. She decided she no longer liked all the make-believe things and shifted her interests into purple and Taylor Swift and learning how to play the guitar and piano at the same time. She focused her time on writing poetry as if she'd suffered through a break-up when the extent of her heartbreak didn't go beyond a dispute with her friends over who the cutest BTS member is. It crept up on me until one day she requested a trip to Home Depot for a can of amethyst purple paint to slather over the large princess castle decal I put up at the head of her bed when she was three. She'd moved onto the next stage of her life where she'd need me less and demanded more privacy.

"Did you pack your curling iron?"

Sadie nods, her arms elbow deep in her duffel bag resting atop floral print bedding. The ones that replaced her princess comforter right before she started junior high. "And I made sure to bring enough tampons," she says.

"You got all of your toiletries too?" I ask, taking a quick peek into her bag, trying hard not to hover. "Toothpaste, toothbrush, shamp—"

"Yes, Mom. I got it all." She walks away to pack up the rest of her things, gingerly placing her acoustic guitar in its case and stuffing away a few pages of sheet music.

I peer at the digital clock at her bedside. "Your dad should be here any minute."

Just then, we're interrupted by the distant sound of a horn honking. Three short beeps, signaling Leo's arrival outside.

I pull Sadie in for a long hug. "Call me whenever you want," I mumble into her hair. "I don't care if it's two in the morning and you just want to say good night. Or good morning."

"I will, Mom."

"Have fun and learn loads," I add.

She lets out a loose giggle. "I will!"

Another impatient honk interrupts our embrace, and I unwillingly let her go before reaching for her duffel bag. Sadie follows suit, slinging her guitar case over her shoulder. When Sadie walks out the front door and I follow close behind, I see Leo walk cautiously toward us. It's so strange to see this man, the man who used to walk through this house in his tattered pajamas, walk the steps of the driveway now with so much heed.

"Hi, Sadie bug," he calls as she lowers her guitar case and runs into his open arms.

"Daddy!" she squeals. It's like she's that little six-year-old girl again, obsessed with putting stickers on her dad's face along with glitter lip balm and pink nail polish.

I see a small crack in Leo's reserve when he holds Sadie in his arms. It's the same soft spot that would make my heart weaken. Forget about those long nights in a cold bed or canceled dinner dates. And for the first week after I found out about his affair, it was the reason I considered working through this. For our family. Until the resentment lingered like rotting mold.

"Can we get some Starbucks on the way?" Sadie asks, handing off her guitar case to Leo. "I'm craving a caramel macchiato."

"Is all that caffeine even good for you? Doesn't it stunt your growth?"

Sadie rolls her eyes, sliding into the front seat and poking her fingers at the elaborate touch screen inside Leo's shiny new Audi.

The slam of the trunk brings me back to Leo, his cautious eyes peering at me, gauging what's allowed and what's not. And I can't believe this is the same man I used to spend weekends in his small studio apartment in nothing but bed sheets and day-old pizza.

"How are you, Teeny?" he asks. His monotone voice sounds so formal.

"I'm fine," I tell him, responding in an uncomfortably stiff cadence.

He pushes the heel of his hand against the closed car door. Music thumps on the inside, and I get a quick peek of Sadie's muffled voice drowning in the bass.

"I'll pick her up in four weeks," I let him know. "You don't have to make the drive again."

He takes a step closer to me. "Javi's taking Sergio and Annie camping the first week of August," he explains, referring to his brother and niece and nephew. "They got this big RV, and he's driving all of them up to Big Bear for a week or two before school starts. I was thinking of joining them. Bring Sadie with me."

"We have Josh's wedding."

"Right."

"But...I guess you can take her after the wedding depending on when they go," I tell him, the guilt making me offer more than I planned to.

A sad smile spreads across his face. "Thanks, Teen."

I nod. "Have a safe trip." I turn to leave at the same time I see him reach his hand up to touch me, but he stops himself.

"Actually, Teeny." He shoves his hands in his pocket and rocks on the heels of his feet. He's wearing a dark Lacoste shirt, probably something I bought him, with jeans and sneakers. A vast difference from the usual business attire he wears during the work week. Though he's dressed down, I see the small details that show how different we both are from those twenty-somethings that didn't mind buying clothes in bulk at Old Navy or whatever was on sale at Nordstrom Rack. Like the Piaget glinting off the sunlight on his wrist. Or the Tom Ford sunglasses folded and tucked into the collar of his shirt. But the bags under his eyes and his gritty five o'clock shadow can't hide the stress dawdling between us. He can't glitz that up with designer clothes or expensive accessories.

"Yes?" I ask after we'd been standing there for a few seconds too long.

"I was wondering if maybe we could talk."

I hold back the frustrated sigh rising up my chest and cross my arms instead. "What did you want to talk about?"

He shifts his gaze inside the car, checking on Sadie who's still oblivious to our conversation. "Are you free for dinner? Tomorrow night?"

"I'm going to this cake tasting thing for Mina."

"Friday?"

I shake my head. "I don't think that's a good idea."

"Please?"

"Leo, whatever you have to say, just say it now."

"I thought it would be nice for us to be alone." He takes another small step closer to me and a part of me recoils. "Sadie won't be here, and we can talk."

Whatever emotional rage I've been tampering down in an attempt to be cordial starts to climb up my throat, and my chest feels tight with frustration. "I really don't have anything to say to you."

"But I...There are a lot of things I want to talk about. I need to explain—"

"What could you possibly have to explain to me?" I hiss, my hands fisting at my sides.

His palms face me. "Okay," he offers. "I-I'm sorry. Okay?"

"Just go, Leo. If I need to talk to you, I'll call you. Or my lawyer will."

"Are you serious? You're not really going to go through with this."

I glare at him. "Why wouldn't I? You *cheated* on me. You fucked some twenty-two-year-old paralegal because she batted her eyelashes at you and stroked your ego."

"It wasn't like that—"

"No? Because I don't know how you can paint it in a different way. It's pretty clear what happened."

"Teeny—"

We're interrupted by the sudden burst of music when Sadie opens the car door. "*Daaad*! I don't want to miss orientation!!"

Our stiff bodies leaned into an obvious altercation, slacken at the sound of Sadie's voice.

"Yeah, Sade. We're leaving right now."

Sadie looks at me with a furrowed brow, taking in my uneasy stance and flushed face. I force a smile and take a few steps toward her before ducking my head to peck a quick kiss to her hairline. "Send me some pictures when you get there. I want a video of that song you're working on."

She smiles, her giddy grin beaming with pride. "I love you, Mommy."

"Love you too, Sadie bug."

I close the door and catch Leo rounding the car. The somewhat amiable air he tried hard to maintain has dissipated into something unpleasant. Something damaged and irreparable. He looks at me as if barely realizing how broken we've become.

97

The next day, twenty-four hours post-argument with my soon-to-be ex-husband, I'm driving the twenty-minute drive to Just Sweets, the very hipster and very chic bakery handling the three-tier wedding cake Mina and Josh spent a pretty penny on for their wedding. The day's shifting into evening, and the sun is gradually falling behind the hills of Del Mar Heights, peeking through the uneven terrain of homes and rise and fall of the highways. As my Spotify playlist decides what to play from my current shuffle, it's interrupted by the sudden ring of an incoming call from an unknown number through the speaker system.

"Hello?"

"Hi, is this Christine Diaz?" asks a deep, unfamiliar voice.

"This is she."

"My name's Eric Lang. I received your number from a colleague of mine," he starts to explain. "I hope it's okay that I reach out to you like this, but I'm looking into remodeling a large property out in La Jolla and am in need of a designer-slash-decorator."

"Oh, yes," I answer, my mind shifting into work mode. "Yes, of course."

"It's a resort-style hotel, a little run down, but I just took ownership of it last month and am currently planning a whole remodel. You came highly recommended."

"Oh, well, thank you for reaching out."

"Would you be available to meet? Maybe sometime this week?"

"I have to check my calendar, but yes, absolutely. Would it be okay if I get back to you? I want to make sure I don't double book before setting a time and date."

"Absolutely," he answers. "You can reach me at this number anytime."

"Great. Thank you, Eric. I'll be in touch soon."

I press the button to end the call right as I pull into the small six-car parking lot of Just Sweets. The bell dings as soon as I enter the store, announcing my arrival and initiating an eager greeting from a middle-aged redhead in a floral apron.

"Hi!"

"Hi," I respond. "I'm here for the cake tasting. For the Cohen wedding?"

"Oh, yes! You must be Mina."

I wave a hand in her direction to correct her. "Oh, no. I'm one of the bridesmaids. Mina's a bit busy so I'm here to help out."

"Well, nice to meet you. I'm Kelly. Is it just you?"

"The groom, my brother, is on his way," I tell her.

Just then, we're interrupted by the sound of the same chime that sounded when I entered the quaint yet stylish shop. When I turn to face the entrance, I see my brother enter the store.

"This must be the groom," Kelly announces.

Josh reaches my side and nods politely. "Josh Cohen," he says, introducing himself.

"Nice to meet you," Kelly responds. "We'll do the tasting here," she tells us, gesturing to a small wrought-iron table with two chairs set up next to a display case of cupcakes.

Kelly disappears as Josh and I synchronously pull out chairs and sit.

"Thanks for helping out," Josh says solemnly.

"Sure." It's quiet between us, and I don't miss the somber mood radiating off my brother. "Is everything okay?"

He nods unconvincingly.

"Are you sure?"

He hesitates, running his fingertip over the pronged plastic fork sitting in front of him. When he looks at me, his face softens into something that aligns with sympathy. "I talked to Leo."

"Oh."

"He called, asked me to meet him for lunch."

"What did he tell you?"

His brow furrows. "That you kicked him out. And you're talking to lawyers."

I shake my head. "Did he tell you why?"

"Yeah," he answers in a low voice. "He told me he talked to James

99

too. I guess he's trying to recruit whoever he can to convince you to forgive him."

"James didn't say anything."

"I know," he answers. "He said he doesn't want to get in between you two. And you know he's got his own set of issues at home."

"It wasn't just a one-time thing," I tell him. "He was seeing her for seven months before she demanded he leave me. She threatened to tell me. He started having *Fatal Attraction* nightmares and told me he couldn't risk her meddling with his family. Said he couldn't do that to me and Sadie."

Josh scoffs. "That was nice of him."

"It's over." I clamp my teeth over my lower lip. "It's been over. For a long time. Not just because of the affair, but we've grown apart over the years. This was just the tipping point."

Josh reaches for my forearm across the table. "Whatever you want to do, I'm here for you. Me and Mina. We'll get you through this."

"Yeah," I croak hoarsely.

"And I'm sorry."

I tilt my head to the side, a little confused. "About what?"

"If I had known...I wouldn't have asked Everett to be a part of all of this."

My body tenses hearing Everett's name. "Why did you?"

He exhales a heavy sigh. "I just...missed him. He was my best friend, and he disappeared so suddenly. I wanted to catch up, know what he's been up to."

I nod, and Josh offers another apology. "I really am sorry, Teen."

"It's—I mean, it's fine. I'm an adult. I can handle it."

"Teeny, I was there." He pauses to run a hand through his hair. "I was there when you had to pick up the pieces of your heart. You were never the same after. And maybe it's that I'm getting married, and I finally met someone I want to spend the rest of my life with, but I can't imagine hurting Mina like that."

My breath hitches. It's been twenty years and I thought what I went through, I went through it completely alone. Isolated in my own world of heartbreak where I cocooned myself in pain and grief. I never once thought about the people around who witnessed it all.

"If I had known what was going on between you and Leo, I would've never asked him to come. Not when you're this vulnerable."

"I'll manage," I say with a weak smile. "The wedding's going to fly by, and I'll never have to see his annoyingly handsome face again." I try to convince myself of the words caustically pouring out of me. It doesn't matter how little they ring true. I have to be okay with it. I have to be able to face Everett at my brother's wedding. Because the ensuing alternative, the one where I choose to let my past peek through the cracks in the walls I've built, isn't something I think I'll survive.

Josh smirks a tender chuckle, indulging my feeble joke, just as Kelly returns. She places a large rectangular plate carrying various cake slices ranging in different flavors between myself and Josh. "So, we have red velvet, chocolate, carrot, confetti, and vanilla."

I poke a finger in Josh's direction. "No confetti," I say sternly. "Bride's orders."

CHAPTER TEN

Everett

"*PARLEZ-VOUS ANGLAIS?*"

"Purrr—"

"*Par—*"

"Okay, this shit is hard."

We're interrupted by a sharp shushing sound, and Teeny giggles.

"*Parlez-vous,*" Teeny repeats, keeping her voice in a low library voice. She peeks a glance at the librarian who's keeping a watchful eye on us after she'd shushed us for the fourth time.

"Purrrr-lay—"

Another set of giggles erupts from Teeny, but this time she muffles them using the sleeve of her sweater. "You sound like someone who's really badly imitating a cat."

"Can we take a break?"

"We just started," she argues. "Plus, lunch is only thirty-five minutes."

"How about we try again after school?" I offer.

She nods. "You want to come over to my house?"

"Sure," I answer a little regretfully, inwardly hoping I'd be able to lure her away somewhere more private without the inquisitive eyes of her parents. The truth is that since our kiss at the party a week ago, I haven't had a moment to talk to Teeny. We've always been around Josh or the entire varsity team or a grouchy librarian. "Come on," I whisper, leaning close to her. "I have a book I want to check out."

"Oh, okay."

She follows me, leaving our backpacks at the table, and we stop when we reach an empty aisle just around the corner.

"What book are you looking for?"

I huff a shy laugh. "I actually wanted to just talk to you without the warden interrupting us."

She laughs, her nose scrunching with amusement. Blood rushes to the apples of her cheeks, and it's disarming. The charming way she smiles with her whole face travels all the way down to my stomach where butterflies take flight.

I take a step closer to her, forcing her back against a wall of books. My hand moves to rest atop a shelf right at level with the top of her head, and I lean down and kiss her. She responds with a sharp gasp and tilts her face up toward me, letting me explore her mouth.

Kissing Teeny feels like everything around me disappears. I don't feel the weight of being the newest member of the basketball team, trying to find my place within a roster that's already formed and established, or the awkwardness that follows whenever I walk through the hallways of a school that still feels too new and uncharted. In the midst of fluttering heartbeats and the rampant butterflies in my gut, I feel calm. Almost serene.

My hand slides down her arm, trailing to the inside of her wrist where I feel her pulse racing behind her soft skin. It feels rapid, almost erratic and fitful.

The bell rings and we pull apart. Instead of pushing me away, Teeny leans her forehead into my chest. I cup the back of her head with my palm and nuzzle my nose into my hair.

"So, the beach wasn't a fluke."

She peers up at me with a conflicting look of amusement and

confusion, and a small smile twitching at her lips. "What do you mean?"

"I just thought that maybe...the second kiss couldn't be just as good, but I was wrong." I kiss her again, swift and fleeting, knowing we have about two-and-a-half minutes before we need to get to fifth period. "And I'm not getting sand in my shirt."

She giggles, finally pushing me away and leading the way back to our table. I follow her, and we hook our backpacks over our shoulders. "I'll see you after school, Hayes."

As soon as I ring the bell at Teeny's front door, I hear the sound of urgent pitter-patter on the other side. The door swings open, and I'm greeted by someone who isn't Teeny but shares her bright smile.

"Hey, Andrew."

"Everett!" Andrew squeals.

He tugs at my hand, dragging me inside. I follow, closing the door behind me, and when I walk into the living room, I find that it's complete chaos. There are sprinkles of snacks strewn all over the floor. Teeny's brothers, and some other guys I don't recognize, are scattered throughout the large sectional couch, and they're all cheering and shouting at the screen where a soccer game is on full blast.

"Everett!" Josh calls from the floor, a Barq's root beer held firmly in his hand. Andrew joins him, grabbing his own can while mimicking his older brother. "Sit down! We have lots of food."

Teeny comes bounding down the steps, rushing to my side. "Change of plans," she says, squeezing my forearm. "We need to get out of here. James came down with his friends, and they've been at it for the last hour. I don't think it's going to let up anytime soon." She looks annoyed and flustered as she starts to guide me back to the front door. "Some UEFA soccer thing with Barcelona and Westchester."

"MANCHESTER!" a collective round of angry voices calls after Teeny, correcting her in unison.

She looks at me like she's plotting their murder before she reaches for the keys hanging from a small hook near the doorway. "Josh! I'm taking the car!"

She doesn't wait for an answer. She hooks her backpack that was sitting on the floor over her shoulder and shoves her feet in her shoes before walking out the door without a glance back. "I feel like I can finally hear my own thoughts," she says with a sigh once we walk outside where it's much quieter. Her loose hair frames her round face, and she presses her hands to her temples, showing how she was seconds away from losing her mind inside that house. A smile finally peeks through her heart-shaped lips when she sees me holding back a laugh.

"How are your parents able to handle all that noise?"

"They aren't home," she explains, turning to her car parked in the driveway. "They went to some dinner thing, which is probably why it's that loud in there. I don't think they could pull that off if my mom was home."

I take her bag off her shoulder and let it dangle from my fingers. "So where are we going?"

"Hungry?" she asks, all evidence of her aggravation gone with the suggestive smile on her face.

"Yeah."

"Well, come on, Hayes," she calls, skipping to the driver's seat of her car.

I hop into the passenger seat, settling her backpack at my feet, and we buckle up. Teeny pulls out of the driveway. With her focus on the road ahead, I'm able to take her in, no longer surrounded by loud noise and angry teenage boys. She's wearing white shorts, cut off mid-thigh, exposing the warm skin tone of her legs. The tank top she's wearing is a bright blue color, and it shows off the sharp curves of her shoulder, the edges blending in with the lines of her shoulder blades. Her hair is down and a little wavy and damp, like she showered recently, though not too recently with the added bounce to the ends.

She flicks at the radio with her fingers, her nails painted a lavender color, and she stops at a station when she hears a song she's familiar with. I sit back, listening to her hum while she turns down winding roads driven through memory.

"Did you bring all your review stuff?"

"No, I thought I'd wing it," I tell her, a sarcastic tone in my voice. "You know, by the coattails of my badly pronounced French words and your tutoring skills."

She peers at me with a quirked eyebrow. That's when I pry open my French textbook and whip out the study guide Mrs. Fix passed out last week.

"Okay, smart ass." She pulls to a stop in a small parking lot that has a liquor store, a small sandwich shop that's closed for the night, and a hole-in-the-wall diner.

"What is this place?" I ask, stepping out to meet her at the hood of the car.

Teeny links her arm through mine and guides me through the door, the words "Marie's Diner" elegantly painted in cursive across the glass. "They have the best hazelnut waffles. And Coke floats. Unless you're too cool for that kind of stuff."

I scoff, expelling a loud "pshhh" through my teeth. "Never too cool for ice cream and soda."

We're shown to a booth seat where we place our study material on the wood grained table. I sit directly across from Teeny as she politely orders for us, and we start to open our textbooks and highlighters. It isn't crowded inside, which is slightly surprising considering it's dinnertime, but it draws in less attention as Teeny and I start to pour over our study guide.

"So, I think we should start with the vocabulary words," she says, her gaze zeroing in on the stapled stack of papers in front of her. "I'm still struggling with some of the words."

"You?" I ask suspiciously.

"Yeah, why?"

"I highly doubt that," I tell her, folding over my notebook to a fresh page. "Didn't you get like ninety-four percent on the last vocab test?"

"Ninety-six, but that's not important," she tells me, brushing off my skepticism. "The new list of words for this chapter are freaking hard!"

"God forbid your GPA drops half a point."

She shoves at my shoulder from across the table. "Whatever," she teases. "Like you aren't sailing through calculus with flying colors."

I shrug. "I prefer numbers over words."

"I guess we each have our strengths."

We're interrupted by the arrival of our drinks, and we gently push our things aside.

"Moment of truth." Teeny nudges my Coke float closer to me with her index finger and a wide grin. "If you don't like this, I don't think this is going to work. I couldn't handle that kind of difference of opinion in someone I consider a friend."

I push away the inkling in my head that's causing me to flip through all the reasons why Teeny calling me a friend suddenly seems inaccurate. "That's a lot of pressure."

"Are you saying you can't handle the heat?"

I reach for the frosty glass, the bubble of soda mixing with the ice cream overflowing the rim, and take a long sip. "Oh my god," I say with a gasp.

"See?"

"Oh my god," I repeat myself.

Teeny's cheeks turn rosy with a gleeful laugh.

"Seriously. Why didn't you bring me here sooner?"

"I am a lady, Everett. I don't bring just anyone to my favorite dessert spot. You have to earn your place in this booth with me."

I take another long, drawn-out sip. "Seriously. This could resolve all war and conflict in the world. Imagine every world leader meeting over a round of Coke floats from Marie's Diner. They'll forget what they're even fighting about."

She laughs a loud and delighted cackle. The server brings us our waffles, and I turn to face her. "Are you aware these Coke floats could establish world peace?"

The waitress looks at me with a peeved and confused scowl.

"I'm sorry," Teeny interjects. "It's his first time."

One quick smile before she slips away, and I inhale the rest of my drink. "Are the waffles just as good?"

"I personally think they're the best waffles in the world."

"How can you know that? Have you tried every single waffle in existence?"

"I don't need to. I just know."

I look at her with skepticism while she reaches for a fork and hands it to me. "I'll let you decide."

"Ladies first, lady," I say, putting my hand up in refusal.

Teeny takes the opportunity to jab into the waffle, tearing off a large chunk, and she angles it toward me. "Try it."

"You're giving me the first bite?"

She nods.

"I feel so honored."

She jabs the fork in a stabbing motion. "Just take it before I change my mind."

I take it in one bite, and Teeny waits patiently while I chew and swallow. "Jeez, Teen. You've really been hiding this place this whole time?"

She tears off another chunk, and before it can make it to her, I steal it right off her fork. "Hey!" she protests.

"I have no control over my actions right now," I say through a mouthful. "Blame it on the Coke float if you want, but all I can say is you better get your share before I eat this whole thing."

"Absolutely not!" Teeny pulls the plate closer, drawing up a protective shield with her elbow before she takes a large bite. One that's twice as big as the one she gave me. "*Yuf ha enuh!*"

She looks like this aggressive little chipmunk with her mouth full and an angry, determined scowl furrowing her brow. And when I break out into an uncontrolled fit of laughter, she does too. Bits of food spray from her mouth. My stomach starts to cramp at the same time my vision blurs from a misty wave of tears.

"Okay," I surrender. "I'm ordering my own." I flag the server down. She looks a little wary when she approaches our table, taking in Teeny as she continues to protect her waffle from an untrustworthy dinner companion. "Can I order another one of these?" I ask, gesturing a hand to the half-eaten waffles. "And another Coke float?"

"Sure."

"You are going to be bouncing off the walls with all that sugar."

"Well," I tell Teeny. "I guess it'll help me power through this study guide."

After four hours of verb conjugation and terminology memorization, we call it a night. My cheeks and stomach ache with a kind of muscle memory that's different from what I'm used to. Like the slight twinge in my jaw that serves as a reminder of how I almost toppled off my seat when Teeny told me about the time Josh got chased by a chicken when he was six. Or the subtle pang that hits my abdomen when I remember how red Teeny's face grew laughing over my own mishap with a rogue squirrel.

We've pulled up into Teeny's driveway where the noise on the inside seems to have died down. Teeny puts her car in park and starts gathering her hair, securing it with a hair tie that was fastened to her wrist. I watch her, eyeing the fluid movements of her hands and her slender neck, when I see a smear of bright orange paint behind her ear.

"Do you paint?"

"Hmm?" she asks with a confused tilt of her head.

I reach up to run my finger over the paint stain, feeling for a second how soft her skin is. "You got some paint here."

Her hand immediately clamps over the spot, and she smiles sheepishly. "I do."

"Like, for fun? Or do you have a side job painting houses?"

"No." She laughs. "I paint...stuff." I stay quiet, silently asking for her to elaborate. Instead of answering, she opens the car door. "Come on, Hayes."

I exit the car, following her lead to the garage. She opens the door off to the side where it meets the fence dividing our two homes and flicks on the overhead light. Once she takes a few more steps in, she turns on another light, this one much brighter. When I look around, I see an entire makeshift studio. There's an easel sitting in one corner with a canvas tarp lying under it. A small boombox stereo is plugged in on a desk where paint brushes sit haphazardly in a ceramic vase. Various tubes of acrylic paint in different stages of fullness cover the rest of the space on the desk, and a wooden stool is tucked underneath it.

"This is my studio." Teeny stands off to the side of the easel where a canvas painting rests. There's some distorted drawing of shapes and colors that lean toward an image of a shore with sand and a water's edge. "It's not finished," Teeny adds when she watches me take in the drawing. "Far from it, actually. But I'm working on this and a few other pieces for an art show at a really small local gallery."

I start to pay more attention to the colors she used. Bright fuchsia, lavender, navy, golden yellow. All colors that don't necessarily blend well together, but when thrown together through brush strokes and thick smears of paint, it creates this glowing sunset with Del Mar Heights as the backdrop.

"You did this?" I finally ask.

She nods, her head moving up and down in a hesitant movement of reserve. "I have a few more, but they're in my room."

I peer over at Teeny with my fingers hovering over the painting where there are abstract shapes of squares and lines with a bold "18" stamped on it. "This lifeguard tower..."

Teeny nods. "It's that beach we went to."

"And you painted it?"

She takes a slow cautious step closer to me and runs her fingers along the dried bumps and ridges of paint. "To most, it'll look like any San Diego beach. The water and the sand and even the lifeguard tower look pretty generic. It's the details that only I notice, and probably you. Like the number on the tower and those darker spots in the sand." She pauses to point them out, and when I take a closer look, I can see that they're footprints. "They're at the water's edge following a path to dryer sand. Like when we were there."

I take it in, the details, the secret moments brushed onto the canvas that mean something to us. All of it. And I can feel Teeny watching me. Like she's waiting for my approval.

"This is amazing," I finally say.

"Yeah?"

I nod. "Yeah."

She smiles, a soft smile that's shy and gentle. "I'm glad you like it."

I turn, looking away from the painting to face her, and take a slow step toward her. "How come you never told me you paint like this?"

She shrugs. "I guess it never came up."

I reach my hand to cup her face, and my thumb strokes back and forth from her jaw to her neck where her pulse beats frantically. Her lids flutter at the same time a soft sigh squeezes through her lips, and her body sags into me. Watching her become pliant in my hands, all slack and weak, has me feeling the same. Like I'm putty in her hands and I'd do whatever she wants.

"You want to kiss me again, don't you?" she asks softly. The warmth of her breath tickles my cheek, and our lips play this little game of tango, moving around each other in a teasing motion.

"Yeah," I whisper back. "I do." And before she can say anything else, I grip her face in my hands and kiss her. I kiss her like I'm hungry. She takes a small step backward, and I stumble with her. Her butt perches at the edge of the desk, grounding herself to something more solid than the electricity making both of our hands frantic and shaky, and I take that moment to lean my entire body into her. I notice her hand reach back, planting it on the hard surface for leverage. And the way her body trembles a little, I feel it when I softly grip her knee, and it shakes in my hand. I pull away and look at her. She looks like with every sharp gasp, she's trying to catch her next breath, only for it to fall short and keep her breathless.

"Are you okay?" I whisper.

She nods. "Things just got a little...intense." A small smile cracks the nerves that are so apparent on her face, and it feels like she's trying to give me something other than unease through an appeasing smile. "Sorry."

"Teeny, no," I say urgently. I take a step back, giving her space, but she follows, eyeing me with worry. Like I might be upset or mad. "I'm sorry. I didn't mean to make you uncomfortable."

Her hand reaches for my arm. "You didn't," she assures. "This is all just really new to me. I've never had, like, a boyfriend, and I guess I just want to make sure I'm doing things right. I'd hate to disappoint you."

I chuckle. "You're not disappointing me, Teen. Not even close."

She tugs at my hand, and I look at her, both of us wearing silly, bashful smiles. "Really?" she asks shyly, though a hint of excitement shines through when her eyes light up, and her smile widens into a relieved grin.

I nod. "Really."

She nods too.

"But I don't want to keep doing this if you're not—"

"I am," she interrupts. "I'm okay with it. I just needed a moment. That's all."

I tilt my head to the side, studying her.

"Really," she adds. "It's just...is it normally like this?"

I already know the answer to her question, but I play dumb. "Like how?"

"Like...when I kiss you, I get..." She pauses, searching for her next words. "I don't know how to explain it, but I've never felt—"

"No."

"No?"

I shake my head. "No," I answer. "It's never like this."

CHAPTER ELEVEN

Teeny

NOW

"HE STAYED THE NIGHT?!"

I look at Grace, my eyes rolling at her laughable assumption. "Not like that. I zonked out on the couch and he...I'm sure he slept somewhere where he was able to keep a safe distance and make sure I didn't die from alcohol poisoning."

She side-eyes with skepticism.

"Also, that was totally your fault."

"How so?"

"You gave him my keys. *And* address."

Her palms face the ceiling, playing innocent. "You were drunk. I couldn't let you drive." I poke at her shoulder, and she rubs the spot as a smirk slips through the annoyed scowl on my face. "How do you know?"

"What do you mean?"

"How do you know he didn't spend the night watching you sleep like some creepy serial killer?"

"Because he wouldn't, Grace," I tell her, sounding a little exasperated. I take a long sip of the red wine in my glass and pick at the sushi we got for takeout while sitting on the floor of her living room. Buster hides under the coffee table, his tail thumping against the carpet, as he peers up at us, hoping to nab a rollaway salmon roll. "Besides, it's not like that between us anymore."

"What are you talking about?"

"We're ancient history," I explain, avoiding her scrutinizing gaze.

"That did not look like ancient history," she argues, waggling a freshly manicured finger in my direction. "That looked like..."

"What?" I humor her, my face deadpanned.

"Like fireworks."

I snort. "You are so delusional."

"Come back to me after Josh's wedding when he gets to see you all glammed up in that green dress." She jabs her chopsticks in the air, stamping her point.

I groan. "Ugh, don't remind me." My hands move to my face, tension coiling at my temples as soon as I realize I haven't seen the last of him. "I'm going to have to see him with his stupidly perfect face and his stupidly perfect hair in a stupidly perfect tux. All while I'm going to be up there at the altar with him."

"He is pretty stupidly perfect."

"Tell me about it." We each stuff our faces with a sliver of sashimi before I look at her. "Leo came by. He picked up Sadie to take her to camp. Said he wanted to take me out to dinner so we could 'talk.'" I use air quotes when I say the last word, unsure of all the ambiguity behind his request to have a chat with me.

"And did you have dinner with him?"

"No," I say, shaking my head. "I told him if he needs to talk to me, I'll be in touch with my lawyer."

"What did he say to *that*?"

"He got angry. Gave me the whole, 'You're not *really* divorcing me?' spiel."

She rolls her eyes. "Did you talk to my lawyer? You got my email, right? With all her contact info?"

"I called her." I nod and run a hand through my hair. "It's a lot of work. A lot of paperwork, going over our financial history, our assets like our home and cars and investments."

"And Sadie."

"And Sadie," I repeat. My lower lip twists under the pressure of my teeth, and I look at Grace, concern etched on her face. "Can I be completely honest with you?"

She nods.

"What if...what if I just stayed. And I—I just swept this affair under the rug. For Sadie and—" My eyes round into a sad pout, and I suddenly feel ashamed.

"Teen, if that's what you want, then I can't tell you otherwise." We sit in contemplating silence before she adds, "*Is* it what you want?"

"No." More silence, this one more despondent and mournful. "I just... I'm scared to be alone," I tell her, saying the words I've been avoiding for so long. "And what if this is it? Like, what if no one will ever want me, and I'll just be this single mom raising Sadie fifty percent of the time?"

"Then you go be a single mom."

I huff a sad sigh, the first of tears starting to make my eyes blurry. "That sounds like fun," I say sardonically.

"No, Teeny," she urges. "I mean it. I know it sounds scary, but you *can* do it. Screw Leo and his little whore."

"That's not very 'girl power' of us."

"Oh, fuck that shit!" she exclaims, drawing a loose chuckle out of me. "She *knew* he was married. Obviously Leo should be taking the brunt of the fault, but she is a grown ass woman who knew better. And I don't care whatever daddy issues made her go for a married man, she earned that title."

I wipe at my cheek as a tear slips and smile at her, unable to disagree.

"Teeny, you can do it. You can. You are a strong woman, and I know you can do this shit on your own. If you want to stay with Leo because you love him and you want your marriage to work, then that's a different story, but don't stay with him because you don't believe you deserve better."

I nod, realizing how true her words ring. "You're right."

"Of course, I'm right," she answers with a smug smile. She reaches for the wine bottle, emptying its contents between our two glasses before lifting hers up in the air. I follow her lead with a small appreciative laugh. "To strong ass single divorced women."

"To us."

In an attempt to stay busy rather than moping around the house without Sadie home, I spend my Sunday evening with an easy, unintentional drive to my parents' house. It's not out of the ordinary for us kids to come over for dinner. Andrew, being the only single member of the family, is usually the most frequent flier with the free food and Tupperware containers of leftovers he takes with him in heaps. So when I arrive, I'm not surprised to see Andrew answer the door.

"Hey."

"Hey." He peers over my shoulder, most likely looking for my husband and daughter. "No Leo or Sadie?"

"Sadie's at camp, and Leo is...busy."

He nods, not caring further than my explanation, and I enter the house. I find my mom in the living room, surrounded by piles of baby blue and beige in silk and hemp. "What is this?" I ask.

She looks up at me, smoothing her hand over the delicate material resting on her lap. "I had my *hanbok* at the tailor to fix some of the loose hems, and I just picked it up." She urges me to sit in the empty spot next to her, letting me stroke a hand over the dress. "It's beautiful, no?"

My heart melts as she watches me take in the beauty of the dress. "It is." Flash images of my mom wearing the same traditional Korean garb to my wedding floods my mind. She was there, moving around gracefully as she shined as the mother of the bride, smiling proudly at me and Leo.

She holds it up, admiring it as if she hasn't had this dress carefully stored in her closet for the last few decades. "Why don't you try it on?"

"It's yours," I oppose.

"So," she urges. "Come on. The last time I saw you in one of these was when you were a baby."

I give in, unable to say no to her hopeful smile. I slip on the dress, putting on the layers with my mom's instructions and tying the bow at my chest with more of my mom's help. It's like I'm a child again, having her dress me with her gentle guidance and shining eyes taking me in. Before I know it, my dad's brought out the full-length mirror from their room and the three of us are looking at the reflection. It's like no time has passed. I'm that little toddler, proud to be standing between my parents while they beam at me with pride.

"It's really beautiful, Mom."

She rests her hands on my shoulders. "You know, the first time I wore this was to your wedding."

"Really?"

She nods.

"I thought you had this before."

"I bought this for your wedding, and then I wore it to James's wedding, and now I'm going to wear it to Josh's."

"And hopefully Andrew's if he gets his head out of his ass anytime soon," my dad adds dryly.

"How did I get roped into this conversation?" Andrew calls from his spot on the couch, the remote held loosely in his hand and his ankle draped on his knee.

"And maybe one day," my mom continues, ignoring my dad and my brother's harmless banter, "you'll wear one just like this to Sadie's wedding."

I laugh endearingly. To think that I could one day be the mother of the bride, just like my mom was, walking down the aisle with my dad to give me away to the man I planned to spend the rest of my life with.

I realize how different the circumstances would be. Leo and I wouldn't be married any longer. He might even have a new wife, waiting in the aisles for Leo to give Sadie away while I slump back into my seat without a partner to hold my hand or slip me a tissue when I start crying. And then I start to think of all the things we'll have to do as a divorced couple. Handle Sadie's birthday parties and school dances, graduation, sending her off to college. Leo and I wouldn't be holding each other, consoling the other through shared tears and assurances that our baby girl is now an independent adult.

I shove those thoughts away, worried I may blubber into a puddle of tears right into my mom's freshly pressed dress. I remove the dress as my mom starts prattling off the various meats my dad needs to pull out of his decades-old smoker in the backyard. Andrew joins him, hoping to get the first taste of his brisket outside by the pool.

"Have you gotten your bridesmaid dress?" my mom asks me, taking the garment bag I carefully placed all the fragile material in.

"Not yet," I tell her. "But I ordered it, and it should be ready in a week or two."

She nods and walks off to the kitchen to finish preparing dinner. I follow her footsteps, ready to help her with whatever she needs. "I saw Mina's wedding dress," she tells me. "It looks so beautiful. Josh is going to love it."

She's preoccupied, focused on cleaning off some vegetables before she starts chopping away at them on the cutting board.

"Leo has to rent a tux, no? Unless he has one—"

"Leo isn't going to be there," I blurt out.

The clack-clack noise of the sharp blade hitting wood comes to a halt. "Why?"

I take a cleansing breath, ready to rip off the Band-Aid. I give her a look that says everything I need to say. Disappointment, dejection, remorse. It's all there, right between the lines creasing my face and my downturned eyes. She places her knife down and rushes to me. "Oh, Teeny. What happened?"

I expected to cry or break down, but I don't do either. Instead, my voice sounds level and calm as I tell her. "He cheated on me."

A whoosh of breath leaves her mouth, and it's like I can feel the pressure expel out of her chest. "He cheated on you?"

"I kicked him out," I continue to explain. "James and Josh know."

"And Sadie?"

"We haven't told her yet."

She squeezes my shoulders in her hands and forces me to look at her. It's then I start to feel the sting of tears hit behind my nose. "You're going to be fine, Christine. You hear me?"

I silently nod.

"We are going to take this one day at a time, and you will be *fine*."

"Yeah," I croak.

She pulls me into a hug, the sounds of my dad and Andrew bickering about proper meat-smoking temperatures echoing off the walls outside. We stay there, her hand running up and down my back and my chin resting on her shoulder, until I feel like maybe what she said is true. Maybe I will be fine. I'll pick up the shattered pieces of my life, scooping all the fragments and shards into my own little dustpan. And maybe one day, those itty-bitty pieces will turn into something. Something that glitters and shines with hope, and I'll look back at this moment and realize I worried for nothing.

CHAPTER TWELVE

Everett

THEN

WHEN I PLAYED basketball up in Monterey, game day wasn't very ceremonious. It was even a little blasé in my opinion. So when the first game of the season at Torrey Pines High School finally comes around, it's a pleasant surprise to see how the entire school rallies to celebrate. The team wears dress shirts and slacks—tie optional—while Coach roams the hallways in a suit. We also make sure to sit together during lunch while the cheerleaders stop by our classes to offer goody bags with power bars and small bottles of Gatorade.

The attention and commotion are contagious, and I feel just as ready and hyped for the game.

"We're all heading out to a bonfire after the game," Josh informs me excitedly at the end of the day. "The cheerleaders are organizing it. You have to be there."

I watch in amusement, Josh hopping up and down like an eager toddler, his fist punching into the opposite hand while he urges me to tell him yes.

"Yeah," I answer. "My dad's in town to catch the game so I'll probably have to check in with him first."

"Your dad's here?"

"Yeah," I tell him, whipping my keys out of my pocket as we reach the parking lot. "He makes it a point to make it to as many of my games as he can. And since it's the first of the season and he had some time off, he flew down for the week."

Teeny walks into view just then, skipping toward Josh with a gleeful smile. Her friend, Diana, who I've met a few times, trails behind her, eyeing me with a sly smile and her position somehow strategic in the way she's hiding behind Teeny while making sure to catch any glimpse of mine and Josh's conversation. I've noticed a lot of "strategic things" a few of the junior and senior girls do around me. Whispering things to each other in between secret giggles, waving at me in the cafeteria, or even the occasional greeting from girls I don't even know the names of.

"Can we drop off Diana? She's going home before the game. She forgot her clothes for the bonfire." Diana cups a hand at Teeny's ear and whispers something, her gaze on me, and I stand there a bit awkwardly.

"You're going too?" I ask, interjecting her question directed at her brother.

Teeny shifts her smile in my direction, though the way her eyes light up with intrigue changes when she looks at me. "Yes. Why?"

I answer her with a shrug. "Just asking." We continue this silent staring contest, uncaring of Josh's presence as he rifles through his bag, his attention thankfully elsewhere.

Teeny tugs at her lower lip with her teeth, and I duck my head to the concrete, where she can't see the creeping smile cutting across my face. She's the only one of the girls who looks in my direction that makes me feel flustered and shy. No matter how many waves and flirty giggles I get, it's only Teeny that makes the blood rush to my cheeks.

"Yeah," Josh finally answers Teeny, though Diana is already helping herself to the back seat. "I'll see you at the game," he tells me.

We all climb into our respective cars, and I give Teeny one last look as she hops into the passenger seat next to Josh. I catch her watching me, her smile unchanging as I buckle up and turn the ignition on in my car.

As soon as I pull up to my house, I see a shiny black Lincoln sedan parked in the driveway next to my mom's minivan. I walk inside, only to be greeted by tense voices.

"What am I supposed to do? This is my job, Alice."

"Realize that you have a family. Prioritize your wife and your son for a change. What happened last year—"

"I thought we weren't going to bring that up again. I already told you I messed up. What more do you want?"

I don't mean to eavesdrop on my parents. Whatever rigidity that's palpable from the next room isn't something that I want to walk in on, but I fear it's too late. I shut the door behind me with the purposeful intention of making some noise.

"Well, Eddie—"

All conversation comes to a halt.

"Ev, is that you?" I hear my dad call.

"Uh, yeah," I answer, walking into the kitchen where my parents are on either side of the island, their hands braced on the marble surface and their body language weary with frustration. My dad walks over to me, reaching for my hand for a firm handshake.

"First game of the season," he tells me, patting my shoulder. "Nervous?"

I shake my head, unconvincingly smiling at him through my lie. "Just ready to play, Coach."

"Good."

"Game starts at five?" my mom asks, turning toward the fridge, her gaze preoccupied.

"Yeah, but I need to be there early."

"We'll go early too," my dad says. "I want to finally meet your coach in person."

I nod before I head to my room to change. I busy myself with getting ready while keeping my ears open. My parents fighting isn't something new. Their marriage has always been what I've grown to call fragile. With the line of work my dad does, his priorities have always been awry. My mom has always questioned his devotion to us, especially when she's had to step in and take on the usually assumed roles my dad would've taken. As I've gotten older, their arguments have gotten more frequent. Often my mom demanding more of his time and his response being that she's being unreasonable and that she should understand the responsibilities his job requires. Since our move to San Diego, their arguments have been less frequent with the distance between them, but the frustration and resentment from my mom hasn't gone anywhere. In fact, I've seen it linger and simmer without the presence of my dad to reassure her.

An hour later, I'm sitting in the back seat of my dad's rental as we pull into the parking lot of my school. I get out first, letting my parents take their time making their way to the gymnasium. I make it to the locker room, finding that a lot of my teammates are already there. Everyone seems to be basking in the game day hype, and my mood matches the lively, animated energy around me. Which is good since my nerves have been somewhat on edge all day, knowing the scrutiny my dad will have on my skills for four full quarters.

I find my locker, reaching for my fresh, unused jersey. The locker room starts to bustle even louder with pre-game energy. As the clock counts down to tipoff, we all funnel out to the court, trailing behind one another as we start a round of drills to get our blood pumping. The bleachers are starting to fill, and the cheerleaders have already taken their spots on the sidelines, matching the competitiveness buzzing between us and the opposing team trickling in from the other end.

I pause, taking a moment to drink some water before things pick up, when I catch Teeny walking into the gymnasium. She has her face painted with a bright gold falcon on her cheek and her hair is tied up in two pigtails. She has a large poster that says "GO 44" in big block letters.

"Hey, Hayes," she calls, her pigtails bouncing as she lowers her sign, and she plops down a step to meet me at eye level. "You ready to kick some ass out there?"

I smirk and jerk my head to her sign made for Josh. "Where's mine?"

"Didn't think you'd want one," she answers, a sheepish smile spreading across her face.

"Why wouldn't I?"

"Thought people might think it's weird?" she says, her voice unsure.

"Hayes!" I turn to where the rest of my teammates are gathering for our huddle with Coach. "Come on!" he calls.

I turn to face Teeny again. "I want mine twice as big for the next game."

I walk away, my back to Teeny, but look over my shoulder one more time before reaching the now fully formed huddle. Teeny's still watching me, and I fully face her, waving my hand in her direction like a love-sick fool. Teeny waves back and just as I reach the team, Josh eyes me, having caught the entire exchange.

"You good?" he asks.

"Yeah," I tell him. "Just saying hi to Teen."

He responds with a light hum before we're interrupted by Coach.

The game starts, and the gymnasium is pulsating with a waving uproar of noise and suspense. The booming cheers echo off the polished floors, and our pace on the court matches that of the crowd around us. I don't start, just like Coach said, but by the third quarter, right after halftime, I'm in. I look over at my dad, his place right behind where Coach is pacing the sidelines. I notice Coach occasionally walking over to my dad, the two in deep conversation whenever there's a lull on the court. My dad watches me intently as soon as I take my place. Running up and down the court, passing the ball to my teammates while making sure to keep a close eye on my footwork. It's a strenuous game, considering I haven't been in a game with this much pressure since last school year, and I'm breaking a sweat by the time fourth quarter rolls around.

With the last few minutes ticking away on the time clock, the scoreboard displays bright glowing numbers in our favor. Before the last buzzer rings, we're already celebrating our win: 99 to 76. The bleachers start to empty, some of the crowd filing onto the glossy basketball court, and as we're all celebrating the first game and win of the season, I catch Teeny running toward me. Without even thinking about it, I swoop down and lift her into my arms.

"Good game, Hayes!" she squeals. Her elbow hooks over my neck where my skin feels slippery with sweat, but she doesn't pull away. The bows on her pigtails tickle my cheek, and I give one of them a light tug as I set her back on solid ground.

We're interrupted just then by my parents. My dad lands a hard pat on my shoulder, pride bursting from his eyes. "I talked to Coach before the game," he tells me. "Said you're doing really well so far. Might even have you start at the next game."

I eye Teeny, and she grins an encouraging smile up at me. It's a private exchange, her expressing her praise and my gratitude for her seeking me out immediately after the game, something I hoped for as the clock ticked through the last seconds of the game.

"Dad, this is Teeny," I say to my dad, tampering down the urge to pull her into another tight embrace. "She lives next door."

"Oh, hi! Nice to see you again," he tells her. Teeny responds with a polite smile.

My mom places a gentle hand on Teeny's shoulder. "Hi, Teeny."

"Well, we'll let you celebrate with your team. Don't be out too late," my dad warns. He and my mom turn to leave the crowded gym, and I'm left there with Teeny.

"You riding with Josh to the beach?"

"Actually, he's going with some other guys on the team. It's just me."

I smile. "Mind if I hitch a ride?"

"Sure," she says, grinning back at me. "I'll be at my car."

I stop by the locker room to grab my things and change. When I make it to the parking lot and find Teeny standing next to her car, I drop my bag on the concrete and stop inches from her.

"Hi."

"Hey."

I peer around me, making note of the almost empty lot before ducking my face down to kiss her. She responds by tilting her head back and lifting herself up onto her toes. I lean into her, making her take a step backward to her car. We both fall against the window, and I cage her into me with my hands braced against the hood of the car.

I'm slowly learning that each time I kiss Teeny, I discover something new about her. The first time I kissed her, I learned that she was nervous. Like really nervous. I didn't realize it until I kissed her again, and her body wasn't as stiff and unsure. And now that I've lost track of the number of times I've kissed her, I'm noticing that she's become softer, more loose and yielding. Her breathing isn't labored anymore. Instead, it's sensual with her soft sighs and even softer lips. She doesn't lock up anymore, uncertain of how to follow my lead. She lets me move her, guide her, and it somehow calms me knowing she's willing to trust me.

When I pull away, Teeny looks around us. Her wary eyes shift side to side, and I cup the side of her face, refusing to create more space between us than there already is.

"I like you." The words splinter out of me like fireworks. They shoot through my chest, bursts of light going off in loud booms. I feel like my heart is going to explode. And while I tell her that I like her, I don't know how to tell her it isn't as simple as that.

I like her. *A lot.*

Her cheeks flush, and she presses her hand into my chest, leaving it there to rest. "With the way you keep kissing me, I sure hope so," she responds. "Unless you're going around kissing other girls willy-nilly."

I laugh. "No. No, I'm not."

"Good. 'Cause I like you too." More *fireworks*.

"And...we're only kissing each other." She nods with the sweetest smile I've ever seen. "Sounds like something only boyfriends and girlfriends do."

"Yeah?"

My smile matches hers, the fingers resting along her jaw and her neck tracing idle circular patterns. "Yeah."

"Does that mean you want to be my boyfriend?" she asks shyly. She ducks her head bashfully, and I resist the urge to pinch her cheek.

"Is that okay?" I ask. Because I need her to be okay with it. Me, her, us. Me touching her and kissing her. Me playing this much significance in her life. I need to know that all of it's okay with her. Because, until now, she's done nothing but offer solace. She carries this warm glow that somehow silences all the loud and chaos. She's made everything in my life okay. And all I want to do is do the same for her.

"Yeah. Yeah, that's okay."

I lean down to kiss her again. She feels like putty. Her loose neck making her head lull, the light sag in her shoulders, even the slackened sigh that squeezes through her lips. Everything about her screams pliant and willing.

Just as my lips brush against hers, we're interrupted by a loud honk and a burst of cheers. I look behind me when a car pulls to a stop next to us, Kevin, another member of the team, at the wheel.

"Come on, Hayes!" he calls, pushing his hand against the horn one more time at the same time a round of loud whoops sound from the passengers squished inside his SUV. He catches the way my hand is still braced against Teeny's car and Teeny's hand hooked over my bicep.

"Yeah, we're leaving now."

"Hi, Teeny." He waves at Teeny, and Teeny offers a meek smile and a shy wave.

"Hey."

"See you guys at the bonfire!" The tires screech, and Kevin drives off, leaving myself and Teeny in the now almost empty parking lot. There are a few stragglers left, those caught behind the rush of parking lot traffic.

"Let's go," I say.

"Yeah," she agrees.

After a quick twenty-minute drive to Mission Bay, we find that the parking lot nearest to the bonfire is packed. Cars are circling the parking lot and moving onto a lot further down after no luck finding a spot. Teeny gets lucky, pulling right up behind a car leaving just as we enter, and we take a moment to sit in the car before getting out.

"How does it feel to get your first win?" She turns to lean her cheek on the headrest and draws her knee up to her chest. "Your dad seemed really excited about the game."

I mimic her, unbuckling first and resting my hand on the center console between us. "Can I be honest?"

She sits up straighter. "Of course."

"It's whatever." My voice sounds morose, even a little surly.

Teeny gently places her hand on mine and starts stroking my knuckles with her thumb, encouraging me to continue.

"Basketball's really my dad's thing," I explain. "I have fun. Especially with the team here. And I like it enough to have done it for the past four years, but I probably would've given it up a long time ago if I knew my dad wouldn't be so disappointed."

"So, no plans to go pro?"

I shake my head. "Absolutely not."

"Does your dad know that?"

"Yeah," I tell her with a solemn nod. "He knows, and he hasn't fought me on it, but I can sense the disappointment in him. I think he comes to my games hoping it would guilt me enough to change my mind.

"A part of me feels like I do it to keep the peace at home," I add. "My parents...they have their own set of issues. My dad cheated on

129

my mom last year. They don't know that I know, and I can see how it's really messing my mom up. Now that my dad isn't even in the same house, I hear her cry at night. Just today, they were arguing when I got home."

"I'm sorry, Everett." She curls her palm into mine and gives me a gentle comforting squeeze.

"You know, I've never told anyone that? About my parents."

She smiles. "You told me."

"I did." I don't really know why I did, but now, having told her, I feel lighter. Less wound up and queasy. I don't know how to pinpoint the way my body always feels on edge, like my feet are never fully grounded but always bouncing on my tiptoes, ready to jump to action at a second's notice. When I talk to Teeny, all of that falls silent. It becomes quiet and I feel...calm. "Is it weird that I feel comfortable telling you? I don't know. I usually don't have anyone to talk to, and this—" I pause to lightly tap my finger against her wrist. "Thank you...for letting me talk. And for listening."

"It's not weird, Everett," she tells me, reaching to cup my face.

I turn my cheek and lightly kiss her palm.

How is it this easy? I can't remember the last time I felt this at ease. With constantly moving, my dad's work always shifting and my life in a forever tentative state, I don't know what calm feels like. And in this new town in a new school surrounded by people I'm still getting to know, Teeny's somehow made me feel as if I belong. The heels of my feet are slowly touching the ground with the intention of staying there.

"Ready?" I ask.

With a quick nod, we both exit the car. Teeny undoes her pigtails, loosening the ties at her crown. She shakes her head and groans when she runs her fingers through her hair.

"Were those pigtails hurting?"

"They weren't comfortable." She starts braiding her hair down one shoulder while I whip out a hoodie from my gym bag. Teeny finishes up, swiping some ChapStick over her pink lips, and we make our way to the beach. I hook my arm around her, to which Teeny embraces, sidling up to me with ease.

"You know there's going to be a lot of people here," she comments, gripping my wrist hanging loosely over her shoulder.

"Yeah."

"People who are going to see me and you show up together." She lets go of my hand and starts to pull away, but I immediately reach for her, linking our fingers together.

"Yeah." I don't let go, and as we trudge through the sand, approaching a thick crowd of Torrey Pines' student body, I pull her closer to me.

"Hey!" Josh approaches me, glazed eyes and flushed cheeks. His gaze catches me and Teeny linked together, a flash of confusion and uncertainty pulling at the corners of his mouth. "You guys came together?" he asks.

"Yeah," I tell him. Teeny's eyes shift nervously, and the three of us stand there, unsure of what to do next.

"Okay." Josh tips back a cup held loosely in his hand before he walks away.

"That was a little weird, right?" Teeny whispers as we watch Josh peruse a large table littered with chips and a tall stack of pizza boxes.

My eyes pinch into a guilty squint as I scratch the back of my neck. "I should talk to him."

She nods. "Probably."

"You good?"

She nods again, her face shifting into a reassuring smile. "Yeah." She pauses, looking around the growing crowd, and her eyes catch a small group of her friends. "Diana and Holly are here too so I'm going to go catch up with them."

I lean down and place a swift peck on her cheek. "Don't go too far."

"I won't." She gently pushes a hand into my stomach before I turn away, stealing glances in her direction as I approach Josh. He's hovering over a large cooler, shifting through the ice.

"Hey."

"Hey." He's distracted, refilling his drink with something red and fruity smelling. He tilts the unlabeled canister in my direction, and I shake my head. "So, you came with Teeny."

"I did," I answer honestly. "Is that okay?"

"Yeah, man," he responds with an earnest smile.

"You sure?"

He nods. "Just...you know. Be good to her."

"Of course."

"I don't need to talk to you about all of that big brother bullshit, but you know the whole, 'If you ever hurt her—'"

"I don't plan to."

"Good."

Josh playfully pushes his fist into my shoulder, and I stumble a step back, relief replacing the taut tension between us.

"Hey, boys."

Josh and I turn just as Angelica, a member of the cheerleading squad and a senior like us both, steps right between us, not bothering to let us move out of the way. Angelica's hand brushes against my chest, and I think it's an accident, but then she doesn't move away, stamping her place in the sand right in front of me.

"Good game, new guy," she says in a low voice.

"Thanks, Angelica." I move a step back, crossing my arms across my chest, creating plenty of space between us.

"Can you get me a drink?" she asks, her lashes batting in my direction.

"The coolers are like, two feet from you," Josh interjects. Angelica throws a harsh glare in Josh's direction, and I use that moment to leave the conversation.

"See ya," I tell Josh, just as he tilts his head back in an acknowledging nod.

It doesn't take me long to find Teeny. She's surrounded by her friends, a group of about four to five girls huddled around the glowing fire. A few of them have soda cans in their hands, and Teeny has a Capri-Sun gripped between her fingers.

"Hey," I whisper into her ear as I sidle up behind her.

She turns to look at me, my chin resting on her shoulder. "Hey."

I catch the eyes of the girls around Teeny glance in our direction. Some amused, mostly surprised.

"Hello," I say, waving a hand.

"You guys know Everett," Teeny says, eyeing the way not a single person greets me.

"Hi," Diana finally says. A few of the girls follow suit, quietly whispering to each other. I glance down at Teeny, and she rolls her eyes at me.

"We were just talking about what a great game you boys had tonight," one of the girls comments, tipping her plastic cup to her lips.

"Oh, yeah," another adds. They share more glances at each other, something secretive and amusing.

Teeny shivers next to me, bringing her hands to her arms and rubbing over her shoulder for friction. I offer her the hoodie in my hand. "Here."

"You won't get cold?" she asks.

I shake my head. "I brought it for you." I help her slip it over her head, and her face reemerges through the opening of my sweatshirt, the hood capped over her head. Strands of hair fall over her face, and she grins at me. I move the hairs out of the way and place a small kiss at her temple. "Better?"

She nods. "Better." She turns and leans her back against my chest. I start to run my hands over her, attempting to warm her when I catch Angelica watching us through the flames of the glowing fire. She has this indignant look of judgment on her face with a raised brow and pursed lips, and she turns to say something to her own clique who's standing a mere whisper of gossip of distance away from her. A few more heads turn in our direction, and

133

I suddenly feel like we're garnering more attention than I'm comfortable with.

Teeny slips her hand into mine, her focus on her friends, though with the way her fingers stroke my skin and her body still leans into mine, I know I'm somewhere in her line of thought.

"You want to get out of here?" I whisper into her ear.

She turns to face me. "Already?"

I nod, and she smiles.

"Yeah," she answers. She then turns to her friends, letting them know she's leaving. The exchange is quick, and my attention is more focused on leaving, away from the crowd, to somewhere less chaotic and probing.

We make our way to Teeny's car, where I stop before getting into her car.

"You okay?" she asks.

I nod into her hair. "Yeah," I tell her. "Just didn't feel like mingling with the crowd."

"Me too," she tells me.

"You sure?"

"Yeah," she assures. "Did you want to go home?"

"No."

"Did you have some place in mind?"

"No."

She laughs, wrapping her arms around my waist. "So, you just made me leave the party early for nothing?"

"Not for nothing." I swoop down and kiss her, wanting nothing more than to do this for the rest of the night. I don't care where we are or what else we're doing as long as I can keep doing this. "I *am* craving some waffles though."

Her face lights up. "And Coke floats?"

"Absolutely."

134

There's something comforting about the mundane. I've had Marie's more than once since Teeny introduced me to the place, and I've grown familiar with the warm syrupy taste of the waffles and the creamy fizz that comes with every sip of their Coke floats, but I'll never get over how soothing and relaxing I feel with every first bite and sip.

While Teeny and I usually settle ourselves inside a booth, letting the high back seats create a small protective bubble away from the rest of the world, we opted to take our bubble elsewhere tonight.

"I've never had a nighttime beach picnic," Teeny says, her hand slipping into mine as we make our way toward the lifeguard tower I've embedded into my memories.

"Neither have I." I'm dangling the crinkly plastic bag, heavy with our late night treat, and a Styrofoam cup holding a Coke float in my hand. Teeny has her own cup, and she takes a long sip as we come to a stop at the base of the steps leading up the tower.

"Are you sure this is okay?" she asks as I take the first step.

"Who's going to tell us no?" I look over my shoulder, a towel that Teeny had in her car draped over it, urging her to follow. "Besides, you want to get sand all over the waffles?"

She gives an agreeable shrug and follows. I lay the towel down, right along the edge where the railing sits, and we both plop down.

"I always thought the lifeguard patrol would come out with their blow horns and whistles if I even stepped foot on here."

I nudge my shoulder to hers. "Got to learn to live a little, Teeny." I open up our to-go container and hand her her fork. She waits patiently while I pour a healthy serving of syrup over it, and she dives in. An enthusiastic giggle widens her smile, and I watch as the breeze picks up her hair and the moonlight glows against her skin.

I don't know why it happens just then, with her focus on sawing through the crispy edges of the waffle and getting enough syrup to douse her piece, but it does. I realize I'm falling completely and utterly head over heels for her. It starts to spread through my chest, to my stomach, and all the way down to my fingers and toes, and it's

135

nearly debilitating. I can't even pretend to act cool, like she doesn't make the air move in and out of my lungs or that I find every single thing she does fascinating. Even something completely ordinary, like the way she drives or how her lips pucker and her cheeks puff out when she chews.

"What?" she asks, her mouth full.

I shake my head and smile. "Nothing."

CHAPTER THIRTEEN

Teeny

NOW

I'VE NEVER TAKEN GROWING up near the coast for granted. I know for some it's a part of life to the point that it becomes routine. A quick commute through Pacific Coast Highway, an annual summer bonfire, the constant smell of salt air and squawking gulls. Not me. I've always stood in awe of it all.

With the long winding coast to my right and the San Diego hills to my left, I'm taking my time driving to El Cielo to meet Mr. Lang for a quick tour of his newly acquired property and to discuss whether or not I would be a good fit for his vision.

I pull into the parking lot of El Cielo, finding that it's still considerably full given the change in ownership, and hook my leather tote bag over my shoulder before walking to the main entrance to the lobby. I wasn't sure how formal this meeting was so I decided to play safe. A tan knee-length pencil skirt slit up the back and a white button-down blouse, low slingback heels and subtle touches of gold in my bracelets and earrings.

As soon as I reach the reception desk, I'm greeted by a man in his mid to early forties in a steel gray suit, no tie. "How can we help you?"

"I have a meeting with Mr. Lang," I tell him. "I'm Christine Diaz."

He smiles warmly at me, extending his hand in my direction. "I'm Eric. Nice to meet you."

"Hi," I respond cheerfully with a firm handshake in return.

He quickly turns to the woman manning the front desk, telling her something discreetly, before rounding the counter and meeting me. "Why don't we have a seat at the bar?"

I nod and follow his pace. "This is a beautiful entryway," I tell him, peering over me at the tall ceilings and abstract chandelier hanging above the main lobby.

He hums something that doesn't sound like approval. "It's a beautiful property," he concedes. "The original architecture is what drew me into this place. A lot of the older homes nearby in San Diego follow a Victorian, Spanish colonial style, much like Old Town and the San Diego Mission. The property follows that almost to a tee."

I nod along, finding the details he's talking about in the sconces and arched entryways and the clay tile roof that was visible when I walked up to the multicolored fountain at the roundabout up front.

"There's a lot of potential. Especially with the natural lighting and the view of the ocean. With the windows, it looks like the lobby is an extension of the beach." I pause, and Eric follows my gaze as if looking at the space with a new set of eyes. "And I love how the infinity pool is elevated. I bet at certain angles, it's like you're in the ocean."

"It is." We reach a small table in the bar area, the furniture a little dull and outdated. Eric waves a hand at the bartender before we both sit. "I have a silent partner involved in the renovation and a grand reopening I'm slating for roughly January, maybe February."

"So that'll give you roughly five months or so?"

He nods. "Do you think that's doable?"

"Oh, yes," I answer assertively. "That's plenty of time."

"My partner will be joining us in a bit. I was thinking once he's here, we could walk the grounds. There's more than the lobby, and I'd like to see what you think."

"Sure."

Eric waves behind me before standing and buttoning his suit jacket. "He's here now."

I follow suit, straightening my skirt and pushing my chair under the table. As soon as I turn to greet this silent partner, my heart jumps into my throat.

"Mrs. Diaz, this is Everett Hayes."

Everett stops mid-shrug into his navy blazer and peers up at me, a light smirk on his lips and those dark eyes dancing with amusement. "Mrs. Diaz."

"Christine," I answer sharply. "Christine is fine," I say again, this time to Eric.

"Everett is in town from Seattle to help finalize some details to the property before heading back up in a couple of months. We're hoping to have him back once our grand opening is set."

I'm still reeling from Everett's sudden appearance. Like a magician is playing some sick twisted trick on me, focusing on my haunted past and whipping Everett out from a wooden box or a shiny tablecloth. Everett who I thought I wouldn't have to see until the wedding. Everett who I thought would be out of my life after my drunken debacle and the impromptu dessert run. But no. He's standing in front of me as a potential client.

"I was just telling Christine we'll go ahead and take a tour of the grounds and see if her vision for the space would be a good fit for us," Eric continues, turning his attention toward Everett.

Everett responds with a concurring nod, his gaze still on me. Just then, we're interrupted with the urgent steps of the same receptionist who was at Eric's side when he greeted me. "I'm so sorry to interrupt, but Eric, we have a situation with one of the vendors, and they'd like to speak with you."

Eric runs a flustered hand through his hair before he turns to me. "I'm so sorry, Christine. Would you give me a minute? I'll be right back."

"Sure—"

"I'll show her."

Everett's deep voice, so level and calm, vibrates through me, sending my pulse racing and my palms clammy. "I—I really don't mind waiting," I argue frantically.

"I don't want to keep you," Eric answers. "Go ahead, and I'll catch up with you two in a bit."

Before I can protest again, Eric scurries off, leaving me and Everett alone. I exhale a controlled sigh, doing my best to keep my cool.

"Ready?" Everett asks with an innocent smirk, extending his hand in the opposite direction of where I came in from.

Unable to refuse his offer, I reluctantly follow Everett's pace as he takes the lead. I keep a considerable amount of distance between us. I cross my arms, knowing I look unapproachable and aloof, though it's because I don't know how to navigate this. How to do this tour, trying to focus on my work and maintain the best professional etiquette, without losing my shit with Everett.

"This is the main ballroom," Everett explains, pushing open the double doors leading into a large, empty space. It's outdated. Curtains the color of mushed peas with old carpeting to match it, plain lighting that dulls everything rather than brightening it. It's such a vast contrast to the beautiful scenery outlining the hotel grounds and the main lobby.

I remain quiet, taking in the room with a flutter of color swatches oscillating in my mind. Vibrant yellow and emeralds, deep purples and navy, with bursts of ideas interrupting my train of thought. "What do you think?" Everett asks after I've stayed quiet for too long.

"It has a lot of potential."

"That's code for horrible."

I huff a laugh. "It's not horrible," I say. "It just needs some...love."

Everett smiles at me, mirroring the one on my face that slipped after his little wisp of humor. "I think you could do something great with this place, Teeny."

My face falls. "Did you do this?"

"What?"

"This." I gesture my arms angrily around me. "This meeting with Eric. Is this your doing?"

He shakes his head, the smile that matched mine long gone and a look of earnest shadowing his features. "No."

"Are you sure? Because this seems like too much to be just a little coincidence."

"No, Teeny. I didn't." He shoves his hands in his pockets and ducks his head. "I didn't even know that you're a designer. Eric told me about a designer who was referred to him. Something Ellis? You did a restaurant or something?"

"Linguine Lane," I tell him, remembering the entire gut we did of the space of what used to be an indoor trampoline park, stripping everything from windows to drywall to fixtures. It's now an upscale Italian restaurant and gourmet grocery store. It's done really well since opening last year, despite the silly name attached to it.

"But I didn't know it was you." His eyes soften into something that looks like pride and admiration. "You've done well for yourself, Teen."

I start to fidget with my fingers, no longer having my arms crossed across my chest like a barricade. "What about you?"

"What about me?"

"How have you done for yourself?"

"Good," he answers. "Really good."

My brow quirks, that nagging curiosity about Everett's life poking at the hard ridges of my heart, wondering if he's been okay. If he's struggled or if he's skated through life without a hitch. Or if he's done nothing but think about me just as he's never been too far in the depths of my mind. "Well, the hotel business has its perks. Especially in areas like this."

"This is just something I'm investing my money in, and my time too, I guess. Eric and I, we go a long way back. I was actually with InnoDex up until a week ago."

"InnoDex?"

Everett nods with pursed lips, almost like he's withholding something from me. "Are you not familiar?"

"No," I answer, a little flustered. "I am. I just..." InnoDex is the lead tech company rivaling HP and Dell. We use it in our home, in what used to be Leo's office and in Sadie's room on her white, neatly polished, Pottery Barn desk. I use InnoDex products for my CAD software. Without it, I wouldn't be able to do my floor plans and layouts. It's household name level. Of course, I'm familiar. "What, were you like, IT or something?"

"More like CTO."

My hands involuntarily splay in front of me, as if moving around this imaginary well of information to sort it around so that I could somehow understand it. "You're the Chief Technology Officer of InnoDex."

"Was," he corrects, scratching the side of his head with his index finger.

"Everett, that's a huge deal."

He shrugs, adding a small noncommittal hum.

"You just decided one day to quit?"

"Yeah."

"Why?"

His face grows silent and dark, mulling over my question. "Personal reasons," he finally says, sounding so mysterious and evasive, I'm not sure if I want to pry or just take his answer at face value.

"Wow," I breathe. "So, you're just a real ass grown up with a real corporate job."

I expect him to laugh at my sarcasm, but he doesn't. "I'm still me, Teeny."

We stand there, our eyes locked on each other. The large space around us seems to expand wider and wider, bringing to light how alone we are here. How it's just us two without a single soul in our hemisphere to intrude. Just like the moments we had when we were teenagers. When we encapsulated ourselves inside a protective bubble. And along the shadows that line his face, the curve of his nose and the struggle behind his eyes that was always there, even at seventeen, I see him. The Everett that he claims to still be. *My* Everett.

"Teeny..."

My eyes start to mist. I don't even know why. Why these emotions are creating this torrent of hurt and nostalgia and longing. "I shouldn't take this."

Everett's brow furrows.

"I don't think this is a good idea," I elaborate. "Working with you...I don't think I can."

"Teeny, don't worry about me," he tells me, a softness to his words that make me fold. Just a little bit. "I'll stay out of your hair. But...I really think you could do something amazing with this place. I've seen your work, and—"

"My work?" I ask, a little confused as to what other properties I've designed he's seen.

He nods. "Your paintings."

"Oh." I haven't talked about my paintings in so long. When I used to mention them to Leo, he'd respond with a placating smile and a "that's nice" sentiment. I don't think Sadie's even seen my work, unless she's taken a peek at them in my parents' garage.

"Don't turn this down because of me," he adds, making a smile slip from my lips. "And I hear the budget for the remodel is pretty decent. Like, abnormally decent. So it would actually be a really bad career choice on your end if you turned it down."

That gets a genuine laugh out of me.

The doors open with a loud boom, and I jump, the haziness of the room morphing back to reality.

"So," Eric calls from the entrance, his voice echoing. "What do you think?" he asks, his question directed at me.

"I—"

"I was just telling Christine about the budget for this remodel," Everett interrupts.

"Oh, yes," Eric chimes in with a broad smile. "Everett has been a very involved silent investor. We're very lucky to have him. And while he's the one to cut the check for most of the renovation, the creative work will all be yours."

I peer at Everett, his eyes downturned as if he's pleading. When I look back at Eric, waiting for me to answer. "Why don't you show me the rest."

CHAPTER FOURTEEN
Everett
THEN

AFTER THE BONFIRE, it was official. People at school knew Teeny and I were together. Josh seemed okay with it, though around him, we tried to keep our PDA to a minimum, but even that was getting challenging. All I wanted to do around her was touch her and kiss her.

"So, a little birdie told me *Titanic* is going to be on HBO this Saturday."

Teeny gasps. "No."

I nod. "Yup."

"How did you know that's my favorite movie?"

"I think you've mentioned it about...twenty times."

"I did not!"

I laugh, burrowing my nose into her hair with her perched on a bench seat in the courtyard. It's lunchtime, and the crisp fall air with the brightly shining sun allows us to sit outside instead of inside where we'd been forced into during the heavy storm last week. "Movie night? I'll pick up some of those waffles from Marie's?"

She whips her head to look at me, her hazy eyes glazed over with infatuation. I don't even feel bad that I'm using her favorite movie to bait her for a night alone.

"Is your mom okay with it? You know, a three-hour long movie? Her son, all alone with his girlfriend..."

"She isn't going to be home," I tell her. "She's spending the weekend up north with my dad for some charity event."

She peers up at me, suspicion twisting her mouth into the cutest pout. "Did you plan this?"

"If by 'plan this' you mean did I reach out to *the* Home Box Office to play your favorite movie on the one weekend my mom isn't home, then yes. How did you guess?"

"Is *that* what HBO stands for?" She giggles, leaning into me so my nose nuzzles against the soft skin of her neck. It's just us two out here since the usual group we spend our lunch with opted for the more crowded area of the courtyard, so I'm taking advantage of the moment. I'm touching her more, kissing her more, teasing her more.

"You know, when I kiss you right here..." I pause, kissing her right below the ear, trailing down her pulse point. "I can feel your heartbeat get faster and faster."

She shivers. "Yeah?"

"Mh-hmm." I kiss her again, her chin ducking low, making this moment more intimate even as we sit out in the open. "And you get all smiley and dopey eyed."

She shoves at my stomach. "I do not!"

I pull her closer to me. "You do," I argue, tightening my hold on her. "You want to know what makes you squeal and get all jumpy?"

"What?"

I press my lips into her neck, puffing my cheeks and blowing a loud raspberry into her skin. It rattles so loudly it causes a few heads to turn in our direction. And sure enough, Teeny squeals. It's a delighted sound, something that echoes around us while the laughter dances in her eyes. She muffles it with a hand clamped over her mouth, and she smacks my arm.

"You are so embarrassing." Her face is a shade of red so deep, I feel like it'll stay like that for the rest of our lunch period.

She reaches for a Cheeto from the small bag sitting on the table and chucks it at me, just as I feel a low thump hit the back of my head. I turn to see Josh taking the seat across from me and Teeny. "I was just in Coach's office. He wants you to start the next game."

"Seriously?" I feel Teeny squeeze my hand, though she's created some distance between us now that we have an audience.

He nods enthusiastically. "Yeah, he was going over the roster for the next game and asked me what I thought. Told him it would be a good idea."

He bumps my fist, and I tamper down the excitement, feeling a little shy from the attention, but Teeny doesn't let that slide. She pulls me closer, kissing me on the cheek before whispering, "Congrats, Hayes."

I offer a shy laugh, unsure if it's from her praise or if it's because her brother's sitting across from us getting a front-row seat. "Thank you."

Her warm breath skirts over the shell of my ear. A soft giggle follows, and she says, "I think we need to celebrate." Her voice is low enough that only I can hear, but I still feel vividly aware of Josh's presence near us. "Maybe some Coke floats after school?"

"Do you even have to ask?"

She pulls away and wipes at my face, removing the traces of lip gloss on my cheek at the same time Josh's face twists into a repulsed grimace.

"Okay, you guys don't need to be doing that shit in front of me." He grabs a handful of Cheetos and tosses it at us, nearly emptying what's left in the bag.

"Josh, I was eating those," Teeny protests.

He ignores her, resting his forearms on the table and leaning forward like he's about to tell us a secret. "So, we're planning this little party on Saturday," he says, his voice a little low.

"Who's 'we?'"

"Me and a few other guys on the team," he tells me. "But we're having some trouble finding a place."

147

"So, you guys are planning a party with no place to have it," Teeny says, her words dripping with skepticism.

"Yes," he answers with a peevish snap to his voice. He then turns to me. "You think we could...use your place? Since your mom is going out of town?"

Teeny looks at me, and I now have two sets of eyes boring into me. Teeny's look disappointed and gutted while Josh's look hopeful. "Uh, I guess."

"But what about movie night?" Teeny asks, dispirited.

"Oh, come on, Teeny! You guys can do that stuff another day."

"Why can't you have your party some other day?"

"Because," he answers, the two tangled in a full bickering argument at this point. "Everyone is busy the rest of the weekend."

She rolls her eyes at him. "Whatever."

"I'll let the rest of the guys know." Josh takes off before I have a chance to change my mind.

Teeny looks at me, her disapproving look making the guilt spread through my body. "I'll make it up to you," I tell her, linking my fingers through hers. "We can have our movie night on Sunday. We can rent *Titanic* from Blockbuster."

"That's not the point, Everett."

I duck my head in shame. "I know."

"And you told Josh your mom was going to be out of town before you told me?"

"It just came up yesterday during practice."

She stays quiet, giving me the silent treatment with a sideways scowl. When her disappointed frown doesn't let up, I round my eyes and pout up at her like a sad little puppy dog. It gets the reaction I want out of her: a sweet as hell smile and a crack in her restraint.

"You owe me, Hayes." She points a finger in my direction, and I cup her face with both of my hands, leaning in to kiss her. We're interrupted by the shrill sound of the bell. "I'll see you after school?"

I nod before I take her hand in mine, pulling her closer before we part. "I am going to make it up to you."

"Oh, I'm counting on it."

I'll be honest, a part of me was worried about this party. Would I make a horrible host? Do I need to order more than the six large pizzas that were delivered right as the first of the guests arrived? What about the drinks? It's not like I have a fake ID stashed somewhere. What if it gets out of hand and my mom finds out? She would kill me.

Turns out, I didn't need to worry at all. While I provided a location, the guys on the team provided everything else. The pizzas were overshadowed by the overabundance of chips and other snacks, and the drinks were pushed to the backyard discreetly, hidden from prying neighbors, including Josh and Teeny's parents, with coolers and grocery bags. And while the music was loud, I was assured it would be lowered to a non-disruptive level by ten p.m.

Still, the anxiety driven need to please those around me causing an extra layer of worry to my already jittery state has me running from the kitchen to the backyard every ten minutes. It's no large scale party like the ones Jake's been throwing, already on his fifth one since the school year started, but it's still pretty lively. Thankfully, it's somewhat exclusive to members of the varsity team, including some of the JV guys that we're familiar with, so the worry of it getting out of hand has subsided.

"Here." A freshly cracked open can of beer is shoved in front of my face, Josh's reassuring smile joining it. "Relax, man. Just enjoy the party."

I take it, my body sagging at his advice to enjoy myself. "Have you seen Teeny?" I ask, taking a long sip. I guess taking a small load off my feet can't hurt.

"She's heading over in a bit," he tells me. "I think she's just waiting for a few of her friends."

"I hope your parents aren't going to complain."

"They took Andrew to Legoland," he tells me. "They're not going to be back until late."

"Well, I guess I don't have to worry about my mom finding out." I chuckle a loose laugh, my nerves unraveling to the point that I start to enjoy myself, just like Josh told me to. I start to make my rounds with Josh by my side. I mingle with a few people, keeping my eyes on the front door hoping to catch the only person I truly want to see tonight.

After about the fifteenth glance at the door, I finally see her. She walks in with a small group of her friends, all of them laughing at something one of them said, and it feels like time stands still. Like she moves in slow motion, her hair tumbling around her in waves and the gorgeous red dress she's wearing fitting her perfectly. Like it was made only for her and no one else in the entire world. She's wearing makeup. Nothing heavy or overwhelming, but I can tell she took her time. That's probably what she was doing, getting ready in her room with her girlfriends while they gossiped and laughed over something silly but would make it to my ears at some point during the night. Because every word that comes out of her mouth, all the little stories she has saved in her mind, waiting until she can tell me with bouncing excitement, I'd listen to on repeat. She can tell me over and over again about the time she and Diana went to Cold Stone Creamery and the boy behind the register asked for Diana's number. And all the little nuggets of information about Diana and her date with the Cold Stone guy? I don't think I'll ever get enough of it. Because it's Teeny telling me. Teeny with her eagerness in sharing every bit of her life with me. Teeny with the way her eyes light up each time she sees me, like we haven't seen each other in days, when in reality, it's only a few hours between classes.

I make my way to her, my steps moving urgently through the crowd, and she squeals when I lift her in my arms, spinning her in a dizzying circle.

"I missed you," I say into her hair. I pull away, and I notice the little added touches she made to her makeup. The deep purple eyeshadow smeared across her lids, the smattering of glitter on her arms, and the intoxicating scent of perfume on her neck.

I don't let her go, and she wraps her arms around my neck.

"Cold Stone guy is going to be here. I hope that's okay."

"I get to meet him in person?" I say excitedly.

"He has a name," Diana informs us flatly, annoyance clear in her tone. "It's Toby, if you care to know."

Teeny laughs, and Diana and the rest of their friends walk away to the backyard where the thick of the crowd is gathered, but I have other plans for Teeny. I drag her to the only room on the ground floor. The office-slash-den my mom's been using to store boxes and a few of my grandparents' things she hasn't thrown away yet. It's quiet in here without the music, and it feels like everyone else outside is no longer there and I get to have Teeny all to myself for the rest of the night.

"Don't you have an entire party going on outside?"

"Yeah," I answer, our bodies pressed against each other as I guide her to a lone desk in the corner. "I just wanted you to myself for a moment."

"Oh," she exclaims softly. I perch her at the edge of the desk and kiss her. No one's watching, no one's giving us an awkward side eye or telling us we're being disgusting. It's just us two, and I take full advantage of that. Her legs part, giving me access to step in between them, and it makes something frantic and desperate grow inside me. My hands start to cup her neck, stroking her jaw and cheek as I continue to dive deeper. A finger flicks the thin strap of her dress, letting it fall off her shoulder, and I start to tease the newly exposed skin. Her arm drapes over my shoulder, and my fingers follow, guiding her closer to me while I grip her wrist. Her pulse is wild, as is her breathing. Her free hand tucks under the hem of my shirt, and the coldness from her fingertips against my skin zaps through me like electricity.

I've never pressured Teeny to go further than she's comfortable with, but I'd be lying if I said I didn't want things to go beyond these heavy make out sessions. It's unreal the way we react to each other. How the curves of her body shift to fit mine like a perfectly carved out puzzle piece. Or how everything about her becomes frantic and blazing. Her hands, her skin, her breathing, her heartbeat. All of it speeds up with urgency, and my entire body reciprocates with a steady flow. A rhythmic beat that thumps at a fast yet even tempo.

Bum-bum-bum, bum-bum-bum.

She pulls away first, both of us unsure of how far we'd take this even with the party going on outside. "We should get back out there," she says, her gaze focused on my chest.

I cup my hand over the back of her head and duck my head so my nose nuzzles into her hair, finding that the glitter strategically placed on her arms has strayed to her scalp. "Yeah," I whisper.

She takes my hand, leading back outside, and I feel a deep twinge in my chest. I have this impulse to tell everyone to leave, anything to be alone with Teeny. Not just to continue that kiss, but to just hang out with her. To hold her and have her catch me up on her gossip, maybe more intel on her friends and the potential boys they've been instant messaging on AIM. Maybe even watch *Titanic* if it hasn't started playing on HBO.

Instead, we make our way to the coolers out back. Teeny dips into one of them, pulling out two Smirnoff Ices. We crack them open and start sipping. We're invited to start a game of beer pong, and with my rusty techniques and Teeny's novice skills, we're outmatched against Josh and Kevin.

"I want to play again," Teeny says, her speech slurred with her arm slung over my shoulder. I hadn't realized when the alcohol she'd been consuming had transitioned from a happy buzz to her current sluggish state. Her body sways, and her smile looks lazy and relaxed, and I can't help but laugh as she giggles to herself.

"I think you should sit this one out."

Her smile shifts into a pout. "Noooo," she whines, her cheeks growing flushed.

"I'm going to go sit her down somewhere," I tell Josh, letting some of Teeny's weight hang on my arm as her swaying grows sloppy. He answers with a nod and refocuses his attention on the game.

I help Teeny up the stairs to my room, and as soon as we walk through the door, the sounds of the party falling silent once again, she flops onto my bed.

"I'm in your room," she slurs through heavy lids. She yanks at my hand, and I fall onto the bed next to her.

"Yeah."

"Did you bring me up here to take advantage of me?" she adds, some of her words blending together.

"No," I answer with a laugh. "I do think you need to sleep this off."

"Nooo," she protests, pulling me closer to her. "I want you to lie here with me."

"Okay." It comes naturally, the realization that I can never say no to her.

She nuzzles her face into my chest, and I give. I cradle her body against me while her breathing starts to grow heavy. I think she's fallen asleep, but then I feel her shift before she whispers, "Everett?"

"Hmm?"

"Nothing."

I smile into her hair. "What is it?"

"I just wanted to say your name," she answers, the laziness in her words gone and a solemnness in its place.

I kiss her temple, taking a deep inhale of her shampoo, and it causes a significant chain of movements between us. Teeny lifts her face and kisses my collarbone, finding her way to my lips like a moth to a flame. Her hand tucks under my shirt, lifting it as her fingers trail over my stomach and chest. She hooks her knee over my waist, causing her dress to lift and expose her entire thigh. It's fast and swift, the way she pushes me against my own bed and ends up on top of me. She continues to lift my shirt, urging me to

153

remove it completely, and I comply. Because, of course, I'd do whatever she wants. My heart thuds in my chest, and I can feel it claw at me. The way Teeny's hands move across my bare skin. How her hips press into me with need. How my own hands move over her possessively.

"Teeny," I whisper between kisses. "We should stop."

She shakes her head, her fingers fumbling with the buttons to my jeans. "I don't want to."

"But you're drunk, and maybe we should do this when you aren't."

"I'm not that drunk," she responds, her voice insistent and pleading. I stop, holding her face in my hands and pulling away from her. She looks at me, her eyes wounded and worried. "Do you not... you don't want to?"

"No," I answer. "God, no, Teeny. I really, *really* want to."

"Okay then..." I stay quiet, watching her grow nervous and worried. She gnaws on her lower lip. "Is it because...I'm not—because I don't know what I'm doing? Like, I don't have experience—"

"Baby, no. No, that's not it at all," I tell her, urging her to believe me. "I just don't...I don't want your first—our first time to be with a party going on outside." Her eyes mist, visible even in the dim light coming from the small lamp sitting at my bedside. "I want it to be special. I want us to be able to take our time." I sit up and kiss her, soothing away any doubts she may think I might have. Because I don't have a single one. Not even a hint of one telling me that it wouldn't mean as much as I think it would.

She finally nods and smiles. "Okay." The haziness in her eyes returns, and she clamps a hand over her head.

"Are you okay?" I ask, bracing my hands on her shoulders for support.

She nods. "I think I might be more drunk than I thought. I should probably lay down." I place a small kiss on her cheek, and she shies away. "Sorry."

"Why are you apologizing?" She shakes her head, shifting to climb off me, but I stop her. "No, Teeny. What's wrong?"

"I feel like I made a total fool of myself."

"No," I argue, squeezing her palm. "No, Teeny. Don't say that."

She buries her face into her hands. "I'm just embarrassed."

"Teeny, listen." I force her eyes on me. "I love that this is what you want because I want it just as badly, if not more. But I want things to be perfect. For you. And this isn't what I imagined to be perfect."

A small smile peeks through the sadness in her eyes. "What did you imagine?"

"Well, for starters, something quieter."

She laughs, running her hands over my bare stomach. "That would be nice."

"And when there aren't like fifty people in my backyard. Including your brother."

"Yeah," she whispers through a huffed laugh. I kiss her, this time in a way that's more consoling than anything else, and she kisses me back, the insecurities that caused her to pull away now gone. She squeezes her eyes shut and buries her forehead into the crook of my shoulder.

"Are you okay?"

She nods. "I think I should sleep some of this alcohol off before I get home."

"Take a nap here," I suggest. "Josh can take you home in a few hours once you're feeling better." I turn over my comforter and let her crawl inside.

She nuzzles her face against my pillow, and before I've even covered her up, she's sighing into the soft fabric. I turn to put my shirt back on, and lay next to her, using the comforter to create a barrier between us as I watch her fall fast asleep.

Whether she believes it or not, the plans I have for her aren't something hurried with the thought that someone outside might walk in on us. It isn't on a night when we're both muddled with alcohol, her more than me, and the memory of what happens between us will grow fuzzy. I want to remember every detail.

The post-party high came and went. The guys on the team did a pretty good job cleaning up the mess left behind, and Teeny went home with the help of Josh discreetly guiding her to her room without getting caught in her drunken state. And with the traces of the party long gone and the conscious awareness to the end of the weekend, I have nothing to look forward to except to be with Teeny for the rest of the day.

So that's what I have planned. After a quick call to Teeny and finding out that her hangover is just as bad as I thought it would be, I arrive at her doorstep prepared.

"Hi." A laugh bubbles inside of me as Teeny answers the door. She has her hair thrown up in a messy bun, and she's wearing my hoodie and bare legs. A haggard look of fatigue mixed with disgust crosses her face as she turns around and lets me in.

"Ughhh," she moans into a cushion as she slumps into her sofa.

Teeny's mom waltzes in, looking over Teeny with concern. "Maybe it was that Subway sandwich you had for lunch yesterday."

"Mh-hmm," Teeny mumbles into the fabric.

Teeny's mom turns to me. "She's been feeling awful all morning. Probably just a little bout of food poisoning."

I hold back a smile. "Yeah," I tell her, keeping an eye on Teeny. "Could've been the mayo." She nods in agreement and walks away, leaving me and Teeny alone, and Teeny finally lifts her head.

"What's in the bag?" She curiously eyes the brown paper bag I walked in with, and I reach for it, excited to show her the contents.

"Well, I said movie night," I say, watching a small smile peek through her bedridden state. "So I brought a movie." I whip out a DVD copy of *Titanic* from Blockbuster, and her smile spreads wider.

She takes it from me while I dig into the bag once again. "And, to help with that hangover of yours." I say that last part in a low whisper. "Some waffles from Marie's."

She cuddles into me, wrapping her arms around my waist and letting her cheek rub into my chest. I accept her embrace, leaning back into the couch while running my hand over her back. "Thank you," she whispers.

"You're welcome." I waggle the DVD case with the blue and yellow logo on it. "Should we pop this baby in?"

She nods, and I get off the couch to start the movie. We settle with our food, and Teeny brings over a few cans of soda and water, and before we know it, we're joined by Josh and Andrew. It seems Josh isn't dealing with the after-effects of last night's party, at least not as badly as Teeny is, and by the time the Titanic is hit with an iceberg, we're surrounded by another heap full of snacks and drinks.

"Thank you for taking care of me." I look down at Teeny. Her head is nestled into the crook of my arm, and her arm is resting over my stomach. She looks a hundred times better than when I walked into her house a few hours ago. She no longer has the look of pain and discomfort, a contented smile in its place, and her energy is back too.

I kiss the top of her head. "You're welcome, baby."

CHAPTER FIFTEEN

Teeny

NOW

MY KITCHEN ISLAND looks like the drapery and paint department at The Home Depot came together, weathered a run through a wood chipper, and spit out all the shreds in a confetti mess of colors and patterns right onto my counter. Fabric swatches and paint samples and backsplash tiles are everywhere. It's taken me about four hours to sort through every option to present to Eric for our next meeting, ready to move toward a decision with a color scheme for El Cielo's lobby. But it's good. Busy and active and hectic are good.

I realized that my way of coping with things—Sadie being away from me for over a month, my pending divorce, Everett—is to keep myself busy. To occupy myself with work instead of trying to mend all the fragile pieces of my life. To avoid the reminder of how close to rock bottom I am.

My phone buzzes on the counter just as I'm matching up small squares of upholstery fabric to wallpaper samples. My face lights up when I look at the screen and see Sadie's name flash on the screen.

"Hi, baby!" I squeal into the phone.

"Hi, Mommy!"

"How's camp? How's the music going? Are you making new friends?"

"The music's happening," Sadie tells me excitedly. "And some of the girls from last summer are here, so I've been hanging out with them a lot."

"Oh, that's good, Sadie!" I'd been nervous about her making friends, especially with her being away from her usual tight knit friend group here, so it brings on a wave of relief knowing she isn't feeling out of place while being away from home.

"We're actually doing a showcase in a few weeks. I got grouped with two other girls here, and family and friends are allowed to be here. Can you and Daddy come?"

"Yeah, of course, baby. I'll have to make sure Daddy's available, but I'll be there."

"Is he going to be busy?"

"Um, I'm not sure," I tell her, hesitating. "I—I have to see how things are with Uncle Javi—"

"Mom."

"Yeah."

"I talked to Dad on the way here."

My heart sinks. "Uh—um. What did he say?"

"That he did something that you aren't happy with, and he has to give you some space. And that he's really sorry."

My throat tightens. "He didn't have to tell you that," I say hoarsely.

"I'm glad he did. I don't want you to feel like you have to keep things from me. And I'm not mad at you guys."

I laugh a watery chuckle, too disappointed in my life and the remains of my marriage. And the person I cherish most in the world who's in the middle of it all. Being pulled in different directions while Leo and I try to navigate a new relationship status. "When did you get so big, Sade."

I can practically feel her roll her eyes. We're interrupted by a loud call on her end, some distorted announcement through a speaker system probably calling all camp members for the next group activity. "I have to go."

"Yeah, we'll talk again next week."

"Oh! I almost forgot to tell you," she adds hurriedly, "Mina texted me. She wants me to sing at the wedding. She picked out a song for the first dance with Uncle Josh."

"That's amazing, Sadie! You're doing it, right?"

"Yeah, I told her I would. I'm going to practice here during my down time."

"Well, don't work yourself too hard. It's still summer. Remember to have fun."

"I am!" she calls. "Okay, I really have to go. Bye, Mom!"

"Bye!"

I shove away the twinge behind my ribcage in my kitchen surrounded by my quiet home and look at the clock on my microwave. It's already past ten. I'm scheduled to meet with Eric in half an hour, and I finally feel like I have enough material to present to him to move forward with some concrete decisions. My phone buzzes again and I answer it, my attention on the mess in front of me.

"Hello?"

"Hey, Teeny. It's Roberta."

"Hi Roberta. Thanks for calling me back," I respond, itching to knock yet another item off my checklist as I move forward with this hotel revamp. "I know you mentioned that you and Lisa were going on that vacation soon, so I wanted to catch you before you two leave. You still have some of the furniture pieces from the last staging I did? For the open house?"

"Yeah," she answers. "I also have some new pieces too. I've been a little busy-bee in my workshop so I can enjoy Australia while we're gone."

"Ah, perfect," I tell her. "You know how much I love the woodwork you put into your furniture." I do a quick mental calculation. With her trip roughly two weeks away and her beautiful selection of furnishings in her Downtown LA showroom, I need to make sure to secure the pieces I want for El Cielo.

"So, I have an opening this afternoon," she tells me, skipping all the gratuitous shop-talk and getting straight to the point. "If not, you may have to wait until I get back from Australia. And I know you usually like your clients to tag along. You think they'll be available this short notice?"

Today. That *is* short notice. I'm not even sure if Eric will be available beyond our meeting. "I actually have a meeting with him today. I'll see if he's available to head up there with me after."

"Great," she responds. "Just give me a call and let me know if anything changes. Hopefully I'll see you today."

"Yeah. Thanks again, Roberta."

We hang up, and I finish gathering all of my materials before walking out the door. It isn't long before I'm sitting with Eric in a secluded corner of the bar at El Cielo, a large mess of color swatches and fabric samples in front of us.

"I really like the use of gold with the turquoise and navy," Eric says, his hands running over the rough fabrics and strips of paint samples. "I think it would make the space look really airy and open."

"I was thinking the same," I tell him. "With the use of the sheer drapes to open the windows to the view, it'll tie in well with the oceanic theme of this location. I have another client who's currently working on a restaurant redesign, and they're using similar color schemes. It's going to look stunning, and you really couldn't have picked a better place with the large windows."

He nods with an approving smile. "I know Everett's involvement is merely on the financing end, but his input has been really contributive. I didn't know he had such an eye for interior design. Would it be okay if I run these by him before we make a final decision?"

My body tenses at the mention of Everett. "Sure. Of course."

"Great." Eric pauses to check his phone. "He should actually be here in a bit."

"Oh, I didn't know he'd be joining us."

He smiles kindly, maintaining a professional facade while the dregs of my past keep rearing its ugly head in the form of my new client. "I asked him to join us. I hope you don't mind."

I offer a purse lipped smile and shake my head, hoping to shift our conversation away from the boy who broke my heart all those years ago. "I also wanted to let you know, the carpenter has an opening this afternoon. She'll walk me through her showroom, show me some pieces she's working on to see what we can use to fill the lobby."

"Already?"

I nod. "She and her wife complete a lot of the work themselves, so to get the pieces we want, we need to choose them in advance. Plus, they're going on a month-long vacation to Australia in a few weeks. It'll be best to meet with her sooner than later.

"Would you be available? I know it's really last minute."

His brow furrows. "I have plans," he explains. "Birthday dinner with the in-laws." He pauses before adding, "Would you mind going alone?"

"I mean, as long as you're okay with it," I tell him after a thoughtful pause. "I do prefer to have my clients join for input, but I understand if you're unavailable."

"I'd appreciate it. You've done a great job with the color schematics, I'm sure whatever you choose will fit perfectly for the space." An echo of footsteps, ones that sound sure and confident, interrupt us. "Oh, perfect. Everett's here."

Curiosity getting the better of me, I turn to look in the direction of Eric's gaze only to find Everett walking toward us. And, of course, he looks like he's stepped out of a freaking *GQ* magazine. He's dressed in a gray suit tailored to fit his body perfectly. He's in the middle of shrugging his jacket on, making the entire look that much more effortless. His hair is perfectly coiffed without a single strand out of place with a light smattering of stubble lining his jawline.

When I was sixteen, I knew he was the cutest boy in school. The girls in my class expressing their keen interest in my boyfriend never let me forget it. Always eyeing him like he was fresh meat and throwing jealous sneers in my direction. And now, twenty years later, he's aged parallel with every single thing I would find attractive in a man.

"I hope I didn't miss too much," Everett announces as he takes the empty seat between myself and Eric.

"I just made some final decisions on the wallpaper and paint, and Christine was just telling me about the furnishings." Eric gestures to me, silently letting me fill Everett in on our latest developments.

"Oh, uh, yes," I stammer. "I was just explaining to Eric that I have a meeting with the carpenter this afternoon."

"Where's this carpenter?" Everett asks, his tone businesslike.

"Her showroom's in LA."

"Everett," Eric cuts in. "If you're free, maybe you can tag along. Christine asked me to go, but I have that dinner with Connie and her parents."

"That's really not necessary," I start to argue at the same time Everett says, "I'm free."

"Perfect," Eric responds, satisfied that our plans have deviated into a productive afternoon of furniture shopping.

I have nothing. Nothing other than the fact that I don't want Everett with me for longer than necessary. Especially not for a three-hour drive.

"Great," Everett responds with a smile that almost seems taunting. "I'll drive."

"No, no. You—that's okay. I don't have to be there until three."

"But with traffic and all." Everett flicks at his wrist, looking at the face of his watch wrapped in solid titanium. "We should leave now."

I start to panic. "I really don't want to keep you from anything. I'm sure you're plenty busy."

"Nope. Free as a bird." He stands from his seat, buttoning up his jacket once his chair is neatly tucked under the table.

Eric clasps his hands together and grins. "Great! I'll catch up with you tomorrow then," he tells Everett. He then turns to me and adds, "Thank you for your time, Christine. Let me know if you need anything from me, but in the meantime, you're in good hands with Everett here."

I silently watch Eric stand and walk away, leaving me alone with Everett. How did this happen? In one swoop, I'm spending my afternoon with the last person I planned to.

"You need help with those?" Everett asks, gesturing to the mess on the table.

"No," I blurt out curtly. "I got it."

I stand and smooth my skirt out. It's curve hugging, stopping at my knees with a slit running up the back, and I've paired it with a silk blouse that's light and airy to withstand the glaring summer heat. I'm hovering over the table, gathering everything and tucking things back into my large binder and bag. My hands move with unease, unsure of where I'm putting things and just shoving them so I can get out of this situation sooner than later. When I'm done, I take a step back to push my chair in only to stumble my back right into Everett's chest.

"Umph," he groans. His hand grips my waist to stop me, and the familiarity of his touch has my entire body buzzing.

A soft gasp slips through my lips, and my hand instinctively covers his. "Sorry," I whisper, nervously stepping away from him.

He accepts my apology with a polite smile and a dismissive shake of his head. "Ready?"

"Everett, it's really not necessary that you come with me."

"I want to be involved in this," he explains. "Eric's been great, but he's done plenty, and I'd like to help him out when I can. Plus, now that he's gone over the color schematics with you, I think this is a good place for me to step in. Have a fresh pair of eyes."

I sigh, not bothering to hold back my indignation.

"I'm parked right out front." Before he turns to walk out of the hotel, Everett extends a hand toward the bag slung over my shoulder. "I'll take these for you."

"Oh, you don't—" Everett ignores my protest and takes my tote bag, hooking it through his fingers and gently placing a hand on my lower back to guide me to his BMW. It's shiny and new and black, just like his old one. The one with the cushy passenger seat with my strawberry lip gloss and country apple body spray tucked into the glove compartment and my scrunchy wrapped around the gearshift.

My fingers still on the handle of the passenger side. Suddenly, I don't recognize the woman I see in the reflection of the polished window in front of me. I only see the sixteen-year-old girl, too eager to hop into her boyfriend's fancy BMW, ready to be swept off her feet.

"Everett." He's at the back of his car, placing my bag in his trunk, when I call his name and he stops, looking up to face me. "I think I should drive my car."

He scowls, closing the trunk with a light thud. "Why?"

I close my eyes and try my best to hold back the grimace twisting my face. How do I tell him that I might crumble into a million little pieces if I slide right into this passenger seat that's no longer mine? How do I tell him that I'm not ready to sit there and watch him drive with the cool coastal breeze blowing through his hair and his wrist lazily slung over the steering wheel as if it hasn't been twenty years since I last saw him like that? How do I explain the grief already slashed into my heart at the mere thought of it?

I look at him, one hand braced on my hip and the other trailing over my chin to hide the shakiness of my voice. "I, um," I say, that wavering stammer too strong for me to hide with anything other than silence. Everett cautiously makes his way toward me, his hand resting on the frame of his car. He eyes me, letting me work through my words. "I just think that..." I pause, looking at him with the words caught in my throat. The truth resting there where it's been held back for so long. "I can't get in your car," I finally tell him, my voice hoarse. "I don't know if I can..."

He gently hooks his hand over my wrist, my fingers still creating this wall of defense to safeguard all the hurt so visible on my face. His index finger trails over my pulse point for a second before he drops his hand, creating this emptiness I'm all too familiar with.

"Okay," he finally answers. "That's fine." He swallows, and a shadow casts over his features, making him look grave and somber. He walks back to his trunk, popping it open to retrieve my bag, and I lead the way to my car.

An hour later, as we sit in the thick of Southern California traffic, Everett and I fill the silence with talk radio. I let the concentration necessary to navigate through stop-and-go traffic fill my already preoccupied mind and do my best to ignore Everett's presence along with the big pink elephant sitting in the back seat. Everett's doing a much better job at ignoring the burgeoning metaphorical mammal behind us, busying himself with the same swatches and color samples I showed Eric earlier.

"I like the gold with the bluish-green color," he comments, his gaze still focused on everything spread over his lap.

"That's what Eric said."

He responds with a low hum. "And I think a really large focal piece like some artwork or a really out of this world chandelier would go great with what you picked out so far."

"Yeah. I'm already looking for light fixtures that I think might work, and I booked a meeting with a local art gallery for Eric to pick out some pieces."

"When?"

I turn to quickly glance in his direction only to see him patiently wait for my answer. "Most likely in a week or two. They have a show in the coming week, so they wanted to get that out of the way before having any potential buyers in."

"I'll meet with them."

"Eric already agreed to—"

"It's fine," he interrupts. "I'll tell him I'll do it. He's got a lot on his plate with hiring new staff and rolling out the new booking software. I told him I'd take on anything I can help with." I don't respond with an answer. Instead, I remain silent, bypassing a slow moving semi. "Have you talked to Josh recently?"

"I called him a few days ago," I answer. "Why?"

"I had dinner with him and Mina last night. He mentioned something about a bachelor party in Vegas?"

"Oh, yeah. They're doing this joint bachelor-bachelorette party. Mina told me about it too."

"It's still a while before the wedding."

"I know, but Mina's maid of honor is visiting, and it kind of worked out," I explain. "Otherwise, we'd be squeezing in an overnight trip the day before the wedding."

"So, you're going?"

I smirk in his direction. "I think I'm a little too old to be out partying with the youngsters."

"If you're too old then what the hell am I?"

I laugh. "I don't even know if I can get the time off. I'm working on a few other projects. And with this hotel renovation, I'm up to my neck with deadlines."

He smirks a playful simper. "I think I can persuade your boss to give you some time off."

"You know, I don't even remember the last time I took some time off for myself. I spent the last fourteen years raising Sadie."

"Well, now's your chance."

I scoff. "And the gambling capital of the country is the place to go?"

"If you could go anywhere, where would you go?"

I peer over at him, wondering how serious his question is. Is he just making conversation? Or does he really want to know? Does he even care to know? "France," I finally say. "Specifically Paris. Maybe a weekend to the French countryside."

"Paris?"

I nod. "This might seem totally touristy and cliché, but I want to see Versailles. And the Louvre. And the Eiffel Tower at night with the sparkly lights. And eat a croissant with a latte." Everett doesn't say anything, and I suddenly feel embarrassed. I'd told Leo I wanted to go to Paris for our wedding anniversary last year. I told him everything I just told Everett, and he responded with a disparaging scoff. He told me no one goes to Paris anymore. That it's too cheap and tacky and full of American tourists as if he himself weren't American. He'd convinced me somewhere like Dubai or Singapore would be much more glamorous than plain old Paris. It didn't change how much I still wanted to see Paris for all its beauty. "But you know, Vegas is good too. They have their own Eiffel Tower."

I glance over at Everett, just as we merge onto the 10, and he looks at me with a soft smile that's somehow comforting and sad at the same time. "You should go to Paris, Teeny."

"What, like now?"

"Now, next week, next year. Whenever. You should go."

A joke or some self-deprecating comment about my social life, or lack thereof, sits at the tip of my tongue, but when I look at Everett, the earnestness in his words and the look on his face stops me.

I continue driving, exiting the freeway and taking turns down one-way streets, before we finally pull into the back lot of a large warehouse style building. It's eerily quiet here. The lot is mostly empty aside from one car parked closest to the back entrance.

"This is it?" Everett asks, peering up at the building.

"Yeah," I answer, exiting the car.

"Looks a little creepy."

"It doesn't look like much on the outside, but I promise her work is amazing. You really aren't going to find more original work like hers."

"Well then," Everett says, gesturing a hand ahead of him. "Lead the way."

I knock on the large metal roll-up door, the hollow metal clunking against my knuckles, before it opens with a loud clank. It rattles as it rolls up, and I'm greeted with Roberta's bright face.

"Teeny! You're early!" We embrace in a tight hug, and she grips my shoulders in her hands. "How is it that you get more stunning every time I see you? Did you do something to your hair?" She lightly tousles it between her fingers.

"Just trying something different." I fluff my hair and give her a pleased smile with my shoulder turned up. "Roberta, this is Everett. He's the client I'm shopping for today."

"Well, client with all the money, please follow me."

I giggle a small laugh in Everett's direction, and he smiles warmly, making this entire exchange feel less professional and much more like two people shopping for furniture together. And it's so unexpectedly intimate.

"So these are some of the large items I finished last month," Roberta announces as she steps farther into her showroom. "I focused a lot of my attention on making these pieces more modern than traditional. I stuck with more neutral colors for the upholstery, but if you'd like to try different fabrics, I can show you some samples."

Everett studies the sofas and armchairs Roberta's walking us through and runs his hands along the rough fabric. "And these will withstand wear?"

"Depending on the fabric you choose, yes," Roberta answers. "Teeny mentioned your selections are going to be for your hotel? It would probably be best to choose linen. It's the most durable and moisture resistant."

There's a pause in conversation as Everett peruses his options, and Roberta eyes me with an inquisitive eye.

"What do you think, Teen?" Everett asks, looking at me with a fascinated gaze. He has one hand tucked into his pants pocket, and his head is ducked low. As if eager to know my opinion.

"Yeah," I answer, searching for the right words. "Roberta's right. Linen would be a good choice, and it won't look tacky or cheap. And we'll have plenty of color options to match with the wallpaper designs and drapes."

He takes a cautious step toward me, his hand moving over his jaw as he muses over my answer. "Yeah?"

I nod. "If you want to run it by Eric before you decide, we can do that. I can take some pictures of a few potential pieces and go from there."

"Sure," Everett says. "Mind if I look around a bit?"

"Yeah! Of course," Roberta answers, the sudden intensity in her voice echoing around us. "Actually, Teeny. Can I steal you for a minute? There's something...my office. Some new end tables I—Maybe you can look?"

I shoot a confused look in her direction, and she wildly gestures toward her office. "Are you okay here on your own?" I ask Everett.

He looks up at me and smiles a crooked smile. His eyes soften after a bemused scowl had taken over his features over the different fabric options. "Yeah."

I feel Roberta's hand hook over my wrist, and she practically drags me away. Once in her office, behind the closed door, she shoots me an accusative glare. "Okay, who is he?"

"He's a client," I tell her.

"Clients don't look at you like that."

I resist the urge to roll my eyes. "You're so dramatic. He doesn't look at me like anything."

Roberta scoffs. "Are you kidding me?"

"Fine," I say, lifting a hand in a surrendering gesture. "How does he look at me?"

"Girl, like he's mesmerized by you."

"He does?"

She nods aggressively. "So, is he still 'just a client?'"

"There's...history," I finally tell her. "But that was ages ago. We were kids."

"Well, it's a shame that you're married because if someone from my past looked at me like that—"

"We're getting a divorce," I blurt out.

170

Roberta looks at me with a blank stare, flashing morse code like blinks asking me if she heard me right. "What?"

"He cheated on me. Some twenty-something with perky tits and probably no gag reflex," I say sardonically. "But um, I kicked him out." I don't know why I'm telling Roberta all of this. Maybe it's the idea that if I'm garnering even a hint of attention from Everett, it wouldn't be toward a married woman committed to her husband. It would be toward a woman scorned.

Roberta grabs me by my shoulders and guides me to one of the matching armchairs in her office, a set she designed and made herself. She sits opposite me, peering at me with concern and sympathy. "Are you okay?"

"You mean aside from the fact that I'm about to be single for the first time in what, fifteen years?" I blow out a sigh. Fifteen years. That's an entire lifetime. And it's gone. Poof! "Jesus," I say to myself in shock. "Fifteen fucking years."

Roberta stays quiet, her brows raised in agreement.

"I'm way too old to be starting over," I say, a whoosh of breath following my words. "I'm going to be this old divorcée filling my time planting begonias and marigolds and watching *Friends* on repeat while Leo goes and marries someone half my age."

"Okay, now who's being dramatic?"

"It's the truth!" I exclaim, throwing my hands in the air. "We women only get to age and wrinkle and sag while the men around us get to fuck anything with long legs and tight skin."

"You could always join the other team," Roberta suggests jokingly. "We never leave the toilet seat up."

"I like dick too much," I mutter. And we both burst out laughing. I cower forward at the same time my eyes mist over, and I don't know if they're tears of joy or misery.

Roberta looks at me, her face serious now that the laughter has subsided. "Teeny," she says, firmly calling for my attention. "You're going to be fine. It's going to take some time, but you are going to be fine."

I nod, a wave of betrayal returning full force with a golf ball sized knot in my throat.

"Now, come on," she says, nodding toward the door. "Let's get back to your handsome client."

Roberta and I walk out of her office, her giving my hand an encouraging squeeze, and we reach Everett as he's looking over a row of coffee tables. He's examining Roberta's handiwork, focusing on the carvings she carefully whittled into the wood.

"So, see anything you like?" I ask just as Everett sees us. His eyes brighten, rounding into big sparkly spheres as if he's clinging to my every word. I feel Roberta elbow my side, but I ignore it.

"I picked out a few chairs and sofas over there," he says, pointing a finger to the living room furniture portion of the showroom. "But I like some of these coffee tables. I think they'd look nice with the furniture I was looking at."

The phone trills from the other side of the warehouse. "I'll let you two do some browsing," Roberta announces, already turning back to her office. "If you need me, just holler."

Roberta walks off, leaving Everett and me alone. I take a few cautious steps toward him, Roberta's words burning a hole in my head. I stop in front of the table he's hovering over and stoop down to run my hand over the material, my fingers tracing the grooves and glossy finish. "I really like this one," I say in a low voice.

"Yeah?"

I nod, smiling softly at him. "I asked Roberta to carve the same design into my desk at home." I pause, focusing my movements over the curves. "See the waves at the edges? That was a special request by me. And she started incorporating it into her other pieces."

Everett's fingers start following the patterns I'm drawing. "It's beautiful."

His face drifts closer to me where I hear a soft sigh exhale from his lips. I get a deep whiff of his cologne. It's not the Calvin Klein he used to wear, a bottle always kept on his nightstand next to his retainers and wallet. It's something more masculine, formidable.

Something that's a part of this new Everett. The one I'm getting to know all over again.

His hand moves from the wood surface to my wrist, grazing against my skin in careful strokes. We both stand upright, his fingers sliding up my forearm. "I think it would look amazing at the hotel."

"I think so too." My voice is a whisper, and I don't even know why.

Why my words feel like they're caught in my throat. Why my heart is racing like I'm on a stage with a crowd full of eyes on me.

Why it also aches like someone is squeezing it in their fist.

His palm lightly cups my elbow. "I think we'll go with this one."

"Yeah," I breathe. I get sucked into his gaze, and it's hypnotizing. Like I'm in some trance, transported into an alternative universe where the thought of Everett doesn't include pain. Where my heart was never broken and left whole for the last twenty years. Where I was always just...happy. And that thought, the idea that I could've been happy, makes me instantly sad. Like I'm mourning over a life I could've had. Should've had. "We should get going. With the traffic, it'll take a few hours to get back."

"Yeah." He lets go of my arm, and my body gets sucked back to reality.

I turn to Roberta's office and find her and her wife, Lisa, walking out into the showroom. Lisa, pixie cut hair with denim coveralls and working boots, breezily links her arm through Roberta's, and the two walk toward me with knowing smiles.

"Hi, Lisa!" I greet her, pulling her into an embrace. "I'm so glad I caught you before I left."

"Hey, Teeny," she says, pulling away from me. "I wouldn't miss a chance to say hi to our favorite designer!" She takes a quick glance at Everett before extending a hand in his direction. "Hi. I'm Lisa."

"Everett," he responds cordially. "Nice to meet you."

"I think we're just about finished," I tell the pair. "We have enough options to choose from within the next few weeks."

"Great!" Lisa says, eyes ping-ponging between me and Everett. "You need to make it out here more often. Bring us more business."

I laugh. "You know you can always count on me for that."

"Are you two heading out?" Roberta asks.

"Yeah," I answer. "We got a long drive back to San Diego, and the rush hour traffic isn't going to be fun."

"You know," Lisa says with a thoughtful hum. "If you want to wait out the traffic, there's this amazing French bistro around the corner. They have the best burrata and french onion soup."

"Oh, no. I don't—"

"That actually sounds amazing. I'm famished," Everett interrupts me. "We should check it out."

I throw a "what the fuck" glare at both Lisa and Roberta, to which they smile smugly. "I'll text you the address."

Finding that the restaurant is actually within walking distance, Everett and I opt to leave my car in Roberta's lot and trek the two blocks to Le Petit Paris. Sitting between a plate of burrata and two glasses of chardonnay, an awkward silence lingers in the air as does something much more palpable. Something alive and beating with the reminder that Everett isn't just a client, only strengthening Roberta's point, and I'm not just someone Everett hired to make his hotel look pretty.

"How's Sadie?"

I look up from poking at my french onion soup, Everett watching me over the rim of his wineglass. He's taken off his suit jacket, hanging it over the back of his chair, and he has his sleeves rolled up his forearm. He looks lax, a little undone. Even the way he watches me, pensive and observant, looks like he's just taking me in rather than watching me with intent. And I wonder if he too notices the changes in me that I notice in him. The few strands of gray hidden in the waves of my hair. The fine lines fanning out the corners of my eyes.

"Good," I tell him. "Settling in at camp and all. She just told me Mina asked her to sing something at their wedding, so that's pretty exciting." I smile softly, remembering a time when Sadie's determination to learn how to play guitar and piano left me and Leo walking around the house with foam plugs shoved into our ears and how now, her music is sometimes the only thing that brings me solace.

Everett smiles too. "She must be really talented. You know, to be performing in front of that many people."

"She's amazing. She has this showcase at camp, and I can't wait to see what she's come up with."

"She writes her own songs?"

I nod. "She's getting more comfortable with it, and it just sort of flows out of her. I honestly don't know how she does it. Or where she even gets it from."

"You're an artist too, Teen."

My lips twist to one side. "Yeah. I guess I was."

"You don't paint anymore?"

"I haven't. Not for a long time. I don't think since college."

"Why?"

I shrug. "I guess I've just been too busy. At first, at least. And then, I just didn't see the point, so..."

"You should again."

"For what?" I wave a hand in his direction and roll my eyes as if to brush off this need to do something that used to breathe life into me. Something that used to breathe life into *us*. Everett and I bonded over my art. His obsession with watching me paint and him unexpectedly becoming my muse. We thrived on it. On what it meant for us, how our love used to translate into my work. Through the brushstrokes and the little details of us I used to paint into my work. And those details were only for us.

We stay quiet, continuing our meal through the awkwardness that's settled over us like a fog. A thick mist of the unknown that feels comforting for some reason. Until Everett speaks.

"You know, my therapist tells me it's good to have a hobby. Something to keep your mind grounded and level."

"You see a therapist?"

"Yeah," he tells me, avoiding my eyes by fixating his gaze on the table. "I started seeing one in college. After I left, I had some friends who...they thought it would be good to see someone."

"Why—I mean, what—"

"I wasn't...okay, I guess. And talking to someone helped. The meds helped even more."

"You never told me this."

"I couldn't..."

My heart twists inside my chest imagining Everett all those years ago. All alone with the aftermath of us being so much more to take on, on top of the grief of losing what we had. He wasn't okay, not by a mile. The realization cracks a chink in my chest.

"I wanted to, though, Teeny."

"Wh—"

"I wanted to call you. I wanted to—"

"Everett." I say his name firmly. It's an objection. And he roughly runs his fingers through his hair, his face hardening with restraint and frustration. "I just...It's fine. You don't need to say anything. I'm fine."

"Okay," he says hoarsely.

We continue to eat, the need to say something tickling the inside of my mouth. I want to tell him that I think the pieces he chose in Roberta's showroom are a few of my favorites and ones I always beg Roberta and Lisa to have on hand. I want to tell him that I'm craving dessert and would love to split a brownie sundae after this with him. I want to tell him that I have an unopened package of watercolors and a few blank canvases sitting in my closet and that I wish I could take it out without having to think of all the pain in my heart every time I pick up a paintbrush. I want to ask him what he would've said to me if he'd called. I want to talk to him about his therapy. I want to talk about all of these things, filling our time with the same pillow talk that would keep us pushing the boundaries of my curfew when I was sixteen, as if no time had passed. But that's the thing. Time has passed. Time that I thought was the remedy to all the hurt he slashed into my heart. But time has done nothing but show me how much I missed him. How much I loved him.

CHAPTER SIXTEEN

Everett

MY FOOT HANGS off the edge of my bed, my sock-covered toe occasionally grazing Teeny's right calf. I've reread the same paragraph in my textbook six times, some impertinent detail about the year 1775 and The Battle of Lexington. Teeny, on the other hand, her attention is a little harder to sway. With every brush against her skin, I expect a peek over her shoulder or for her to put her paintbrush down altogether and join me on my bed. But all she does is dip her brush into the small mason jar of water on my desk. Or a quick readjustment of her headphones.

One more sweep against her skin.

"You keep doing that, and I'm going to leave."

"After lugging your easel and your stool and your paint and brushes here? What a waste of time."

She gently puts her brush down and swivels on her stool to face me, tugging her earphone out of her ear. "Yeah, but I'd get so much work done if I didn't have you trying to distract me."

I sit up and pull at her hand. "Take a break."

She exhales a deep sigh but gives. "Fifteen minutes, mister." She starts climbing onto my bed next to me and nuzzles her face into my neck. My entire body turns into Jell-O, and I feel her warm breath and her playful kisses all the way down to the pit of my stomach.

"Fifteen minutes is plenty for what I want to do with you."

She giggles. "What do you want to do with me?"

"Have you help me memorize, in sequential order, who signed the Declaration of Independence? Eat the last of the cookies and cream ice cream in my freezer?"

"Well, John Hancock was first," she says, her voice muffled against my skin. "And we can go over the rest over a bowl of ice cream."

"How did you know that?"

"Everyone knows who signed the Declaration of Independence first."

"I didn't know."

She shrugs, looking at me with a smug smile, and I pinch at her waist, making her squirm.

"Everett!"

"Are you making fun of me?"

I pinch her harder, and she giggles into my chest. She's flush against me now and while the moment is a playful one, I have this sudden urge to kiss her. And not a quick peck on the cheek, but something deeper and unhurried.

Teeny moves first, hooking her arm around my neck and tugging me closer to her. She kisses me, pushing her chest into mine, and I grab her arm, pressing her hand into the mattress. My thumb runs over the soft skin of her wrist, where her pulse thuds and races. She's nervous, or anxious. One of those things that makes her heart pound inside her chest.

The way her blood rushes through her, faster when she's excited and more listless and measured when she's calm, feels like an all-access pass to her thoughts. And knowing I'm exciting something in her brain, something that elicits this level of enthusiasm, makes me uninhibited.

My body moves over her, pinning her down, and my hand grips her wrist harder. I don't even realize the low grumble that rattles in my throat, but it cuts through the room and has Teeny pushing her hand into my chest.

"You know, the last time we were in this place, I believe I was a little..."

"Drunk?"

She looks at me with narrowed eyes. "Indisposed?"

I smirk. "Okay."

"And...I just want to say thank you."

"For what?" My fingers move a few strands of hair away from her forehead.

"For making the right choice for me," she says softly.

"Yeah?"

She nods. "I don't want to say I would've regretted it, but I don't think I was as ready as I thought I was."

"I'd never pressure you to do anything you're not comfortable with."

"I know." She kisses me, her lips moving gently and carefully. After a thoughtful pause, she looks at me before saying, "Can I ask you something?"

"Of course."

She takes a deep breath. A quiet, preliminary pause before she segues into her question. "Have you been with anyone? You know..."

I laugh awkwardly, and my heart suddenly feels like it's ricocheting off the walls of my chest. "Um, yeah."

We both sit up, and Teeny draws her knees up to her chin. She peers up at me, the mood now shifted into something more quiet and earnest.

"It was sophomore year," I tell her. "This girl in my algebra class. We started kind of seeing each other. I think she liked that I played basketball. But then I moved, and we lost touch."

"So, she was your girlfriend?"

"'Girlfriend' is a little strong. More like...'girl who was a little more than a friend.'"

The silence between us lingers noisily, hard to ignore or snuff.

"Is that...okay?"

Teeny shrugs. "Your past is your past."

"And I don't talk to her."

"Okay." She smiles at me, her eyes soft and understanding.

I sense a moment of unease. A tight tension she doesn't feel comfortable with. A change in subject feels good right about now. "You want to tell me about what you're working on?"

She sighs, letting a small, relieved smile slip, and we both turn to look at the painting. It's not finished, made obvious by the white patches of the canvas. What's colored is a blend of blues. Turquoise, navy, sky blue, indigo, periwinkle. "It's for my show at the gallery. This is my last piece, and I need to have it done just after New Year's."

"So, you have a little over a month?"

She nods. "And I feel like I'm kind of losing my creative groove."

"What are you talking about? It looks almost done."

Teeny stands from the bed, walking over to the painting. She traces a gentle finger over the drying painting, hovering over it with care. "I'm having trouble getting the right shade of green and blue to mimic the ocean. The darker colors of the deep water and the waves...no matter what I use, I can't seem to get it the color I want."

I follow her steps, sidling up behind her and wrapping my arm around her stomach. "It's beautiful."

Her fingers thread up my neck and into my hair, guiding my chin to rest on her shoulder. "Thank you."

"Can I ask you a favor?"

"Hmm?"

"We have an away game up in Irvine in two weeks. Right before winter break. Can you be there? Maybe bring that big sign with my number on it this time?"

"Yeah," she says, her voice is soft and light and airy. "As long as you come to my show."

"Yeah."

"Yeah?"

"Of course." She turns to fully face me, and I cup a hand over her cheek. "I'll be back from visiting my dad on New Year's Day."

"My show's on the second," she says, an apologetic look sweeping across her face.

I place a quick peck on her cheek. "I'll be sure to be back in time."

"Are you sure?"

"I won't miss it, Teeny."

She tilts up on her tiptoes and kisses me, opening her mouth and letting our tongues sweep and tangle. She sighs deeply, and her lips become persistent and urgent. And this time, she doesn't push me away.

The game day bustle hasn't changed, not even as we head into game six. And as we ride a bus on the hour-long drive to Irvine, it's entirely filled with loud chitter-chatter and the boisterous excitement of pre-game jitters. The bus finally pulls into the parking lot of University High with a loud sigh, and we all file out, a round of cheers following our exit. As soon as my feet hit the parking lot, my eyes scan over the long row of cars, looking for the same maroon Pathfinder Teeny and Josh share.

That's when I spot her in the parking lot with her hair tied in the same pigtails she had at the first game, but no sign. She's wearing a hoodie zipped up to her neck, and when she spots me, she bolts into a sprint right into my arms. I lift her, spinning her in a dizzying twirl and she squeals.

"You made it," I whisper into her ear.

"I did." I set her back on solid ground and peer over her shoulder.

"So, no sign?"

She smiles smugly. "I have something better." She takes a step back and swiftly unzips her hoodie. She flashes me with a big sparkly red and gold eight colored with some patterned fabric and puffy paint. Teeny beams at me with a proud smile.

My face lights up too, and I give in to the urge to kiss her. Right there, in front of the entire basketball team, including Teeny's brother. A loud whoop sounds around us, and Teeny laughs against my face.

"Sounds like we have an audience."

I stand back, taking in the shirt she'd made herself. Spent time planning and painting and drying. "I can't believe you did this," I say softly, still disbelieving of this enormous gesture that makes me feel like I could move mountains.

I'm suddenly shoved forward, a force of brawn pushing me into Teeny. "Stop making out with my sister," Josh teases. "We have a game to win."

I lean into Teeny and her face shifts into bliss. Into something so happy, I feel it all the way down to my toes. And my heart feels like it's going to burst. Like all I ever want in life is to see Teeny like this. Happy and completely elated. "I'll catch you after the game?"

"Yeah." Teeny pulls away and lands a soft punch to my arm. "Now go get 'em, tiger."

My face twists into a grimace. "'Tiger?'"

"Sport?"

"Ugh," I respond. "Why is that actually worse?"

"Go, Hayes. Before they have to drag you."

"I like Hayes," I tell her, taking a step backward. "Let's stick with Hayes."

She rolls her eyes and clamps her teeth on her bottom lip, shoving a hand into my stomach. I throw a wink in her direction, and I feel like I could win this game all by myself. Just me against the whole University High basketball team, fueled by Teeny's smile.

The entirety of the game—the fast accumulating points, the

cheers and buzzers, the fleeting but very noticeable glances at Teeny on the bleachers in the thick of the crowd, the halftime routine—happens in a blur. Next thing I know, the time clock has run out, and the scoreboard is showing Home 81, Visitor 116. By the time I've changed in the locker room and walked out into the parking lot, I see Teeny waiting by her car.

"I'll see you back home," Josh says in a low voice, patting a hand on my shoulder. He walks past Teeny, never missing an opportunity to annoy his little sister by mussing up her hair. Teeny shoves a hand against his head before he turns to a commotion of guys waiting at a nearby car. With the bus going home only half full, the parking lot is more hectic. Parents and friends picking up some of the guys on the team, waiting to celebrate yet another win. I see Josh walk onto the bus, leaving Teeny all to myself.

"Hey." I come to a stop in front of Teeny's car, dropping my duffel bag to the ground.

"Hi."

"Josh isn't riding with us?"

She shakes her head. "He said he'd rather take the bus back."

My smile spreads into the widest grin. "Let's go."

The drive back feels like I'm sitting in the passenger seat on a big fluffy cloud. Music blasting on the speakers, all the windows down, Teeny's now loose hair blowing in the wind, my hand grazing over hers as it rests on the center console between us. We've been talking in random tangents, the topics running in different variances, and skipping through different subjects as they pop in our minds like a barrel of bingo number balls. Teeny's voice grows tired and raspy as the late afternoon transitions into darkness, and it makes her sound all loose and sexy.

Before I know it, we pull up right onto the curb area dividing our homes.

"Thank you," I tell her, my voice lazy, matching hers, "for coming out today. It really means a lot to me."

"I had fun." Her eyelids fall a little heavy when she turns to face me. A contented smile is plastered on her face, and the glow from the dashboard reflects off her eyes, making them shine in a lax and placid way. I unbuckle my seat belt and lean closer to her, cupping her nape as I kiss her. I kiss her deeply, taking my time while pulling the last bits of her energy from her lips. It feels incredible, feeling her mouth on mine. I get small hints of sweet watermelon, most likely the pink gum she'd been chewing since we drove past Carlsbad. I feel her shift her gum in her mouth and my tongue sweeps against hers, searching for more of that taste I can't get enough of.

My hand starts to travel into her hair, gripping a small fistful at the root, and a soft whimper squeezes from her throat. Her hand hooks around my neck just as a fresh wave of energy bursts through her. I feel it in the way she shifts closer to me, unbuckling her own seat belt to close the space between us. She starts to climb over the center console and positions herself over me, her thighs straddling mine.

"Teeny," I whisper while my lids fall heavy, just as her nails grate through my scalp. "I love that you wore this." I give a playful tug at her shirt. "You look so damn cute with my number on you."

I feel her lips transition into a smile. "You better like it, Hayes. I spent a lot of puffy paint on this baby."

"Then you should wear it every day so you get your money's worth."

A bubbly giggle erupts from her, but I immediately drown it with another kiss. A flood of urgency is there as she presses herself into me. She takes a fistful of my shirt in her hands, bunching it at my neck like she's trying to claw it off me. My hands find the rough edges of her jeans, meeting the soft skin of her waist, and they trail up and up and up until I feel the clasp of her bra in the middle of her back. Her body stiffens, and she pulls away to look at me. Her eyes are wide, so much swimming in them, and I can't tell if she's scared or worried or exhilarated.

"Sorry," I whisper, pressing my forehead to hers. "I'm sorry."

She shakes her head, brushing off my apology. "Um," she says, taking large gulps of air like she's having trouble finding her words and catching her breath at the same time. "I, uh..."

"Hey," I urge, trying to regain her attention. She runs a distracted hand through her hair, and she fiddles with the collar of my shirt, keeping her gaze away from mine. "Teeny, it's fine. We can stop."

She finally looks at me and gives me an appeasing smile. I feel her fingers trail up my neck and trace over my jaw and then my cheek. "No, it's okay. I was just going to say..."

There's a long pause, and I worry things may be moving a lot faster than she's comfortable with. Especially after the last time things got this heated. "I'm listening," I tell her.

"I was thinking that...I want—I'm ready to...you know..." Her flustered words are cut off when she kisses me, distracting me, or quite possibly herself. "Do other stuff? Besides just kissing and things."

A worried and uneasy sigh has my chest expanding, followed by a deep scowl of disappointment. "Teeny, I'm not thinking about that. You don't—"

"Are you saying that you don't? That you changed your mind?"

"No, no." I pause to kiss her, gently pressing my lips to hers in a soothing manner, attempting to snuff those thoughts from her mind. "I mean, I am..."

"Then?"

My throat moves a rough swallow and my jaw tics, searching for the right words for her to understand how I feel. How the conflicting thoughts are causing a struggle, and I'm not sure which side I want to win. "I don't want you to say that just because you think that's what I want to hear. I want you to want those things too."

"I do."

My thumb runs across her cheek, stroking her soft skin. "Are you sure?"

She nods. "I mean, not right now, but you know, if the opportunity arises..." A shy smile casts over her features. "And I promise I won't be drunk this time around."

I laugh before I blow a little bubble with the gum in my mouth, and she gasps, moving her tongue against the inside of her cheek. "When did you get that?"

I watch her blush just as I answer, "When you were a little distracted."

And we fall into a heap of soft laughs and gentle reassurances as she leans herself into my chest.

CHAPTER SEVENTEEN

Teeny

NOW

THE HOTEL REFURBISHMENTS were slowly but surely moving along. Restoring the original trim to look new and modernized. Working with the contractor to make sure the installations for new carpeting, drapes, and countertops were completed on time. Getting my hands a little dirty with minor paint duty and some maintenance cleaning. Finalizing the last of the furniture orders with Roberta. I've been keeping myself busy, making sure to be present during the more important renovations. It's more than I usually do. Normally, I'd let the construction teams check in with the design-build contractor and I drop in on an as-needed basis, but this project feels different. I want to be there. To make sure things run smoothly. To make sure I'm available if anyone needs me.

There's also this niggling, poking thought in my head. Maybe I'll run into Everett. Maybe I'll see him in passing. Ever since our trip to LA, I've been more and more curious about his life. What he talks to his therapist about. If it has anything to do with us, what happened and what drew us apart. If he's okay. A small fraction of the persistent worry that's been consuming me thinks maybe he's not okay. Maybe even after all that time he's spent in therapy, he's still not who he used to be.

I'm overlooking the new curtain and drapery installation in the grand ballroom, making sure the layers are arranged correctly, when my phone buzzes in my hand.

"Hey, Mina," I say, answering the phone with a smile.

"Vegas, baby!" A loud hoot follows, and I pull the phone away from my ear. "Are you excited?"

"Yes, Mina. Baking in 112-degree heat at Encore, stewing in a pool at a day club with a hundred drunk people, and the DJ playing loud ass house music is my ideal weekend. And let's not forget those thirty-dollar drinks I could be mixing together at home for free." I release an exasperated sigh, regretting this weekend already.

"Come on, Teen! Be excited! It's my last night of debauchery as a single woman."

"So why is your future husband joining us?"

"To ward off all the weird men, duh. Anyway," she adds. "They're going to do some gambling while we do some shopping."

"Now that I'm excited for."

"What time's your flight tomorrow?"

"Noon," I tell her. "I just have to come back to the hotel and check in on a few things before I head to the airport. What about you guys?"

"We're driving."

My face twists into a disgusted grimace. "Ugh, on a Friday? Have fun sitting in six hours of traffic."

"That's why Josh is driving, and I'll have plenty of snacks." A loud boom interrupts us, and I turn to see one of the workers add to the pile of rubbish full of dusty fabric and rusty metal rods. "Where are you?"

"I'm at the...uh, the hotel. The one I'm—"

"Oh, you mean Everett's hotel?"

"Yep. That's the one."

"So, um," she says in a low whisper. "Josh told me about Everett. You and him."

"What did he say?"

"That you two were..." She sighs before adding, "In love." She says it like she's talking about a fairy tale. Some far-off happily ever after Everett and I got to live out where we parted ways amicably, and we remained fond of each other and the memory of us.

"It's so much more complicated than that. You have no idea."

"Well, he told me you two were disgustingly cute. And he thought you two would end up together until you met Leo, and—"

"Mina," I interrupt, begging her to stop. "Me and Everett—"

"Me and you, what?"

My heart shooting up into my throat has me gasping for air. I grip my hand against my stomach, hoping that too won't jump out of my body with the sudden appearance of Everett. It's almost like he has some Spidey sense, and they started tingling as soon as his name was spoken into the air. "Everett!" I shriek, turning around only to come face-to-face with his amused smile.

"Everett's there?" I hear through the phone.

"Uh, um. I'll talk to you later, Mina."

"Okay, call me," she instructs.

My eyes stay glued on Everett's. "Yeah, I'll text you when I get to Vegas too."

I hang up, letting my phone sit heavy in my hand after I feel like my limbs have lost all control. I haven't seen Everett in weeks. I also haven't been able to stop thinking about him, and it's like I conjured him from my thoughts in his pressed dress shirt and drifting cologne.

"So, you're going?"

"Huh?"

He nods at the phone. "Vegas. Decided you aren't too old for a weekend of club hopping?"

"Yeah," I say, taking a step back, creating more than the two inches of space sitting between us. "Grace and Mina guilt tripped me into going, so..."

He tucks his hands into his pockets, and that smile hiding a secret, shifts as he takes me in. I opted for comfort today, prepared to get my hands dirty if needed. That meant skinny jeans and a white-collared button-down tucked in at the waist. My hair is tied up in a loose ponytail, much like I used to have as a teenager, reminding me of what I must look like to Everett. Like the Teeny he met when we were just kids.

"And Eric told me he could handle things here while I'm out of town," I add, feeling the pressure from his gaze. "It's the weekend, so a lot of the work will be held off until Monday anyway. But I'm available if you guys need—"

"I'm going too."

"Right." *Of course, he's going.* "Anyway, I got an update from Roberta on the pieces you picked. I was going to go over them with Eric, but since you're here and you chose them, you want to take a look?"

He nods. "We can have a seat at the bar. Grab a drink?"

"Sure." I sound soft, affable. Friendly even. And I realize I can't remember the last time I felt that simmering anger, that resentment and bitterness I had when Everett came back into town. It's all been replaced with a keenness I can't seem to hide. But it's confusing me. I feel like I should be angry. Like I should still demand answers and keep this wall up around me, protecting myself like I've always done. But now, with Everett around, I have this urge to deconstruct parts of that wall to create the smallest of openings. Just wide enough for him to fit through.

Everett and I make our way to the bar area right around the time the workers in the ballroom break for lunch. He signals to the one server working the bar area, and I order a cup of coffee while Everett orders a club soda and lime.

"You don't want to eat?" Everett asks, gesturing a hand to the menu sitting offside on the table. "We have a pretty decent lunch menu."

I shake my head. "I actually need to head out in a little bit. Sadie has her showcase, and it'll be a bit of a drive to LA."

"Okay," he answers. "So, do you want to show me the pieces?"

"Oh, right." I power up my iPad, tapping away at the screen before nudging it in front of Everett. "The coffee tables are almost finished. And they'll be perfect for the main lobby area, especially with the furniture and upholstery you picked." I swipe across the screen, showing him the progression of the tables as Roberta adds the final touches. She's been sending me regular updates, asking about Everett in a non-professional inquiry.

"They look good," he comments, his eyes on the screen. He takes over, swiping along the images before swiping too far, and he lands on a picture of me, Leo, and Sadie. "Is this him?"

Him. He doesn't say "your husband," and it feels intentional. I nod. "Sadie was four, and it was her first visit to Disneyland."

Sadie's smile beams with the sun shining above us. She has a set of too large Minnie Mouse ears sitting lopsided on her head, and Leo and I sandwich her tiny little face stained with chocolate. "I forgot that was in there."

"That's a beautiful picture." He hands the iPad back to me.

"Thank you."

Our drinks arrive, and we sip in silence. My spoon scraping against the ceramic mug and the ice clicking in Everett's glass creates a buffer of noise, but after a moment too long of silence, it only magnifies the quiet.

"You're driving out to Vegas?"

"Flying," I tell him. I take a slow sip of my coffee. "I don't have the patience to sit through that drive."

He smiles. "I'm flying too."

"Oh."

"Maybe we can take a cab to the hotel together," he suggests. "You know, if our flights get in around the same time." He reaches into his pocket for his phone and taps away at the screen. My eyes widen when he slides it across the table to me. "Go ahead and put in your number."

I should decline his offer. It would actually be the polite thing to do since it would be such an inconvenience for him to track me down

192

at the airport. But I don't. Instead, I take his phone in my hands, carefully inputting my number before sliding it across the table back to him. He takes it in his hands, and my phone vibrates in my bag.

"That's me," he says, nodding his head in the direction of the buzzing noise. "Let me know when you get in."

I take another sip of my coffee instead of answering him. "I should actually get going," I tell him, setting my cup down.

"Of course." We both stand, our cups full and barely touched. My coffee has steam rising from it, and the condensation on Everett's glass is still frosty, no beads of water dripping down it quite yet, showing how fleeting this exchange was. "I'll walk you out."

I lead the way, Everett following a step behind me. I feel his hand graze over my lower back, something I think is instinct. But he quickly moves it away, as if he's realizing it shouldn't be there.

"I'll reach out to Eric if there are any updates," I tell him as soon as I reach my car. "And I'll talk to that gallery for the artwork. Set up an appointment."

"Call me," he tells me casually. He gestures a quick nod to my bag, reminding me that I now have his number. I have a way to reach him.

He stoops down to reach for my door handle and opens it for me. We're quiet as I step in, securing my bag in the passenger seat, and I look up at him with a grateful smile.

"Thank you."

He nods in response and closes the door behind me. And he doesn't walk away. Instead, he stands there, watching me as I pull out of the parking lot. I see him in my rearview mirror until he disappears when I turn out on the main road.

"Mommy!" Sadie squeals, her voice echoing off the walls inside the main building at the School of Creative and Performing Arts. Her body crashes into me, and I feel a conflicting wave of bliss and melancholy.

"Hi, baby." I pull away to take her in. It seems she's grown even bigger in the short weeks we've been apart. She's no longer my little girl. No longer that four-year-old toddler, still mixing up her words and throwing tantrums over more hugs and kisses from her mama and dada. "Are you nervous?"

"Nope," she says confidently. She links her arm through mine and guides me to the main auditorium where other parents are slowly making their way to their seats. "Is Dad here?"

"I don't know," I tell her, searching over the room. "Did he not call you?"

She shakes her head. "He said he was coming though."

"Well, he must be stuck in traffic."

Sadie suddenly waves wildly at a small group of kids her age, all gathered near the stage. "I have to go, Mom. The rest of the band is here."

"Break a leg, Sade." She gives me one last hug before sprinting to her friends.

The seats in the large space start to fill. I finally find one in the middle, two seats sitting side by side. I don't know why I do it. Maybe after fifteen years of being married to the same person, it's hard to break the habit of consideration. Always making sure my husband is taken care of whether it be a fresh pair of socks when the dirty laundry pile is getting too big or saving a seat.

The lights dim, signaling the start of the show, and still no Leo. The seat to my right still sits empty, and I get a few judgmental glares as people look over the available spot before heading to the back of the auditorium to the standing-only space. Frustration starts to bubble inside of me. What could possibly be keeping Leo from seeing his daughter's first showcase?

I catch Sadie walk onto the stage. She takes her spot on a small stool in front of a keyboard while the rest of the members of her newly formed band take their spots. One in front of a microphone stand with a guitar slung over their shoulder, and another behind a drum set. The entire room stills as Sadie, her mouth settled in front of a mic propped in front of the keyboard, makes introductions.

"Thank you all for being here," she says, her voice a little shaky and nervous, though she refuted any anxious nerves a mere ten minutes ago. "We are Ultraviolet here to perform 'Brilliant.'"

Music sounds immediately as Sadie presses her fingers on the keyboard. The three band members on stage start to sing at the same time, their voices harmonizing evenly in a fluid way that makes me wonder how they found each other. Those nerves in Sadie's voice disappear instantly, and I see her fall into her element. I forget about Leo being late, about how disappointed she'll be once she finds that her dad isn't here. About how many more moments like this will add onto the slabs of letdowns she'll have to suffer as she gets older.

She's a woman up there, using the power in her voice to express herself. She grew up right before my eyes, and I feel my nose start to sting with tears. She grew up despite my urges not to. For her to stay my baby forever. She grew up regardless of the rift drawing the two people she looks up to the most apart.

As soon as the band finishes, I clap. I cheer and holler, and I see Sadie blush from the attention inside the auditorium. They all bow, their hands linked together at the edge of the stage, before walking off. I reach into my purse for my phone to text Leo, to let him know he missed his daughter's performance, when I see a new message from him.

LEO

I got caught up at work. Tell Sadie I'm sorry.

I resist the urge to groan. My frustration turns into anger, and I'm reminded of the Leo I've always known. I should've expected this.

"Is this seat taken?"

I look up to see a woman, her hopeful eyes urging me to answer her as set changes are made on stage for the next performance. "No. Go ahead."

The flight into Harry Reid International was smooth. Thankful for the short flight and the aisle seat I was able to snag, I exit the airport with my carry-on in tow. As I order my rideshare, I hesitate. Should I call Everett? He *is* the one who suggested we share a ride when we get in. Maybe he's here, somewhere in this airport, hesitating just the same as he questions whether or not to check in with me before sliding into his own rideshare.

I choose the less conflict-inducing choice and order my ride. It would be really weird if Everett and I showed up at the hotel together. If my brothers were to see me stepping out of a car with my ex-boyfriend as if we'd planned the whole thing, they'd be sure to give me their two cents.

When I arrive at the hotel, I check in and go to my room. It's nice, a single king-size bed with plush bedding and small bottles of Fiji water at the mini bar. It's still early, and I know Mina and Josh won't be here for another few hours, muscling through the Friday afternoon traffic onto Las Vegas Boulevard. Grace is set to arrive soon too, though she has her own plans with a different hotel on the strip. Something about a comped room.

So to beat the heat and kill some time, I change into my bathing suit and head down to the pool. With my large sun hat, mesh cover-up, and a few magazines in my small tote bag, I find a spot near the bar with the perfect amount of shade and away from the gaggle of children cannonballing themselves into the water.

I flag a server walking by, requesting a white wine spritzer, before sliding my sunglasses on and laying back. I leave my magazines, the unanswered emails, and the book I've been lugging around with me in my bag. The heat is stifling, but under the shade and with the occasional gust of a mellow breeze, it's relaxing, and I eventually start to laze into the rough yet plush fabric of the lounge chair I've flattened.

"Enjoying yourself?"

I know it's Everett before I even see him. From the way his voice melts over me, making my insides warm and gooey. Or his sure stance, standing over me with confidence. His presence feels almost...pervasive. Hard to ignore and overpowering.

I face him with a proud smile, the smugness radiating off the way I don't bother covering up or moving about in a flustered state. Instead, I leave my arms draped over the back of the chair and cross my leg over the other. "Very much."

"Mind if I join you?"

"Go ahead." I gesture to the empty spot next to mine. As Everett lays down a towel and adjusts the back of the chair to his liking, I take him in. He's traded his neatly pressed dress pants and fancy shoes for swim trunks and a loose-fitting button-down. He's wearing sunglasses as well, Ray-Bans that make him look cool and even a little trendy. In the overbearing heat, his skin looks sun kissed. And the muscles that run along his calves and forearms look nearly indecent.

"You just got in?"

"Mh-hmm," Everett hums. "Thought I'd check out the pool to beat the heat." My drink arrives, and Everett orders one for himself. I lay back, sipping my wine while trying to ignore the way Everett's hair blows in the wind almost as if it's got a mind of its own. Or how the light stubble around his chin makes him look unruly and roguish rather than unkempt. "When did you get in?"

"Just now," I tell him. "I checked in and came straight down."

"Do you know when Josh'll be here?"

"They barely left like two hours ago. With the traffic, they probably won't be here until close to seven."

I reach for my sunscreen out of my bag and start applying it on my arms and legs. I move to my back, barely reaching the center, before giving up and applying more to my neck and chest area.

"Did you need some help?"

I look at Everett as he points an indistinct finger to the tube of lotion in my hands. I hesitate but then consider his offer. It's an innocent one, something my parents used to do before I raced into their pool, yet there's something underneath it. An undertow of caution I'm too aware of. "Sure," I finally answer.

He takes the tube in his hands at the same time I turn to face my back to him. I hear the cap pluck open and a blubbery staccato noise of the sunscreen being squeezed out, and before I know it, Everett's hands are on my skin.

My muscles jolt at the contact, but I adjust quickly, finding that his fingers move skillfully. I start to wonder if it's because of a past that involved numerous partners where he performed a similar act in hopes of some intimate favors. Or maybe it's that his hands have always known how to touch my skin. He never unlearned how.

I feel his hand tuck under the strap of my bikini top, moving along the dip in my spine, and those fingertips kneading the lotion across the spots I couldn't reach. And I realize, I don't remember the last time I was touched like this. So intimately and with so much care and tenderness. It makes me wonder how his hands would feel on other parts of my body.

I feel his breath sigh over my shoulder blade, and I instinctively lift it, as if to move closer to him, hoping he'd dip his face to press his chin or even his lips to my warm skin. A gentle pat to my hip signals the end of his task, and when I turn to face him, he's extending the sunscreen in my direction.

"Thank you," I whisper, taking it from him.

He nods and sits back in his chair.

I lay back down, brushing off the moment by stretching my toes to a point and exhaling an indulgent sigh, even letting a small hum slip through my lips. "This feels so good," I say quietly.

"You look relaxed."

I perch my sunglasses on my head and look at him with a cheeky smile. "As opposed to how irate and bitchy I've been for the past month?"

"No," he argues. "You don't look wound up. You look good. You should go on vacation more often."

"I agree," I respond. "Just maybe somewhere where walking the Las Vegas strip in six-inch heels isn't on the itinerary."

"It can't be that bad."

"Let's just say I'll need a few cocktails before Mina has me dancing on any bar top."

Everett chuckles, the throatiness of his laughter causing my insides to liquify even more. Maybe it's the soothing summer heat or this much needed vacation away from real life. Or maybe the ideology of what happens in Vegas, stays in Vegas, but I feel loose. Amenable to anything.

"Want to go in for a little dip?" I remove my large hat, exposing the matted mess of my hair underneath it. Everett looks at me, watching me stand from my chair while I tie my hair up in a haphazard knot.

"Sure." He sits up, unbuttoning the top two buttons of his shirt before pulling it over his head. His hair comes out a little disheveled, but he smooths it out and readjusts his sunglasses.

I don't understand how his body, unlike this face, hasn't changed. He still has those familiar muscles lining his stomach, and the sharp edge of his collarbone that used to dig into my cheek when I'd nuzzle into him too aggressively. There's a light smattering of hair on his chest now, slightly obscuring a tattoo on his left peck. With his deep wavy hair and his hipster swim trunks showcasing his massive thighs, he looks the part of an annoyingly, almost obscenely, attractive bachelor enjoying a weekend of debauchery in Vegas. In comparison, I look like a mom on a weekend girls' trip to escape the realities of motherhood. My too pale skin from the lack of sun exposure and the faint stretch marks I never saw coming lining my outer thighs really are the cherry on top, as are the high-waisted bottoms I chose to hide my loose mom pooch.

I walk ahead of Everett, feeling him close behind me. I hurry, hoping if I submerge myself in the water, I won't stand out in stark contrast to him. As soon as I'm waist deep, I turn to see Everett carefully taking the steps inside. I catch a few ladies admiring him, turning heads as they walk by, but he doesn't seem to notice.

I coast my hands through the water, causing it to ripple around me, and Everett inches closer. He sinks in all the way and when he reemerges, his face is inches from mine. I giggle, and he squirts water from his mouth, dousing my dry cheek.

I laugh, shoving a hand into his chest, and he laughs too. "You are such trouble."

He shoots a flirty little grin at me. "How so?"

I choose not to answer him, my eyes flitting to his chest instead. "When did you get this?" My fingers trail over his chest, outlining the dark lines engraved into his skin. It's waves, ripples of water that look chaotic, colored in different shades of blue. Turquoise, navy, sky blue, indigo, periwinkle. I didn't even know tattoos could be this vivid and kaleidoscopic.

He looks down at my hand, and he lays his over it, his fingertips brushing over my wedding ring as if reminding me that I'm not his to be touching. "After college."

"It looks nice."

He nods, tracing his thumb into my palm and trailing it down my wrist. Drops of water land around us, making light plunking noises that echo in my ears. I feel our legs and feet touch in the water where it doesn't feel as wrong as it should. It's probably the shrouded cloak of the sparkly surface creating an out of sight, out of mind effect. Or that there's so much going on between us, our feet playing an accidental game of footsies feels trivial.

I can't see his eyes through the veil of his sunglasses and droplets of water covering the lenses. My heart races and words feel like they're stuck in my throat.

"You're nervous?" he asks, his voice low and cautious.

I nod. "I don't know why..."

"It's just me, Teeny."

"I think...that's what I'm afraid of."

His hand slides behind my back, pushing me closer to him, and he rests his forehead against mine. My heart seizes inside my chest. But I don't push him away like I should, too scared to face the hurt and pain carved into the parts of my heart where I tried to forget my past. Instead, I hook my hand around his neck. This feeling starts to become all too familiar. Me in Everett's arms where I never wanted to leave but didn't have a choice but to.

"Why did you come back, Everett? After all this time? Why?"

"I missed you," he whispers.

I want to tell him I missed him too. That I still do. But I can't. Too confused and unsettled to have him looking at me, waiting for me to say something, I turn my cheek, letting it brush against his. I feel his mouth coast over my skin, leaving behind a torrid heat in its wake. He doesn't do more, but I feel his lips. Like fingertips reading braille, scanning and studying and absorbing.

We stay there, the water moving around us in waves from people coming and going. Families frolic in the water, lovers coast by in each other's arms, people laugh and squeal, but Everett and I don't move. We're fragile, the pieces of us barely held together with something weak and vulnerable. And if we move, if we break this trance, all those pieces may fall apart and become irreparable.

Okay, so maybe those heels I was telling Everett about were more like four and a quarter inches. Nonetheless, they're going to kill me by the end of the night. But boy do I look sexy in them. These shoes paired with my bandeau top and short skirt, I look like a very single woman who is ready to mingle.

Holy shit. I'm a single woman. Well, technically not until this divorce is finalized, but once it is, I will no longer be Leo's wife. I'll just be me. I don't even know who *me* is. Who am I if not Leo's wife? Sadie's mom? Am I more than that? Well, tonight, I'm just a member of the bridal party, here to show my full support as the bride and groom embark on yet another celebration.

I give my hair one last fluff, making sure my blowout looks runway ready, and grab my small silver clutch before leaving my room. When I make it downstairs to the lobby where Mina had instructed me to meet with the rest of our entourage, I find I'm the first one there.

I'm scanning the room, hoping to catch Grace when she arrives from her hotel a block over, when I feel a light tap on my shoulder.

"You look lost," I hear a deep voice say. When I turn, a set of glossy eyes with a sloppy moving mouth and clumsy hand gestures wait for me to say something in response.

"No. I'm fine," I tell the drunken stranger as he smirks through a hiccup. "I'm just waiting for someone."

He doesn't take my dismissal well, and he grabs my arm at the same time I recoil from his touch.

"Oh, come on," he says, his voice getting more slurred by the second. "Let me buy you a drink. Looks like you could use one. Might loosen you up."

"I'm—"

"Teeny." Everett reaches my side, his steps urgent yet calm and collected. His eyes dart to where this drunken stranger has his hands on me. His eyes narrow, and I see his jaw tic. "Is there a problem here?"

The man's eyes round, dropping my wrist. "Nah, man. Just making sure she's okay."

"Like I said, I'm fine," I snap at the man. He raises his palms in my direction and backs away with his tail between his legs. I turn to Everett, and he looks at me with his brow raised in amusement. "I could've handled that on my own."

"I know."

He peers down at me, starting at the crisscross straps of my shoes up to the too short hem of my skirt and finally stopping at the cleavage rounding my top, far below my neckline. "You look nice." His voice cracks, and he tries to hide it with an unsteady hand through his hair.

I fidget with my clutch and smile politely, a little uncomfortable from the attention. He's wearing a suit, of course, cut and tailored against the curves of his body. It's a light gray color, and he paired it with a black dress shirt with the top two buttons undone. And I just know if I were to peek just an inch down his shirt, I would get a glimpse of that tattoo on his chest. "You clean up pretty well yourself, Hayes."

I don't realize it slipping from my lips, calling him something that used to come so naturally to me. Everett doesn't respond with a pleased smile or chuckle. Instead, his eyes bore into mine, his gaze darkening with the furrow in his brow casting a shadow.

"Teeny!" Mina's body collides into mine, making me stumble a step back, and I laugh into the wavy curls of her hair. I catch Josh from over Mina's shoulder, walking toward us at a leisurely pace. "Girl, you look fucking hot!" she says, taking a step back and gripping my elbows in her hands. "Doesn't she look hot, Everett?"

"Mina!" I hiss.

"What? You do."

Too embarrassed to argue with her, I reach into my purse instead and pull out the magenta-colored BACHELORETTE sash I stuffed in there. "Here," I tell her, lifting the looped part over her head. She takes it graciously and smooths her hand over the wrinkles before adjusting it.

"What else you got in there?" I hear a low whisper graze the shell of my ear. I push down the dull shiver that starts at my shoulders and turn to face Everett.

"You know. Just the necessities," I tease. "A hat rack, my house plant...a Tide to Go Instant Stain Remover."

We share an intimate pause meant only for me and him, and it feels so dreamlike, I want to bottle it up. Drop it into a silk pouch so I can hold it in my hands when I grow lonely and scared.

He doesn't have time to sneak in a little quipped remark because Grace struts through the sliding glass doors like she's walking a runway. With her true to words six-inch heels and body squeezing bandage dress showing an almost indecent amount of cleavage, she outshines us all.

"Okay, now *she* definitely looks hot," Mina gasps. Grace has her hands behind her back, hiding the fluffy tulle veil she and I planned to go along with her shiny satin sash. She holds it out for Mina, to which the bride adds to her ensemble with a rumble of excitement through clickety hops on the marble floor and giddy giggles.

"Where's everyone else?" Grace asks, fixing Mina's hair and making sure she doesn't have a single strand out of place.

"The rest of the bridesmaids are meeting us at the club," Mina tells us.

"And Andrew too," Josh adds. With James unable to leave Kendall at home alone with the baby, it looks like it'll be just Everett and Andrew keeping Josh company tonight.

"You guys ready?" Grace asks, walking toward the busy casino area to take a shortcut to the club.

"Actually," Everett butts in. "I got a car for us."

All of us look at Everett, mixed looks of amusement, confusion, and curiosity. "What do you mean, 'a car?'" Josh asks.

Everett tilts his head in the direction of the sliding doors where hotel attendants are handling luggage and drunk patrons are stumbling across the concrete. Once we're all outside, following Everett's lead, all our mouths gape.

"This is your definition of 'a car?'" Josh grins and grabs Mina's hand before bolting for the shiny black limo parked out front with the driver nodding a hello at Everett. Everett nods in return before the driver opens the door and Mina scurries inside with Josh at her tail.

"Can you run by me why you two broke up again?" Grace whispers at my side. I nudge her gently with my elbow, avoiding her question with a little deviation. She ignores me and throws a wide grin over her shoulder before following the betrothed couple inside.

"This is very generous of you," I tell Everett, taking slow teasing steps to his side.

"Only the best for the bride and groom."

I chuckle, looking up at him with something that's playful and even a little dangerous. "Well, thank you," I tell him softly. "I appreciate you doing this for them."

"Hope you enjoy it too, Teeny."

"First time in a limo?" I smooth a hand over the lapel of his jacket and smile. "Of course I'm going to enjoy it."

The distance to the club is short, which makes me question why a car was needed in the first place, but I don't argue the indulgence of being drenched in LED lighting and expensive champagne. I sit next to Everett during the quick ride while we're able to each sneak in a small flute of bubbly. The limo shifts during a sharp turn, and when I lean into him, I feel his hand brush against my hip to steady me.

I ignore it, though it takes a significant amount of effort with the alcohol slowly coursing through me. I tilt back the rest of my glass and place it on the mini bar. As soon as the car pulls to a stop, Josh and Mina pour out, the two giggling with their hands all over each other, drunk not only on the champagne, but also on love.

Grace hooks her arm through mine after she adjusts her dress, the act looking racy and seductive as she runs her hands over her curves. "Ready to be my wingman tonight?"

"I believe the PC term is 'wing person.'"

"Whatever," she says, waving a hand in my direction. "Just help me get laid."

"Yes, ma'am." I laugh, throwing a sloppy salute at her followed by a complying flick of my wrist.

As soon as we bypass the thick velvet ropes and walk into the darkly lit foyer of the club, I can barely hear my own thoughts let alone what Grace yells over the noise.

"What?" I yell.

"I said two o'clock! By the large ficus!" She looks at where she's gesturing to, urging me to look too, and I see two men standing next to a tall decorative plant. They're dressed in suits, dark and somewhat statuesque, and they're looking right at us.

"How do you know that's a ficus? It could totally be a fiddle leaf!" She looks at me like I've grown horns out the side of my head, and I offer a sheepish smile. She ignores my question and turns to throw a little wave in the direction of the questionable tree and the two men.

"What are you doing?!" I hiss loudly, gripping her hand midwave.

"Getting a little attention!"

"Well, get a little attention alone! When I'm not around!"

"Come on, Teeny! What happened to my wing woman?"

"How about if I just present you at the DJ booth with a cowbell and my starting offer?"

She cackles at the same time a laugh bubbles inside of me. I guess this is what I needed. A night away from reality with my family and friends. And Everett.

"Ready?" I turn just as Everett hovers over me like I've summoned him with my thoughts. I feel his hand at my back, and Grace and I look at him, unsure what we're supposed to be ready for. "They're showing us to our table."

I hadn't even noticed him talking to the hostess, too caught up with some unwanted attention, but next thing I know, we're being escorted through a noticeably crowded room painted in strobe lights and bad decisions. People are dancing on top of high surfaces, men are approaching women, peacocking their way into their hearts, or their beds.

We stop once we arrive at a private booth, away from the dance floor where I can actually maintain a conversation without feeling like I'm talking over a wood chipper. We sit on plush seats wrapped around a small table filled with ice buckets with hard liquor and more champagne.

There's a small moment of peace where we decide where we're going to sit and what drinks we'll concoct out of what's available for us before we're interrupted by the gaggle of the remaining wedding party. Mina's bridesmaids enter the booth before stealing her away to the dance floor, to which she goes willingly.

"I'm going to go back to see if our new friends have made their way to the dance floor," Grace tells me, her hand cupped against my ear. "You want to join me?"

I eye Everett, him and Josh exchanging some words I can't hear over the noise. "You go ahead," I tell her. "Just be careful. And use protection!"

Grace slides out of the booth and scurries off without a second glance.

"Andrew's here," Josh announces, his eyes on his phone. "He's having some trouble getting past the bouncer. I'll be right back."

Josh leaves, and it's just me and Everett. Me and Everett and enough alcohol to lower not only my inhibitions but also my restraint with about twelve inches of space between us.

"You want a drink?" Everett says, his voice heightened and enunciated.

I nod, and he reaches into one of the buckets, lifting the top of a drink hidden under all the ice. He pulls out a single serving bottle, and I cackle a laugh.

"A Smirnoff Ice?"

Everett smiles, and something blooms inside me. It feels familiar and good. Like really, really good. "Only the best."

He twists off the top with his fingers and hands it to me before retrieving a bottle of his own. "For old times' sake."

I clink my bottle to his with a wide, cheesy grin. I take a sip at the same time Everett does, our eyes locked on each other, and when we pull our lips away from the narrow opening, our expressions are pensive, almost disapproving. "Did it always taste like that?"

Everett laughs. "Perhaps we need something more fitting to our matured taste buds."

He takes the bottle from me and sets it down on the table. "Did you want something else?" He gestures a hand toward the bottles in front of him.

I shake my head. "I think I'm going to go to the bar," I tell him. "Maybe see if Grace needs rescuing."

"You want me to come with?"

His offer feels tempting but a little risky, especially after our afternoon by the pool.

"I'm good." I stand before I change my mind on his offer and head to the main bar. It feels like it's gotten even more crowded within the fifteen minutes we've been here. I bump into a few carelessly moving elbows before I make it to the bar, no Grace in sight. I set out to order myself an espresso martini, hoping it'll wash out the tangy taste of the Smirnoff Ice, just as a set of arms wrap around my waist.

"Teeny!" a shrill voice screeches into my ear. "Come dance with me!"

"No, no," I protest, turning to see Mina and the entourage of bridesmaids at her side. Her tiara's lopsided, and she now has a beaded necklace around her neck. The kind that people throw around at Mardi Gras. Only this one has a flimsy plastic shot glass attached to it. "No dancing for me. I'm just going to order a drink."

"Come on!"

One of Mina's friends, who I haven't had the opportunity to meet yet, gently tugs at my hand. "Hi! I'm Cecelia! Maid of honor!"

"Oh, hi! It's nice to meet you!"

"Mina said we need to get all the girls on the dance floor," she tells me, playfully tugging at my hand again.

"And we never say no to the bride, right?" I answer, laughing at the way Mina has her arms in the air like those blow-up guys at car dealerships with wide smiles and lanky arms.

I reluctantly walk away from the bar and follow Cecelia's lead.

I'm standing there, awkwardly swaying, while everyone moves along to the music, some pop remix I can barely recognize over the thumping bass. Just as the crowd thickens to the point of sardine can crampedness, I'm pushed forward at the same time the heel of someone's foot decides my bare toes are a good place to ground.

I suck in a loud breath, though it isn't heard over the noise. No one sees what's happened, but I turn to Cecelia. "I'm going to use the bathroom," I tell her, holding back the grimace from the pain shooting up my foot.

"You want me to come with you?"

I shake my head. "I'll catch up with you guys in a bit," I say over the noise. "Keep an eye on the bride."

We both turn to see Mina with her arms wrapped around a woman we don't know. They're both swaying in an embrace like they're lovers, and Cecelia steps in to intervene.

I turn back to our booth, trying my hardest not to limp, when I see that there's blood lining the knuckles on my toes. When I finally make it to where Josh, Andrew, and Everett are sitting and sipping on glass tumblers filled with something amber colored, they all turn to see me hobbling to the edge of the cushioned seat.

"What happened?" Andrew asks.

"Someone stepped on me on the dance floor," I explain, reaching for a napkin to wipe away the blood now pooling around the open wounds. "I warned Mina about my rusty dancing skills."

I pull away the napkin to see that the gash is a lot bigger than I thought. What the hell? Was this person wearing cleats? My second and third toe start to look mottled with red and purple spots, the telltale signs of the swelling and bruising to come, and I just hope that's the extent of my injury instead of broken bones underneath the surface.

Warm hands wrap around my ankle, carefully undoing the straps of my shoe with calm and ease. Next thing I know, I see Everett kneeling in front of me with a large cloth napkin wrapped around a bundle of ice pressed to my toes. I flinch from the painful pressure, and Everett peers up at me with worried eyes.

"Are you okay?" he asks, though I can barely hear him. I can read his lips, talking to me with concern. Yet his hands move calmly, a complete contrast to the stress covering his face.

"Um, yeah," I tell him, my foot still in his hands. "I'm fine. But I think I should call it a night. I can just take a cab back to the hotel."

"We can take the limo back," he tells me.

"We?"

He turns to my brothers, the three exchanging a quick set of words, before they nod at Everett. "I'm going to get you back to the hotel," Everett tells me. "And I'll send the car back for them when they're done."

"Oh, no. Everett. It's really fine. I can go on my own." I take my shoe laying on the floor and start to carefully guide my foot through the tight straps. When the hard buckle grazes my cut, I wince.

Everett ignores my protest and wraps his arm under mine, easily hoisting me up and supporting my weight. "Just let me take you."

One look at Everett, and I know it's a pointless objection. He's dead set on getting me back to my room himself. I give up and wave at Josh and Andrew as we walk by. "Tell Mina that I'm really sorry," I tell Josh. "And I'll make it up to her tomorrow."

"Don't worry about it," Josh says.

"And make sure you ice that," Andrew instructs. I throw them both a thumbs up and shuffle off in Everett's arms.

Once we're outside, it's about twenty feet from the door to the car waiting on the sidewalk, but it feels like a hundred. I take the first step slowly, using Everett for support. After the first five steps, I feel my feet sweep out from under me.

"What are you doing?" I gasp, my eyes round in shock as Everett scoops me up against his chest.

"It's easier this way."

"Oh my god, Everett," I cry, covering my face with my hand. "Please put me down."

"We're right here, Teen."

"This is so embarrassing."

"Stop complaining," he playfully argues. "Plus, it'll keep the drunk creeps away."

"Oh, so that's the plan," I comment. "This has nothing to do with the damsel in distress situation I'm in."

I feel Everett's chuckle rumbling through his chest, and I laugh too. His cheeky smile, my awkwardness, our easy playful banter. It all makes me feel like a kid again, my heart so full of hope and optimism. So blind to the future that lies ahead of me.

The driver standing with his hand clasped in front of him opens the door for us as soon as we reach it. I hop in, being careful not to bump my already feeble foot against yet another hard surface, and Everett follows.

The car pulls out of the narrow driveway in front of the club, and we leave behind the loud noise and flashy lights and expensive alcohol. Well, I guess not the expensive alcohol since we seem to have quite a selection inside the limo. Everett reaches for the open bottle resting in the bucket of ice dripping with condensation.

He takes a long pull and shrugs. "Can't let it go to waste."

I extend my hand, requesting a share. "I guess not."

"So, I guess I was wrong."

I take a long sip. "About what?"

"About walking around the Las Vegas strip in high heels not being such a bad time."

The alcohol starts to course through me, and I hand the bottle, now more than half empty, back to Everett. He takes it by the narrow neck and tilts back another long pull.

"I warned you."

He nods. "You did."

Before we know it, the bottle's empty and we've pulled into the entrance of our hotel. I urge Everett to refrain from carrying me, and instead ask that he help support my weight to the elevator. Once inside, I remove the heel from my uninjured foot, looping the straps to both shoes to dangle from my fingers.

"I'm sorry you had to leave early," I say quietly inside the low hum of the ascending elevator.

"It's fine." His words are spoken so gently, the last thing I feel like is a burden. Almost as if he would've chosen this had it been up to him. But then again, I guess it was his choice. He could've let my brothers handle things. Let them help me into a cab and send me back to my hotel, but he's the one who offered his help. Like he'd been waiting for the opportunity to be my knight in shining armor, and he simply swooped in at the first chance to come to my rescue.

We remain quiet, the tension filling the small space to the point that it feels suffocating. We arrive on my floor, and I expect Everett to watch me get off and be on his way, but he doesn't. He gets off with me. We reach my room at a slow pace with my limping and Everett matching my steps. The dimly lit hallways make the moment more intimate than it should be just as I reach my room, I pull out my key card.

"Thank you. For walking me back." My back is to my door, and I peer up at Everett. Without the added advantage of my heels, he's even more overpowering. His broad shoulders cage me backward like a scared animal, and his eyes look at me in an almost predatory way, flitting up and down my dress with a shadow of darkness and hunger. He hovers over me, inching closer and closer, and he finally stops when he has his hand resting on the door above my head.

His eyes dart to my lips and back to my eyes. "You're welcome."

My chest rises and falls, pushing against the tight pressure of my top. I feel my heart racing, and I don't know what to do. I know I should say good night. I should turn around and swipe my key card against the reader and close the door firmly behind me, but my feet feel like they've been set in cement.

Everett doesn't move away either, and I feel like the space around me is getting smaller and smaller by the second. I press a hand against his stomach, trying to create some distance between us, but it causes him to lean into my touch.

"Ev—" My words are cut off when Everett's lips crash into mine. My hands immediately grip his waist, tugging him closer to me until our hips are aligned with each other. His hands move over me just as urgently. They start at my back, pushing me against him, and thread up my neck and into my hair. A loud, helpless whimper sounds from the base of my throat, and I feel my back slam into the hard door.

I didn't know time machines could be real. I thought they were something that only existed in science fiction movies. Usually starring Christopher Lloyd riding through time in a DeLorean or Mr. Peabody giving Sherman history lessons in the WABAC. But right here, kissing Everett, I know I've stepped into the most undeniably real time machine to ever exist.

His lips move like they know me. Like they've only known me. And his hands roam over parts of me that only he knows exists. Like the curve of my hip or small hollow between my shoulder blades. He lets out a near vulgar grunt that sounds more like a low growl, and I feel him stoop down to my level, deepening our kiss. I respond with a tilt of my head and a swipe of my tongue against his lips. He takes it as an invitation, reading into the moment exactly how I wanted him to, and he tangles his own tongue alongside mine.

My room key is still in my hand, grasped against my palm, and I clumsily tap it against the reader. When the telltale chime of the door unlocking sounds, Everett hoists me up, and I wrap my legs around his waist.

He finds the bed quickly, his footing catching on the carpeted floor, before we both land on the soft comforter with a light thud. We don't stop kissing, and a part of me feels like if we did, it would be over. We'd hop off the time machine after a whirlwind trip back to our past, no matter how badly we'd want to stay inside this imaginary capsule.

My fingers start to move frantically down his shirt, undoing each button with shaky hands. He follows my lead, removing it over his head before I'm done with the last few. He presses his forehead against mine, and just like I predicted, this pause gives room for a realization. An interruption we can't ignore.

"Sorry," he says through heavy gulps of air. "I'm sorry, Teeny. I couldn't help it. I—I had to kiss you. I couldn't hold back anymore."

My fingers trace over his chin, his mouth, his cheek. And he watches me, taking in the way I let my hands relearn the terrain of his face. It's all muscle memory. Like knowing where the dip is that connects his ear to his jaw. Or the tiny freckle that's at the corner of his left nostril.

I don't know what to say, so I decide to stick with the truth. "I missed you too."

He doesn't kiss me again like I expect him to. Instead, he smooths my hair away from my face and cradles my head, cupping his palm to my crown like I'm made of glass. Like he's been handed this fragile delicate thing, and he'd risk everything to keep it in one piece.

He moves so he's lying at my side, and I turn to face him, leaning on his bicep with his free hand still roaming over me. Over my hair, along the column of my neck, down my arm. I start tracing along the lines of his tattoo, following the patterns and colors.

"Is this okay?" he whispers into my hair.

I nod. "Yeah, it's okay."

CHAPTER EIGHTEEN
Everett
THEN

IT'S crowded and stuffy inside the large mansion sitting atop a hillside, overlooking glinting lights and distant fireworks popping off at random. People wearing pressed suits and sparkly dresses standing around a room cased in marble flooring and a chandelier that probably costs more than my car reminds me that I'm far from the place I now call home. The dress shirt my parents forced me into, along with the tie strangling my neck, is causing the night to become weary and tiresome.

The occasional smile from those passing by, an acknowledging tilt of their head or a "How are you, Everett?" is adding to the lingering fatigue. As are the sporadic formal introductions letting me know who they are and their connection to my dad. I've been at it for almost two hours, and I feel stiflingly overwhelmed. Like I'm suffocating. And the only person I want to spend tonight with is five hundred miles away.

"Everett!" I hear my name just as I reach the main foyer. I turn to see my dad calling for my attention with a proud and determined smile, a man in a lopsided plastic party hat and a grin matching my dad's at his side. "Meet Francis. He heads the facilities department over at ARCO."

I politely nod and shake Francis's hand. "I hear you'll be at UC Davis next year," he says, giving my shoulder a stern pat. "Your dad is really proud of you."

"Yes, sir," I answer. "Got my admission letter last week. I'm very excited." It feels rehearsed, almost monotone and fake, yet I've said it enough times tonight that I'm not sure how much of it's true, even as it's spoken from my own mouth.

"Good. You should come by the arena next week. Hang out for a game. We can get you some courtside seats."

"Everett is actually heading home in a few days with Alice, but he'll be back next month. We got a tour scheduled at UC Davis, and he promised he'll catch a game while he's here."

I glimpse at the large clock displayed over the mantle and see it's almost midnight. New Year's. We're interrupted just then when a wait staff walks by with a tray full of champagne flutes filled with gold bubbly.

"I guess we're gathering in the main room?" Francis states, grabbing a glass.

My dad reaches for two and hands me one. "Since it's a special occasion."

I give a low chuckle and watch them walk away. Instead of following their lead, I sneak off to an empty room where I can get a moment to myself. A moment to think without all the noise and attention. Without the buzzing in my head, like a low whirring noise, that doesn't seem to go away. But even with the spirited chitter chatter stifled behind a closed door, my body feels on edge. And that feeling, the one where I feel like my feet are never fully grounded and I'm ready to jump into action, magnifies.

The room I'm in looks like an office. There's a large wooden desk at the far wall and opposite to it is a floor-to-ceiling bookcase filled to the brim with leather-bound books. I reach into my pocket and dial Teeny's number.

"Hello?" I hear her voice on the second ring.

"I was hoping you'd answer."

She laughs. "I've been waiting by the phone."

I set my glass down on a small side table situated next to a leather couch before I plop onto the cushy seat. "I finally snuck away," I tell her. "I'm hoping the ball drop will keep my parents from looking for me."

"Well, I got my Martinelli's in a mug and the party hats my mom got us."

"Your parents aren't out tonight?"

"Nope," she answers. "New Year's is strictly a family event. Plus we're going to my grandparents' house early in the morning."

"How early?"

"Seven-ish?"

I grimace. "Is this a usual thing?"

"For us? Yeah. New Year's is a big thing for my grandparents. We go to their house, pay our respects, eat a lot of food."

"Huh," I respond. "Well, I'll be sleeping in until noon. Or later, depending on how smashed my parents get."

"Lucky."

"I miss you," I finally say after I feel like I've been holding it in for so long.

"I miss you, too," she responds, her voice hushed. "When does your flight get in?"

"Around eleven."

"In the morning?"

"Yeah."

She breathes a sigh of relief. "I thought you were going to miss my show."

"I'll cross oceans to be there."

"Actually you'll cross a few deserts and Fresno," she says in that teasingly sarcastic tone I love so much. "And Bakersfield, I believe."

"Since when did you become a geography whiz?"

"Since I paid attention in fourth grade."

The noise outside feels distant now. As if this room isn't simply a room in this large mansion I feel completely out of place in, but as if

217

it's a sanctuary. Something Teeny created through a phone line despite the distance between us. My feet don't bounce anymore on the fancy rug underneath me. They're grounded, sitting in place as if something's telling me it's okay to stay rooted right now. While I'm on the phone with Teeny, in this hideaway that's secluded me away from the noise, it's okay that I be who I am when I'm with Teeny. I wish I could know if she feels the same way. I wish I could know if her heart is beating calmly. If it's steady and measured because she's talking to me, if I have the same effect on her as she does on me. And suddenly, I can't wait to get back to her.

"Oh, ten seconds," she says excitedly.

We both start counting down.

"Nine, eight, seven, six..."

I miss you.

"Five, four."

I can't remember what my life was like before you.

"Three."

I'm falling for you.

"Two."

I don't know what I would do without you.

"One."

I love you.

As predicted, I woke up past noon on New Year's Day. After spending the rest of the party on the phone with Teeny, I drove my parents home in their inebriated state. "Home" feels a bit generous. With the thirteen-foot-tall ceilings and formal dining room, it feels like a museum rather than a place I'm supposed to call home. Even my room, mostly empty with all of my belongings back at Del Mar Heights, feels cold and vacant.

I trudge out of bed and down the winding staircase to the large kitchen with an industrial-sized refrigerator to find a note on the island.

> *Went out to brunch with Mom. Call my cell if you need anything. -DAD*

Without the pressure to wake up and be presentable, I reach into the fridge for a bottle of orange juice, drinking it straight from the spout. I slump onto the sectional couch in the TV room where we have a projector set up in place of a TV. It takes some troubleshooting before I learn all the bells and whistles, and I finally figure out how to play a DVD. I consider calling Teeny but then remember her plans with her family.

So, I'm left alone in this house that will always feel new to me, like a tumbleweed rolling through a lush forest. After about two hours of mindless TV watching, I mosey back to my room, feeling a little restless. I'm about to call Teeny, hoping she's finally back home, when I hear the front door open.

"I can't believe you, Eddie!" I hear my mom hiss at my dad followed by the door closing and my dad's urgent steps at my mom's heels.

"Alice, I told you. Nothing's going on."

"You are so full of shit. I saw how she was looking at you last night," my mom openly argues. "And today at the club. What the hell was that?"

"You're being ridiculous."

Something, probably a cabinet door, slams shut with a bang. "*I'm being ridiculous?* Are you kidding me? You didn't see the way she kept touching you and laughing at your jokes like you're her own personal comic. Do you know how inappropriate that looks? You're married, Eddie. And so is she."

"Well, maybe it's nice to get a little attention every now and then."

"Oh, you want attention? That's the problem?"

"Alice, keep it down. Everett is going to hear you."

I've been sitting at the top of the stairs, my knees drawn up to my chest with my back against the wall, reverting back to when I was a kid, and this was how I coped with my parents' arguing. Sitting offside, trying to blend into the wall like a spider in its web while getting a front-row seat to their marital problems.

"Well, maybe he needs to hear how his dad is a cheat—"

"Alice." My dad's tone turns dark and threatening. "Stop."

"You can't keep shutting me down every time I bring it up! You can't treat it like it wasn't a big deal!"

The high-pitched blast feels like an explosion. Glass shatters, skittering across the hard floor.

And the room falls silent.

It's like a snowstorm. When it snows, it's silent. It isn't like rain where the fat drops of water hitting the ground sound menacing or even deafening, especially during long bouts of thunder and lightning. It's quiet even though you expect noise.

"I'm done." I hear my mom's shaky voice. "I'm leaving. You can stay here in his big house all on your own and do whatever the hell you want, Eddie. I'm done."

"Alice, I'm sorry."

"No. Just stay away from me."

"Fine! Leave!" my dad responds with a gruff growl. "Go back to that house that's burning a hole into our lives!"

"You think it's burning a hole in our lives?"

"I told you to sell it," my dad continues. "I told you to get rid of it and stay here."

"I've been here for almost twenty years doing whatever you wanted. Following you around like some goddamn Stepford wife. I wanted to go back home, Eddie. I wanted to see my parents before they died, but I couldn't because we always had to do what you wanted. You couldn't give me that."

"Then do what you want, Alice. Go back to your home."

The silence rings inside the house again, and it isn't just snow this time. It's a blizzard. My parents' angry words flurry around me like a howling wind.

So many times, I saw the end coming. The fight that became their breaking point. I always think it's going to be the last one, but then they work through it. They talk it out. But in those moments when I think it's over, I have this wave of relief wash over me. Like getting off a really scary rollercoaster. While on it, I feel the high of the ride. Christmas mornings, family vacations, movie nights watching *Homeward Bound* or *Casper*. But in between those moments, the adrenaline feels too much. The fighting, the yelling, the name calling. Those drops and loops are unbearable. Then I get back on. Because my parents work through it, and the thrill of the ride starts to become appealing. I forget about all the scary parts.

The rest of our visit is filled with tense, frigid silence. I see it in the way my parents brisk past each other with a cold shoulder and how I instinctively tiptoe around the house. I spend the rest of the night in my room, picking up dirty clothes and the loose CDs scattered about in silence. The drive to the airport the next morning is just as quiet. My dad drives us, much to my surprise. He doesn't say anything, and when we pull to the curb, he doesn't get out of the car. He pops open the trunk from his seat and watches me lug the heavy luggage out before driving off.

My mom doesn't react. She doesn't huff out in anger. She doesn't cry. Instead, she reaches for her suitcase and turns toward the airport.

When we get back home, my body moves about like it's on autopilot. I watch my mom sit at the kitchen table, looking over a stack of mail with a blank look on her face. It seems both of our bodies have grown numb from the shock of how the new year is already starting to play out.

It starts to become almost unbearable, and I feel like I need to leave. I know I have some time before Teeny's show, and I should at least call her to let her know I've made it home, but I don't. Instead, I grab my keys and drive. I drive along the breezy coast, feeling like my feet need to keep moving. If I stay settled for too long, it'll all catch up to me. The inevitable uprooting, the constant impermanence of my life. Anything can change in a heartbeat.

I finally stop when I pull into a parking lot on the beachfront. The one Teeny and I came to with the lifeguard tower, not realizing where the impromptu getaway would lead us. I sink into the sand, focusing on the soothing coolness, on the hazy sky painted a mural of oranges and purples and blues.

I thought when we moved to San Diego, this feeling would be more fleeting. That maybe it was more isolated to my life up north. But you can't run from your problems. They'll just follow you. And what if after all this, I end up back to my old life. Under the appeal of a new school, I forgot that I wouldn't be here forever. I forgot that I'd have to say goodbye to the place that finally felt like home. I'd leave for college, and I'd miss the beach and my grandparents' home.

And Teeny. What would I do without her? How am I supposed to go off to college for four years without her? And when I graduate, what of us then? I have no idea how to plan for a future when everything feels so unsure.

I see a couple sitting at the edge of the lifeguard tower, much like Teeny and I did. One is wearing a red lifeguard uniform while the other, a girl, dangles her feet with a large beach towel wrapped around her shoulders. They laugh at something, toss some chip crumbs at a lone seagull, and my heart twists thinking about how much I miss Teeny.

I start counting down the minutes until I see her. Until I'll be able to hold her and kiss her. It won't be long—

Shit! Teeny's show!

I dig into my pockets for my phone only to realize I'd left it at home. I rush to my car, shoving the key into the ignition to see the dash light up with the time. Four o'clock. *Fuck!* I was supposed to be at the gallery at two. I rush down streets, risking those yellow lights while hoping I don't get pulled over.

When I finally pull into the parking lot of the small gallery, I spot

Teeny's dad's car in the parking lot and exhale a sigh of relief. She's still here. It takes a few moments, a few deep breaths before I collect myself enough to walk in without looking like a ball of anxiety. I spot Teeny right away, talking to some people, her parents standing offside sipping on some bottled water. She looks engaged in whatever conversation she's having with a polite smile. As soon as she sees me, her smile drops.

I make it to her and wait. Wait for her to acknowledge me, to talk to me. To, hopefully, forgive me.

"Everett," she says coolly as she finishes her conversation.

"Teeny," I urge. "I'm so sorry. I lost track—"

"We'll talk later," she says in that same distant tone I don't like. "I have to...mingle." She says that last word with a smirk and a hint of annoyance, even throwing a small eye roll in my direction. She doesn't seem like she's as mad as I thought she'd be. More like... disappointed. And it almost feels worse.

"But I'm sorry," I say, ducking my head so only she can hear.

"I know."

I don't push. Instead, I stay. Somewhere she can see me, call me if she needs to, but with enough space to let her know that I'm giving her what she asked for. I see her talking to her parents, another older couple who I don't know but seem important to her based on the way they fawn over her and gush in hushed tones. It isn't long until the crowd dwindles down and the gallery seems to be emptying that Teeny gives me her full attention.

"My parents drove me," she says, after she's said her goodbyes to them. "Do you think I could get a ride home with you?"

"Sure."

I lead her outside to my car, and she keeps a noticeable amount of distance between us. I help her in, round the hood to get into the driver's seat, and we sit in silence. The drone of cars passing by and others walking to their cars stay on the outside while we sit in this disconcerting silence.

"Teeny—"

"You said you'd be here."

"I know."

"This was really important to me."

"I know." She turns, facing the front of the car, avoiding my eyes. "I really am sorry."

She doesn't answer me but silently nods. "How was your trip?"

I spare her the gritty details. "It was fine."

"And your dad? How's he doing?"

"Uh, yeah. He's good."

She finally looks at me and smiles. "I'm not mad at you." I smile weakly, and she laughs. "Okay, maybe a little. But you could've called if you were going to be late."

"I know. I left my phone at home. And I didn't realize what time it was."

"You weren't at home?"

I shake my head. "I went for a drive." I morosely tell her my vague explanation of my whereabouts, and something twinges in my chest. It tugs and coils, and I want to tell her about it. How when I feel this ache inside me, I don't know how to put it into words. But if I could, it would be for her. I only ever want to be able to explain it to her. How I'm constantly drifting and floating when all I want to do is sit and be calm.

"Is everything okay?"

"Yeah," I tell her. I reach for her hand, placing a soft kiss into her palm. "You want to just go home?"

"Yes and no," she tells me, a shy smile teasing her lips. "Can we maybe go to your house? Is your mom home?"

"Yeah, but it's okay."

"Okay."

I start the car and drive in silence. Teeny plays with my radio, keeping the volume at a low hum, and I hold her hand in mine. I steal glances in her direction, finding no resentment or anger, but my girlfriend. The same girlfriend I love and who would stand by me, never dismissing me out of spite.

I pull into my driveway to see all the lights are off. Next door, Teeny's driveway sits empty.

"My parents drove my grandparents back home," she tells me.

"Is that who that was? At your show?"

She nods. "My grandma grew up in Korea. She loved to draw and paint, but it was a struggle for her. Especially after the war. She couldn't afford oil paints or anything fancy, so she'd use twigs she'd find outside. She would burn the tips and use the charcoal ends to draw." She pauses, smiling fondly. "So, she's always been really supportive of my artwork. When I was five, she was the one who convinced my mom to send me to art school after she let me play with a bunch of her watercolors. Said I had a natural talent for it.

"I was so excited for you to meet her today. When you didn't show up, I told her that you were still up in Sacramento with your dad. That he needed you and you couldn't make it. And she said, 'Good boy. He put family first.' So, I didn't want to introduce you when you showed up late. I didn't want to tell her that you just... didn't show up on time."

We've been sitting in my car, the engine turned off and the radio all the way down, and my heart sinks to my stomach when Teeny tells me this. This was so much more than just me being late for her show. She expected me to be there.

"I really am sorry, Teen."

"I know." She cups my jaw, and her soft eyes make the guilt in my gut brew to a thickness that's hard to digest. "And I'm not telling you this to make you feel bad. I just want you to know how important this was to me."

"I knew. I promise I knew. I was just dealing with...some things."

"I know, Everett. I know you think I don't notice, but I do. And whatever you're dealing with, I wish you'd tell me."

"I'm trying. I'm figuring out how to put it into words so you'd understand."

She pats my thigh, gesturing for me to make room, and I pull the lever to the seat, making a loud cranking noise as it moves all the

225

way back. She climbs onto my lap and grips my face in her hands. "Try."

I exhale a deep breath as my palms rest on the outside of her thighs. I feel her eyes searching mine while my fingers trail nervous circles over the skirt of her dress inching dangerously higher as she situates herself on top of me. "I guess...I feel like I don't know what's going to happen. With this house, my parents. Even with college. Like, I know I'll be back up north in the fall, but you know...what about us? And all of this makes me feel like I have to be on my toes. Like I need to be prepared, and I don't even know for what."

She stays silent, and my hand moves to her lower back, pressing her closer to me as I try to figure out my words.

"And sometimes I don't even feel like I'm inside my body. It's like I'm hovering over it and watching everything happen, and my body's frozen in time, and I can't do anything. I watch my parents fight, and I just sit there, not doing a single thing. I feel like such a coward when that happens. I know I should do something, but I can't."

My body starts to shake, and my skin feels like it's crawling with a thousand tiny bugs under the surface. She takes my hand, wrapping it around her wrist where I feel her pulse. It's steady, unlike mine. I match my breathing to the easy moving thumps, and my body sags in her arms.

"You don't need to worry about us," she tells me, the softness in her voice making her words ring so true, I can't even try to argue it. "I'm going to miss you, but we'll figure it out."

A calmness washes over me, and it feels like a placid lake. The small ripples that disrupt the surface don't feel chaotic as they pop and plunk inside me. Instead, they magnify how all the scary things in my life aren't actually scary at all. As long as I have Teeny by my side. We really are going to figure it out. And, at the end of it all, we're going to be just fine.

"Yeah," I respond. "I know." After a long pause, one that makes me feel like it's there to let us absorb this understanding between us, I whisper, "You."

"Me?"

"You ground me."

Her lips press into a soft line, and her eyes round, waiting for me to explain.

"When I feel like I'm hovering and I'm frozen, you bring me back to earth. And sometimes, just the sound of your voice makes me feel like everything's going to be okay."

She smiles, and it glitters. Like a thousand diamonds glinting in the sunlight, making everything luminous. It's the only way to describe her smile. The way her eyes warm and twinkle, or how I can see every emotion through the small wrinkles that bridge her nose and the corners of her eyes. She's so beautiful, and a dull throb starts to pulse in my chest. It looms over me like a dark cloud before I push it away, focusing on how her chest rises and falls with the soft sighs that filter through her pretty lips.

"I love you. And I know we're, like, super young, and people are going to say we're just kids and shit, but I really do. I've literally never felt this way about anyone—"

"I love you too," she interrupts me. "And who cares about what people say."

That twinge behind the barricade of my ribcage fades into bursts of fireworks. They go off in my chest, and I feel like I'm going to grow rocket thrusters on my heels and shoot up into the sky. I love her. With my entire heart, I love this girl. And she loves me.

"You love me?"

"Yes."

"You love me?" I ask again. My brows bounce in a menacing manner, and it shifts everything around us. This is us, in our purest form. Our hearts have been stripped bare for each other, and it doesn't feel scary or unsure. It feels right.

She shoves a hand into my chest with an adorable chuckle, playing into my taunt. "You're so silly," she teases, and I see a redness creep up her neck even in the dark.

I laugh too, leaning forward to kiss her. "But you do."

"I do what?" she asks, her voice breathy and soft as our kiss deepens.

"You love me."

She nods into my lips. "I do."

She starts rocking, back and forth, creating this ache inside me I've been trying to douse with the urge to never push her. My fingers find the bottom hem of her dress, finding that it'd ridden so far up her thigh, I've officially reached underwear territory. My thumb strokes her soft skin, matching the rhythm of her shifting on my lap. Back and forth, back and forth.

"Teeny, I think we should stop," I tell her with a strain in my voice that makes me sound wounded and anguished.

But she doesn't show any signs of stopping. In fact, she starts to move more frantically. Tugging the hair at my scalp, letting her teeth scrape against my lower lip, moaning a hopeless and urgent sigh into my mouth.

"Can we go inside?" she asks, her chest heaving against mine.

"Inside my house?"

She gives a small, indifferent shrug. "I was thinking your room."

"Really?"

She nods. "Please?"

"Yeah," I whisper. "Let's go."

We attempt to calmly collect ourselves and get out of the car, moving quietly, like we might get caught, though we aren't doing anything necessarily suspicious. When I open the door to the house, it's eerily quiet. The only sounds are coming from the small den with the glowing lights reflecting off the TV.

"Everett! Is that you?"

"Yeah, Mom."

"I left some pizza in the kitchen if you want some."

"Okay. I'm just going to head up to my room. I'm kind of tired."

"All right."

Teeny grins at me, following my quiet steps up the stairs to my room. Once inside, I lock the door. "You think she'll be mad if she knows I'm here?"

"Nah, don't worry about it," I tell her, though I'd probably get a small lecture on bringing Teeny over this late and how her parents would react if they assumed my mom allowed it.

She looks over my room, catching a small box that was once neatly wrapped in paper meant specifically for a birthday with the colorful balloons and party hats printed on it. The torn paper now sits messily on my desk, and she peers into the box, poking her finger inside the nest of tissue paper with inquisitive eyes. "Was there...a special occasion?"

I walk over to her, picking up the box and taking out the iPod still wrapped in its packaging and plastic film. "My dad gave it to me while I was visiting," I explain to her. "Early birthday gift."

Her eyes round, and a smile cuts across her face. "It's your birthday?"

"Not for a few months. In March," I tell her shyly. "My dad...I think he just feels guilty about this year. Us being down here and all of that shit. Probably why he got me the new car."

She nods. "Well, happy early birthday."

"Thank you," I answer with a smirk.

We stand there, our bodies tentative and shy, very much unlike how we were just minutes ago in my car. Until she makes the first move. She reaches for my hand and leads me to my bed, guiding me as if this isn't my room. We lay down, side by side, and she kisses me. With the way she touches me without a beat of hesitation, it feels like she's moving in a single sweeping fluid motion. No pauses. No moments that make me wonder if she feels the same flicker of nerves crawling under my skin. All I feel is how deep her love runs, and I can't ever imagine a time when I'll question how much she loves me. Or how much I love her. All of this...it feels like a sure thing.

Teeny pulls away, her breathing desperate and loud. "Do you have..."

"What?"

"Um...you know," she continues, her chest pressing against me. "Protection?"

"Oh." I huff a nervous laugh. "Um, yeah. Actually, I do."

Her timid laugh matches mine. "Yeah?"

I nod. "My mom...she got me some."

"What?"

"That's totally weird, isn't it?"

"A little," she responds through a laugh.

I tuck my chin toward my chest so that my forehead leans against the crook in her neck, snuffing my embarrassed chuckle. "I swear, I didn't ask for them or anything like that."

"So, she just...gave them to you?"

"She's noticed you and I have been hanging out," I tell her. "And she didn't like, hand them to me with a long speech on safe sex practices. They were just on my bed when I came home one day."

"Hmm," she responds, her body relaxing against my comforter. "Nothing like having your mom be your wingman. Definitely doesn't scream 'mama's boy.'"

A light pinch to her side and she squeals, quickly stifling it with a hand to her mouth. I lean down and run my nose along her cheek. "Is this a diversion technique?"

"What do you mean?"

"We don't have to do anything if you don't want to, Teeny. If you're not ready—"

"No," she interrupts. "No, I am. I just want to make sure we're prepared."

"You sure?"

"Yeah." She tilts her head up and kisses me, angling her head to the side while running her hand up the center of my back. Everything starts to move in a blur, but I'm here. I'm in my room with Teeny. In her arms, like she's anchoring me to earth. In a place where I belong.

Quiet whispers of "Are you sure?" and "I want to," and "You're amazing," float into the air. It hangs and hovers, creating a bubble of hope and confidence that we can survive anything. I could take off to college for four years, be hundreds of miles apart, and we would somehow still survive it all. I would eventually find my way back to her. My place is with her, no matter what.

We pull back the covers of my sheets and slide under a cocoon, burrowing farther into the place where I finally feel at home. We undress, taking our time, learning each other's bodies while knowing this won't be the last time. We'll have more moments like this...forever.

We both know this is fundamentally physical, whatever teenage hormones running rampant in our blood, but it feels so far from it. It's charged with some cloyingly visceral thing that I can't quite place. Because I've never felt this. I've never felt this close to another living soul in my entire life.

When we're done, Teeny lays against me, her bare body flush against mine. Her hair sprawled across my pillow where I know I'll be able to smell her when I go to sleep tonight.

"I'm so in love with you, Christine."

She giggles into my chest. "So formal."

"I am," I tell her, smiling into her hair.

"I know," she responds. "I love you, too, Everett."

CHAPTER NINETEEN

Teeny

NOW

VEGAS BECAME A DISTANT MEMORY. My foot injury scabbed over and healed. And my kiss with Everett stayed in Vegas, right on top of that luxurious goose-down comforter. As soon as we came back to the real world, after a weekend of alcohol, long hours spent in chlorinated water, a tinge of a sunburn, and even more alcohol, my night with Everett turned into a heavy mass I carried around with me. And I kept it at my heels, like dragging a suitcase on wheels, as a constant reminder.

I'm a married woman. I'm still Mrs. Christine Diaz. And yet, it's taken one moment of weakness for me to realize how little that title means to me now. Fifteen years ago, I wore it like a badge of honor. I introduced myself as Mrs. Diaz to everyone I met. I stood proudly by Leo as his doting wife. As the mother of his child. And now, I'm questioning it all. Did it all mean nothing to him? Was I just a placeholder for him? Someone to fill the role as his wife so that he'd slide perfectly into what he envisioned for himself: a successful man who had it all. A reputable lawyer and a family man. And I played into it all.

With the pending meetings on my calendar with Grace's lawyer, I knew I needed to talk to Leo. As much as I wish I could just shove a stack of divorce papers into Leo's face and have my lawyer handle things, I owe it to my marriage to talk to him. No matter his infidelity.

Right now, I have to push all of that aside to meet Everett at Allegra Augustus Gallery in La Jolla. I'd set up the meeting quickly after my return from Vegas, and Everett jumped at the opportunity when I texted him to let him know about the earliest opening.

I'm looking over a large canvas, probably spanning close to fifty inches wide, with abstract florals. It's just the kind of art I would've painted. Something I would've drawn up in my head and let it linger there until I finally let my hands talk. But that was a lifetime ago. Something Everett is more familiar with than I am.

Allegra Augustus, the gallery owner herself, is meeting with us today to personally show us the current pieces in her gallery. As I'm perusing the relatively familiar space, I hear the bell on the door trill as it opens and closes. My heart flip flops. There's that time machine again, plopping me right back into my sixteen-year-old self, giddy with excitement over seeing my boyfriend. Waiting for him to meet me after basketball practice or at the door to Mrs. Fix's class.

I can't hold back the completely silly grin on my face. "Hi," I say softly to Everett, waving a hand in his direction.

"Hi."

He'd texted me a few times. Simple exchanges asking me how my foot was, if I made it home okay. If there were any more encounters with unmannerly men who didn't understand the concept of consent. I've been responding with one-sided answers, too confused to egg on a more flirtatious banter. And Everett being Everett, he seemed to take my lack of engagement as a silent request for space instead of urging for more of my attention. Something I appreciated with my entire gut.

I hear faint clicks of shoes echo against the stark white walls in the gallery, coming from the back offices away from patrons. "Christine," Allegra calls, approaching me with a kind smile. "It's so good to see you!"

"Hi, Allegra," I say, greeting her with a quick embrace. "Good to see you too." I turn to introduce Everett. "This is the client I was telling you about. Everett Hayes."

Everett is all professional and gentleman-like, shaking Allegra's hand, and I can almost feel his charm radiating off him. My heart does another flip and another flop, reminding me how in love I was with this man at some point in my life.

"Nice to meet you," Everett says, throwing in a little extra of that charm with an easy simper.

"So, we have some pieces in the back. Ones I usually save for more serious buyers," Allegra explains. "We can start there and work our way up front."

Allegra turns on her heels, and Everett and I follow.

"You didn't tell me this was the gallery," Everett whispers, ducking his head close to my ear. I keep my eyes on the floor while our steps move in synchrony on the hardwood floor.

He remembered.

I silently nod, smiling at my plum-colored shoes standing out against my white wide-legged slacks. When I turn to look at him, his eyes are on me with that smile I can't seem to shake out of my head.

"Is your...work still here?"

I nod. "There's still one piece," I tell him, my voice shaking. We come to a stop at the back of the gallery, and there it is. It isn't as vivid as it once was, and the golden tones of the sunset look more canary than the amber color it once was. But the lifeguard tower is hard to miss. Everett sees it, and he veers right into it. He's not here anymore. He's at the beach, right next to that tower, his footprints leaving marks on the wet sand just as they once did.

"So, this—"

"Everett is familiar with this piece," I gently interrupt Allegra. She politely nods, giving Everett a moment, and I walk up to him. "They never sold it," I tell him. "I offered to take it back so it didn't take up space in the gallery, but the previous gallery owner said it was okay. And when Allegra bought the gallery six years ago, she decided to keep it on display."

I don't know if Everett heard me. He gives no indication that he did. So I stay quiet, giving him a moment longer.

"I'll take this one," he says to the piece.

Allegra and I share a look. "It's actually not for sale," she explains.

That gets Everett's attention, and he looks at Allegra with a steel look of determination. "What do you mean?"

"It's the only piece that came with the gallery when I took ownership of it, and it's really a part of the space," she tells him. She looks at him apologetically, her body already angled toward another piece on the opposite wall.

Everett and I follow, and a deep scowl covers Everett's features.

Allegra explains in a skillful voice, going over the different painting techniques and art styles. We move on to some sculptures, and Everett hasn't said a single word. I can feel Allegra grow more nervous as we move along the gallery, and I realize Everett hasn't made a decision on another piece aside from mine.

"Well," Allegra says, her voice a little defeated. "I'll give you two a minute to talk things over."

I reach for Allegra's arm for an appreciative squeeze. "Thank you, Allegra." I turn to Everett, his scowl turning pensive and preoccupied. "Did you not see anything you like?"

"Maybe some of the sculptures," he says, his voice distant and distracted.

"Okay," I tell him, trying to sound encouraging. "Did you want to look at them again? Maybe you can pick some—"

"I'm okay with whatever you pick, Teeny," he interrupts. His tone is clipped, like he's displeased.

"Sure. I'll talk to Allegra, and we'll go over some pieces. See what'll be a good fit."

I stop by Allegra's office and give her some details on the hotel design changes and the entire remodel. I tell her I'll be in touch with some decisions on the pieces, and we part ways. With that, Everett and I leave the gallery. We're standing in the parking lot, my back against the door to my car and Everett standing about two feet from me. My eyes are back on my feet, noticing a small chip of nail polish on my middle toenail.

"I should get go—"

"How are you?" Everett interrupts, ignoring my pending departure.

"I'm okay." I sound so timid and scared, and maybe I am. Maybe Everett's presence, while it makes a flurry of butterflies grow rampant in my stomach, also terrifies me.

He nods, and I fidget with my car keys.

More silence sits between us. I finally look at him, and I realize why I'm so scared. I'm scared of my past. I'm scared it's going to careen right into me when I've spent the last twenty years avoiding it. I'm scared that after all this time I spent safeguarding my heart, it was all for nothing. And I don't know if I'll survive it again. I don't know if my heart will survive. People die from a broken heart. I've seen it happen in movies, in books, and that could be me. It could kill me.

"I really do have to go," I say again, my hand already pulling at my door handle. "I'm picking Sadie up from camp."

"She's coming back?" he asks.

"Yeah," I tell him. "Just in time for the wedding."

He smiles. "That's good. I'm sure you'll be happy to have her back home."

"I am."

"I guess...I'll see you soon?" he asks tentatively.

"Yeah."

I don't understand the impulse that has me reaching for him, but it happens despite the nagging voice in my head telling me it's a bad idea. I place my hand lightly on his forearm, giving it a gentle squeeze. He looks at me with an observant gaze, and before he can do anything, like give my hand a reassuring pat or even something as bold as an embrace, I turn and get into my car to leave.

The entire drive to LA is a blur. I don't remember what roads I took, what street signs I passed. I don't even notice the usually irritating freeway traffic. All I see is Everett's face. How solemn his expression turned as soon as he saw my painting. How he looked like he wanted to ask me more than how I've been. Maybe he wanted to ask me if I've been thinking about him. About our kiss. About those stolen glances in the pool around everyone else, hoping we didn't look suspicious. And a part of me wished he asked me. Just so I could tell him that it's all I've been thinking about. But also to tell him that I'm still scared.

As soon as I walk onto the campgrounds and head over to Sadie's dorm room she's been sharing with three other girls, I go right into mom mode.

"Sadie, your clothes are a mess in here." I'm sifting through her duffel bag, finding that her clothes have been thrown in there without a care.

"I'm going to wash them all anyway, Mom," she argues.

I huff, sorting through her things to make room for the rest of her belongings. We finish packing, and she says her goodbyes to her camp friends. They exchange hugs, promising to stay in touch and keep each other updated on their music. Before I know it, I'm filling the three-hour drive back home with a demo Sadie recorded at camp, played through Bluetooth on her phone, and a complete Taylor Swift singalong that she and I duet.

When I pull into my driveway, I'm surprised to see Leo's car there.

"Dad!" Sadie squeals as she bolts out of the car before I'm even able to put it in park.

"Whoa, kiddo," Leo exclaims, embracing our daughter in a tight hug. "You go away to camp for the summer and suddenly I'm 'Dad?'"

Sadie rolls her eyes, the only appropriate response from an angsty tween, before she helps me with her bags from my car.

"I thought we could go out for burgers," he tells me, eyeing me cautiously. "It's been a while since we've had a milkshake from Ruby's."

"Yes!" Sadie exclaims. "I'm so hungry."

Leo's eyes don't leave mine. "Why don't you get your things inside," he instructs Sadie. "I need to talk to your mom for a second."

"Okay." She takes her guitar from me as I remove it from the trunk, and she walks into the house through the open garage.

"Sadie told me she was on her way home," Leo explains. "She texted me when you two left camp."

I nod.

"Anyway, are you okay with some burgers? Or we can go to that sushi place you like."

"You can go with Sadie," I tell him. "I'm sure she's excited to see you. You know, since you missed her showcase."

"I'm sorry about that."

I huff. "Tell her."

Leo awkwardly rubs his knuckles into his palm. "I, uh, talked to James a few days ago."

I already don't like where this is headed. "And?"

"He told me you guys went to Vegas."

"For Mina and Josh's bachelor-bachelorette weekend, yeah."

"And he, um...he mentioned that your old boyfriend was there."

My body stiffens. "Yeah, he was."

There's a long pause of silence. I can tell he wants to know more. Not the details he already knows. Like that Everett was the one who got away. That he was the one who had my heart in shambles when Leo and I met one weekend during the summer after junior year when James brought him over to the house. That when he saw me moseying around the house in a state of grief and misery, we bonded over my heartbreak and his incredibly welcoming shoulder to cry on.

"Is that all? You came here to tell me what James passed along to you?"

"Is there something going on? With you and him?"

I scoff. "I don't think that's any of your business."

"You're my wife—"

"Your soon-to-be *ex*-wife," I spit back. "Your soon-to-be ex-wife who you *cheated* on. Or did you forget that little detail?"

His hands fist at his side, and I can see his face flush red with anger and frustration. "I don't care what I did. You're still my wife, and if you're cheating on me to get back at me—"

"I am not *cheating* on you!" My voice raises, and I see him taken aback by the brazenness of my words. "I'm not cheating on you, because we aren't together anymore. We are done. I don't know how else to make things clearer, but this—" I point a finger back and forth between us. "It's over."

"Teeny, don't say that."

"Why?" I throw my hands in the air, looking for the last bits of my will as I search for the words that'll finally make him understand how far we are from reparable. "You're going to honestly say that this is worth salvaging? That there's something there worth fighting for between us?"

He responds with silence, and it's the answer I need. "But you're...we're married. You're the mother of my child. What...what am I going to do without you?"

"Maybe you should've thought of that before you cheated on me, Leo." I start to feel tears prick at my eyes, and my throat tightens, making me near speechless. I didn't want him to see me like this. Hurt and suffering from his betrayal, but I don't know how to hold it back any longer. I wipe at my cheeks, trying to hide the evidence of my tears before Sadie comes back outside, and Leo takes a step closer to me.

"Teeny, please." I feel the emotions swell in his voice, his eyes on the brink of his own tears. All I can do is shake my head, too tired and weary to fight anymore.

The door from inside the garage opens, signaling Sadie's exit from the house. I quickly wipe at the last bit of my tears, smoothing it over with a forced smile in Sadie's direction. "Don't

239

have too much ice cream. You know all that dairy makes your tummy ache."

"You're not going?" Sadie asks, a hopeful look on her face. And under different circumstances, I might have changed my mind. I might have pushed aside my hurt and resentment from Leo's betrayal for the sake of our daughter. But I couldn't. Not after everything we'd just said to each other.

"No, baby," I tell her apologetically. "I have to make some calls for a client, but you enjoy your time with Daddy."

I can feel Leo watching us, his presence suddenly unwanted in a way that feels unsettling, but I ignore it. I said what needed to be said, and as much as it disturbed what little truce we silently settled on, I meant it. I should at least look him in the eye and bid him farewell before he leaves, if not out of politeness, then at the very least for Sadie, but I don't. Instead, I embrace Sadie in a tight hug before she scampers off into Leo's car. And I walk right into my house without a second glance.

I start picking up the mess in my house. Loose shoes strewn in the entryway, empty coffee mugs in random parts of the house, small bits of littered trash on the floor. I do that while I try to process the reason for the aching twinge in my heart. Wondering if it's a spasm of guilt or if it's a cluster of anger building and growing into something hard to ignore. I start to become exasperated and irate toward Leo. At his assumptions, his hypocritical accusations. And then that pain shifts completely into anger. I start stomping around the house, muttering under my breath all the things I wish I could say to Leo's face. That he has no right to go around still calling me his wife. That he should start getting more familiar with the term *ex-wife* or mother of his child instead. And how dare he accuse me of cheating on him! As if he has the right to even question something like that. And yet, there's a lingering guilt brewing in my gut. Because I couldn't deny his question, asking if there was something going on with me and Everett. Not after that kiss. And maybe the fact that the guilt that should've been pointed in Leo's direction is now

240

teetering a little toward me has me more hot and bothered than I should be.

I try to stay busy, washing Sadie's clothes, tidying around the house, putting away all the little toiletries I still had stashed away in my makeup bag from the Vegas trip. Before I know it, Sadie's home. Leo doesn't walk her in, and I take it as a sign. Maybe he finally got the hint that his actions caused all of this. This rift, this tension.

As I'm folding Sadie's laundry while she's fast asleep in her room, that guilt starts to claw at my chest. Leo's right. I *am* a married woman. And Everett should've respected that. My mind starts to play this violent tug of war, unsure of what I should be feeling. And by the time it hits one a.m., I'm still stewing. I've moved on to sorting through the clothes in my closet, filling a garbage bag of items to donate to Goodwill, when this nagging voice tells me I need to talk to Everett. I need to clear this up. Because if that kiss meant more than just a kiss, more than some form of closure I've been convincing myself that it was, then it makes me no better than Leo.

"Teeny?" Everett answers on the second ring.

"Were you sleeping?" I ask, suddenly realizing the time.

"No."

"Okay."

There's a pause, and I hear the rustle of bed sheets. "Is everything okay?"

"Mh-hmm," I answer, giving nothing away.

"Are you sure?"

"Yeah." I hesitate before saying, "I don't...really know why I called."

"That's okay." I don't know how to explain it, but he sounds so... understanding. I feel like I can confess my darkest, deepest sins and he'd somehow convince me I'm at no fault.

"Leo came by," I finally tell him. "James told him that you're in town and that you were in Vegas with me."

"How did he take it?"

"He asked if there was something going on with me and you," I answer. "He...knows about you. He's known about you for a long time."

"What did you tell him?" I can hear the cautious tone in his voice. It's there in the hesitating pause and the quietly whispered question.

"I told him no," I say firmly. "I told him it wasn't any of his business. And he told me that he didn't care because I'm still his wife."

He lightly scoffs instead of the expected string of curses directed at Leo, showing some restraint on his end. "It doesn't change the fact that he still cheated on you, Teeny."

"I know," I tell him. "And I reminded him that I won't be his wife for much longer."

"Good."

A smile that feels completely foreign in place of the perpetual scowl I've been wearing all day tugs at my lips. "But...after what happened, it doesn't make me any better than him, Everett. I stooped down to his level."

"Was that what that was? Trying to show him up? Or get back at him?" he asks. His voice isn't threatening or accusatory. He sounds like he's genuinely asking. If not out of pure curiosity, then to clarify what our kiss meant.

"No!" I answer quickly, and I can almost hear him smile. "No, Everett. That's not what that was at all. Me and you—"

"Then you haven't stooped down to his level," he assures me.

"Okay," I say, sounding unsure of myself. "I should go," I tell him after a pregnant pause. "I'm sorry I called you so late."

"It's okay, Teeny. You can call me anytime."

My heart squeezes inside my chest, and I want to fall into a heap of tears. "Good night, Everett."

"Night, Teeny."

I hang up, and as soon as my phone lands on my bed, the tears start to flow. I can't pinpoint why I'm crying. If it's because of Leo and our broken marriage. If it's because I miss Everett so damn much and crying is the only way to express the pain I'm feeling from his gaping absence. Or if I'm finally saying goodbye. To Everett and our past, and this is the mourning period I never got to have. Or to my marriage, all the good years we had before everything went to shit.

Or maybe it's the tidal wave of emotions that's finally hitting me. All at once, like a tsunami. I feel too many things. Anger, regret, sadness, grief, resentment, relief. All of those feelings are coming together, only for me to realize how weak I've become. I'm tired, completely spent from trying to keep my shit together.

My nose starts to blubber with snot, and the tears run down my cheeks, soaking my shirt. I bury my face into my pillow, letting it stain with the remains of my sadness. I don't know how long I've been crying, but I'm interrupted by an alert on my phone. I pick it up to see a new text message from Everett.

> EVERETT
>
> I'm outside.

The tears stop cold in their tracks, and I reach for a tissue to wipe away at the mess on my face. I should question his message. There should be some kind of emotion that aligns with panic and worry coursing through me knowing that Everett is at my doorstep while Sadie's sound asleep in her room, but I don't. I feel the opposite. I feel relieved.

My body's on autopilot as I walk down the stairs to my front door, and when I open it, Everett's on the other side. He's wearing a black hoodie and jeans, his hair a little disheveled and that five o'clock shadow outlining his jaw perfectly.

"Hi," he says grimly. His eyes look tired and sad, almost mirroring mine.

I know I look like a mess. Cheeks stained with tears and my nose a blotchy red color, all evidence of the sobbing fest I had up in my room, but I don't care at this point. The dam breaks, and the tears come in a fresh wave. As soon as my face twists and a sob breaks from my chest, Everett steps forward, pulling me into him. I don't know what to do. I don't know how to make the tears stop, and when the sobs become louder, he pulls me outside, closing the door behind me.

"Is Sadie home?"

I nod into his chest.

"Okay," he whispers. "Shh, it's okay, Teeny," he continues softly into my hair. It helps, his soothing voice, his hands moving over my threadbare night shirt, and next thing I know, I'm looking up at him. He smooths away the hair on my face and wipes at the tears. "I'm here, okay? And I'm not going to hurt you. Not again."

My body sags, landing with a heavy thud into a safety net. I feel safeguarded. Like I can weather an entire storm and come out the other end unscathed. I can't explain it. The way it courses through me, exposing my heart by placing it right on my sleeve, but it's there. The last few bricks of the wall I spent so many years building crumble to the ground, and it's just me. It's just me and Everett. And for some reason, it feels so right.

"Why did you?" I say, my voice so low, I don't even know if Everett heard me. "Why did you hurt me?"

He cups my face in his hands and forces my eyes to him. "I didn't know any better. I didn't know how to stop the hurt inside me, and it made me hurt you instead." His eyes mist over, and they start to rim red. He closes his eyes, a wince taking over his features with his tight jaw and furrowed brow. I see a tear trail down his cheek, and he rests his forehead against mine. "I don't regret a lot of things in my life, but hurting you is something I wish I could take back. All of it. I wish I could go back in time and change everything." He pulls away, and the tears continue to fall. "I miss you so much, Teeny. God, I missed you." His voice cracks and it's enough to break me.

I pull at his neck, bringing him closer, and kiss him. And it feels like I've come home. Right onto the plush purple rug in the middle of my childhood bedroom, surrounded by half-empty tubes of acrylic paints and bristly paintbrushes. Everett's arms wrap around my waist, holding me so tight I can barely breathe. It's suffocating, but he doesn't loosen his grip. He grunts into my mouth, letting that little bit of reserve he was clinging to fall apart. My entire body presses into him, seeking more than just this kiss. I want to mold into him. I want to feel every part of him to every part of me as if there'd been no time spent away from him. As if I'd spent the last twenty years by his side and I knew his body as if it were my own.

Everett lifts me, his hold on me growing impossibly tighter. I follow him as his steps move backward toward my driveway. He fumbles his hand against the door of his car, but not the front seat. He veers to the back, and I don't even protest. I follow willingly because I don't think there's a place on this earth I wouldn't follow him to right now. I'd follow him right into the ruins of our past if it means more of this.

Everett goes first and I follow, naturally situating myself on his lap. When I do, my thighs straddling his, he takes a moment to look at me. To run his hands over my skin, trailing goose bumps over the exposed areas. He doesn't say anything, and for some reason, that silence says more than any words possibly could. I try to kiss him again, going for his lips, but he stops me.

"Sorry," he whispers. "I just need a minute."

My hands thread into his nape and up to his hair. "Do you not... do you want to stop?"

"No," he answers urgently. "No, Teeny. I just...I can't believe this is happening. I've thought about this moment for so long."

I watch the way he studies me under the glowing moonlight, his eyes looking at me as if he's committing everything to memory. The way my skin gleams in the light streaming in from the windows and the way my chest heaves against my too-thin shirt. And I wonder if he notices me too. All the changes. Like the fine lines that etch my face or the body that withstood motherhood with stretch marks and saggy skin. Or if he doesn't see any of that. If he still sees the girl next door he fell in love with.

"I can't lose you again, Teeny," he finally says. A fresh wave of tears gloss over his eyes, and I see the pain pulled to the surface.

"Please tell me what to do. I don't know what to do, and I'm scared that what I do might hurt you again. And I can't—"

I cut him off with a deep kiss, pressing my hips into his. Tears roll down my cheeks, and they mix with his, making our kiss salty and wet. My hands reach for the hem of his sweatshirt, and he pulls it off. I'm taken aback when I see that he's not wearing anything underneath, but that passes quickly, and my focus shifts to his tattoo. In the darkness, I trace it with my fingers, appreciating the fine lines and colors that stand out even in the veil of the night.

"It was the only way to keep a part of you with me," he whispers, watching me. "I walked away from everything, and your paintings and this place and you...I wanted it all to stay with me forever."

I look at him, his words firing every nerve ending in my body until my limbs buzz with electricity. "You got this..."

He looks at me, waiting for something, anything. When all I can do is look at him in awe, he inches closer, moving cautiously. In that moment, I realize how deeply we're meant for each other. The moment I laid eyes on him, it was set in stone. Regardless of our journey, of the different paths we took, and the fork in the road that drew us apart, we were always meant to find our way back to each other. This is what soulmates are made of. The invisible string tugging at our hearts, tying us to one another to connect us whenever we lose our way.

My hands start to fumble at the button of his pants, and he quickly follows my lead. I reach into his boxers and grip him. I feel his arms slacken around me, and he lets out the most erotic moan I've ever heard. It shoots straight into the pit of my stomach, making it tumble and roll.

His hands snake up my back, under my shirt, against my bare skin, and all the way to the opening at my neck. The movement lifts my shirt, exposing more of my skin, and he ducks his head, taking my nipple in his mouth through the almost see-through fabric. My back arches, and I swear I see stars on the ceiling of his car. I want him. I need him. I need him like I need air to breathe.

This is becoming more than just our bodies wanting each other. It's becoming a way of sustaining life. We need each other to survive.

He trails kisses up my chest and when he reaches my neckline, his tongue caresses my skin all the way up to my earlobe. He takes an indecent taste between his teeth, and it feels like numbing pins and needles low in my stomach. My body begins to feel desperate.

I start to climb off of him, removing the loose sleep shorts I was wearing, exposing the bareness of my entire bottom half. He watches me, his eyes turning dark and hungry. I move so that I'm straddling him again, and my hand is on him, stroking him, learning how to do this all over again.

Everett suddenly grips my wrist in his hand to stop me. "Shit!" he mutters, cursing under his breath. "Fuck. Teeny, I don't have a condom."

"I have an IUD," I tell him quickly. "Unless you don't think we should..."

"No, I do," he answers, that urgency back in his voice, full of desperation. I wait for him to continue. "Are you sure?"

"I trust you," I tell him, finally realizing how deeply I believe those words. I trust him. With my entire body, I trust him. And suddenly, all the pain, all the hurt falls into the shadows, drawing the curtains closed as if they've done their part. I'm safe now.

"I trust you, too."

With that, I position myself over him, and we both gasp. Everything inside me grows wanton. I claw at his bare shoulders, needing something to ground myself to. I feel like I'm going to float away on a big fluffy cloud, and this will all be a figment of my imagination.

Everett kisses me, crushing his lips into mine. His hands tremble against my waist, and I realize his entire body is shaking. I wrap my arms around his neck, drawing our bodies even closer together. I start to move, my hips seeking friction against his.

"You feel...incredible," he groans. "Jesus, you feel fucking amazing."

I shift so he hits a spot inside me that makes my entire body jolt and quiver. He notices how I react, his gaze growing dark and heady.

"There?" he asks. He gives a rousing thrust upward, testing his question only to find the answer in my reaction.

"Mh-hmm," I whimper, nodding while my lids fall heavy. I shudder and fall slack on his lap, shivering through the overwhelming sensation from how skilled he is even at an angle where I'm at the advantage. "Touch me, Everett."

He watches me, pressing his index and middle fingers against my lips. He pushes further, prying my mouth open, and I feel the smooth pads of his fingers grate against my tongue. My mouth responds with a loud pop as soon as he withdraws his fingers, and I feel them between us.

"You are so goddamn beautiful like this," I hear him whisper while his fingers stroke and tease. He fists my hair with his free hand and wraps it loosely around his palm, tugging it back to angle my jaw to the ceiling of the car. My hips start to move in circles and the back of Everett's head hits the headrest. "*Ohhh*, fuck. You're driving me insane."

"Just keep touching me," I demand. "And don't st-stop. Whatever you do, do—don't stop moving."

He continues his rhythm, those thrusts moving in and out with a steadiness I'm finding fascinating. My breaths start to come out in shallow gasps, just as my body begins to tense and seize. Those pants that were leaving my lips in desperate gulps of air become loud, turning into aching cries. I cry out his name, some line of curses I can't even remember, and even a prayer to a higher being as I fall apart right on Everett's lap. Even inside his car, I know it's getting loud, to the point that if someone overheard, we wouldn't be able to disguise what we're doing. Everett's hand clamps over my mouth and my cries turn into screams. Screams that scrape against my throat, creating a deliciously satiating sting.

My body starts to relax as I come down from my high, and Everett scoops his palms right behind me and lifts off the seat. He dizzies me in an agile pivot, and I'm suddenly on my back, Everett hovering over me in the small space of his back seat. My knees fall open, welcoming this new position, and Everett picks up his pace.

"You're amazing," he growls, his focus on maintaining a steady tempo that feels delectable and wicked. "And you're so fucking beautiful." He ends his sentence with a harsh kiss, smashing his lips to mine. His hips start to meet mine, thrust to thrust. I hear a rhythmic grunt rattle Everett's chest, matching the beats to the racy slaps of my skin against his. The indecency of our movements, the sheen of sweat lining our foreheads, the recklessness and desperation of our fucking has a crescendo effect, making it build.

It was never like this between us. We'd always find ways to make our lovemaking sweet and wholesome and tender. But this...it's rousing, injecting electricity straight into my veins. All these years, I've been missing out on this kind of sex. This kind of compulsive, addictive sex.

"You gonna let me come inside you?" he asks, a dark and lustful gaze filling his eyes. It hardly sounds like a question, but more like a threat. And if I said no, there'd be consequences.

"*Yes*," I answer, my voice breathless. "Please."

His hand moves above me, bracing himself against the window. It gives him the leverage he needs as I start to feel his movements become frantic and wild. My moans mingle with all the sounds inside Everett's car. My bare skin against the leather seat, our choppy breaths that blend the fine line between a gasp and a shriek, the lewdness of the squelching noises we're creating with the in and out motion of his thrusts.

"*Fuck!*" Everett groans noisily, pressing his forehead into the crook where my shoulder and neck meet, rattling everything from the inside out. I don't care anymore that anyone outside can hear us. All reason and sense leave my body, and what remains is this desperation clinging to my body that I want more.

But then our bodies come down from the high. Like a deflating balloon, and I realize how we acted completely on carnal urges. It was all about our bodies craving something our hearts told us we'd already had enough of. We became glutinous and caved.

I push him off me, searching for my underwear and shorts. I quietly put them back on, the mess already growing slick against my thighs. I watch Everett do the same, tucking himself away and zipping up his pants.

I reach for the door, but Everett stops me. "Teeny."

"I should go," I tell him, my eyes on the handle.

"Teeny, look at me."

I do, and my chin trembles. "I'm sorry, Everett."

"You have nothing to be—"

"I'm so fucked up," I interrupt, my voice shaky and scared. "This is all so fucked up, and I wish things weren't the way they were."

"I love you, Teeny."

My face twists, and it feels like a dagger shot straight through my chest.

"I never stopped loving you," he adds. "You are, without a single doubt, the love of my life. It's always and only been you."

"Don't tell me that."

"Why?"

"Because..." I look at him, my eyes glassy and sad. "It's too late."

CHAPTER TWENTY

Everett

THEN

BASKETBALL SEASON CAME AND WENT, which helped ease my thoughts into a calmer, lighter state without the constant motion of practices and games and celebratory parties. I made my trip back up north to tour UC Davis, walking through my future school with a lingering edge I couldn't place. I'm not sure if it's the thought of being in another new place in another new school with an entirely different student body or if it's because this time, I'm actually going to miss the place I leave. It feels like time and senior year and all the important milestones around me are happening while I just stand here, watching it fly by.

When I sent out college applications, I had a plan. My year in San Diego was meant to be temporary. But now that I've settled in, the last thing I want is for all of this to be temporary. I've been considering my options. What about a transfer? Somewhere closer to San Diego. Or maybe even a year off? Then Teeny and I can start college together, maybe at the same school? But then what would my parents say? My dad was so proud when I'd gotten into UC Davis, and my mom. She wouldn't take the news well.

I tried talking to my mom about it, hoping she'd understand should I choose an alternative to my current plans, and maybe let her know why I'd grown so apprehensive about college and the reasons behind my lack of enthusiasm when she becomes excited about some minor detail. Like the student center equipped with a pool table and pinball machine or the Target within walking distance from my dorm. But when I tried to tell her how the impending changes to my life after graduation made me feel like there was a never-ending hamster wheel squeaking away in my insides, I'd clam up. I couldn't explain it to her.

I was better at keeping my emotions under control before moving down here. I was able to breathe through the nerves that left me on edge. I was able to isolate myself in my room, listen to music, go for a drive, and it would be enough. But now, I feel like I'm constantly chasing after normal. It'll be at my fingertips, I'll touch it and maybe even grasp it, and then it'll inch further and further away as soon as the dread of the future washes over me. And it leaves me feeling like my skin is crawling and my insides are going to spill outside of me.

I keep asking myself, what's changed? What's brought on this sudden dread of having to leave my new home? I realize it's this shift. When I'm here, not thinking about what's to come, I don't feel like I'm on edge anymore. I feel grounded and...normal for a change. And it's all because of Teeny. She's become this unexpected anchor, holding me down instead of letting me drift off into the unknown where things are dark and scary.

It's easy to forget about the future. In my room, where Teeny's scent lingers on my bed. Short moments after school before her parents come home from work and long hours on the weekend when my mom's out, we lie in bed. Our hands always touching each other, our clothes strewn on the floor, and I wish time could stop. Just so I could stay grounded a little longer. So I don't have to release the anchor holding me down.

With plans to see Teeny tonight, and hopefully get some of that alone time I've been craving more of lately, I hop in the shower. My phone rings on my nightstand just as I'm getting out with a towel wrapped around my waist. I reach for it and see Diana's number pop up on the caller ID.

"Hello?" I answer.

"Hi. It's me," Teeny answers from the other end. Her voice sounds meek and scared. "Um, can you meet me at the diner?"

"Oh, are you not going back home?"

"I—I'm here at Diana's. We were just...I'm going to leave in about an hour or so," she answers, her voice still low and distracted. "I'm... can you just meet me there? And we can go to the party after, I guess."

"Sure," I tell her, doing a mental count of our change of plans before heading to Jake's pre-spring break party. "I just got out of the shower, and my mom needed me to get a few things at the store before I head out."

"That's fine. If I get there before you, I'll just wait."

There's a pause between our back and forth. I hear her sigh a heavy breath. It sounds shaky and tense.

"Is everything okay?"

"Mh-hmm," she answers. "I'll just talk to you later."

"Okay." I hang up my phone, tossing it on my bed. I start to play out a dozen different scenarios in my head, worried that I may have done something wrong. Something that may have upset Teeny. My movements become hurried, wanting to get to her sooner than later. As soon as I'm dressed, I reach for my keys and wallet and head out the door. Just as I land at the bottom of the stairs, I hear my mom's tense voice coming from the kitchen.

"Eddie, what are you talking about?"

I halt my steps, turning to the kitchen instead.

"Oh my god." My mom's voice sounds completely devastated. Like the ground beneath her gave out from under her. "Oh my god. I can't believe this is happening."

My entire body freezes, and my feet are bolted to the hard floor at the doorway leading into the kitchen. My mom's back is to me, and I can see the fear and pain ripple through her whole body.

"Eddie, how could you do this to us? You have a family. What am I going to tell Everett?!"

She starts to sob, her cries wailing through the emptiness of the house. Her body sags, and I reach out to her just as she collapses to the floor. She doesn't even seem to notice that I'm there, but she leans into my chest as I guide her to the ground slowly.

"Mom," I call. Her face is buried in her hands, and I don't know if she hears me. I'm right next to her, my voice right up against her ear, and I don't know if she even realizes that I'm here.

I take the phone she's dropped to the ground. "Dad?"

"Everett," he answers. "Is your mom okay?"

"What happened? What did you do?"

"Let me talk to your mom."

"Dad, tell me what happened!" I feel like my insides are thudding and pounding. My heart is beating so hard and fast that it rattles through my entire body.

He sighs through the line and my anger toward him starts to simmer. "Look, I wanted to tell you with your mom, but...I guess you need to know sooner than later. I met someone here."

A numbness starts to course through my body.

"And I just found out she's pregnant."

"What?" My voice sounds like it isn't even coming from my own lips. It sounds like it's echoing off the walls, spoken by someone other than me.

"And this woman, she's threatening to go public with this. She's already spoken to the PR manager of the team. I—"

I hang up the phone. I can't stand to hear his voice anymore. Not while I look at my mom, her disheveled hair splayed over her tear-stained face.

"Mom," I call, urging her to look at me. With my hands braced on her shoulders, I force her to look at me.

Her eyes grow misty and her chin trembles. "He said it wouldn't happen again. He said..." The last of her words are drowned in an inconsolable wave of sobs. She cries and cries, and I hold her. I hold her until exhaustion takes over, and she's just a heap of fatigue and betrayal. I don't know what to do. I want to tell her everything will be okay, regardless if it's the truth or not. I want to call my dad and yell at him. Tell him how royally he fucked things up and how I will never be able to look at him the same. I want to go to Teeny. The only person who could hold my hand and somehow make things okay. Even if she's just sitting next to me, her hand in mine while we sip on a Coke float.

With my mom still crying, I walk her to the couch. She slumps into the cushions, her limbs heavy and lifeless. With her legs drawn up to her chest and her face pressed against the arm, she stares blankly. At the floor in front of her, at the coffee table scratched up from the years my grandparents owned a tabby cat, at my foot firmly rooted on the carpet as I watch her completely fall apart.

She slowly falls asleep, her breathing steadying, and her face growing lax. I reach for a blanket to cover her with and set about getting a hold of Teeny. As soon as I find Diana's number on my phone, I walk into the kitchen to avoid waking my mom.

"Hello?"

"Hey, is this Diana?"

"Yeah."

"It's Everett. Is Teeny still there?"

"She just left."

Shit. "Okay. That's fine."

"Okay."

I hang up, realizing I have no choice but to leave.

When I get to the diner, I find Teeny in our usual spot. She has two Coke floats sitting in front of her and has her arms crossed on the table with her chin resting on them. Her eyes look vacant, like she's processing something in her mind that she can't manage to wrap her head around in a crowded diner filled with clanking silverware and boisterous chatter.

For some reason, looking at her reminds me of my mom back home. The way her eyes don't seem to focus on anything, not even the ice cream spilling over the rim of the milkshake glass or the crinkled straw wrappers scattered in front of her.

"Hey," I say, reaching her and placing a small peck on her temple. "Have you been waiting long?"

She shakes her head, her gaze still in front of her. I reach for one of the Coke floats and take a long sip. The waitress comes to the table, asking if we want anything. After a quick glance at Teeny, I tell her no and thank you.

"Is everything okay?"

She nods again.

"Teeny."

She finally looks at me, and her eyes look so sad, I think she might start crying.

"Hey," I urge, standing from my seat across from her and taking the one by her side. "What happened?"

I'm answered with silence and a quiet sniff as she wipes the sleeve of my hoodie she's wearing across the tip of her nose. My hand runs over her shoulder, attempting to soothe away whatever's causing her so much difficulty to tell me what she needs to say. "Teeny, whatever it is, you can tell me."

Another swipe across her nose and she looks at me. "I'm, um...I think I'm late."

"What are you talking about?" I ask, confusion lining my words.

Her fingers fidget on her lap, and she exhales a shaky sigh. "I hadn't realized...I guess I was a little busy or something, but my period...I think I'm late."

"Like how late?"

"I-I'm not sure," she stammers. "A few days? Maybe a week? I don't really keep track—"

My heart plummets to my stomach. "You're pregnant?"

"No," she says quickly. "I mean, I don't know."

"What do you mean, 'you don't know?'"

"I haven't taken a pregnancy test or anything," she explains. "I just know I'm late. And I was wondering if—"

"What the fuck, Teeny," I shoot back, my voice growing louder. This shit cannot be happening right now. Not right *fucking* now. "How could you do this to me?"

She starts to cry and a desperate sob breaks from her quivering lips. "Everett, I'm sorry."

She reaches for my hand, but I recoil. I'm so fucking angry. So pissed at my dad, at myself. I rise from the booth, and stand there, needing to put some distance between me and her.

Another sob cuts into the space between us. She inches closer to me. "Everett, please," she begs. "Please. Just sit down so we can talk."

"I have to go," I say angrily. My entire body starts to tense and spiral into a bulging knot of frustration, and I don't want to say something to Teeny that I'll regret. "I can't be here."

"Everett," she cries.

"I'm sorry, Teeny."

I don't remember getting to Jake's. I barely remember the four shots of Jameson I practically funneled down my throat within the hour I arrived and the bottles of beer I drank after. Even once I've slumped onto the couch in the living room, the TV playing some music video on MTV with the sound blasting through the surround sound speakers, my memory feels muddled in a foggy haze.

"Everett!" A high-pitched squeal, one that's overzealous and fake, grates through my ears. It sounds stretched, like there's four extra syllables to my name in addition to the given three.

I lift one eye wider, taking in a blurry figure with dark hair and a red dress, to see Angelica hover over me.

"Where's your girlfriend?"

A zap zings through my chest at the mention of Teeny. A garbled sound gurgles up my throat. Something like, "I don't know," though it sounds closer to, "*Ah uh no.*"

I feel hands on me, sloppy grazes against my shirt reaching across my chest to my shoulder. A thud of a head landing on my arm followed by giggles. It's so loud, I can barely make out anything aside from Angelica's wobbly laughs with her cheek pressed against mine. I smell the acrid scent of alcohol on her breath, and my stomach churns. I try to turn away, lifting my arms to shove at her, but all I do is flop my hands. By the time I've given up on my fight, my hands land on her bare thigh, and my fingers itch to create some distance between us.

My head feels like it's resting on a spring instead of my neck. The cushion behind me catches the back of my head as it lands with a soft thump. Everything starts to spin, and I feel like my insides are liquifying, making the alcohol spread all the way down to my toes. I don't think I've ever been this drunk.

But who the fuck cares. Who the fuck cares if I end up in the hospital, my stomach pumped with my mom by my side, realizing how much of a fucking disappointment I am. How much I've become my dad with an illegitimate child on the way. I'm going to be a fucking *dad*. Right alongside my own. The man who single-handedly ruined our family is going to share this experience with me with his own baby. How did things get so fucked up? How the fuck am I supposed to be a dad? Oh god, my child *and* my brother or sister are going to be the same goddamn age. They're going to grow up not knowing who's Dad and who's Grandpa. I feel sick just thinking about what our family dynamic will look like. All the judgy stares and whispered gossip about all of us. My dad, my mom, Teeny, our child. This is such a fucked-up situation.

And Teeny. I ruined her life. Forget her art, something that she's passionate about with her entire heart. Forget college, not just for me but for her too. I can't believe how I treated her. Leaving her in tears while she begged me to stay. I should've stayed. I should've held her and told her we'd figure things out. That we'd be okay as long as we stuck by each other. Regardless if this was a mistake, we'd make it work. Because I love her. I love her so fucking much, and if a surprise like this was the result of how much we love each other, then so be it.

There isn't a problem with me wanting to be with Teeny. The idea of spending the rest of my life with her, living in our own home while watching our baby grow, springs this sudden thrill to course through my body. Forget my dad and his affair. Forget all the shit my parents are going through. My priority is with Teeny and our baby.

Everything feels dark. In the flurry of my epiphany, I see flash images of our future. Bringing an infant home, gingerly moving the car seat from the car to a rented apartment somewhere north of San Diego. Somewhere close to home yet far enough that we have a sense of independence. Me working and juggling school, tired but focusing on the reward of coming home to my family every night. Teeny finding time to paint in the moments I carve out for her by taking on responsibilities at home, so she doesn't lose her zest for her art.

"What the fuck!" I hear a grating screech next to me. I start to sputter, ice cold water hitting my face and shooting up my nose. The darkness suddenly clears, a burst of cold and light crashing into me like a Mack truck.

I feel the heaviness of limbs over my chest and thighs, scrambling against me in a clumsy manner. My eyes pry open, and I see Angelica right next to me, her red dress darkened with water stains as she wipes away at it with her hands. I barely register her standing from the spot next to me and walking away. That's when I see Teeny standing over me, an empty cup dangling from her fingers.

Even in my drunken haze, my blurry vision obscuring not only my sight but my judgment too, all I see is how beautiful Teeny is. Her face is red, the anger making her cheeks flushed. Her hair is tied up in a messy knot, and she's swimming in my hoodie, and all I want to do is wrap my arms around her. I want to tell her how sorry I am and how badly I regret how I reacted to her news. I want to tell her about what happened with my dad so she'd understand and hopefully see how troubling it was for me to handle the news of our own possible pregnancy. I want to tell her that we'll go right now to take a pregnancy test, just so we can confirm her assumptions and celebrate instead of dwelling over all the scary things that come with this unexpected surprise.

I want to tell her that I love the name Daniel for a boy because it was my best friend's name in kindergarten, and the name is linked to so many happy memories for me. And last, I want to tell her that I can't wait to watch her become a mother. To see her stomach grow bigger knowing it's our baby in there while anticipating the day that I get to see her holding him or her.

But I don't say any of that. Instead, my mouth moves in slow motion when I say her name. "Teeny," I slur, barely lifting a hand.

Then she chucks something into my chest. My hand moves by reflex, catching it as it tumbles down to my stomach. I lift it up to my hand, using a monumental amount of strength to clear my head and register what I'm looking at.

"It's negative, asshole," I hear Teeny say icily.

She walks away, and I blink about twenty times before I realize that what I'm holding is a pregnancy test. One line waves at me through the little window, and my body suddenly aches. Every bone, every muscle feels like it's twisting and turning. When I look at where Teeny walked away, she's gone.

CHAPTER TWENTY-ONE

Teeny

NOW

THERE'S BEEN a cloud hanging over my head for the past few days. It isn't dark or menacing, but it's more just there. Gray and lingering, following me around like a bundle of balloons tied to my wrist. I'd been calling in a lot of my work, corresponding with my clients via email, making sure Roberta's first batch of furniture arrived at the hotel without a hitch. I returned to Allegra's gallery, unable to walk all the way to the back to see my painting, and purchased some pieces with her receptionist, linking my selections with Eric for his approval.

I took Sadie shopping for her dress for the wedding, the one she'd wear while she sang "Unchained Melody" accompanied by the baby grand piano Mina arranged to have at the reception. I listened to her practice and practice in her room, perfecting her already performance-ready voice to sound angelic. We were ready to celebrate yet another union within our family.

Picturing my brother and Mina swaying in the candlelight and the romantic ambiance of their rustic wedding brought on an entire onslaught of my past. There was so much of myself that I buried when I let go of the idea of me and Everett. Something in me died, snuffed there alongside those glimmers of hope I reserved for love. I convinced myself that love isn't real. That it's an illusion. Something for people's hearts to feel warm and fuzzy around. But the true ideology of love? It's all a lie.

But is it? Is love really a lie? Because if it is, what is Everett doing here? After all these years, why is he here if not for love? And if not for love, then what am I doing letting him back in?

I shove all those questions, swirling in my head like a torrent, aside as I pull to the curb in front of James's house. Sadie has a box of Sprinkles cupcakes on her lap, and she exits the car carefully as we both round the hood to walk up the driveway.

"Hey," James answers the door, a pink elephant plush in his hand and a look of confusion on his face. "What are you guys doing here?"

"I texted Kendall to see if we could stop by."

He opens the door wider to let us in. "Come on in," he says, eyeing the box in Sadie's hands. "Sophia just woke up."

We walk in, carefully tiptoeing through the hallway littered with baby things. A folded stroller, stacked diaper boxes, an activity table out of its original packaging with parts of it not yet completely built. As soon as we enter the living room, I catch Kendall leaning back on the sofa. She has Sophia resting on her chest, a burp cloth hooked over her shoulder, with her hand lightly rubbing Sophia's back.

"Hey," she calls softly as Sadie curls up to Kendall's side, her face inches from Sophia's. "Are those for us?"

Sadie hands her the cupcakes. "Yup. Can Sophia have some yet?"

Kendall laughs. "How about we start with some pureed carrots first." She looks at me over her shoulder. "You want some tea? Coffee?"

"Coffee sounds great."

She starts to stand, but James stops her. "I got it." She smiles gratefully at him, and James presses a kiss on Kendall's temple before walking into the kitchen.

"Can you get Sophia's bottle too please?" she calls after him.

"I'll see if he needs any help," I tell Kendall. "Still not sure if he can do two things at once."

"I heard that," I hear from the kitchen. I leave Sadie cooing at Sophia to follow my brother. "You take cream and sugar?"

"Yeah," I answer. I watch him reach into the fridge for a bottle of creamer, and I sit on one of the barstools surrounding the island. "Leo came by the other day."

"Yeah?"

I nod. "He mentioned you told him about Vegas?"

"Yeah," he answers, his focus on filling the coffee maker. "We went out for a couple of drinks, and it came up."

"Yeah, well, he got pretty upset."

His face twists in disapproval. "Why?"

"Because Everett was there."

"Oh my god. That's outrageous." I stay quiet, fidgeting with a silicone teether resting on the counter. "I mean, you two are married. He has nothing to worry about."

"You know, I had that same thought at one point," I say, a sarcastic undertone beneath my words.

He looks at me, pressing the brew button and letting the machine garble as the water inside heats. "Yeah, I know." He pauses, watching me with his hands braced on the counter. His lips twist to one side and his brow furrows. "I mean, he has nothing to worry about, right?"

I answer with more silence.

"Teeny, don't do this."

"Don't do what?"

"Don't use Everett to get back at Leo," he says, the tone in his voice annoyed as if he assumes I've already considered this.

"I'm not."

"Look, I've been trying to stay out of this because it's really none of my business," he says, that annoyance gone and in its place a voice of reason and genuine concern. "But if you're going to end it, then end it. Don't drag it out to punish Leo, and don't involve Everett."

263

"I'm not dragging it out, and I'm not punishing Leo," I argue. "But these things take time. A divorce isn't like online shopping. There's a process."

"So, you're going through with it? The divorce?"

I look away, my focus on the bumpy edges of the teether made for soothing irritated baby gums. "It's been over, James. This affair was just...It's not worth looking past. I don't have any fight left in me."

The kitchen starts to fill with the warm, chocolaty smell of the coffee dripping into the glass pot. "And Everett?"

My knee jerk reaction is to deny what he's insinuating. Even get upset that he'd question something that feels so absurd. But I realize how *un*-absurd his assumption is. "I don't know."

"Teen, what's going on?"

I shake my head, the sting of tears hitting the bridge of my nose.

"Did something happen with you and Everett?"

I don't know how to deny it, so I look at him just as the first tear trails down my cheek. He lets out a heavy sigh, showing how concerned he is for me. "Teeny," he says, his voice void of judgment. "I'm not opposed to this whole thing with Everett because you're married or whatever the fuck. I know what Leo did and...it's inexcusable. But Everett..."

I reach for a napkin and dab at the corner of my eyes, unable to stop the tears as they flow freely. I draw in a loud sniff, and I feel it in my chest. How much of my pain has resurfaced. How those old wounds never healed. They didn't even scab or scar. They're still fresh.

"Does he know?"

I shake my head. "I never told him."

"Teeny, what he did..." His voice trails. "And you were so damn young. I honestly don't think I would've let that shit go if Leo hadn't come around. But I did. Because Leo stepped in and he...he brought you back.

"I think you need to talk to Everett. He needs to know the truth."

I nod, unsure if I can even utter the truth to myself let alone to the man who's held on to the weight of my past for the last twenty years.

CHAPTER TWENTY-TWO
Everett
THEN

MY HEAD FEELS like it's about ten times its size. I don't even know how I made it to my bed. But somehow, I'm nestled on a soft surface surrounded by cushions and a thin blanket. Hopefully my mom didn't see me stumble home. But when I open my eyes, I realize I'm not in my room. I'm not even in my house. I'm still on Jake's couch, only without the haze of darkness and flickering lights and loud music, and it makes me feel low and regretful.

A tumble of empty cans and glass bottles clatter somewhere, and the sounds feel like a fighter jet flying over me. My head starts to pound as I sit up.

"Jesus," I mutter, my throat feeling like it's full of coarse desert sand.

"You all right there, Hayes?"

I twist my neck to look behind me but immediately regret it, my shoulder aching like hell from the distorted position it was in on Jake's couch. "What the fuck happened?"

"I have no idea," Jake answers, looking just about as bad as I feel. "I woke up to pee and found you here."

I scramble for my phone in my pocket to check the time. It's just after ten o'clock. "Shit!" I mutter. "I need to go." I stand to leave when something hard and plastic crunches under my shoe. I lift my foot to find a pregnancy test. Teeny's pregnancy test. I pick it up, further examining the dark line cutting across the little window, and last night comes flooding back to me. Teeny looking at me, her eyes filling with tears and this tangible hatred toward me. She's never looked at me like that. Like she wishes me dead while hoping I'd somehow survive her bid. And I just sat there, nailed to the sofa while she walked away.

I rush to my car, running a hand through my disheveled hair, and buckle in, racing back home. I park my car in my driveway, seeing my mom's car parked next to mine, and rush to Teeny's house.

I ring the doorbell and wait as patiently as I can, fidgeting with my keys and tapping my foot against the doormat. When the door finally opens, I see James on the other side.

"Uh, hi," I say awkwardly. "Is Teeny home?"

He eyes me warily. "She's in her room."

"Can I talk to her?"

He opens the door wider, and I rush past him, not bothering to appear calm. I take two steps at a time up the stairs to Teeny's room, knowing I'm probably breaking a rule by being up here. It looks like Teeny and James are the only ones home, and it brings my nerves down a notch knowing her parents aren't around.

When I reach her door, I find that it's open, left slightly ajar. I knock gently before pressing a hand to it. Teeny's there, roughly shoving some of her things into her backpack, and she watches me as I walk in. Whatever sad expression she had on her face sours into that hate and anger again.

"What do you want, Everett?" she asks coolly.

"Teeny," I say, inching toward her only to find that I suddenly feel unwelcome. "I'm so sorry."

"About what?" she asks, her hands moving angrily around her. "For getting drunk and cozying up with Angelica? For getting mad at me because you thought I was pregnant?" She stops what she's doing, turning to face me. She throws a blow to my chest, shoving

267

me a step back. "For blaming *me* because you thought I ruined your life?"

My hands loosely grip her wrists. My fingers trail her skin, skimming over her pulse point, but she pulls away before I can feel the beat of her heart. "All of it. I'm so sorry."

"I don't care." She zips up her bag and hooks it over her shoulder.

"Where are you going?"

"I have to go to Diana's," she tells me, her eyes trained on the door behind me. "We're working on a project for English that's due after spring break."

"Teeny, please," I plead. "Talk to me."

She chucks her bag on the floor, finally looking at me. It's then I see how much last night took a toll on her. Her eyes are puffy, swollen and red from a night's worth of tears. Her hair is all over the place, strands matted to her forehead, and she's not wearing my hoodie anymore. She's changed into something of her own, and of all the details of her appearance, that little bit hurts the most. "You hurt me so bad," she finally says, her voice wavering. "And you go and embarrass me like that."

My head hangs between my shoulders, so ashamed of my actions even as I acted in a drunken fog. "Teeny, I'm so sorry."

"You know what those girls said to me?" she asks, her eyes growing misty. "They told me that you finally got the girl you *really* wanted and led me right to where Angelica was practically straddling you. They shoved in my face that you cheated on me."

"I didn't cheat on you—"

"That doesn't matter!" she shouts. "That was so humiliating! I stood there, watching her touch you and throw herself all over you while you did nothing! All while I went and—" Her words are cut off by a sudden sob. "I went and got that pregnancy test by myself. I stood there while the cashier looked at me and judged me. And I took the test all by myself when all I wanted was for you to be there for me!" I reach for her to wipe at the tears now trailing down her face, but she leans away from me. "I needed you last night, but you..." She stops, her body sagging like she's exhausted. "I need to go. I already promised Diana I'd meet her."

"Teeny, please. Don't go."

"Just leave, Everett. I have nothing else to say to you."

Teeny brisks past me, and I don't stop her. When I hear the front door open and close, followed by the sound of her car starting, I leave her room. I awkwardly walk past James in the living room, giving him an uncomfortable nod, before walking over to my house.

When I see my mom in the kitchen, she's sitting there, staring blankly at a steaming cup of coffee. She looks up when I walk in, and her face shifts to confusion. "Did you just get in?" she asks, her voice hoarse.

I nod.

"Jesus, Everett," she says, somehow sounding even more exhausted than last night. "What the hell were you doing out all night? Were you with Teeny?"

"No." My answer is curt as I reach for the fridge for some juice.

It's quiet in our house, though the silence isn't in any way comforting. I move about the kitchen, my steps sluggish and weary, as I pull up a stool in front of my mom. Both of us sit there, the exhaustion evident in our posture and our slackened expressions. I don't know what to say to her. If I should ask her about my dad or what's going to happen moving forward. And I think she feels the same way about me, wondering why I'm in such a morose state as if my heart is as broken as hers.

"We're going back home."

I feel like I've been sucker punched. "What?"

My mom's grave and grim expression matches the level tone of her voice. But when she finally looks at me, all of that's swiped away. The formidable way she said we're leaving and the stone-like expression that said she means business. It's all gone as she looks at me, as if silently asking me if she's making the right decision. "We have to go back."

I start to panic. "Why? Mom, why do you want to go back?"

I see her hands start to tremble and just how badly her exhaustion is taking a toll on her. The dark circles around her eyes, her chapped lips and sunken cheeks, her disheveled hair and the same clothes she was wearing yesterday. She's been brewing over this. All night. She didn't get a wink of sleep, and she's come to this decision in the delirium of insomnia.

"I have to fix things. I have to talk to your dad and let him know that this was just a mistake."

"Mom, what are you talking about? He ch——"

"No, Everett!" she says harshly, shutting me down in an instant. "It was a mistake. It's my fault."

What the hell is she talking about? How is this whole situation her fault? I watch her as she convinces herself to take full responsibility for my dad's actions. I see it in the way her eyes shift as she says the words, an underlying shakiness that accompanies them. I can tell she's been repeating them to herself all night. I don't know how to dispute her at this point. I don't know if she'll even hear me, let alone let me get in a word through the fog of her misconstrued blame.

"I should've never come back here," she continues, her words not necessarily directed at me. "I gave him permission to be with someone else. Especially after he'd already done this, I should've known better."

I realize then that this woman isn't the same woman who raised me. The same woman who taught me to be confident and humble, always reminding me who I was and where I came from despite whatever challenges life threw in my direction. She would've never let me lose sight of who I was, no matter what. And she especially would've never let me shoulder another person's faults when I was clearly the victim.

Now, looking at her, I see how weak she is. She let my dad shrivel her down into this broken version of herself, willing to take the blame for the sake of her marriage.

"We're leaving tomorrow." Her voice is cold, and the iciness of it drains all the blood from my body.

"What?"

She stands from her seat and walks off up the stairs. I follow close at her heels. "I got a flight leaving first thing in the morning," she continues, not bothering to look me in the eyes as she tells me she's uprooting me once again. "Pack what you can, and I'll come back for the rest. Or I'll send someone."

"Mom, this is ridiculous," I plead. I start to feel clammy and shaky. I don't know what to do or how to convince my mom to change her mind. We can't leave. We just can't.

"No!" she shouts.

She turns to face me, a darkness cast over her features. It shadows the warm, loving woman who never raised her voice at me. Who used to laugh and play with me and hold me when I woke up in the middle of the night from a scary nightmare. "Everett, we are leaving. This is not up for discussion. I'm not going to stay here so you can stay out all night with your little friends while my marriage falls apart! You are just going to have to make this sacrifice!"

She ends her sentence by turning away and slamming the door behind her as soon as she walks into her room.

I'm dumbfounded. Completely speechless. I can't believe she'd say that to me. As if I'm some martyr in this whole mess, taking the brunt of everything like I'm being punished. As if she and I aren't the ones suffering after what my dad did.

I start to think of ways to work through this mess. How am I going to pack all of my things in less than twenty-four hours? And what about school? Am I just going back to my old school? Or finish out the year from home? My mom has to have thought about that before coming to this decision.

Or maybe...maybe it doesn't have to be this way. Maybe I can convince her to let me stay. She wouldn't have to worry about transferring schools, and it'll only be for another couple of months until I graduate. I'll be eighteen soon, in a little over a week, and I can be here on my own in this house. I can promise her I'll be good, be on my best behavior. I can finish out my senior year and go off to college like I've been planning. And maybe once I fix things with Teeny, we can talk about her joining me up north. She hasn't told me where she wants to go to school, and maybe we can have that discussion as soon as things settle at home.

I just need to talk to Teeny. Let her know what's going on so...I don't know. Maybe she can hold my hand through this? I can't do this without her. I need her on my side.

I just need to talk to her.

I've been sitting at the curb between mine and Teeny's house for the past two hours, waiting for her to come home, hoping I can get a minute with her. So I can tell her what's happening and my plan. We can figure this out as long as we have each other. We'll work through this.

My head jerks up when I hear a car pull into the cul-de-sac followed by the familiar rumble of the engine from the car Teeny and Josh share. She sees me as she pulls to a stop at the curb, and her eyes turn cold as she looks at me through the passenger window. I stand as she exits the car and hooks her backpack over her shoulder. She ignores me, beelining to her house, but I stop her.

"Teeny, can we talk?"

"I don't really want to talk to you," she says, her back turned to me.

"But you have to let me explain—"

"Everett," she interrupts, whipping around to finally face me. She has a hand cut across the space between us, her stance concise and unbending. "Look, I've been thinking, and maybe this is for the best. You're leaving for college in a few months. There's no way this would've worked."

Confusion starts to edge its way into every nerve ending in my body. My jaw twitches with the effort to not argue with Teeny, and my face transitions into a full scowl at her assumption. How could she think this? And how long has she thought this? This whole time, while I've been planning visits back to San Diego during long weekends and holidays in the fall, plotting the quickest route from Sacramento to her, and even looking up flights so we could make the most of my short visits, was she already thinking about ending things?

"Teeny, how could you think that?" I try to keep my voice calm and collected, wanting to make sure I stay as levelheaded as possible so we can figure out a way for me to stay, but I'm buzzing with the urgency and desperation to fix things. My chest feels like it's being compressed, making it hard to breathe, and my hands start to feel numb and clammy.

"You're going to have your own life up there, and you don't need an annoying girlfriend hundreds of miles away, calling you all the time and wondering where the hell you are."

"You know it's not like that." I focus on Teeny's eyes. Dark pits of chocolate with golden whiskey rings, and layers and layers of different shades. Mocha, chestnut, bronze, sepia. Even with the sadness and hurt cloaking them, they somehow ground me. Right here, between our homes and in her arms. I can't lose her.

Her lips purse and her chin trembles, evidence that she's holding back her tears. "I don't know if I can trust you."

"What are you talking about? Of course you can trust me."

She responds with silence, creating a barrier between us by crossing her arms.

Not knowing what else to say to convince her, I tell her, "I'm still me."

"Are you?"

"Of course," I plead, stooping down to meet her at eye level. "I still love you. I still want us to be together. I still want to make this work after I leave."

"I don't know if I want that anymore."

"Are you serious?" Everything evaporates. All of the plans I laid down for us, me staying here and finishing school so I can be near her, all of it revolving around my life with her. It disappears into thin air. She wants nothing to do with me.

Her lips pucker as she exhales a shaky breath. "I can't be here wondering if you're going to be hooking up with girls, going to parties, and getting drunk. I can't—I wouldn't be able to stand it if you..."

"I'd never hurt you."

"But you did."

"Teeny, it was a mistake," I tell her.

"And how many more mistakes are there going to be before we realize it isn't going to work?"

"So this is what you want?"

Everything about her body says yes. Her squared shoulders, her arms still braced over her chest, the firm line her lips are set in. But not her eyes. They tell a different story. *Fight for me*, they say. "Don't you think it's for the best?" she finally responds with a shrug, letting that uncertainty ring higher.

"No," I tell her. "No, I don't."

That speck of hope that glinted in her eyes begins to waver. They start to well with tears, and a moment passes where she considers it. My plea, my regret, my guilt and remorse. Her face softens as if she's going to break, letting me have that chance that I want with every fiber of my being.

But then it fades, the stone-like restraint reminding her of the night she had.

"Everett," she whispers. She closes her eyes, and a tear slips down her cheek. "I don't want to make this any harder than it needs to be. Please, just give me some space. Let me get over you and move on."

I stay quiet, letting her words echo and ring in the air. I watch as she turns away and walks inside, never looking back at me once.

CHAPTER TWENTY-THREE

Teeny

NOW

JAMES SAID I could leave Sadie with him. She could stay for dinner, watch a movie, keep Sophia entertained while he and Kendall set about their bedtime routine. He even offered to let her stay the night if I needed to. Just so I could get a moment alone with Everett.

I make it to the hotel at an easy pace. I'm not rushing, I'm not buzzing with anxiety in anticipation to see him. For the first time in a long time, my body just feels...ready. To walk away from my past. To close a chapter so I can finally move on.

As soon as I reach Everett's room, searching the marked numbers based on his instructions, I knock on the door. Even my knuckles rap with a calm hollow thump.

"Hey," Everett calls as soon as he sees me across the threshold.

"Hi."

He opens the door wider to let me in, and I walk past him, getting a hefty whiff of him. He smells clean, like a lavender scent, mixed with something spicy. Like aftershave. I find that his room isn't just a simple accommodation with a single king-size bed and the usual amenities, but more of a penthouse suite with a formal living room.

"You have all this space to yourself?"

He smirks. "Gets a little lonely sometimes." He's the embodiment of a lazy Sunday afternoon with his low hanging sweatpants and undershirt. There's a slight dampness to his hair, evidence that he either just got out of the shower or he'd done some strenuous activity. Though with his appealing eau de Everett fragrance wafting around him, it's likely the former.

I perch myself on the sofa, the soles of my white canvas shoes firmly set on the carpeted floor, and Everett sits across from me.

"Is everything okay?"

I nod, picking at one of the purposely slashed tears on my faded jeans. "I know I sounded really vague over the phone, but I needed to talk to you in person. I just felt like you deserved an...explanation? Or at the very least, more than just a cold shoulder after last week."

He nods too. "Okay."

"I think you've been giving me some space to think things over, and I really appreciate that," I continue. "It's given me time to think about what I want to say to you."

He stays quiet, though if he spoke, I feel the words, *"Tell me everything,"* would match the forbearing way he looks at me.

"What happened between us was...a little impulsive, I think."

His brow lifts and his forehead wrinkles. "Impulsive?"

"I feel like maybe we should've talked about things before we let it get that far."

"Yeah, I agree, but I don't regret it."

A small smile slips, and I don't know what it means. If I'm agreeing with him or if it's something more reassuring and appreciative. "So, I guess, I'm here to talk."

"Okay," he says again. His patience doesn't waver. And if it does, he's doing a damn good job of hiding it. He's sitting across from me, his posture completely open with his knees angled in my direction and his shoulders leaned forward to give me his full attention.

"I loved you," I say, my words spoken fondly. "I loved you with my entire heart. And when I was sixteen, I really thought I was going to spend the rest of my life with you. When you were planning for college and everything, I really wasn't scared because I knew we would figure things out, no matter how far away you'd be.

"I didn't expect things to turn out the way they did, and it happened really fast. Looking back, I think it was a lot to take on at such a young age."

We sit there, letting my words hang around us. They aren't big or scary, all the things we've been holding back for so many years. Instead, they're just there, waiting for us to sift through.

"I thought you'd come back," I add. "At some point, I thought you'd call me or something."

"I wanted to," he says, his voice sounding loud after his resigned stretch of silence. "Things went to shit with my parents, and after it settled, I wanted to come to you."

"Why didn't you?"

He shakes his head in a motion of uncertainty. "I don't know," he says, his gaze on his hands bracing his knees. "I know I was scared, but I couldn't get over it. I just felt like I'd let you down so badly, and I didn't know how to make things right. That whole pregnancy scare...I handled it so horribly. And when you told me to leave...you said you thought things would be better if we broke up, and I didn't know how to argue that after everything I did."

"I know," I say, the first of my tears starting to gather. "And a part of me thought you'd fight for me. I know what I told you, but I thought you would try to convince me to...change my mind."

"Would you have?"

Now it's my turn to be uncertain. "I don't know."

"Maybe I should've come back sooner," he says, his voice sounding more urgent now. "Maybe I should've at least called or something, but..." He stops talking, looking at me with so much sadness. "I didn't know how."

His words hit me like a warm balm. Something to soothe and ease the pain. I wasn't going through it alone. I wasn't the only one

277

suffering, spending night after night crying in my bed. He was going through the same heartbreak I was. And I know it's now or never.

"I was."

His face turns soft with concern and confusion. "Was what?"

I swallow the ball lodged in my throat. "I was pregnant."

I see it the moment my words hit Everett like a wrecking ball. I see it in the way his face falls slack and his eyes grow blank. Even his breaths that were coming in and out of him at a steady pace start to become choppy and ragged.

"What?" he whispers.

"Ye-yeah," I start to explain. "I don't know if the first test was faulty or maybe my body wasn't ready to test positive yet. At least that's what the doctor said. And um...James was home for a long weekend, and I started getting really sick. My parents were out of town. They went to Florida to see my Aunt Annabelle. That really eccentric one with the red hair and tattoos. She had all those parakeets in her living room. She was throwing a party for an anniversary or a birthd—anyway," I say, interrupting my rambling. "That's not important.

"James got really worried when I kept saying I felt dizzy and weak. And he said I looked so pale. He took me to the emergency room and um, yeah. He was there when they told me."

His body slumps to the floor, on his knees like his weight gave out from underneath him. "Wh-what," Everett stutters. "Where..."

"I didn't—I took care of it." I say the words boldly, my heart pounding in my chest. "James—he took me in, made sure everything went okay. Luckily, I didn't need my parents to consent for it. I guess that was a plus.

"I tried to wait until I told you first. I went to your house, but you weren't there. I wanted to call you, but I thought it wasn't the kind of thing you say over the phone, so I waited and waited. After a few weeks, I saw a For Sale sign go up in your front yard.

"You never came back, and I just couldn't do it. I couldn't have a baby all on my own." I feel...ashamed and chastened and even guilty.

The same way I felt when I told Leo after he'd pressed on why James told him that my ex-boyfriend was a "sack of shit." But Everett doesn't look at me the way Leo did, eyes sifting through the dozens of responses to make sure he doesn't sound judgmental or pious. Everett looks at me as if his entire world is falling apart.

"No, no," he starts to mutter. "No. That can't—" His chest starts to heave, his back and shoulders moving up and down to help him move the air in and out of his lungs. His fingers grip his temples, and he lowers his head toward his own lap. His hands shake violently as he curls into himself like he's taking shelter. Those pants begin to sound desperate, and it starts to scare me.

"Everett," I say, landing on the floor on my knees right in front of him. "Everett, what's wrong?" I put my hands on his arms, and the trembling skates along his skin, making his entire body rattle.

His breathing doesn't calm, and his eyes look frantic as he searches the ground below him. I shake his shoulders, trying to get his attention, but his entire body is locked. It's like he's in his own little bubble of panic, and I can't seem to get him out.

"Everett," I say his name again firmly. "Look at me."

He doesn't look at me. Almost as if he's still bouncing around in that bubble, and I need to catch him so I can finally bring him back down. But I don't know how. I used to. At one point in my life, I knew how to ground him. How to make him realize that he just needed to put one foot in front of the other and walk through life while holding my hand, but I haven't been that person in a really long time. I don't know how to be that person again. And the realization that I'm no longer that person, and that quite possibly he doesn't have anyone to ground him like I used to, makes the same panic in Everett's eyes spread through my own body.

"Everett!" I shout. I grip his face and urge him to look at me, desperately calling his name and forcing his eyes on me. "Please! It's me. I'm here. Please, just look at me!"

I see a small nod bring him back to me. His eyes finally focus on mine, and something in him clicks. I'm here. I'm here to bring him back down. To ground him to something solid instead of feeling like he's drifting away.

"Baby," he cries softly. "No, no, no..."

"I'm here," I whisper, making sure to keep my eyes on his. I pull him close to me, cradling his head against my shoulder and letting his breathing even out. His hands start to move, first hesitantly, and then with more assurance. But it's still cautious in the way he makes sure I'm okay with it before getting closer. He starts at my hips, his fingertips moving over me like he's making sure I'm here, and then they wrap around my back. He encircles his arms around me like he's holding onto me for dear life. And then it becomes desperate. He grasps for me, his fingers clawing at my shirt like he's trying to catch me, but I keep slipping through his fingers. And when his hands finally find their place, like an anchor being dragged across the bottom of the ocean only for it to finally find purchase on a rock or some other solid part of the earth, he calms. I feel his body sag against mine, and his breaths start to even out.

"It's okay," I whisper against his temple.

"Teeny..."

"I'm okay now." I sound sad and scared and completely unsure, but it doesn't matter how I feel. I need Everett to know that I'm okay. He needs to know that I'm okay. I couldn't live with him living like this. Worried about me when he should be searching for his own footing so he could finally find a place to land.

He pulls away and looks at me. "I'm so sorry."

My throat tightens at the sound of his voice. "It's okay, Everett," I tell him as I start to cry. "I'm okay now."

"I'm so sorry." He grips my face in his hands. "Baby, I'm so sorry."

I force a smile, though it's wobbly and faint. "It's okay," I repeat through a shaky voice. "It's okay."

"I'm so sorry," he says again. "I should've been there."

"It's okay."

"You went through that all alone." He places a hand over my heart, and I don't know why, out of all the reactions and emotions he's working through, this is what breaks me. It's as if he's surveying that damage. After all these years, he's looking at the wreckage only to find that it's no longer reparable.

"It's okay. It's okay." I repeat it, over and over again. And I don't even know if I believe it. If, after all these years, I'm still mourning over something that could've been. But I have to be. I have to be okay with it. I have Sadie, and my life, and so much more that I wouldn't change a single thing for, and for all of that, I have to be okay.

He starts to kiss my face. On my cheek as the tears pour, on my chin as if he's catching them before they fall into the space between us, on my forehead, soothing away whatever guilt he's held onto all these years.

"It's okay," I say one more time.

"I should've been there."

I don't know how long we've been lying here on the couch with our bodies pressed against each other, but I can tell the sun is slowly setting outside. I see the orange glow mix with the purple haze of dusk streaming in from the floor-to-ceiling windows. Everett's fingertips graze my arm, moving in slow, drowsy strokes while my arm rests lazily across his stomach. Our legs are loosely tangled around each other, and this feels like the most carefree I've been in a long time.

We've been talking on a random tangent, saying things on our minds as they pop up without any direction or path. I ask him about his mom's new husband. He asks me to tell him about Sadie's birth, like how long I was in labor and who she looked like when she came out. He chuckles when I tell him she looked like Hasbro came out with a russet potato model of a Cabbage Patch Doll. And I giggle when he tells me about his mom's sixtieth birthday when his stepdad surprised her with a new puppy who chewed through her favorite pair of cowboy boots.

"Daniel."

I nuzzle my nose against his chest. "Hmm?"

"If it was a boy, I wanted to name him Daniel."

I look up at him, turning my face to see his gaze is fixed on the recessed light fixtures on the ceiling. He finally looks at me, those deep brown eyes melancholy and mournful.

"When you told me you weren't pregnant after all, I was a little disappointed," he continues. "I mean, a part of me was relieved because we were kids ourselves, but I started planning this future for us. Moving into a small one-bedroom apartment just outside of San Diego, somewhere where your parents and my mom wouldn't meddle and let us have our own lives. And I got excited to see you with a big ol' pregnant belly."

"But you..."

"I know I was upset," he says, explaining himself. "My dad...he cheated on my mom. Again. And he got this woman pregnant. I kept thinking how I'm no better than my dad. That I couldn't be responsible enough to avoid an unwanted pregnancy, and how badly I'd let my mom down. But after I got over that initial shock that my own kid and my dad's baby were going to be the same age, I started to realize how much I loved you. How this meant we could watch each other become parents, and that there'd be this little baby that's half you and half me."

"Why didn't you tell me? About your dad?"

He shakes his head. "I was so embarrassed. He'd obviously not learned his lesson. Turned out that the woman was just trying to blackmail him, and there was no baby at all. And my mom...she was so desperate to make things work. She kept saying it was all her fault, that she threw him into the arms of his mistress. She tried so hard to make it work. That's why we went back home. She...she thought by going back, he'd realize what he was missing."

"I'm sorry," I say softly, my cheek pressed against him. "I'm sorry you went through that alone. And your mom...I know it couldn't have been easy on her either."

"I guess we both needed each other." He pauses before adding, "I had my first panic attack in college. I was walking to class. I was a little late and rushing. At first, I thought I was just winded from walking too fast or something, but then I felt like...I wasn't ever going to catch my breath. It felt like I was dying, and I was vividly aware of it.

"I saw a doctor. I thought I was getting asthma or something, and they told me I should talk to someone. Like a therapist."

"When's the last time it happened?"

"About six years ago," he answers calmly. "I've been getting pretty good with working through it before it gets out of hand." After another short pause, he adds, "Josh doesn't know, does he?"

"How did you know?"

"He wouldn't have asked me to come if he knew," he says. "He wouldn't have forgiven me."

"James did."

"Yeah," he says morosely. "But it's different. Josh was one of my best friends."

"Do you regret coming? Reopening our past like this?"

"Teeny." His hand is cupping my face, forcing me to look at him. "I came back for you. Whatever past you want to bring up, I came to face it."

"But you knew I was married..."

"Yeah, I knew."

"And you still came?"

"I had to see you," he says hoarsely.

I don't know how to feel or what to think. He did exactly what I wanted, just twenty years too late. After I've moved on. After I've lived an entire lifetime. Built a home with someone else when I desperately wanted it to be him at one point.

He's here for me, right when my life hit an unexpected crossroad, leaving me confused and uncertain. But what if I decided to let

Everett in? What if him coming back right now was for a reason? Those questions and all the wrong in my life swirl like a big scary tornado in my head, and I feel like the air around me is being siphoned out of the room. Facing this, my past, my marriage, my future, feels suddenly daunting, and I just want to step away from it. Out of sight, out of mind feels like the perfect solution right about now.

I start to push away from him and sit up, and he follows. "I should go. I left Sadie with James."

"Yeah." He sounds reluctant. Like he wants to convince me to stay but isn't sure if it's allowed.

I stand and walk to the door with Everett close behind me. When I reach the door, I turn to face him. "Thank you for...letting me tell you, I guess."

"Teeny, you don't have to thank me."

I nod. "I know things are really complicated. For me, for us. And it's all really confusing to me."

"I know."

"Okay."

"Teeny." I look at him, feeling so lost and scared. "I'm here," he says, his eyes soft and gentle. "I know it took me a really long time to come back, but I'm not going anywhere."

My fingers find his hand, tracing over the wrinkles lining his knuckles and the bumpy ridges of his veins. He lets me, giving me a moment to study the hands that used to touch me without permission. With his hand in mine, I look up at him, wishing I could find more than just the solemn look on his face. Maybe answers.

I expect him to do something. Anything that'll help those confusing fitful thoughts to become quiet and hushed, but he doesn't. Instead, he gently dips his head to place a small, gentle kiss at the top of my head before opening the door for me, and I'm left feeling bereft.

"I'll see you at the wedding," I say softly as I turn away to leave.

"See you at the wedding."

CHAPTER TWENTY-FOUR
Everett
NOW

I NEVER THOUGHT about having kids. It didn't feel like something that was meant for me, and I never really met anyone I could picture that life with. Weekend trips to the aquarium, after-school pickups, coaching the local youth basketball league, having make-believe tea parties in a room decorated in glitter and purple.

If the possibility of that life ever scraped my mind, it would've only been with one person.

Teeny was pregnant. With my child. And whatever path she chose for her future, that baby wasn't a part of it. And neither was I. Not because she had a choice in the matter, but because I chose for her. I left and never came back. No matter what I do, no matter how hard I try to prove to Teeny that I should've been there, that I should've known, it won't change the fact that the trajectory of my life changed the moment I left.

What if I was meant to be a father? Even at seventeen with nothing but our love for each other to fuel the rest of our lives.

I'm not usually a "what if" type of thinker. I make decisions based on reasonability and the likelihood of an advantageous outcome. I don't tend to look back and second guess my decisions, wondering if I had chosen a different path, would it have led to a more favorable result. It's gotten me this far in life, and to be completely honest, I've gotten pretty far.

Except with Teeny. I've spent the last twenty years wondering what if with her. What if I came back? Without my parents or the issues that tied me to them, but on my own. What if I realized sooner that I needed Teeny in my life? Instead of working through the heaviness of my anxiety on my own, those panic attacks, the long drawn out therapy sessions making me wonder what the fuck was wrong with me, all of it taking years and years for me to finally realize that I just needed the only person in the world who could ground me. I spent the last twenty years skimming the surface, hoping something would finally bring me back to a place where I felt solid. Where I felt like I could function without feeling like I was going to catapult into space and never find my footing.

All of those what ifs crashed into me the second Josh called me. His voice, full of nostalgia and genuine happiness for our reconnection, tethered me to something. He pulled me in until I finally found Teeny again. Now that I'm here, I don't care about all the what ifs. All I want is for Teeny to be back in my life.

My phone rings on my bed, right on top of the goose-down covers rumpled from a restless night's sleep, jolting me back to my hotel room.

"Hello?" I answer, recognizing the number from my old office back in Seattle.

"Everett," I hear on the other end, the deep voice cautious yet somehow impatient and stern even with just the sound of my name. It's Victor Storm, the executive chairman at InnoDex. A.k.a. the board of directors's head honcho. "How are you?"

"I'm good," I answer. While his name may sound like a fictional superhero, he's anything but a child's comic book character come to life. In fact, I don't think he's ever even flipped through a comic book or gone to see the latest Marvel movie with his commitment to his work. He has a no-nonsense attitude about a lot of things and is persuasive and direct in the boardroom, making me that much more wary about this call.

"Good."

"Victor," I say cordially, regarding him with an air of modesty. "Unless you're calling to borrow my place in Lake Tahoe again, I believe we've already said everything we need to say to each other."

He offers a good-natured chuckle, letting some of that heedfulness dissipate in me. "Just hoping I could change your mind."

I shake my head. "I've already made my decision," I tell him for what feels like the hundredth time.

"I understand," he answers, his voice still hopeful. "But we still haven't filled your position. And replacing you is no easy task."

"I'm sure you'll manage."

"Yes," he agrees. "I'm sure we will. But—"

"I need to take some time to figure things out," I tell him, hoping it's enough of an explanation as to why I decided to leave after six years with the company with practically zero notice, citing "personal reasons" in my resignation letter. As bittersweet as our conversations are, and while I appreciate the sentiment of his calls, it makes the words difficult to say each time I have to decline his offer.

"Well, don't expect us to give up just yet. I'll call you again soon."

"Maybe give it an extra week next time. Give me some time to miss your voice."

He chuckles again before hanging up.

It wasn't a decision I made very soundly. In fact, it happened overnight. After Josh called, we chatted for hours. Catching each other up on the last twenty years. Like my dad's retirement four years ago after he took a coaching job in Florida. Or that he'd met the love of his life and wanted me to be a part of their special day. I tried to stay composed when he brushed over the details that involved his family. Like that Andrew, the perpetual baby of the family, is still spending his days partying like he's some frat boy. Or that his nieces are the stars of the family, something he hopes to add to in the near future. And then there was Teeny. Teeny who'd become a wife and mother. Who moved on and had the life I repeatedly thought about over the years. Come to find out, it could've all happened with me.

It was a rash move, but after all this time, all I could think about was going back home. And when I approached the board of directors at InnoDex, I was surprised at how naturally the words came out of my mouth. It might have been the coincidence of Eric, a fellow UC Davis alumni, reaching out to me a month prior, asking me about property management and hospitality experience, and whether or not I had any interest in investing in said property. Or even the idea of going back to a place that held too many memories. But deep down, I knew it was for Teeny. Just the idea of seeing her, even though she was happily married. Or so I thought.

And now, here I am, the day before Josh and Mina's wedding, ready to begin the festivities with their rehearsal dinner. It isn't long until I'm dressed and ready, walking through the lobby of El Cielo and to the outdoor patio offside to the pool. There's an expansive view of the ocean, the string lights above the strategically placed tables fighting against the setting sun and floral arrangements that make the space look like its own secret garden.

When Mina and Josh were looking into local restaurants to hold a casual rehearsal dinner, just close friends and family, mostly members of the wedding party, I offered the hotel. I told them I'd handle the details, the food and drinks and set up. As a wedding gift, and in part, to thank Josh for bringing me back, though he doesn't know how heavily he contributed to that minor detail.

When I step outside, I see most of the hired staff still setting up. Placing wineglasses on the tables, arranging the last of the floral centerpieces, setting up the bar area near the pool. And in the corner of the outdoor area, near the lounge chairs and patio heaters, I see Teeny. Her back is to me, facing the ocean ahead of her, and her hand is wrapped over her shoulder as the breeze picks up her hair. She doesn't hear me approach her, so I'm careful with my steps, making sure I don't startle her, but she knows I'm here anyway.

"It was a girl." Her voice is so quiet and low, I barely understand what she's saying. Until she turns to me with a smile so sad, it's nearly void of life. "I wasn't supposed to know because it was so early and...but the tech was there with her up on that little screen, and she asked me if I wanted to know. She wasn't even a hundred percent sure, but she started pointing things out and—

"I almost changed my mind," she continues. "Thought about calling you or even doing it on my own. But then I couldn't. And I spent the last twenty years hating you because of it. Because I couldn't call you and tell you. Because I had to go through all of it on my own. Because I loved you so much and you—" Her words are cut off by a soft sob. I want to hold her, run my hand over the curves of her back, and tell her how sorry I am. But my body's frozen. The guilt of hurting Teeny starts to wind down my body, keeping my feet planted, and I don't know what to do. I don't know how to fix this, how to make things right with the woman I love. "I don't know how to trust you again. I don't even know if I should, but I feel like...I want to."

I reach out to her, hoping to soothe some of this ache. But she recoils. It's subtle in the way her shoulders lean back and her arm crosses her chest. I know this isn't an opening to comfort her. It's simply my time to hear what I've done.

She lightly dabs a fingertip to the corner of her eye and looks at me. "They're going to be here soon," she says hoarsely.

I nod and turn to walk away, but Teeny surprises me when she touches me. Her fingertips sweep across my jaw, cupping it gently. She doesn't say anything but just looks at me with the same smile I've memorized. The one with the small dip in the middle and the corners pointing up like little spears. And those teeth that press lightly into the fullness of her bottom lip. I can't believe this is the same woman I fell in love with twenty years ago. The same woman I haven't stopped loving.

My hand reaches for hers, my thumb running over her wrist where I feel the murmur of her pulse. It's steady and calm, just like her eyes looking at me with so much pain and hope. And I realize then that I can't give up. Not now.

I turn my head to kiss the inside of her palm just as we're interrupted by the clatter of footsteps and excited voices. We step apart from each other at the same time.

"Everett!" I hear Josh's stunned voice call my name. "Are you kidding me?" He has his hands outstretched in front of him and Mina at his side, her mouth open in shock as she takes in the scene.

"I can't believe you did all this," Mina says with a grateful smile. She reaches Teeny, giving her a quick squeeze. "Where's Sadie?"

"She's coming with James and Kendall," Teeny tells her. "I came a little early to check on some things here."

"This is amazing," Josh adds, facing the ocean view. "Thank you, Everett." He shakes my hand, patting a hand on my shoulder.

I nod a simple acknowledgment for his gratitude. "You guys want a drink?" I look to the bar, an attendant waiting patiently behind a neat row of bottles. We walk over as a group and I order a round, opting for the Patrón as Josh and Mina nod in approval. "To start off the celebrations," I tell them, distributing a round of shot glasses filled to the brim.

Teeny takes one, looking at me with a contradictory smile, marked with a small smirk and disapproving shake of her head. "What did I say about hard liquor?"

"Come on, Teeny," Josh interjects. "I'm getting married."

A small eye roll and Teeny raises her glass in the air, joining us.

"Cheers to...the married life," I say, smiling fondly between Mina and Josh.

Josh clinks his glass to mine. "And to old friends."

"To old friends." I tilt my glass back, keeping my eyes on Teeny as she takes a grimacing gulp. "You good?" I ask with a laugh.

She nods, though the sour contortion on her face says otherwise. She throws her hand in my direction, her thumb and pointer finger making a little circle with an a-okay sign. "Superb."

More people start to enter the space, the rest of the wedding party and friends and family members. James enters with his wife and Sadie following close behind, a baby attached to her hip. They join us, James ordering two glasses of wine for him and his wife. Sadie reaches Teeny's side where she takes the baby from her with absolute glee.

"This is Sophia," she tells me, running the back of her index finger on the baby's bulbous cheek. She places a soft kiss at the side of Sophia's head, and my heart flip flops at the sight of Teeny with the baby. Her motherly instincts adjusting the adorably small yellow dress while smoothing the fine strands of her hair away from her face.

"Hi," I say sweetly, waving a hand in front of her. Sophia reaches for my thumb, firmly gripping it in her fist, and she starts to bring it to her mouth.

"Oh!" Teeny exclaims happily, prying Sophia's death grip away from my hand. "You want to hold her?"

I hesitate. "I don't think I've ever held a baby before."

"It's okay," Teeny encourages. "I'll make sure you won't drop her."

"Jesus, I was worried she'll start crying. Now I gotta worry I might drop her?"

She giggles just as Sophia extends her hands toward me, her chubby fingers pointed in my direction. "There's no going back now."

I take baby Sophia, letting her bottom rest firmly on the crook of my arm. She plays with the lapel of my suit jacket, her focus on the hemmed edges like she's examining it for defects, and without any warning, she rests her head on my shoulder, patting a hand at my chest. Teeny watches me, placing her hand on Sophia's back with wonder at how easily I slipped into the role as an expert baby carrier. "See? Total natural."

Teeny looks at me, and I know we're thinking the same thing. How this could've been us at one point. With a little girl of our own.

One who would've had her eyes and smile, and hopefully something of mine. Like my attachment to her mother.

"We should take our seats," she whispers, her head dipped low, watching baby Sophia slowly doze off in my arms.

Teeny walks to the tables, and I follow, moving about carefully while balancing the baby in my arms. James and his wife have already found seats, Sadie staying close by, and Teeny finds her own seat at the same time.

"It looks like Sophia found a new friend," James's wife comments, the two watching as I sway side to side to avoid waking Sophia up. "Do you need me to take her?" she offers.

"I'm good."

A cool breeze picks up, and she reaches for a blanket, walking toward me and draping it over Sophia's shoulders. She shifts, almost waking while I hold the blanket against her so it doesn't blow away.

"I'm Kendall, by the way," she says quietly as to not wake the baby. "You must be Everett."

"Nice to meet you."

"Let me know if you get tired," she adds. "She might be small, but twenty pounds can get heavy really fast."

"I will," I say with a chuckle. "Thank you."

Kendall looks at James with a small slump of relief and a satisfied smile, but James doesn't reciprocate. Instead, he looks at me, a wary look of uncertainty and mistrust on his face. I don't know how to say sorry to him without saying sorry. For hurting someone he cares about while taking the entire brunt of the situation I put Teeny in. He saw every detail unraveling in real time. Every tear, every cry I didn't answer.

Dinner moves along. Sophia wakes up and cries for her mom, and my hands are free. I sit around a table that consists mainly of the wedding party. Teeny sits across from me, Sadie close by her side as she makes periodic attempts to gain Sophia's attention perched on Kendall's lap.

"In case I haven't said it yet," Josh announces to the table over slices of strawberry cheesecake and chocolate lava cake distributed among the crowd. "Everett put this whole dinner together. So we should all thank him."

He's actually said this multiple times, attributing the success of tonight's dinner to my connections to the hotel, and it makes me rather timorous with all of the attention on me.

"Please," I protest, shaking my head with a grateful smile. "It's really not a big deal."

Josh stands, clinking his spoon against the glass tumbler in his hand to get everyone else's attention. The low rumble of chatter stops, every pair of eyes on the groom.

"I just wanted to take a moment to thank you all for coming tonight," he says, his voice echoing off the side of the building. "A lot of people don't know the story about how I proposed to Mina, and I guess now's the best time to tell everyone how it went down.

"Mina turned me down."

Laughter fills the air at the same time Mina takes Josh's hand and places a comforting kiss on the back of his hand.

"She told me, 'Ask me again when you mean it.' I guess asking in a spur of the moment while we were covered in strawberry smoothies after a mishap with my blender didn't help. But the thing that Mina didn't know was, I knew I wanted to marry her by our second date. We were sharing a hazelnut waffle at Marie's, and I noticed how she saved the last piece for me. And she listened to all of my basketball stories like I was talking to her about Ryan Gosling."

Another round of laughter.

"Ryan doesn't hold a candle to you, baby," she coos in his direction.

"Say that again when you're watching *La La Land*." He lets the laughter die down before adding, "Mina is my soulmate in every way possible. I would choose her in every lifetime, and I can't wait to live the rest of this one so we can continue on in the next." Josh raises his glass at the same time as everyone else, and Mina stands to kiss him.

A round of claps and cheers fill the air, and I catch Teeny's eyes from across the table.

It suddenly feels like this is the next lifetime Josh was talking about. After having failed so miserably at the first, I've landed right in front of this one. This second lifetime where I learned from my mistakes. One where I choose Teeny over and over again, and we get to see this play out between us. And I can't even begin to imagine a lifetime where I don't choose Teeny.

"I can't believe I never thought to learn how to tie a bow tie."

I chuckle, my focus zoned in on Josh's Adam's apple where I'm working the knot through the loop to make sure it's even and secure. "I don't think very many people know how to tie a bow tie."

"You do," Josh points out.

"Yeah, well, I've been to my fair share of events and shit, so." He scoffs just as I finish adjusting the ends of the bow tie and give his shoulder a pat. "Look at that. Now you look like you belong on the top of a cake."

"Thanks."

He turns, looking at the mirror placed strategically so we're sitting under the perfect lighting for this time of day. Just outside the window veiled with sheer curtains, lies the expansive view of the coastal vineyard where Josh and Mina are having their wedding. Myself, Josh, James, and Andrew have been confined to this room until we're given the go-ahead for the ceremony, and with the antsiness of the bride and groom's big day, we're all eager to get things going.

"You ready?" I ask, smoothing a hand over my jacket to dust off any residual dust after running a lint roller over pressed lapels.

"Yep." Josh leads the way, all of us following at his heels as he exits the room and maneuvers down hallways to the foyer leading outside.

We're ushered to a canopy set up for the wedding party where we get a glimpse of the guests waiting patiently for the ceremony to begin. I have no idea where Teeny is, though she's most likely with Mina and the rest of the bridesmaids. And even though she has her own duties as a member of the wedding party, I can't help but search for her, hoping to get a glimpse of her before we stand on either side of the altar.

Before I can track her down, the processional music starts. It begins with the brighter chords of a violin, followed by the lower tenor of a cello. We step out, following Josh with his mom's arm hooked through the crook of his right arm with his dad matching his steps to his left. I trail last with Andrew and James ahead of me, and we're finally waiting for the rest of the wedding party to enter.

I know the star of the evening is the bride. With her extravagant dress and meticulously planned out hair and makeup, it's a title every bride deserves. But right now, all I can think of is Teeny. She steps out behind the rest of the bridesmaids in her stunning green dress, and she looks achingly beautiful. She smiles at someone in the crowd, adding a small wave of recognition, and something tugs at my chest. It feels like my past. Like a thread where one end started twenty years ago and the other end is wrapped around my heart, reminding me of what we had. The nights spent huddled under the covers in my room, wishing for time to stand still so she wouldn't have to leave me. The small moments in the hallways or in class where we glanced at each other, like we were exchanging a secret. And all those times I found myself with Teeny holding me down, letting me know I was so much more than the fear and trepidation that bundled my life into what it used to be. I'm not whole without her. I was broken pieces before her, all those fragments being swept along with the barely there will to focus on my future. She put me back together. And I broke us up, making those shattered pieces irreparable. Until now. Somehow, I'm learning how to glue myself back together.

The sounds of the wedding sound muffled, my attention solely focused on Teeny. She stands at the other side of the altar where my view of her is obscured by the ceremony at hand. Next thing I know, Josh is dipping Mina in a dramatic kiss with the cheer and laughter spurring on a longer-than-necessary kiss.

We make our exit out of the ceremony, the bridesmaids and groomsmen linking arms to walk the same path of the aisle, and I realize that I'm paired up with Teeny.

"Hi."

"Hi," she responds softly. She smiles at me before hooking her hand over my arm, and all I want to do is veer her away from all the people just to get a moment alone with her. I want to ask her about her day, what she had for breakfast, and how she spent her morning getting ready. I want to take her on a long walk along the vineyard, searching for secluded corners where I can just listen to her talk.

We walk while I keep my eyes on her, ignoring the people slowly filing out of the rows of folding chairs, and once we're at the end of the aisle, it's a flurry of pictures. We're guided away from the guests and enticing cocktail hour, toward the scenic area of the vineyard where we spend the next hour posing for pictures.

"You look beautiful," I whisper to Teeny, my hand gently resting on her lower back as we pose for what feels like the hundredth time.

"Thank you," she responds, her words coming out through a gritted smile.

I let my thumb smooth over the soft material of her dress, not realizing I'm doing it until it's already done, and Teeny looks up at me. "You don't look too bad yourself."

I smirk. "I tried."

She smooths her hand over my jacket, adjusting the boutonniere pinned to the lapel, and we look at each other. Our gazes lock and smiles widen, and just as I dip my head to tell her green is definitely her color, we're interrupted by an overly exaggerated "ahem." Teeny and I turn our heads to the photographer, who's giving us an impatient look like that of a parent who's had to repeat themselves more than once to their child.

"Can the both of you step about half a step to your right?" Her impatient voice matches the awkward tensions surrounding us. I get a few curious glances from Josh and Mina, wondering what the holdup is. And I get another glance, this one much more narrowed and concerned, from James.

Teeny and I follow suit, using the positions of the other bridesmaids and groomsmen as our guide, and discipline ourselves like young children in a classroom: with a lot of effort and small slip-ups of stolen smiles.

This feeling, the covertness of our smiles and whispers, the moments hidden beneath the surface where we think no one can see, feels like we're kids again. Like we're sitting in the library, our elbows brushing up against each other and our pencils scribbling notes across a shared table while we talk in voices barely above a whisper.

I feel high. Off champagne, cake, and life. I feel like I'm floating on a big fluffy cloud, the shimmery glow of candlelight creating a halo effect on everyone. And then there's Teeny. She has the same glow as everyone, made brighter with her smile and laughter, and she looks like an angel, flitting around like a dream.

I've been keeping my distance, though it hasn't stopped me from catching glimpses of her throughout the night. As she showers Sadie with praise for her performance. As she embraces her family members, her grandparents especially, over glasses of wine and the delicious four-course meal. As she too steals glances at me from across the room with consciously aware looks and shy smiles.

After the three-tier cake has been cut and the wedding music has transitioned into something less raucous and more placid and tender, I find Teeny.

"Could I trouble you for a dance?"

She'd been sharing a laugh with Grace, who she looks at as if requesting permission, which Grace grants with a subtle nod.

"Make sure to have her back by midnight," she says as Teeny takes my hand.

I smile gratefully at Grace, appreciative of her approval as Teeny's friend and someone who'll always have her best interest. "Yes, ma'am."

Teeny giggles as I lead her to the dance floor. It's fairly empty, those who'd been involved in a vigorous "Cha Cha Slide" dance now taking a breather, and it feels serene with Teeny's hand loosely gripped in mine and my hand pressed to her back.

"She must like you," she says, a smile dancing on her lips. "I thought you'd have to fight her before she let me go."

"I'm easy to like," I tell her, ducking my head so my words brush over the shell of her ear.

"Debatable." I give a small pinch to her waist, and she squirms in my arms. It's fluid, how she moves with me. How she turns her face at the same time I bring our joined hands to the small space between us. My thumb runs lazy strokes over her wrist, feeling the slow steady thumps of her heartbeat. "You know this is the first time I've danced with you."

"No," I argue, a rise of perplexity causing my brow to furrow.

She nods, a smug look of incontrovertibility on her face. "Prom wasn't really what I thought it was going to be."

My heart falls, realizing all the moments I missed out on because I wasn't there to be a part of them. "Would it make it any better if I tell you...I had some pretty big plans for your first prom?"

"Did you?" she asks, skepticism written all over her face in the way her brow shoots up and her smile turns cheeky.

"I did."

"Well, tell me, Hayes. What were these plans?"

"A limo."

"That's a good start."

My forehead meets hers. "Dinner at a fancy restaurant."

"With dessert? Something of the chocolate variety?"

"Of course."

Her eyes close and a shallow exhale slips through her lips. "What else?"

"A hotel room," I add softly, boldly heading into territory that needs to be tread cautiously.

"Yeah?"

"Mh-hmm."

"That sounds so much better than a night spent in my pajamas with a pint of Ben and Jerry's."

"You didn't go?"

She shakes her head. "I couldn't..."

My hand cups her nape, my thumb moving across her jaw. I start to dip my face at the same time her chin tilts up. But then we realize where we are. Surrounded by her family and friends, watching us as we take a painful stroll down our past.

We continue to sway through the changing songs and the movement of couples dancing around us. We know we should part ways, go back to our respective seats, and sip wine and enjoy the vanilla cake making its way to each table before we start to garner more looks and attention than deemed appropriate, but it's hard to let go. It's hard to watch Teeny walk away when all I want to do is whisk her away somewhere quiet. Somewhere we won't need to think twice about what we want to do.

CHAPTER TWENTY-FIVE

Teeny

NOW

"SHOULD YOU BE MANNING THE GRILL?"

Andrew looks up at me, a wounded look on his face. "Why shouldn't I?"

"Didn't you burn the burgers last time we left you alone with a spatula?"

He scoffs. "That was like, ten years ago. I've learned my lesson."

"No, Teeny's right," James cuts in. "I can't risk you burning all of these precious short ribs." He snatches the tongs from Andrew's hand just as he protests.

"What the fuck!"

"Hey, watch your mouth in front of your mom," my dad warns, his back to us but his ears on high alert.

"Whatever," Andrew says glumly. "I'm going to get a beer."

"Get me one too," James calls, and Andrew responds with a middle finger thrown over his back.

I take a sip of my own beer when my phone buzzes in the pocket of my dress. I pull it out, swiping through it to an alert showing a new text message from Leo.

LEO

I'll be there in about fifteen minutes.

ME

Okay. Sadie's swimming but I'll tell her to get out.

"Is that Josh?" James asks. "I thought he'd be here by now."

I shake my head, nudging away the disquiet of having to see Leo and focusing on ways to remain cordial through our pending exchange. "It's Leo. He's picking up Sadie."

"Here? He's coming here?"

"Yeah. He's going camping with Javi and their kids, so he's taking Sadie too."

He nods, his focus on the sizzling meat in front of him. "That's good. I'm sure Sadie misses him."

"Yeah." There's a bit of an awkward pause between us, but I fill it by rearranging some of the grilling tools my dad laid out for us to use. Even clacking the hard bottom of my beer bottle onto the surface of the fold-out table, right next to a tray of salad and other side dishes my mom prepared.

"James." Both James and I look toward the inside of my parents' house, the sounds of water splashing and Sadie and Sophia playing in the pool mixing with the warm summer breeze as we all lazily enjoy a post-wedding celebration my parents put together for Josh and Mina. My mom has her head poked out the side of the glass doors, looking at James. "Can you take out the trash?"

He's in the middle of flipping a few short ribs, the sweet marinade scent mingling with the cloud of smoke surrounding him. "Yeah," he answers, his movements turning rushed. "I just gotta turn these."

"I'll do it. Can you tell Sadie to get out? Maybe she'll listen better to you than me." James gives me a small smirk and a nod as I turn to the inside of the house to collect the gathered bag of trash resting by the entryway. I heft it in my hands and drag it outside the front door.

It takes some heavy lifting for me to heave it into the bin, and I miss on the first try, causing the bag to land on the ground where a pool of trash juice leaks out the bottom.

"Shit!" I mutter under my breath.

"You need some help there?"

I look over my shoulder to see Everett strolling up the driveway. He looks cool and easygoing in his warm sun kissed skin, sunglasses perched on the bridge of his nose, shorts cut high above his knees with a shirt that stretches across his chest, discreetly showing off his broad shoulders. His hair looks a little messy yet laid back, making him look more chic than disheveled as he walks toward me with ease.

"I think so," I confess sheepishly. He takes the straps of the trash bag from me and swings it in one go while his other hand flicks open the lid effortlessly, not a single muscle straining in the process.

"Okay, you don't need to show off."

He chuckles, the deep throatiness of his laughter making my insides warm and gooey. "Is everyone here?"

"Except the newlyweds."

"I guess they had an exciting night in the honeymoon suite."

I cringe. "Don't talk about my brother and his wedding night."

His laugh becomes infectious as he takes a step closer to me. One that feels guarded and wary. I take a step closer to him too, though my movements are less hesitant, and I realize how much of this is on me. Because Everett isn't pushing me. He isn't asking me for anything I'm not willing to offer, only taking moments like this as they come. And that gives me a sudden unexpected boost of confidence, making me bold and a little dizzy.

"I didn't thank you for the dance last night." My hand reaches for the belt loop poking out from under the hem of his shirt and I tug at it, gently pulling him closer. We both look down at my hand where the tan line from my wedding ring is too glaring to ignore. My heart twinges at the memory of taking it off last night after the wedding, carefully stowing it away somewhere safe, knowing how much it's weathered. A wedding, motherhood, hours of baking cookies with Sadie and doing dishes, even a mishap when I thought I'd lost it only to find it fallen behind the toilet tank. It had a good run.

"Is this you thanking me?" he asks. I can feel his eyes search mine through the dark lenses of his Ray-Bans while I avoid the scrutiny of his gaze.

I nod. "Thank you." I smile up at him, and he lifts his glasses, slipping them off and letting them dangle off his fingers. I finally see his eyes, warm pools of whiskey that light up against the early afternoon sun. And for some reason, the reality of his words hit me at full force. Like a freight train or a missile, crashing into me in a way I can't ignore any longer.

He loves me. He's always loved me. I'm not just some girl he dated in high school, filling his time until he found something better. I am the love of his life. And maybe he's mine.

"You're welcome." I playfully shove at him, and my lips twist into a bashful pout, suddenly feeling shy. "Come here," he whispers, pulling me into a deep embrace. His large hand cups the back of my head, and I feel him kiss my temple, a heavy sigh expanding his chest. My hands snake up his back, sinking into his arms like I've come home. For some reason, everything feels incredibly right.

"Teeny?"

Like a zap of lightning cutting across a midnight sky, we're broken from this trance-like spell that made me forget where I was. For a second it felt like I was sixteen again, finding solace in the warmth of my boyfriend's arms after he got home from basketball practice. Or I was doing the usual mundane teenage chore of taking out the trash, and he stopped me from the front steps of his own home next door, finding any excuse to garner some of my attention. And now, it feels like I've been caught doing something I wasn't supposed to be doing.

"Leo."

"What's going on?"

"Uh, I—uh..."

"Who the hell is this?"

Everett steps forward with his hand extended toward Leo, his closeness suddenly so loud and blatant, and I feel ashamed of how comfortable I'd gotten in his arms a second ago. "You must be Leo. I'm Everett."

Leo recoils, the anger spreading across his face with his flared nostrils and flushed face. "What the fuck, Teeny?"

"Leo, this isn't what it looks like." I don't even know why I'm defending myself. Why I feel the need to contradict all the accusations swirling in my husband's mind as he walked in on what was meant to be just a simple hug with...my friend?

"Are you sure? Because it looks like you're over here with your ex-boyfriend while I'm trying to pick up our daughter."

"I know—"

"You're married," he interrupts. "In case you forgot. You're my wife."

My blood starts to simmer at his words, and I realize that none of this should matter. Because he's the reason I'm in this place. He's the reason I'm finding comfort in the arms of someone else. "Did *you* forget?"

"What are you talking about?"

"You were *my* husband," I point out angrily. "Until you cheated on me."

"Oh, come on, Teeny! I already said I was sorry. What more do you want?"

"I don't want anything from you. I already said this is over. I don't know why you're here, telling me I'm your wife when I've never felt further than being your anything at this moment."

"So that's what this is? You're cheating on me because I cheated on you? You're trying to get back at me?"

I groan, my frustration building in heaps inside of me, making skin crawl and my heart race. "No! You are absolutely ridiculous! I am *not* cheating on you! Nothing is going on with me and Everett. So don't go and minimize what you did as if it's not a big deal. You broke us!"

"What do you mean, 'I broke us?'" he questions with an incredulous tilt of his head. "You're the one who kicked me out. You're the one who wants a divorce. I'm over here, willing to work through this and get past what happened."

"And I'm not, Leo." All kindness and affection have left my bones. I've been wrung dry, and it doesn't even hurt. I just feel numb. "I'm not willing to look past what *you* did. I don't want to anymore."

"Then don't spew this bullshit that I broke us when you're the one giving up."

"Fine. I don't care anymore. Go back to your mistress, or go find some new side piece who's going to give you the attention you want so badly. I don't give a shit anymore."

"Teeny—"

"No, Leo. I'm *done*. I've been done for way too long. Maybe it was a good thing you cheated on me. I can't imagine how badly you would've badgered me into staying if I at least didn't have that to hold against you."

"I—"

"And for some fucking reason, it's still not enough," I cut him off, not even caring what he has to say anymore. I'm on a roll, my words spilling out of me, right alongside the resentment I no longer care to hold back. "Even with you being caught red-handed, it's still not enough. You still can't seem to understand how badly you hurt me and Sadie. All you can focus on is that I'm being unreasonable and shoving aside the blame on me."

"Teeny, don't—"

"I'm serious, Leo. I'm so goddamn done. If I need to talk to you, I'll go through my lawyers."

"Teeny, please." He takes a lunging step forward, his movements desperate, and my body instinctively recoils. He wouldn't hurt me, he's never laid hands on me, and I can't imagine he'd resort to any sort of violence, but with the desperation and rage dancing in his

305

eyes and his sudden jerky movements, my arms go up to shield myself.

And that's when Everett steps in. "I think you need to leave," he says, his voice icy and rigid.

"What? Are you going to force me to leave? Kick me out? You don't even belong here. Last I checked, I was her husband."

Everett stays quiet, positioning himself between me and Leo, acting like a shield with his back to me. He's standing firm on his request for Leo to leave before things get out of hand and the rest of my family bears witness to this downfall of my marriage.

"Well, come on!" Leo shoves Everett in the chest, and Everett barely leans an inch back. "Tell me to leave again! You want me out of here so badly. Let's see you force me out." Everett doesn't fight back. Instead, he stands there, his hands braced at his sides with his face hardened like stone.

"Leo!" I shout. I was merely frustrated before, irate due to his inability to take responsibility for his infidelity and his deftness as shifting the blame on me, but now I'm livid. "Get Sadie and leave before I call James out here."

Leo looks between me and Everett, an incredulous look of shock taking over his features. "Are you kidding me? You're going to let him tell me to leave?"

"No. *I'm* telling you to leave."

"Christine," he says, calling my name with a seriousness I hate hearing from him. "Don't do this."

"It's already done." I pause and finally look at him. I notice how Everett's posture softens next to me, letting me finish what I want to say so I can get the last word in. "Please, make Sadie your priority. She needs you, and I can't watch you break her heart like you broke mine."

I didn't mean for it to happen like this, with Everett's steely presence fixed to my side, but I'm thankful for him right now. I don't think I would've been able to say what I wanted to say without his confidence and sympathetic gaze.

I turn to walk away, not bothering to wait for a response from Leo. I feel Everett trail behind me as I walk into the kitchen. It's empty, thankfully, as everyone is outside now gathering around the food. I ignore Leo as he walks through the gate from the back, saying a polite hello to my parents and brothers and collecting Sadie.

This man who I vowed to love for the rest of my life is now walking through my childhood home as if he's a stranger. The same home he helped move me out of when we got engaged. The same home we visit on the holidays with our arms full of gifts. And the idea that this separation isn't just about me anymore, it's about my family and Sadie, brings on an onslaught of guilt. Maybe he's right. Maybe I did break our family. I let my insecurities and hatred for his actions dictate our future.

My heart wrenches in my chest, and the tears start spilling before I can reach for a paper towel to catch their fall down my cheeks. The rip of the rough paper mingles with my harsh sniffles and whimpers, and I know it's no use in trying to hide it anymore.

"Teeny." Everett's soft voice feels like a balm to all the pain twisting inside of me, and it makes the tears fall harder. My back is to him, too embarrassed to show my face to him. I'm dabbing at my eyes over the sink when I feel his reassuring hands on my shoulders. He starts to turn me around, not forcing me but guiding me to face him. "Are you okay?"

I shake my head, my chin trembling violently. He sighs, pulling me to him, and my cries start to come out in sobs. My tears stain his shirt, and I feel like my entire world is crumbling while he runs his hand up and down my back.

"I'm so sorry," I say, my voice weak and watery.

"Why are you sorry?"

"That was so humiliating. You didn't need to see that, and—"

"Teeny," he says, his soft voice somehow comforting even though all he's said is my name. "You have nothing to apologize for."

My hands cover my face where I muffle a sob I have no control over, and it sounds so painful and hopeless even to my own ears.

Everett lifts my face to his, all while the tears stream down my cheeks, and he wipes at them with his fingers. I look at him, all the sadness and regret pulled to the surface, and he looks back at me, urging me to say all the words held at the tip of my tongue.

"Everett..."

"Yeah?"

"You said—you told me before...you love me?"

He nods.

"Even after all this time?"

He nods again. "I don't think I've spent a single day not loving you. Wondering what you were doing, thinking about where you were and who you were with." He pauses and I cry, though much lighter this time as the hope in his words makes its way through the ache in my heart, letting me see for the first time in a long time what it means to love with my entire heart. He stoops down, and I tilt my chin up, and we kiss. Lightly at first, testing the waters in this territory that still feels dangerous and frightening, and then it becomes eager and ardent. Like we're finally pushing away all the reasons this shouldn't be happening. The fact that I'm still a married woman. Or that we have no idea where this could go, what the future has planned for us. And maybe that's okay. Maybe I'm willing to do what I can to figure it out.

"Teeny." Josh's trembling voice, level and stern, cuts through the kitchen. I jump away from Everett, creating an arm's length of distance between us while I wipe the back of my hands across my cheek, unsure if I'm wiping my tears or the evidence of our kiss. I look at Josh, but his glare isn't pointed at me. It's all directed at Everett.

"What did Leo just tell me?" Josh asks, his eyes still on Everett.

"What?" I ask, confused.

"You were pregnant?"

My heart sinks to the bottom pit of my stomach. "What?" I ask again, this time more shock and fear plaited in my voice.

"I just saw him on the way in," he explains. "He looked pretty upset. He said he ran into you and Everett outside." His voice cracks and shakes as anger visibly rattles through him. A flash of a wince crosses his face before he finally looks at me. "He said you were pregnant. And it was Everett's."

I stay silent, unable to deny everything he's saying.

"Teeny, tell me that's not true."

More silence. And I nod, my eyes trained to the linoleum floor underneath me. "Josh, it was a long time ago," I tell him, my voice trembling and scared.

"So he's telling the truth. You were pregnant. That's why you..." The pain of watching me, his baby sister, live through the trauma of what I went through at such a young age is evident in the way his entire body softens. His face, his voice, all of it feeling every bit of the ache that tore my heart apart twenty years ago. But then it's like a switch. He remembers the person who caused all the pain is standing right next to me. "You piece of shit!" It happens in a blinding flurry. Josh lunges for Everett, gripping him by the collar of his shirt. He starts to shove him into the nearest wall, slamming him against it with enough force to knock the wind out of him. "You got her pregnant, and you fucking took off!"

Everett doesn't fight back, even as Josh's reddened face comes within inches of his. "I listened to her cry every night. I just thought she was having trouble getting over you, but you fucking got her pregnant and *left* her!"

"Josh!" I cry out, pulling at his arms as he continues to shove at Everett. "Stop!"

Josh ignores me. "And you're over here kissing her, acting like you're not the one who tore her heart to shreds! Why the fuck did you even show up after all these years? What, you wanted to have another go? Once wasn't good enough? You have to come back and hurt her all over again?"

He throws the final blow, his fist meeting Everett's jaw with a loud crack. It's then James comes rushing past me, putting his hands on Josh. He pulls him off Everett with much better success than I had.

"That's enough," James's stern voice warns us.

"Are you kidding me? This fucking—"

"I know," James tells him.

"What do you mean, you know?"

"Let's talk outside."

"No. What do you me—you knew?" James looks at him, silently begging him to stop. "You knew? Did Mom and Dad know?"

"Teeny." I hear my dad's deep voice slice through the kitchen, turning off the chaos like a firm finger snap. "What is he talking about?"

I turn around to see everyone gathered around the entrance to the kitchen, my parents' shocked faces looking at me with so much sadness and disappointment. I want to fall to my knees and beg for forgiveness.

I watch my mom's eyes well with tears, betrayal painting the edges of her sad frown. "Christine, is this true?"

"I—I, he..." My words are caught in my throat, and I feel like the room is closing in on me. I don't know how to tell my parents everything that happened. That I was stupid enough to get knocked up at sixteen, and I had to have my brother help me during a time when Everett should've been there. That I've been keeping this secret for twenty years, struggling with the aftermath of that heartbreak by covering it up with a marriage that feels like a sham now.

Unable to speak, I walk out. I leave the room, avoiding the concerned stares from everyone around us. I hear Josh call after me, James stopping him, and the urgent sounds of footsteps following mine, but I ignore it all as I walk out the front door.

"Teeny!"

I don't turn around. Instead, I keep walking. Down the narrow pathway that leads into another neighborhood, away from everything that unfolded in my parents' home.

"Teeny!" I hear again just as strong hands grip my arm. He

caught up to me. He came for me this time. Just when I thought it would be like last time, waiting around for him to show up and tell me how sorry he was, he proves me wrong by coming for me. I turn around to face Everett, and he doesn't let me go. "Where are you going?"

I shake my head. "I just need some air. I need..."

"I'll take you home," he offers, his hand lightly tugging me back toward the house.

"No." I pull my arm from his grip, and a wounded look of uncertainty casts over his features. "Everett, I need time to think. I just need some distance."

"Okay," he answers calmly. "Let me take you home. I don't think you should drive like this. I don't think it's safe."

"No, Everett." I pace the sidewalk, trying to find the right words because I don't even know what they are right now. I don't know what I want to say to him. I don't know what I want from him, but everything feels wrong. I shouldn't have kissed him. I shouldn't have turned to him in a moment of weakness. He shouldn't have told me he loved me. He shouldn't have come back. "This was a mistake."

"What are you talking about?"

"I shouldn't have kissed you back there. I shouldn't have slept with you. I should've never told you about me and the—It was all in the past, and I should've left it as it was."

"Teeny, don't say that. I had a right to know."

"And you should've never left!"

His head hangs between his shoulders, and he lets my words hit him at full force. He doesn't bother to draw up a shield to help dull the pain of the truth. He doesn't try to argue with me or even show any sign of contradiction. As if he's willing to take the brunt of it all at once. "You should've called. You should've come back for me!"

"I know."

"No, you don't! You have no idea what I went through. And you think you can just come back after all this time and act like nothing happened. As if a simple apology is enough and I'll run back to your arms?"

"No, Teeny. I don't think that."

"Then why are you here?"

"I told you—"

"Yeah, you told me you missed me," I cut him off. "So?"

"What do you mean?"

"You think you can just swoop in with your fancy hotel and win me over?" He stays quiet, letting my words sink in. "Well, you can't. The damage is done. You broke what we had, and there's nothing you can do to fix it."

"Teeny."

"No. Josh was right. All you're going to do is hurt me all over again," I tell him. The realization washes over me, and it hits me like a ton of bricks. I won't survive that again. I can't live through that type of betrayal from someone I was willing to give my whole life to. "There was a time in my life when I was willing to give you every-thing. I was willing to go wherever you went. I would've followed you to the end of the earth, but now, I can't trust that you'd love me enough to let me."

"Teeny, I *do* love you."

"It's not enough," I say, the pain of my words making me realize how badly I wanted him to love me back the first time. "I can't trust that you'll love me enough to...never hurt me again."

He takes a step closer to me, the desperation in his eyes making me want to take it all back. His hands grip my shoulders, and he crouches down to meet me at eye level. I watch him as his eyes grow misty, and his throat bobs as he swallows back the tears. "I'd never hurt you. Not again."

"I don't believe you," I whisper. I say it like it's a fact. Like saying the sky's blue or the grass is green. I can't dispute it, and I don't know how to make it disputable. I don't know if I'll ever be in a place where we could discuss this. If he could ever convince me to trust him again. Wounds like these don't heal. They just sit there, open and weeping, poking at my heart with the reminder of my past.

"Teeny, please," he cries, his voice hoarse. He takes my hand in his and presses it against his chest. He holds onto it, linking our fingers together and running the pad of his thumb down the curve of my palm, like he can turn the memory of the lines and shapes into a piece of me he can keep. "I just—I just got you back."

I shake my head at the same time I start to feel his heart rattle on the inside. It's desperate and frantic, showing the devastation coursing through him.

"You never..." Our eyes lock, and all I see is the boy who once had my entire heart. It was never something he had to question or worry about, but now...How could I ever be his again? "You never had me back."

"Teeny," he cries, a loose sob following my name. "I-I can't...how am I supposed to live without you?" He squeezes my hand, crushing my fingers together with his own trembling fingers. "Without these hands." He brings my hand to his lips, pressing a tear-stained kiss into my palm. "Without your beautiful face. And your smile, and—" He drops my hand and cups my face, stroking his thumbs over my cheeks. His hand trails down to my chest, resting over my heart. A broken cry, one that can't be feigned or forced, rattles my heart, making it vulnerable, and he adds, "Without your heart?"

I don't waver. "I can't, Everett." I place my hand over his and gently lift it, needing the space between us so I can say what needs to be said. Because if not, I'll change my mind. "I—If you hurt me again," I say, forcing the words through the pang stabbing at my heart. "I don't think I could handle it. I can't go through that again..."

He stands upright, pulling me close to him, and I allow it. I break in a small moment of weakness, wanting to remember how it feels to be held by him one last time. I cry into his chest, and I hear him sniffle back his own tears. We stay like that, letting time stand frozen before I finally pull away and look at him. I watch as he presses the heels of his hands to his eyes, another painful sob making his lips tremble through a cry. I swipe my finger at my cheeks, brushing away my own tears.

"Okay," he says hoarsely. His hands cup the sides of my head, and he looks at me. Like he's seeing the pain for the first time. He's always been aware of it, always been conscious of what he did, no matter how much time has passed. But he's finally seeing the visible, physical damage. It's there in the way my eyes glisten with tears and the way my dry lips catch the ones that have fallen, following a continuous pathway before falling off my chin. I'm broken, and it's because of him.

I watch him hesitate, like he wants to hold me or kiss me, knowing it's not allowed. And I almost want to tell him it's okay. One last time. Just so we can remember how we were and all the moments that could've been.

"Okay."

CHAPTER TWENTY-SIX

Everett

NOW

EVERYTHING FEELS STILL. Even as the waters crash onto the wet sand, it feels eerily quiet in the late night surrounded by nothing but the moonlight and the ocean breeze.

When I came back, I knew this was a possibility. Hell, I expected it. I was ready to watch from the sidelines as Teeny bounced around with her happy little family while I continued my role as the pushed-aside ex-boyfriend who got everything he deserved. But I got a glimpse of it. I tasted the life we could've had. I got to touch it and breathe it and exist in it. And just as quickly, it slipped away.

I wanted to grovel right there in front of Teeny. Beg for her to give us a chance. Because we deserve it. But I couldn't. Not when she's this vulnerable. I didn't want to take advantage of a weak moment only for her to regret a decision that would've been made through the anticipation of disappointment. I can't even blame her. Her heart is still healing, mending from the damage I sliced through it, and now I'm paying the price for those wounds.

I feel so lost. I don't know what to do now. Teeny let me go. The pain of holding on to me and our past was too much to bear for her, and I can't even fight her on it. She's right. I hurt her in a way she can't look past, and to ask her to wouldn't be fair. I don't know

315

where to go from here. Going back to my hotel doesn't feel right, and being here by the rampant waters feels the opposite of cathartic.

So, I get in my car and drive. I drive, following the roads I used to take when I was seventeen, finding solace in the familiarity of the winding paths and unforgettable landmarks. And suddenly, I'm standing in front of Josh's house. The lights are off, which makes sense considering it's close to midnight, but I make my way up his driveway and knock at his front door.

It opens, the hinges creaking slowly, somehow showing how fragmented our friendship has become. "Hey."

"Hey," I respond. We stand there, looking at each other. The anger in his face has shifted into disappointment. A part of me expects him to shut the door in my face or even yell at me, but he doesn't. Instead, he opens the door wider, letting me in.

I follow his steps as he leads me to his living room. The lights are low, only one or two lamps lit in the far corners of the room next to the large flat screen and a few tall floor plants. We both sit on his couch, our postures tense and nervous.

"How's your jaw?"

I run my hand over my chin. "A little sore."

"Good," he responds with an impassive smirk.

"How's Teeny?"

He shrugs. "She won't talk to me."

"Why?"

"I don't know," he says, his gaze focused on the floor. "She hasn't talked to anyone."

"I know this doesn't make things any better, but I didn't know."

He finally looks at me, a line cutting through his forehead as a confused scowl shifts his features. "She didn't tell you?"

I shake my head. "She mentioned she thought she might be back then, and I—I got mad. I shouldn't have, but I got some news about my dad, and I was in a bad place." I pause before adding, "It's not an excuse. I ended up pushing her away, and that's why she didn't tell me. It's my fault. I should've been there, but I was too in my head about my own shit."

He offers a small nod and a lingering silence that isn't tense or angry. It's just there, sitting between us while we figure out how to move on from this. "You still love her, don't you?"

I nod. "I don't think I'll ever stop loving her. These past twenty years have been...nothing. It felt empty and pointless, and when I came back..." I inhale a deep breath. It's difficult to find the right words to describe what it felt like to have Teeny back in my life. But I try. "Things just seem to make sense now. Even without my job, I feel at ease, and—"

"What happened with InnoDex?" Josh asks, concern etched on his face.

"I resigned."

"Why?"

"I needed to be here."

"For Teeny?"

I nod.

He exhales a heavy sigh, and I'm not sure if it's relief or frustration. "Everett, you have to understand why I'm mad."

"I know."

"If it were anyone else, I would tell you to stay far away." He chuckles morosely before adding, "Actually, I'd probably beat the shit out of you."

"And I'd deserve it."

"Yeah," he scoffs. "You know you don't deserve her."

"I know."

"And I will actually beat the shit out of you if you break her heart again."

"I know that too."

He looks at me, a smile cracking through his older brother façade ready to do anything to protect his baby sister. "So, what's your plan?"

"I don't know," I tell him glumly, realizing I'm all out. There's

317

nothing else I can do to convince her she can trust me again. As much as I don't deserve another chance, I'd crawl to her on my hands and knees to earn it, but I don't know if that'll be enough. "She told me...me loving her isn't enough. She doesn't trust me to not hurt her again. And as much as I'll do whatever it takes, I don't think it's enough to convince her to trust me."

"You're going to have to make it enough."

A small smile teases my lips, a little surprised at his change in attitude. "What happened to kicking my ass?"

"Oh, don't get me wrong, I'll still kick your ass if I need to," he clarifies with a mocking chuckle. "But...I can't imagine you doing what her idiot husband did to her. Or anything even remotely close."

"Yeah," I answer with a scoff.

"And she might not trust you. At least not yet, but a part of me does, and if you give it all you have, you might be able to convince her to start trusting you again. Once she does, once she realizes what you're willing to do for her, then maybe you can earn the rest of it back."

CHAPTER TWENTY-SEVEN

Teeny

NOW

IT'S A BEAUTIFUL SUMMER DAY. The kind that's not stiflingly hot with the beaming sun but more breezy and tolerable with the occasional waft of cool air rolling through to pick up the ninety-degree weather.

In contrast to the weather, my mood might as well be described as a storm cloud. A cumulonimbus floating over me with the threat of a storm, matching the cyclone twisting away at my insides. Everything hurts. My head, my muscles, my heart. It all aches, reminding me that pain doesn't really go away. As soon as there's a twinge in a familiar place, like right in the center of my chest, it all comes back like muscle memory.

I'd just texted Sadie to remind her to wear sunscreen when I hear a knock at my door. I trudge off my couch, shuffling around in my sweatpants and loose T-shirt with a tattered image of 98 Degrees on it, Nick Lachey's flirty smile disappearing into the creases, and answer the door to find Josh on the other side.

"Hey," he says, taking in my haggard appearance. Bags under my eyes, hair being held together by an overstretched hair tie, a crusty coffee stain on my thigh, right next to the Nike logo, and a smear of peanut butter from the peanut butter and jelly sandwich I made for dinner last night. "Can I come in?"

"Sure," I say, my voice hoarse. I turn around and walk to the couch, my feet sliding across the hard floor with the lack of pep in my step. I slump into the cushions and pull the throw blanket I'd been wrapped up in for the last forty-eight hours before peeking at him through the tattered edges. "If you came here to check on me, I'm obviously fine."

Josh settles into the armchair facing me, slouching forward and resting his elbows on his thighs. "Are you?"

My throat tightens, my emotions threatening tears. "Yeah," I whisper.

"Teeny, I wish you would've told me."

The first tear falls, seeping into the knitted fabric of my blanket. "I didn't know how."

"I know," he says, the kindness in his voice almost too much to bear. "But I wish I would've known. I wish I could've been there for you. Me and James, we could've been there for you together.

"You didn't just lose Everett. You lost...I mean, I know it was your choice, and given the circumstances, it was probably for the best, but it doesn't mean you aren't allowed to mourn."

A sob breaks loose from my chest, and I realize what he's saying. I didn't just lose Everett. I lost something that was a part of us. While I didn't go through with the pregnancy, the idea of this baby that could've been was swiped away the second I decided for us. And Josh is right. It was probably for the best, but I'd be lying if I said I've never thought about the what-ifs.

What if I had gone through with it? With or without Everett. I could've possibly been a mother to two beautiful girls. I would've had a part of Everett with me for the last twenty years, reminding me that something good came from our love. And what if I called Everett, braced myself for the possibility of yet another rejection with the news that he'd fathered a child? Would he have come back then?

Josh lets me cry, letting me bury my face into the cushions while the tears continue to pour out of me. He moves from his chair to the empty spot next to me, and I shift so I'm wrapped in his arms. As close as we are, we don't do this. We don't use physical affection as a way to comfort each other. It's usually done through cheeky insults or the occasional physical blow, especially between my brothers, but it seems necessary right now. Because he isn't just comforting his sister, but he's comforting a woman who's suffered through a loss and is finally coming to terms with it twenty years later. He's letting me find the closure I needed after all this time, guiding me to that place so I don't feel ashamed of my choices.

"Do you still love him?"

I don't even need him to clarify the "him" he's talking about. I nod. "But I'm so scared," I tell him, my words carefully trickling out of me in small drips, too reluctant for them to mean anything. "I want to trust that he'll never hurt me again, but if I'm wrong, and he hurts me again...Josh, I don't think I could survive that."

So what if I love him?

I'm realizing it doesn't matter whether or not I love him. How far can that love go if I can't trust him? It almost feels like loving him is the easy part, but deciding if giving us another chance is worth it? That's the true dilemma.

"That's completely understandable, Teen. You don't need to explain yourself," he tells me calmly, letting me feel all the things I want to feel.

"What if this doesn't pass?" I ask him, and I realize that's my biggest fear. Because what if I walk away from this and another twenty years pass only to realize that even with all of the time between us, I still love him? The thought of loving him so deeply and not having him in my life makes the hurt twist and coil inside me.

"Then you take your time. He's not going anywhere."

"How do you know?"

He shrugs. "Just a hunch." A watery chuckle rattles through the sad tears, and Josh smiles bleakly at me. "Want to go somewhere? I'm craving some Sprinkles."

A smile matching his stops the tears. "Sure."

I'm sitting in the front seat of Josh's Jeep, a box of Sprinkles cupcakes resting on my lap. I managed to change into something more presentable, jeans and a top that wasn't a portal to my late-nineties boy band obsession, and the smell of sweet cupcakes is starting to make my mouth water. The music on the radio is something I don't quite recognize, and Josh sifts through his playlist as we turn into an unfamiliar neighborhood.

"Where are you going?"

He keeps his eyes on the road ahead of him, his throat bobbing with a forced swallow. "I just need to make a stop somewhere." I lift the lid to the box, peeking inside for the fourth time. "I told you, no eating in my car," Josh scolds. I catch him glancing over at me, a side-eyed warning attached to his words.

"You know, they have handheld vacuums. Amazon sells them for like, fifty bucks."

He ignores me, taking a few turns down a winding road, driving deeper into a neighborhood filled with large homes and fancy cars.

"Seriously, where are we going?"

He pulls to a stop in front of a house with a for sale sign on it, a bold "SOLD" stamped across the marker with some real estate agent's corporate smile and her phone number.

It's a beautiful home. A wide cobblestone paved driveway with in-ground lights along the edges leads up to a three-car garage and brick siding lining the side of the house. Small palm trees are planted along the curb, and the grandness of the house is near overwhelming with the large pane windows. Leading up to the entrance of the house sits a small set of stairs and a two-door entrance. And Everett.

He's sitting along the steps with his elbows braced on his knees. He's wearing jeans and a gray T-shirt, exposing his tan arms. He looks up at Josh's car at the same time my eyes land on him.

"What is he doing here?" I ask Josh, the two of us still inside the safety of his car.

My reaction is to lock the doors and demand Josh to drive off, or even slouch down so Everett doesn't see me, but then I see him watching me as he pushes himself off the steps and walks down the long driveway in our direction. Those jeans he's wearing hug his hips and thighs almost indecently, and all I notice is the way his narrow waist sways seductively, no matter that it isn't his intention.

His steps are intentional as he reaches the car and waits at the end of the sidewalk. He nervously shoves his hands in his pockets, rocking on the balls of his feet, and his triceps muscle bulges as he squares his shoulders. I almost roll my eyes at the absurdity of how attractive he looks, even with the confusion and uncertainty swirling in my head.

"He wanted to show you something."

I look at Josh, unable to comprehend his involvement in this. "You planned this?"

"I just facilitated an opportunity."

I huff a scoff. "Whose side are you on?"

"Yours. Always yours," he answers with no hesitation. "But I think it's worth a shot to hear him out."

"Don't. Go. Anywhere," I instruct him, using the same tone our mom uses when she's told us something for the third time. "I'm coming back in five minutes." I stamp the end of my sentence by holding out five fingers between us.

He raises his palms up in my direction. "I'll be right here."

I sigh, my breath coming out shaky and nervous, before I open the door. I gently place the box of cupcakes on the seat and throw one last glare at Josh. It's a mixture of a warning and a death stare so he knows we'll be talking about this whole behind-my-back setup when I come back, but also so he doesn't steal one of my cupcakes.

"Hi," Everett says just as I turn to meet him. His expression looks solemn and pensive, though there's a softness in the way his eyes aren't narrowed, and his jaw is relaxed.

"Hi," I answer, squinting up at him from the blinding sun. I take him in, noticing that he's trying to read me, and how it makes him look worried and sad. It causes my heart to soften, wondering if he's okay. I want to ask him, but I know I shouldn't. "Is this another property you're renovating? Really digging into those real estate investments there, aren't ya?"

He smirks, ducking his head toward the ground. "Can I show it to you?"

"Sure." I sound the complete opposite of sure as I take one last glance back at Josh before turning away. He gives me an encouraging smile, and I follow Everett where he takes a key out of his pocket and unlocks the front door.

It's even more stunning on the inside. A split-level staircase leads up to the second floor, and the foyer breaks off to a living space with a large open floor plan covered in a clean gray-toned white oak wood flooring. The ceiling has to be at least ten feet high, and hanging over the main dining area is a glittering chandelier that looks like it's dripping with diamonds. Showcasing the glimmering pool and breathtaking cliffside view, the floor-to-ceiling windows lining the far walls cause a light gasp to climb up my throat.

"Everett," I whisper. "I—" I press a hand to my chest, imagining Everett in this home. Building a life here, maybe even meeting someone one day and bringing her home and raising a family. "It's a beautiful home."

I peer over at Everett as he watches me take everything in with my hands braced along the kitchen counter. The way my eyes go gaga over the kitchen with the farmhouse sink and glossy wood grain finish on the cabinets, and more windows letting in natural light.

A sudden pang twists inside my chest, and it spreads through my entire body. Why am I here? Why did I get out of that car as if I'm ready to face Everett like this? I know I'm not ready to see him or talk to him. I don't know if I'll ever be. I need to leave.

"Everett—"

"There's more outside if you want to take a look."

I turn to face him, and I swallow back the tears making my throat tighten and my breath hitch. I'm ready to tell him no. To tell him that Josh is waiting for me outside. To tell him that I can't do this. I need to be able to move on. But then I look at him, his eyes urging me in a way that I want to say yes. Because I don't see the man I don't know how to trust or the man who came back for me even though he wasn't sure I'd be here for him.

Instead, I see the boy I fell in love with with my entire heart and soul. That menacingly messy hair that laid rumpled on his pillow and those brown eyes that watched me as I drifted off next to him, surrounded by the warmth of his arms. He promised me the world then. We talked about our future like we'd never not be a part of each other's lives.

"Sure." This time I sound less unsure and more placating, hoping that we can at least be in the same room without the reminder of how much hurt we've suffered through in our past. Because the thought of letting another twenty years pass without ever seeing him actually hurts more than this. It's self-destructive, this idea that he can remain a constant in my life while believing I can actually move on, but the latter. The thought of never seeing him again...It suddenly feels calamitous.

He slides open the large glass door leading outside, and he takes a few steps ahead of me to what looks like a small pool house. I step carefully around the edges of the pool, noticing how beautiful it is with the infinity edge. He opens the door to the pool house, holding it out for me to enter first, and when I do, I see that it's the only place in the entire property that's furnished.

There's a small love seat sitting on one far wall, right next to a wide workstation. There's an easel positioned right next to an entire wall of windows, floor to ceiling, where all the natural light flows in.

"What is this, Everett?" I finally ask.

"It's your studio."

"*My* studio?"

He nods. "I spent a lot of time wondering where home was," he starts, and I'm taken aback by the calmness in his voice. The genuine frankness and vulnerability. "I used to let my work dictate where I lived, and it never really bothered me. But then I came back here, and I saw what I've been missing." He takes a step closer to me, gauging my response with heed as he watches me for any signs of protest. When I don't give any, my curiosity outweighing any doubt or reservations, he continues. "And I realized that this place is the closest thing to home I'll ever have.

"I'd like to say it's the weather or the sandy beaches, but...it's home to me because you're here."

My throat tightens, and I feel like giving up. I don't want to fight this anymore. I don't want to search for all the reasons I shouldn't be here, listening to this man while he tells me how he feels about me.

"So, this is where I'm going to be."

"You bought this for yourself?"

He nods. "I'm not going anywhere this time." I exhale a shaky sigh, and my chin starts to tremble. "And, this may be a bit presumptuous, but this home is yours too."

"Mine?"

He nods. "If you'll have it."

"Everett, I told you," I cry. "I can't..." I start to cry, wiping away at the tears spilling out the corners of my eyes while working on the last bits of my resolve to stand my ground.

But even as I stand on the brand-new wood flooring, I can feel it start to shake. It's starting to break and crumble, making me want to run into Everett's arms. And I realize the fear of never getting over Everett is completely valid. It isn't some irrational thought I'll look back at one day only to learn I just needed some time to get over the greatest love of my life. I will never move on.

"I know," he answers, taking a step closer to me. "And I'm not here to badger you into changing your mind. I'm just here. That's all Teeny."

It's then my eyes catch a large, covered canvas. The corners of it peek out through the torn paper it's wrapped in, and I recognize the colors pop even from the small, exposed inches of the painting. I walk over to it and lift the ripped corner, tearing it back. The loud harsh sound echoes around us, and I feel Everett stand behind me.

"You bought my painting?" I remove the last bits of paper, pull at the twine holding everything together before taking a step back to take it in.

I don't know why, but it's more beautiful than when it was hung in the gallery. Where it looked commercial and manufactured on display for sale. Here, it looks like it's at home. To be enjoyed by the only two people it was meant for. The blues and yellows and purples glow with a warm fluorescence, and that lifeguard tower stands out as a reminder of the Teeny and Everett we used to be.

"I was storing it here for now," he explains, his warm breath close to my ear. "I thought maybe you'd want to decide where to hang it, so…"

My shoulder blades brush his chest, and I feel my body lean into him. I want so badly to give in. To let my weight fall against him, to let his arms wrap around my stomach while my head tilts to the side and his chin rests on my shoulder. I'm suddenly back in my garage, Everett's looming presence there to listen to me talk and learn about all the things that I loved. To be engrossed in whatever my hands and fingers were bringing to life.

"I thought it wasn't for sale." I turn around to face him, and I see him hanging on to my every word. To my movements, my breathing, the way I'm taking everything in, the way the tears have stopped but my cheeks remain stained.

"I made a pretty good offer." He thinks to himself before adding a reserved smile and, "Actually a really good offer."

"Why?"

He lifts his hand to cup my cheek, his movements keen yet

somehow apprehensive. Like he's gauging my reaction as he moves, wondering if the way my shoulders sag or how a sad smile twitches at my lips is a sign that it's okay for him to touch me. I curve into his hand, letting his warmth sink into my skin. And that feeling that everything feels right returns, making me realize how I don't ever want there to be a time when he has to think twice about touching me. How it should be second nature for him, like breathing or sleeping.

"Teeny." His voice is almost mocking, shoving aside every question in my head wondering why he would go to such lengths to buy my painting. "How could I not?"

I reach up to lay my hand over his, turning my cheek so my lips press a soft kiss into the palm of his hand.

"I'm scared," I tell him, the truth too conflicting for me to keep inside.

"You have every right to be."

"I'm going to be scared for a really long time," I continue. "And I might rub it in your face until you become sick of it."

He nods.

"To the point that you'll wonder why I even considered giving this another shot. And you're going to wish you never spent all that money on the painting or this house."

"Teeny, there will never be a life where I would regret another chance with you." He pauses to smile softly, a flash of our life scrolling at lightning speed across his glistening eyes. "You're it for me. And I will wait the rest of my life for you to come back to me."

My chin trembles. "Don't break my heart, Everett."

"I wouldn't dream of it."

He kisses me, softly and gently, taking his time relearning the ways to kiss me, knowing there's no time constraint to worry about. We have the rest of our lives.

CHAPTER TWENTY-EIGHT

Teeny

NOW

I FEEL Everett's fingers fidget over my lower back. He's not doing it to soothe or comfort me. It's more for him as he eases his own anxiety.

"Why are you so nervous?"

He looks down at me while we stand on the stoop of my parents' front door. "Because the last time your parents saw me was when they found out I knocked you up twenty years ago."

I roll my eyes. "It's going to be fine, Everett. I'll explain everything. Plus, they love you."

"I don't know how much they'll love me after this."

The door opens with a rush of air, and we're greeted by my mom's stunned face from across the threshold.

"Hi, Mom," I greet her meekly.

"Hi, Mrs. Cohen."

She lets a discontented sigh slip through her lips before she opens the door wider for us to enter. We walk into the kitchen where my dad is hovering over what looks like the ingredients for cheeseburgers, and when he sees Everett and me walk in, hand in hand, a hard, disapproving scowl covers his face.

"Christine and Everett are here," my mom announces as she

329

follows our footsteps. It doesn't sound like she's announcing our arrival, but more like giving my dad a warning.

"Hi, Daddy."

My dad drops the plump tomato in his hand and crosses his arms over his chest. He's joined by mom, their matching stone-like faces looking over us.

"What's going on, Teeny?" my dad asks, the tone of his voice matching his rigid posture.

Though the question is directed at me, it's Everett who speaks. "Mr. and Mrs. Cohen, I know you both must have a lot of questions. And while we're both happy to answer them, I want to say something first."

My parents share a look. An exchange asking the other whether or not they're willing to hear him out.

"I love Christine," Everett continues. "I've loved her my whole life. And though things happened between us that drew us apart, I've come back hoping that she'd give me another chance."

He's answered with more silence from my parents, and a wave of anxiety rolls through me. Maybe this was a bad idea. Maybe I should've given it a few weeks, let the dust settle before explaining to them that I plan to have Everett in my life for a very long time. Perhaps forever.

"And uh," my mom finally says. "Is this...what about you, Teeny? What do you..." The cautious tone of her voice feels like the smallest of gaps. One that both Everett and I can squeeze through, hoping that my family will accept our reunion.

"I love him too," I confess.

Everett's brow springs up to his hairline. I grip his hand firmly, giving him a light squeeze to warn him. *Keep your cool.*

My dad cuts into the moment with a harsh cough into his closed fist. "Teeny, I know you're an adult, and you're fully capable of making your own decisions, but we—" He pauses, looking at my mom, hoping to find the right words with her. "We want to make sure you've thought this through."

"What your dad means is that we don't want you to..." My mom moves closer to me, cupping my face in her hands. The pitying look on her face causes the air around us to shift, and suddenly, I feel like I'm a child again. "We don't want you to get hurt."

"James told us about what happened," my dad adds, "and we want the two of you to work through what you went through before jumping into something."

"We have," I tell them. "This isn't some rash decision we settled on overnight. Everett knows what I expect of him, and we're working through things."

"And I don't plan on leaving Teeny."

My dad levels Everett with narrowed eyes, and I almost stifle a laugh. It reminds me so much of when he used to be greeted with the same look by my dad. Especially when Everett's presence in our home became more consistent as he followed me around like a puppy dog.

"You say that now, but what happens when something more important comes up," my dad accuses. "You had no problem leaving before."

"He bought a house," I tell him.

My dad's face softens a bit, and I hope that it means we're getting through his stern exterior.

"It's beautiful. It has a pool and this beautiful view that over-looks a cliff. And there's more than enough room for..." I stop, realizing that we haven't really decided on *my* living situation.

"You bought a house?" my mom asks, confirming this news with Everett.

I nod.

"I bought it for Teeny," Everett explains, extinguishing any doubt I had about moving in with him even though I haven't officially accepted his offer to make his home mine as well. "I want to build a life here with her, and that means I'll be wherever she is."

The tension dissipates, and I can see the beginnings of approval edge its way into my parents' apprehension. My mom shrugs at my dad. It surprises me how well they're able to have a whole conversation with their eyes and body language.

"Well, I'm hungry," my dad announces. "We can talk more while we eat."

"Have you had lunch yet?" my mom asks. "We're cooking some burgers."

"No, we haven't," I answer.

"We'll get the grill started. You kids finish up the vegetables," my dad instructs. There's still unease laced into his tone, but with my mom's uncomplicated attempt to move forward with an invitation to lunch, he goes along with it.

My parents pick up a tray of uncooked patties and walk outside toward the grill. Everett and I are left in the kitchen.

"That could've gone worse," Everett comments.

"I told you, you had nothing to worry about."

He leans down and places a small peck to the corner of my mouth. "You said you love me."

I give a playful pout. "Was that not already obvious?"

"No, it was," he agrees. "But it's nice to hear you say it."

"Well, I love you."

He kisses me again, but this time, he lets it linger and settle. "Say it again."

"I love you."

He closes his eyes, and his forehead meets mine, and I can almost feel all the disquiet and fear dissipate off of him. "I love you, too, Teeny."

Teeny

NOW

"WHAT?"

Everett innocently shrugs a shoulder, ducking his head just as a smirk lifts the corners of his lips. "Nothing."

"Then why are you staring at me?" I lift my champagne flute, letting the cool bubbly tickle my throat, relishing in the lavishness of this European getaway.

"Because I can, Mrs. Hayes."

My heart does this thing where it stumbles and stammers, skipping a beat at the sound of the words "Mrs. Hayes." I can count on one hand the number of times I've heard it. The curt ticket agent at the check-in counter at San Diego International Airport, the attentive flight attendant walking the aisles along our first-class seats, the bubbly front desk clerk at Shangri-La Paris as her eyes caught the attention of our wedding rings and eyes misted over with giddiness. And now, Everett. It seems he's added it to the long list of endearments handpicked for me. Baby, when we wake up in our king-size bed facing the bright morning San Diego cliffside. Sweetheart, when I'm fighting him on something minor and trivial, like who it was that left the garage door open (usually me). Honey, when we're in front of

Sadie and he doesn't want to gross her out with the more corny sentiments.

My brow shoots up, and I stave off a cheeky smile with a dismissive shake of my head. "I'm going to have to get used to that one."

"What?"

"Mrs. Hayes."

"I hope it doesn't take too long," he says, leaning into my hair and whispering the words against my goosebump-ridden skin. "Because I plan on calling you Mrs. Hayes every chance I get."

"Say it again," I tease against his cheek. "Maybe I need to hear it over and over again, and it'll feel more instinctive. Second nature."

"Mrs. Hayes." His voice tickles my ear, and I giggle, wrapping my arm over his neck. "Mrs. Hayes. Mrs. Hayes."

A light knock to our door has me pressing my hand to his chest. "I think that's our luggage."

"They can wait," he mumbles into my neck.

"Everett," I scold with a playful shove.

He reluctantly pulls away from me, landing a light smack on my ass. I feign a shocked squeal, and he peeks over his shoulder, watching me as I settle into the plush linens of the bed. I kick off my heels and let my toes press a groove into the fluffy sheets, my head falling back against the cloud-like pillows.

This is my life now. Me and Everett. Him touching me whenever he wants and me always getting my way. It almost feels like a pinch isn't enough to confirm this reality.

Two years after we've settled into our new lives, Everett and I finally sealed the deal with a beautiful Malibu wedding topped off with a stunning ocean view along a secluded cliffside. Surrounded by our friends and family, we placed our love story at a vantage point it deserved. It took some time for my parents to get over the double whammy of my divorce and the illegitimate child that never was, but once they saw how amiably Leo and I worked through co-parenting, they warmed up to the idea. And it definitely helped having Everett's mom around, rekindling a friendship long forgotten, to erase the painful stain of my past with something brighter to replace that memory.

Sadie's growing into a woman as she starts her junior year of high school in the fall, embarking on yet another milestone I feel honored to witness. I sold the house I shared with Leo shortly after our divorce, not wanting to hold on to those memories of my past, and I moved in with Everett. We started to build a life together, my trust in us slowly and surely growing with each passing day.

Everett started his own tech company, something from the ground up, and with his experience and networking skills, ProTech Solutions is becoming a widespread specialist for companies small and large to meet their tech support needs. Sadie adjusted to the divorce, and even offered her support when Leo announced he'd met someone while on a business trip to Toronto last summer.

While I support Leo's choices and how he wants to live his own life, I minimize our interactions to an as needed basis. While we've maintained a cordial air between us, it feels as if the chapter of Teeny and Leo has been officially closed.

It seems all the colors in my life have turned bright and shiny. It's all Technicolor now, making all the light beam out of me without a single moment of hesitation. Instead, it pours and flows with enough to share.

"Sadie said they just landed," I announce, my phone wedged in my hands. Everett saunters back to me with the bellhop having moved our luggage quickly and efficiently inside, Everett handing him a hefty tip. He watches as I roll onto my stomach, my feet kicked up in the air and my skirt ridden up my thigh, resting just below the curve of my ass. "She just sent me a picture of the Statue of Liberty from their cab."

I turn the phone over to show Everett, and his hand glides over the exposed skin of my calf, traveling up slowly and meticulously.

"She's going to have an amazing time," he says softly as he leans down to place a soft, wet kiss behind my knee.

"Thank you."

"For what?"

"For organizing their trip." He trails a kiss from my shoulder to my neck, letting a shiver travel up my back. "She's going to have so much fun with Lauren. And Mina's always wanted to visit Manhattan."

"You don't need to thank me, Teeny." He tugs at my wrist, letting my head fall to his shoulder where he presses a kiss to the top of my head. "I just hope this was enough to convince you to come to Paris on our honeymoon without feeling guilty for leaving Sadie behind."

"Oh, so that was the plan," I contest teasingly. "Send my daughter off so you can have me all to yourself."

"Plus send her on a trip she's been begging to go on," he disputes. "With a responsible chaperone."

"Hopefully responsible enough that she won't let Sadie get that nose ring she's been asking for." I end my sentence with a kiss, my lips finding Everett's. I follow a path that started at his collarbone, all the way to his jawline, finally settling on a flirty nibble to his bottom lip.

"She's sixteen, babe. I think she's old enough for a nose ring. It's not like she's asking for a tattoo."

I jolt up from the bed. "Don't even speak that into existence."

"What's wrong with a tattoo?" he protests. "You like mine."

"Because it's meaningful and thought out." I tuck my hand under the small opening of his collar, running my fingertips over the tattoo I know is there underneath his clothing. "She'll probably get something she'll end up regretting in twenty years. Like the words 'Live, Laugh, Love' or an infinity symbol."

"Have a little more faith in her, Teen," he whispers, yanking me back down and hovering over me. He covers my lips in a debilitating kiss, running his hands over my hips possessively.

"Okay," I gasp between kisses. "Whatever you say."

I feel him chuckle, his nose traveling over the shell of my ear. "Have you seen the view yet?" he murmurs.

"You're worried about the view? *Right now?*"

"You don't want to miss it." He abruptly stands from the bed, urging me to follow. We mosey toward the french doors leading to the balcony, and the view takes my breath away.

"Are you serious?" I squeal, grinning like a love-sick fool in Everett's direction.

Just below us are the streets of Paris. Cobblestone pathways line the beautiful streets where lovers skitter through, drunk on love. Just like me. Steep-hipped rooftops and arched windowpanes bring the nineteenth-century Parisian architecture to life, showcasing its original beauty. And the Eiffel Tower, standing in all its glory right outside our balcony. "Everett! It's beautiful!"

"It's going to look even more stunning at night."

I turn around to face him, crushing his lips to mine. He kisses me back, gripping the iron guardrail behind me and caging me between his arms. I start to untuck his shirt, furiously undoing the buttons and running my hands over his stomach.

"Mrs. Hayes," he protests weakly. "People can see us."

"I don't care."

It doesn't take much to convince Everett to go about our very public display of affection. He glides his hands over my bare thigh, lifting my skirt just as I hook my knee over his hip. His lips travel down my neck, nipping at my collarbone in teasing nibbles, and I feel his hand grip my ass.

"Are you sure, babe?"

"You're going to say no to *the* Mrs. Hayes?"

He chuckles. "Never," he answers. "Whatever my wife wants, she gets."

Everett
NOW

MY WIFE.

It feels surreal. Teeny's shimmering platinum wedding band, cool and assuring, grazing over my day-old stubble as she runs her palm over my jaw. Even as she wraps her legs around me, letting her feet hook over the small of my back, her hands travel at a slow, delicious pace. They move with confidence, never stopping to hesitate or ask for permission. And it's like a dream. One that I've been playing on repeat for twenty years. And now, it's a reality. This is my real life. Teeny is my wife, and I get to touch her and kiss her and hold her and tell her I love her every single day.

My stomach dips when Teeny's hand tucks into my unzipped pants, and I grunt a harsh groan into her mouth.

"Mrs. Hayes."

"You know, I think I'm getting used to it." I feel her smile against my cheek, and that instantly fades into a breathy moan when I slip her panties off and let them pool at her feet.

"See? That wasn't so hard."

My legs start to feel like Jell-O the instant Teeny's fingers trace over my most sensitive areas, and suddenly, I feel like a ravenous animal. My own fingers do their own exploring, teasing and stroking her until all I'm left with is a squirmy, very impatient wife.

My pants start to lose their give and loosen around my hips. Teeny yelps when I swing her around and trudge back into the room, my pants hanging dangerously low around my thighs and slipping further and further down. I shouldn't be surprised when they start to tangle at my ankles, making me stumble and fall onto our bed in a heap of mirth and giggles.

"Oh!" Teeny exclaims and giggles. "You okay?"

I nod.

"You sure? 'Cause it looks like you almost lost a foot there."

I nod again, completely pushing away the fact that I almost suffered a minor injury. It seems the lengths I'd go to just to make love to this woman is getting pushed further and further with each passing day.

The concern mixed with the tiniest dollop of a taunt vanishes the second my kisses travel down her stomach and the bunched-up fabric at her hips. In no time at all, I'm tasting her, her moans filling the room like a symphony of sounds I could play for the rest of my life.

Urgent, desperate fingers rake through my hair, tugging at the roots at my scalp as the sharp jerks direct where she wants my mouth. How she wants me to lick and suck and bite.

"Everett," she gasps. "We can skip all that. Can you please just fuck me?"

My head pops up from between her thighs. "You've got quite a mouth on you, Mrs. Hayes."

A grumble blends with a chuckle on her beautiful face, and she gives my hair one last tug. "Shut up and—"

"Fuck you?"

She nods frantically. "*Yes.*"

It seems I don't move quickly enough for her because she starts to pull at my shirt collar, dragging me up her body until our noses bump.

"Hi."

Teeny giggles. "Hi." She claws at my shirt, undoing the buttons and yanking at the last ones until she's finally gripping at the sleeves. I do the same, lifting the pretty floral blouse she's wearing and exposing the choice negligee she's wearing to display everything she's hiding underneath her clothes.

"This new?" I ask.

A teasing eye roll and a hand shoved into my chest is my answer. It's followed by her gripping me, giving a painfully seductive stroke. I respond with a groan muffled into the crook of her neck just as a jolt of pleasure ripples down my stomach and straight to my groin.

"Okay, okay," I mutter.

"Why are you stalling?" she whines.

"Because it's fun watching you beg for it."

Anger flushes her cheeks, and with one quick swooping move, I'm on my back with Teeny straddling me. I watch her, mesmerized by the sated glaze of satisfaction in her eyes and her bottom lip clamped under her teeth as she guides me inside her.

"Hmm," Teeny hums, a low rumble vibrating through her as her hair falls over her chest. I can't take my eyes off the delicate lace details pressing against her swelling cleavage. How I can see the protruding outline of her nipples through the thin material cupping her breasts. Even the shadows of her ribs bulging and relaxing as she takes in heavy gulps of air.

I sit up, leaning back on the heel of one hand and tracing her neck with the other. "You're so damn beautiful," I whisper against her collarbone. I let my tongue glide across her skin before kissing her lips. "And you drive me so fucking crazy with your body."

Her movement stills, the rocking motion of her hips coming to a stop as she smirks with a wicked grin. "Oh, now look who's begging for it."

I deliver a sharp smack to her ass, and she yelps. The surprise in her face dissolves as I thrust upward, and her head falls back

340

between her shoulders. "Right there," she gasps. Her fingers start to move between us, getting herself off while I do my part. "*Right there.*"

I lean forward and yank at the cup of her bra, pulling at her nipple until it pebbles and grows rigid against the length of my tongue. I start to feel her body seize and tense.

"Oh god, Everett," she whimpers, her voice sounding weak and restrained.

"Let it out, baby," I urge. "I want to hear you get loud for me."

"*Everett!*" I feel her come around me, the pulsing contractions of her orgasm gripping me so tight that I follow right behind her, taking pride as second place in this race for pleasure. I feel dizzy. High on this life that revolves around a dreamlike reality where I married Teeny.

"That was fast," I comment.

A long, breathy sigh and a concurring nod is Teeny's response. "I've been waiting since we left San Diego for this."

"And you've been so patient," I tease. I feel Teeny's body shake, and an amused laughter fills the air. "What?" I ask, resting my chin on the hard part of her sternum.

"Just..." She rests her palm on her forehead, eyes pointed to the ceiling as if she's looking for the right words. "I can't believe we're married."

"I know."

"If I could go back in time and tell my sixteen-year-old self that you're my husband, I'd throw a fresh Coke float in my face."

"We're really married, aren't we?" I mumble against her soft skin. She wraps her arms around me, cupping the back of my head and cradling me against her.

"Yeah," she whispers into my hair. "We really are."

Hours later, once we've satiated enough of our "appetite" to get dressed and leave our hotel room, we're walking hand in hand down the streets of Paris. It isn't too crowded. A lot of the narrow pathways consist of small stores rather than the larger chain ones with more foot traffic. We mosey our way into a quaint café after Teeny's adorable plea for an authentic French croissant.

"*Bonjour. Je prend deux croissants*," she tells the cashier. "*Et un café crème, s'il vous plaît.*" She manages to get the words out with such fluidity, my chest beams with pride.

"Thank goodness I didn't have to brush up on my French before our honeymoon," I say low to Teeny's ear as we veer away to a small round table and two cushioned chairs.

"What French?" she asks, skepticism holding back a bemused laugh.

"I learned some stuff in high school."

"Oh, you mean how you could barely say, 'My name is Everett?'"

The tips of our elbows meet at the middle of the table like lovers exchanging a sweet Eskimo kiss. I reach down and give her knee a soft squeeze to which she jerks away with a delighted giggle.

"You never did miss a chance to make fun of my French, did you?"

"It's just so easy," she croons, leaning forward for a kiss.

"Well, maybe you can help me while we're here," I suggest, pecking the corner of her mouth.

"Again? But you're such a lost cause!"

"Yeah, but maybe I can throw in some incentives," I tease. "Teach me how to order a croissant, and I'll buy you a puppy as soon as we get back home."

"Keep talking." Teeny tilts her head down as my kisses travel to her ear.

"Teach me how to say that 'Pur-lay voo—'"

"*Parlez-vous,*" she corrects.

"See? I need you, baby."

She giggles. "It's okay. Just stand there and look pretty. I'll do all the talking."

I cup my hand to her face and stroke her cheek. "I love you so damn much, Christine."

Her nose scrunches through her smile. "So formal."

"But I do."

"I know." She places a gentle kiss into my palm. "I love you too, Everett."

A Look at: Best I Never Had

BEST I NEVER HAD BOOK ONE

Sometimes, the one who got away is closer than you think.

Natalia Marquez thought she'd left her high school memories behind—
awkward lab partners, football jocks, and the lingering sting of unspoken
feelings. Eight years later, she's navigating life in New York City, mending a
broken heart and trying to find purpose in a job she doesn't love. The last
thing she expects is to run into Hayden Marshall, the boy who made AP
Biology unexpectedly thrilling.

Once the school's star athlete, Hayden has traded touchdowns for chef
whites, carving out a life in the culinary world. But his move to the city isn't
just about career aspirations—it's about starting over. When fate reunites
Natalia and Hayden, the connection they once shared sparks anew.

As their friendship deepens, so do the unspoken truths they left behind. Can
they reconcile who they were with who they've become? And will revisiting
the past risk their fragile present—or unlock a future that could be the best
they've ever had?

AVAILABLE NOW

Acknowledgments

First off, to all of my friends and readers, you are the heart of this book. I poured so much of myself into this, and in the process, relearned what it felt like to fall in love with writing. It didn't feel like I was wielding a keyboard but rather a paintbrush against a blank canvas. So thank you, from the bottom of my heart, for taking such tender care of my babies. I hope this is another one to add to the collection.

To my author friends who have kept me sane and, more importantly, included, I LOVE YOU ALL! It takes a different kind of heart to accept someone who is essentially a stranger and create a community that feels like family, and a little bit like a trauma bond. Because this author shit is SO FUCKING HARD!!! Hazel, Kaye, Melissa, Bianca, all my OC writers. I feel so blessed to have all of you to turn to when I need you all the most.

The biggest thanks to my alpha/beta-readers: JESSICA, HAZEL, KATY, SAM. You are my heroes. You swooped in with your superpowers (reading romance books) and capes and saved me and my manuscript. Teeny and Everett are who they are because you helped mold and shape them. Thank you!!!

To my publisher, Love N. Books Press, Ellie and Kayla. Thank you for taking a chance on this itty-bitty baby author. Your faith in me and my work is inspiring, and I hope one day to make you proud to have me be a part of the Love N. Books family!

And to my babies. I say this every time I publish a book, and I will never stop saying it. I hope that one day, you two are able to come to me and tell me about a dream you have for yourself. It can be anything. To become an astronaut or a figure skater, travel the world or climb Mount Everest. WHATEVER YOU WANT!! I will stand by you and help you reach for the stars. Just like Daddy does for Mommy.

JEANNIE CHOE
ROMANCE AUTHOR

Specializing in new adult contemporary romance novels, Jeannie Choe offers stories ranging from angsty and emotional to heartfelt and outright adorable. Because who doesn't love a happily ever after filled with squeal-inducing moments of romantic gestures?

Living off an endless number of paperbacks, cold brews, and 2000's rom-coms, Jeannie lives in Southern California spending her days with her family and two attention-seeking elder dachshunds.

www.jeanniechoeauthor.com